TILL NEXT TIME

CORA BRENT

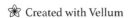 Created with Vellum

ALSO BY CORA BRENT:

KEEP IN TOUCH!

Sign up for my newsletter and get early news on releases, cover reveals and special giveaways...
CORA BRENT'S NEWSLETTER SIGNUP

I always love hearing from readers so contact me at:
corabrentwrites@yahoo.com.

Check out what's happening on Facebook:
www.facebook.com/CoraBrentAuthor

Join my exclusive reader Facebook group:
https://www.facebook.com/CoraBrentsBookCorner

Add future releases to your TBR list:
https://www.goodreads.com/CoraBrent

Follow me on Instagram: CoraBrentAuthor

TILL NEXT TIME

I met Colt Malene when I was fourteen years old.
And it seems I've never recovered.
He became the headstrong star quarterback in a town that
idolized high school football titles.
Meanwhile, I was the coach's dutiful perfectionist daughter, never
daring to step out of line.
We should have stayed far away from each other but we didn't.
And the volatile fallout was unbearable.
More than a decade has passed and now my father is dying.
He wants to make amends.
He wants to be forgiven for the role he played in Colt's ruinous
downfall and my painful heartbreak.
To give a dying man some peace, Colt and I agree to a plan.
While Colt is here in town, we pretend to date.
We pretend to like each other.
We pretend that the past is buried and forgotten.
But with one reckless, passionate act we carve a new future.
Leading to a fate we never suspected.
In the middle of a storm we never saw coming.
And an ending no one could have predicted...

PROLOGUE

COLT

M y sister tries to stop me from leaving. "It's too dangerous. Listen to the sirens."

Nobody needs to explain the meaning of the sirens.

We heard that metallic wail once when we were kids. Back then, the funnel cloud that teased its way to the earth only grazed a barn north of town.

The front door is open and I stand at the threshold, watching the sky shift with furious speed.

The emergency alarms keep screaming.

A terrible, unwelcome instinct whispers the cold truth.

The town of Arcana won't be as fortunate this time.

I'm already holding my keys, reflexively squeezing the silver charm I've carried everywhere since the age of fourteen. If the smallest gleam of luck remains, it is desperately needed right now.

Deadly tornadoes are uncommon here, but they happen. The twister of 1982, remembered clearly by all of our parents, was a monster that tore open the summer sky and carved out a neighborhood only blocks from the high school. Ten people were killed. And in a town the size of Arcana, ten people is a hell of a loss.

Tori tugs on my arm and pulls me back, forever the big sister. "Colt, wait!"

But Jace and I lock eyes. He understands that I can't wait. He wouldn't wait either.

I nod at him. "I'll see you soon."

My best friend cradles his infant son in one arm. He protectively folds his wife into his other arm. Tori's wide eyes dart from me to Jace and back again. She gasps when a torrent of nickel-sized hail cracks against the front porch.

"Be careful." Jace's voice is mild, like he's wishing me well on a road trip.

"Sure," I answer him, just as evenly, and then sprint out to my truck before Tori can follow. Jace will keep her safe, both her and my tiny nephew.

But I need to get home.

I should never have left earlier, thundering out the door in the wake of angry words. Like a clown. Like a jackass. Like a childish fucking punk who has never deserved the girl who loves him and sure as hell doesn't deserve her now.

I left her alone.

That's right, I left her alone with her tears and her anguish and her swollen belly. I should have known better. I should have behaved better. And now I'm cursing the wind and the sky and every horrifying second that separates us.

My phone is useless, the battery dead. This too is worth cursing and again, the failure is mine. For so long I was a careless nomad, indifferent to people, unconcerned with the future.

Honestly, I was a selfish dick.

I still am.

But I'd willingly crawl over every inch of the world on my knees while begging for one more chance to get it right, to be worthy of her.

The wind answers with a ferocious laugh that rattles the bones of my truck. A layer of dust is scraped from the floor of west Texas and swirls through the air. I punch the gas anyway and rocket down the private country road, away from my sister's house. The steering wheel requires both hands and it's still a battle to keep the truck straight. When I reach the end of the road, I hang a sharp right toward Arcana and finally get a clear view of what's coming.

A furious mass of dark clouds has collected directly over the vulnerable heart of my hometown. I'm not far away, less than three miles, yet immediately I know I won't get there in time. All I can do is watch with powerless dread as the sky swirls and comes to a decision.

The change is abrupt and furious.

I've only ever seen this phenomenon from a comfortable distance. Accelerating in its direction is beyond reckless but this doesn't matter. All that matters is what might be forever lost in a moment. That's all it takes, only a moment for a catastrophe to reach down from the heavens and engrave itself on the landscape below.

"Please," I whisper. "Please."

This is the only plea I know how to make.

It's not that I've forgotten my prayers.

No, I never knew them in the first place.

The truck is being battered while I keep fighting with the steering wheel. Visibility evaporates. The wind shrieks through the cracks, blotting out all other sound.

I understand I'm in danger.

I don't fucking care.

I would trade my safety for hers. My life for hers.

This is the bargain I make, to anyone who might be listening.

It's not an even trade. My wife is worth ten of me.

Maybe that's why the offer is ignored.

The front tire catches the edge of a ditch and pitches down with a thud. Flooring the gas does nothing but spin the wheels. A tree branch spins out of the vortex and dents the hood of my truck. The smell of the dirt and the roar of the wind is consuming.

I should be afraid and I am, but not for myself. There are things worse than dying.

Then the dust clears and I see it; a thick, churning nightmare, indifferent to the agony it generates. It's a monster more terrifying than anything invented in Hollywood. It is as heartless as it is unstoppable.

There's a flash of electricity as the dense cloud intersects with a stoplight. The tornado abruptly spins to the west and begins to fall apart. In another minute it will no longer exist.

With a savage yank on the stick shift, I try to reverse. The truck lurches but remains stubbornly stuck in the ditch. I curse and try again. And again. Finally, a small miracle nudges the truck back to solid ground. The thick overhead clouds depart with the storm and the sunshine peeks through as I race over roads I could navigate while blindfolded.

A chunk of downtown Arcana is a scrambled mess of destruction but there's no time to focus on this right now. Trees have been bent to the side and in some cases beheaded entirely. Debris is hideously clumped in some areas and nonexistent in others. One building will stand untouched right beside its ruined neighbor.

This storm, like all storms, was a fickle bastard.

The streets beyond downtown are a mixed bag. Some paths are blocked entirely and I need to roll over curbs and through front yards. Here and there, dazed people emerge and blink at the sky. Some of them I can recognize. Some of them might need help. And I'll help them, all of them. I'll help every soul in Arcana until my fingers bleed once I know she's safe, her and the baby.

I'm two blocks from home. The damage isn't so awful here and my chest lightens with hope. Some broken trees and displaced lawn furniture. A single white minivan that has somehow been pushed on its side. But all the homes are standing.

Two right turns later and my whole world implodes.

The scene is a cruel spectacle. The north side of the street is pristine, the houses slightly assaulted but intact. The south side has suffered the brunt. Erratic and brutal, the twister saved the worst of its fury to inflict right here.

Right here. *Right fucking here.*

Right where I assembled a crib for my unborn child earlier today.

Right here where I last saw my pregnant wife.

Just before we fought.

Just before I ran out on her.

My heart splinters and my skin is numb.

I'm vaguely aware that the truck has stopped, that I eject from the driver's side and stagger the last terrible feet to fall to my knees in front of the fatal pile of wood and glass and random unimportant things. I see the warped horror that used to be a house and understand that there is no storm cellar and no basement. No one could have survived in there.

Still, I will dig frantically through every last shard and plank.

I will do this until I find her.

But first, I tilt my head back and with all the useless, miserable heartbreak that has now damned me to this waking hell, I scream her name at the sky.

ONE YEAR EARLIER....

1

SUSANNA

Whenever I wake up in this room, part of my brain is convinced I'm still a teenager.

After all, everything looks the same as it did then.

My old bedroom is unchanged because that's how my father left it, even after my mother divorced him the year I bolted to college and rarely visited.

Before making the leap forward to the present, I'm irritated by the noise coming from the kitchen. Drew Toledo has always risen with the sun. There must have been a thousand mornings when I'd be jarred awake by the slamming of the kitchen cabinets or the clatter of dishes in the sink as he hurried through his breakfast, his mind not on any sleeping inhabitants of the house but distracted by the football strategies constantly running through his head. He'd be thinking of his players and the team and the pressures of an expectant town that drools over state championships, budgeting far more for the high school football program than for the high school science department.

The slow shuffle of slippers on tile and a loud grunt of pain reminds me of the way things are now. I toss the covers back, pull an oversized hoodie over my pajamas and hurry down the stairs in my bare feet.

He has spilled juice on the counter and wears a tight grimace as he reaches for a dishcloth to mop up the mess. My breath sticks in my chest, as it sometimes does when I'm confronted with the sight of my father as he is now instead of how he used to be.

"Dad, I'll clean it up. Sit down." I don't mean to sound like a weary parent and I'm afraid that I do so I add a gentle "Please," at the end.

My dad glances over his shoulder and rewards with me with a ghostly smile. "Sorry, Susie."

He gingerly takes a step toward the nearest wooden chair and fumbles when the edge of his slipper catches the table leg. Instinctively, I reach for his arm so that he doesn't fall. Three months ago he was doing nothing more strenuous than frying eggs when he dropped the spatula and lost his balance trying to retrieve it. The fall fractured his left wrist and radius. Yet the damage could have been far worse. His hospital scans confirmed what we already knew; his bones are riddled with cancer. Fracturing a hip or a femur wouldn't take much and would be far tougher to recover from.

Recover.

An illogical word when dealing with terminal illness. The indomitable Drew Toledo – high school football coach, teacher and local hero – won't be recovering.

The day I received the call about the kitchen mishap was the day I left San Antonio and returned to Arcana indefinitely. He had already been sick for nearly two years and I waited longer than I should have, always stopped by my father's stubborn insistence that he doesn't need help from anyone and especially not from his only child.

He doesn't resist when I hold his elbow to help him into the chair. He leans back as if exhausted and rubs a hand over his jaw.

It's an effort to keep my face neutral as I turn and wipe down the counter. I'd never want him to know how I defeated a shudder of dread when my fingers sank into the flaccid flesh of his arm. My father was always a powerful, dynamic man who could easily intimidate other men with one look. But those thick layers of muscle have melted and now the skin sags from his tired bones.

One of the few meals he'll still eat is steel cut oatmeal with fresh berries. He makes no objection when I begin to prepare a bowl.

"Are you sure you feel up to going today?" I slice off the top of a strawberry with a butter knife. "Everyone will understand if you need to rest."

"It's Jace's wedding," he says in a way that suggests he'll crawl there if he must. "Of course I'm going."

I slice the strawberry in half and feel lucky that the knife blade is so dull or I might have pierced my finger.

Naturally, this day means a lot to my dad. He coached Jace to the state championship in high school and then watched with supreme satisfaction as Jace excelled in college, was drafted into the NFL and then led his team to a Super Bowl victory. Even if the Arcana High football team could only boast of a mixed record of winning seasons during my father's tenure as head coach, he always had the miracle year that brought a state title home and he could always point to Jace Zielinski, his crowning accomplishment, his pride and joy.

The monologue inside my head sounds bitter.

Perhaps it is, just a little.

Jace is not at fault. We went to high school together and while we weren't exactly friends, we weren't enemies at all. In fact, we had something in common when we both suffered devastating heartbreaks at the same time. Jace was a decent guy back then and from what I can tell, he's a good man now. Last year he shocked the world when he quit football at the height of his career and moved back here to Arcana. At least twice a week he checks in with his old coach and I know he's sincere when he urges me to let him know if there's ever anything at all he can do for my dad. Jace Zielinski is actually quite impossible to dislike. I just wish I got along with my father as well as he does.

After slicing one more strawberry, I present the bowl to my dad, who frowns at it.

"Not really hungry, Susie."

I retrieve a spoon anyway and hand it over. No one else calls me Susie or ever has. "Just a few bites. You get dizzy when you don't eat."

He throws me a stubborn look but accepts the spoon. I pour two glasses of juice and take a seat at the table. My dad quits stirring his oatmeal when I push one of the glasses across the table. He sighs.

I'd like to sigh too but manage to stop myself.

The mood has become awkward and I wish I had my phone, or a newspaper, or even a cereal box. Something to look at so it doesn't seem like I'm hovering and hoping for just a few ounces of that spongy oatmeal to find my father's mouth.

He fills about a third of the spoon and relays it past his lips slowly, taking a long time to swallow. He scowls when he notices that I'm watching. We have the same eyes; a deep, clear green framed by dark lashes, although lately his look dull and bloodshot. My mother would always exclaim over the luck of my green-eyed inheritance and then she'd scold me for failing to wear makeup properly.

"Susanna, did you spend any time at the mirror this morning? You could at least capitalize on your best feature."

If my dad was in the room when she dropped such comments, he would glare at her and announce in his thunderous Dare-You-To-Argue tone that I looked just fine. Having his support meant the world. We shared an alliance, or so I thought. Even as my social butterfly mother fretted over producing such an ungainly daughter, my father beamed over my stellar grades and seemed forever pleased every time he found me immersed in a book.

But my mother would pout when he contradicted her, which he did more and more, leading to an increasing number of arguments.

There was a time when they loved each other. I'm not sure when their troubles began but I do know for certain that they never planned to have only one child. And I'm sure they never planned to become so unhappy with each other that divorce became the only logical next step.

As for the so-called alliance between me and my father...

That was destroyed a long time ago, right here in this house.

The man sitting here struggling to eat a bowl of oatmeal is still my dad. I still love him no matter what. I will never regret giving up my life in San Antonio and returning here to care for him when he has no one else.

But we're both aware that we never did recover and return to the way we once were.

"You should come today," my father says, setting down his spoon in a sign that he might be finished trying to eat. "Jace and Tori invited you."

I know they have. Tori Malene even called last week with a personal invitation. Hearing her voice again after so many years was a strange dose of nostalgia. Tori and I were never best buddies but we were friendly back in high school, both of us members of the Student Council and Honor Society. I always liked Tori. She was direct and confident and had no patience for gossip. Last year she and Jace reconnected after many years apart. They were high school sweethearts.

No, that sounds inadequate.

Tori Malene and Jace Zielinski were the most epic of love stories. They grew up next door to each other, their families hopelessly intertwined. When they fell in love, they fell in love completely. And when they all fell apart, the wreckage was tragic to see. The fact that they have overcome all those old wounds and lost time is a victory. They are a walking, breathing happy ending. Who wouldn't want to see that?

"Colt will be there," my father adds, as if that piece of information is something I would be unaware of.

Of course Colt will be there. He's the groom's best friend. He's the bride's brother.

He's also the boy I was once madly, desperately in love with and haven't seen in a decade.

Colt Malene doesn't live in Arcana. He hasn't lived here since he was a kid and I don't have a clear picture on where he actually does live now. Colt moves around a lot. I'm told he visits often now that Jace and Tori have settled down on a nice piece of property right outside town.

My father watches me with eagerness, thinking that perhaps the temptation of Colt Malene will change my mind. The guilt weighs heavily, even after all these years. Or maybe it only really began bothering him when he discovered he was dying.

There was a time when Colt Malene's name was part of our everyday conversation. Colt was more than his prodigy, his future star quarterback. My dad took a sincere interest in all his young players, but Colt was special. Colt was like the son he'd never been fortunate enough to have. He even invited Colt to live here when Colt's mother announced a plan to move fifty miles away to Bredon.

But it wasn't to be.

Drew Toledo has many fine qualities, however tolerance isn't one of them. When Colt broke an important rule, my father didn't hesitate to exile him in a very cruel way. And no amount of heartbroken tears from his only daughter made any difference.

Still, ten years have passed between then and now. For a little while Colt and I shared something wild and wonderful, but it ended horribly in a whirlwind of painful drama. I doubt that Colt has thought of me much in the years since. I can't say the same.

My eyes stay focused on a worn spot on the table where the finish has been rubbed off and I trace the shape with my fingernail. "I really can't. I've got too much to do."

Silence from across the table. Then the clink of the spoon scraping the side of the oatmeal bowl.

I lift my eyes in time to see my father shovel an oatmeal-covered strawberry into his mouth. He tries to chew and makes a face. A pang of sorrow overwhelms me and I stand up, feeling helpless. "Is the oatmeal too thick? Or would you like me to add some brown sugar?"

"Nah." He swishes the food around for a long moment and manages to swallow. "Told you I'm not that hungry this morning."

I can't very well force feed him. I change the subject. "Is Paul still able to give you a ride to the wedding this afternoon?"

"Yeah, he gets to be my chauffeur today."

My dad was displeased when I took the keys to his truck last month. I had no choice. One day he limped outside, climbed behind the wheel and promptly mowed down three innocent recycling bins that could have easily been people. Confiscating his keys was not a pleasant moment for either of us and a miserable reminder of just how completely our roles have shifted.

While my dad continues to make a bleak attempt at ingesting his oatmeal, I toast two slices of whole wheat bread and top them with a drizzle of honey. As expected, he shakes his head when I offer him one.

We never ate together in the morning as a family. I'm not sure families do that at all in real life. Typically, my mother would still be asleep when I dashed in here to hunt through the pantry for something shrink wrapped and portable. If football season wasn't underway, then I could usually catch a ride to school with my dad. But during the playing season he tended to live on the field or in the weight room or fastened to the chair in his closet-sized office beside the gymnasium, eyes glued to a laptop screen while he dissected footage from the most recent game. Football is my father's religion. It comes with the territory. There's no end to the pressure to produce a winning season in a small town obsessed with the sport.

"What do you need to do?"

The questions startles me. I was chewing my toast and reminiscing. Now I realize my father has probably been studying me the entire time.

He raises a greying eyebrow. "You said you couldn't go to the wedding because you have so much to do."

Dry toast crumbs stick to the roof of my mouth and I sip my juice to buy a few seconds of time, trying to invent an excuse. "Work tasks. That's all."

"Right." He nods with a frown, leaving me to wonder if he's figured out that I'm not on sabbatical like I claimed. My sabbatical request was denied. I quit the following day. Admitting to my father that I'd sacrificed an excellent position and slapped my condo on the market before returning here to take care of him would only make him unhappy.

I don't put up a fuss when he pushes his food to the side of the bowl in order to make it seem like he's eaten more than he really has. He rises from the table and he's clearly tired, so tired. He says he's just going to sit out back on the creaky wicker lounge chair and watch a movie on his iPad. This might sound like an unremarkable way to spend the morning, but only to someone who never knew my father in his prime.

An hour later, I check on him and find that he's fallen asleep, the iPad balanced precariously on the arm of his chair. I relocate the device safely to the nearby picnic table and my dad grimaces in his sleep. He's in the shade of the patio pergola and the weather is clear and warm, not a cloud in the sky. Jace and Tori will have a beautiful day for their wedding at Capstone Park and I'm happy for both of them. I'm told that Jace hired security to keep the press away. The wedding is to be small, only friends and family. Colt will no doubt be standing at Jace's side as his best man.

There have been moments of weakness when I searched for any sign of Colt on social media, hungry to see what had become of him. I've never found any internet evidence that a man named Colt Malene even exists. For many years his fate was entirely private, and entirely a mystery.

Paul Elkins shows up promptly at two in the afternoon. An Arcana fixture and longtime close friend of the Zielinksi family, he's thrilled to be entrusted with the task of escorting the bride down the aisle today. Paul's law office has occupied a central location in the tiny downtown commercial district for decades. He must be in his seventies now but time hasn't cost him much except his hair while adding a network of wrinkles to his face. He is bright-eyed and healthy and I can't help but compare his vitality to that of my father, who is more than twenty years younger.

The suit my dad retrieved from the depths of his closet no longer fits him properly, but he's in good spirits and I bite back the urge to instruct him to stay hydrated and not tire himself out. A short reception beneath a tent in the park will follow the ceremony and Paul promises to return before dark.

"These old bones require a lot of rest to function," Paul says with cheer and although I doubt this is true, I give him a smile because I suspect he intends to cut his own night short in order to bring my father home early.

The carefully wrapped wedding gift is one that I chose on a trip to the Plainsfield Mall. I was at a loss what to buy for a millionaire NFL champ but finally settled on something sentimental; a wooden cutting board engraved with their names and wedding date, along with a matching set of coasters.

I stand just outside the front door and watch my father slowly carry the wrapped gift to the vintage gold Cadillac waiting at the curb. Paul waves at me after getting my father settled in the passenger seat and I keep watching until the car's taillights disappear around the corner.

The fragrance of newly blooming lilacs is a tempting incentive to remain outside. The single file line of lilac bushes were tiny when we moved in the summer before I began high school and now they've grown into a dense hedgerow. Andrea Wilkerson jogs by on the side-walk and waves. I wave back and feel relieved when she bops past without stopping to chat. She knew my mother in high school. Arcana is my mother's hometown, not my father's. He's from Okla-homa, an only and unexpected child of parents who were approaching retirement by the time he finished high school and died before I was born.

Impulsively, I walk across the tousled and overgrown lawn to break off a handful of lilac stems. I'll find something to use as a vase. The interior of the house has remained frozen in time ever since my mother moved out. Lately there is a vague but horridly sweet smell of sickness, difficult to describe but detectable none-theless.

Carrying a fistful of lilacs, I reluctantly duck back indoors. I will spend the afternoon mopping and dusting and rotating cycles of laundry. The weather is pleasant enough to keep the windows open and I clap on a pair of wireless headphones with plans to finish the audio book I started yesterday. Romance is a genre I rarely read but I'm enjoying this lighthearted romantic comedy about a quirky small town in Vermont. I'm sorry when it ends and automatically select the next book in the series.

Whether in books or in real life, romance isn't often on my mind. My longest relationship, just shy of a year, ended recently and was anything but passionate. Nate and I never even had sex. Since college I've dated sporadically but nothing ever seems to escalate. I'm aware that much of the fault lies with me. I've been accused of being too clinical. Stuffy. Aloof. Now and then when I'm out in public, I examine random couples relishing their bubble of contentment and wonder if I'll ever rediscover the ability to fall in love, to feel that overwhelming connection with another person.

When such thoughts cross my mind, so does Colt Malene.

And instantly I feel ridiculous. We were so young. So much time has passed. Besides, Colt's memories of me might be more bad than good. It's unlikely he dwells on them much at all.

There's a lot of square footage in a five bedroom house and after two solid hours of scrubbing and mopping and dusting, my cotton shirt sticks unpleasantly to my sweaty skin. This place is far too large for a single man. It was even excessive for a family of three when we moved in. My parents were still hopeful that more children would miraculously show up. I wonder if the two of them would still be together had that been the case.

Possibly, but I doubt it.

My dad was twenty-four and an assistant coach at UT Austin when they met. My mother was a student who loved her sorority but disliked the academic side of university life, switching majors every semester. Within a year they were married. She was glad to leave her studies behind when he received a job offer at a junior college in Arizona. My earliest memories are of Arizona, of heat and tiny lizards and the muted colors of the desert. From infancy I was a spectator at college football games, seated right beside my mother, outfitted in pigtails and little cheerleading costumes. The rules of the game were taught to me early but the action on the field never kept my interest.

No, my spellbound eyes would stay glued to my father as he paced the sidelines and barked at the referees and hollered encouragement to his players. At home, my dad enjoyed quiet surroundings and simple things like watching a pink sunset from a backyard lawn chair with a cold beer in his hand. On the field, my father became a lion. His love for the job was stamped into every move and it was impossible to imagine him doing anything else. We might have stayed in Arizona, if it weren't for funding cuts that hit the athletic department of his small college. Ultimately, he was enticed back to Texas by a head coaching job at a Dallas area high school.

The cracks in my parents' marriage likely predated the move. My father was endlessly working. My mother was endlessly dissatisfied. We lived in a handsome brick house on a peaceful cul-de-sac and when their tempers flared, they tore each other apart. I would retreat to my pink and cream bedroom and find solace in my latest stack of library books, blotting out the furious shouting.

While my mother and I were always rather incompatible, I adored my father. Nothing motivated me more than his proud smile when I presented yet another academic accomplishment. I was so far ahead of the other students that a big meeting between my parents and the administration was called where it was decided that I should skip the fifth grade. The idea of skipping a grade did not appeal to me. I had few friends as it was. My father, however, was ecstatic.

"That's my daughter, Susanna, the genius."

I knew I wasn't exceptionally pretty. Nor was I remotely athletic. But I was *smart*. I was reading at age three and never met a test I couldn't ace. Disappointing my father was inconceivable. I agreed to skip the fifth grade. I even pretended to be excited about it.

To me, life in Dallas was mostly pleasant, despite hearing the quarrels of my parents while being the constant project of my hopeful mother. She dragged me to ballet class. I ran off the stage in the middle of a recital. She pushed me into gymnastics. I fractured my wrist on a fall from the balance beam. My mother loved me. I knew that. She didn't *want* to feel disappointed in her only child but she did. She spoke endlessly of Arcana, like it was a magical land instead of a fading small town in west Texas. If only she could raise me in Arcana, where she grew up, then everything would be different. Everything would be better.

When Arcana High announced a search for a new football coach, she was sure this was a dream come true. My dad wasn't convinced. He was happy where he was. But she begged and pleaded and ultimately he gave in, accepting a pay cut and a less prestigious position. I was thirteen when we moved to Arcana, with its lackluster downtown, obsessive football devotion and inadequate high school. My parents' marriage hung on for another five years but wound up being doomed anyway.

I hope that last fact wasn't partly my fault but I suspect that it was.

Last week while searching for my father's medication, I discovered that he keeps a photo of my mother in the top drawer of his nightstand. It's an old photo, taken in their early dating days and now left carefully face up, like he wants to be able to open the drawer and gaze at her face whenever the mood strikes him. She wears a sexy red bikini while a gerbera daisy flops over her left ear and her lips are parted in a laugh.

The photo strikes me as an intimate one and I'm not sure he'd want me to know he keeps it close. My mother now lives an hour away with her new husband and never visits the town she was so desperate to return to. It's my dad who has remained in here in Arcana alone. Or at least he *was* alone. I won't let him be alone for what little time he has left.

True to his word, Paul deposits my father at the front door before twilight sets in. I'm plumping the sofa cushions for the second time when my dad strolls in with a broad smile, looking happier than I've seen him in ages.

A smile spreads across my face in return. "How was the wedding?"

He shuts the door behind him. "Terrific. I'm glad I went. Tori was a gorgeous bride. Paul's granddaughter sang with the band."

"Oh? That's nice."

"Yup. We're having a guest for dinner tomorrow."

The abrupt change in topic is so surprising that I drop the pillow I was holding. "A guest?"

He's still smiling even though his bony shoulders are hunched with exhaustion. "Don't worry about cooking anything. He said he'd pick up some pizzas from Giorgio's."

I'm glad the couch is right behind me because I have an urgent need to sit down. The pillow I dropped a moment ago gets pulled into my lap. My fingers dig into the scratchy upholstery. "*Who* said he'd pick up pizzas?"

I don't know why I asked. I'm ninety nine percent sure I know the answer.

"Colt Malene," replies my dad, clearly delighted and expecting me to be delighted too.

Pulling off a poker face is a challenge right now. Fortunately, my dad fails to examine my expression as he rattles off an explanation.

Colt is remaining in town while Tori and Jace are on their honeymoon. The newlyweds will be traveling the western United States in a luxury RV and Colt volunteered to stick around in order to watch their dog. He'll be staying only two miles from here, in a house that used to belong to Jace's grandmother.

I remember that house on Tumbleweed Lane. It's where Jace Zielinski grew up, raised by his sweet, if slightly eccentric, grandmother. Gloria Zielinski was on a first name basis with the entire town and managed most of the Arcana High fundraising events. She always had a smile ready whenever she saw me. She would often declare that someday I would make our hometown famous.

Of course, I did nothing of the kind. I dutifully applied myself in college and earned a well paying, if rather dull, job with a pharmaceutical company. I have no complaints, but I've certainly done nothing worthy of fame. No, instead it would be her own grandson, the NFL quarterback and Super Bowl champion, who put Arcana on the map.

Gloria Zielinski passed away suddenly about a year and a half ago. My father mentioned her funeral during one of our rare phone calls. At the time, I did wonder if Colt showed up at the funeral but I could not find the nerve to ask. In any case, Gloria's house wasn't the only Tumbleweed Lane landmark known to me. The Malenes lived right next door.

While my brain has been preoccupied ever since my dad dropped the dinner bombshell, he has kept up a cheerful Colt-based monologue. Eventually he notices that I have not uttered a word.

"Susie?" His forehead creases.

My pulse races but my voice is calm. "What time is dinner tomorrow?"

The lines in his forehead smooth out. "I told him six o'clock would be fine. Is it fine?" He sounds so worried, and so eager.

The couch pillow remains in my clutches. How fortunate it has no feelings because the death grip of my fingers would otherwise be painful. "Of course it's fine."

Relieved, he lowers himself carefully into the leather armchair opposite the large screen television. "Good."

In just twenty-four hours our bland living room will be hosting Colt Malene. He might be sitting right here in the spot I'm currently occupying on the sofa. This is difficult to imagine.

I flex my fingers and give the pillow a break. "I'll bake something for dessert."

I'm not good at baking and don't enjoy it but the offer makes my father happy.

His dry lips split into a grin. "Perfect."

I've known all along that returning to Arcana would come with the possibility of seeing Colt again. I should be prepared. Yet somehow I'm not prepared at all.

There's no reason to cook dinner tonight since my dad claims to have eaten at the wedding, which may or may not be true. He's tired, more tired than usual, and by the time the streetlights flicker on outside he's ready to retreat to his bedroom.

"Good night, Susie," he murmurs and then suffers a harsh coughing fit that leaves him struggling to inhale. Yet he waves me away with irritation when I try to help him. Thankfully, his bedroom is on the first floor. He hasn't been able to manage the stairs for weeks.

"Good night, Dad." I'm standing awkwardly in the hallway. Once his door is closed, I look around for something to do. The kitchen is spotless but still I wipe down the kitchen counters with a square of cheesecloth and swallow hard to banish the bubble of nausea in my gut. I know I'm not sick and this feeling is one I've become accustomed to. It's a precursor to the inevitable grief that awaits at the end of this journey.

It's one thing to logically understand that your father is dying.

It's quite another to watch it happen in slow motion.

I wish suddenly, and urgently, for siblings. Our family is small and has never been close. I do have one cousin, the son of my mother's deceased older brother. He's a Navy SEAL now and isn't really in touch. My small pool of friendships tend to be work oriented and superficial. Normally, I'm not bothered about being alone but right now I'm very bothered. Even a friendly voice on the phone would be welcome and I consider calling my mother until I remember she's currently vacationing on a river boat with her husband.

Empty rooms feel lonelier when darkness falls and I switch on the television set for company. An upbeat show featuring an energetic couple searching for beachfront real estate hums in the background while I take a seat at the kitchen table with a bowl of dry cereal and scratch out a grocery list. I'll go shopping in the morning. Early.

The list is short and I set the pen down. The television couple bickers over whether they should choose the four bedroom Tudor style cottage set back from the shoreline or the modern home with walls of glass facing the ocean. They share three sons and they've been married for fifteen years. He teases her. She laughs. They choose the cottage.

I wonder what Colt is doing right now. It's strange to think of him nearby. The rowdy, hilarious, impulsive teenage boy with a devastating smile might have little in common with the man he's become.

All I know of Colt is what I've learned secondhand. He wasn't seen in Arcana for many years. He moves around often. He and Jace were also estranged for a long time. Evidently, he now likes the company of dogs. And apparently he still eats pizza from Giorgio's.

Other than those vague scraps of intelligence, Colt Malene is unknown to me. I have no idea what to expect when he shows up tomorrow.

Back in high school, we had little in common. We were fascinated with each other anyway. It's possible we have even less in common now.

In fact, there's a strong likelihood that Colt and I may have nothing to say to each other at all. Given the way he was treated by my father, and then by me, I can't imagine why he would choose to spend an evening here.

I'm afraid to find out.

2

COLT

I've seen only two weddings in my life.

Ten years ago, I got baked off my ass in order to watch my mother exchange corny vows in a cheap reception hall with one of my nondescript stepfathers.

That was the first wedding.

The second wedding was yesterday.

There was *nothing* corny or cheap about yesterday.

On average, I'm about as sentimental as a tree trunk. But damn if I didn't have to blink back a film of tears and breathe through the tightness in my throat as I watched my sister marry my best friend. I'm not a believer in soul mates and destiny and shit, but when I look at Tori and Jace I'm forced to change my mind. There's no one more deserving of a storybook ending than the two of them and that's exactly what they got.

Tori was beautiful in her dress. Jace got choked up when he delivered the heartfelt vows he'd written himself. Their day was a long time coming. They fought the odds for the right to stand up in front of everyone they care about and declare their promises to one another.

Naturally, there were some uninvited guests. Jace expected there would be. Some of those asshole paparazzi were caught slinking around the perimeter of the park right before the ceremony, trying to snatch photos they could sell for a quick buck. As the best man, I considered it my job to make sure they got escorted out of sight real quick. Jace announced his retirement from the NFL last year but he's still an object of extreme interest. After all, why would pro football's most talented quarterback quit right after he led his team to a Super Bowl victory? The move didn't make a damn bit of sense to most people.

But it made perfect sense to me.

Jace never wanted to wear the crown of the national football king in the first place. He was always happier standing outside the center of attention. He wanted privacy, away from the spotlight. He wanted to be a writer. He wanted to spend his years beside the girl he'd been in love with since we were all kids bashing around the dull streets of Arcana together. He has sworn to me that from now on, his number one job is to make my sister happy. He gets all my respect for that.

I can't guess how differently things would have gone for him, and for Tori, and for me, if our trio hadn't been shattered a decade ago. Were like the Three Musketeers; fiercely loyal, always together, assuming no matter what kind of rotten crap the whole world and our shitty parents decided to throw our way, we'd always have each other.

Until we didn't.

Not everything that happened next was my fault but some of it was. That's always been a tough cross to bear, understanding that I'd failed them both. We all had our problems back then, but I was the goddamn president of the Fucked Up Teenager Club. When the dust settled, I'd destroyed my friendship with Jace and my sister could hardly bear to look at me. I figured the best thing I could do for them was to stay out of their lives and that's how things stood for a long time.

And then fate extended an olive branch.

Last year Jace showed up at a remote Wyoming job site where I was employed for the season. He had tracked me down for a reason. And what he had to say changed everything.

While I was off in the woods building homesteads for people I'd never even meet, my sister had gone through hell while living in California. After surviving a brutal assault from her boss, she'd become addicted to pain meds. She also suffered from PTSD as a result of the attack. She needed help.

More than anything, she needed her brother.

When Tori and I were kids, sometimes people would think we were twins. We're not. We don't even have the same father. Like all siblings, we fought now and then, but I would have done anything for my sister. Had I known what had happened to her, I would have been at her side in a heartbeat. However, Tori and I hardly ever spoke anymore. I had no fucking clue what was going on until Jace paid me an urgent visit out of the blue. He and Tori were together again, another fact that almost knocked me flat. Jace came armed with an important request.

"Come home to Arcana."

I didn't need any convincing. If my sister needed me, then I would go.

Jace was right. Tori did need help. Together, Jace and I drove her to an exclusive rehab facility where she would have the chance to get well. Then we barreled straight to the California coast and paid a visit to the sociopath who figured he would never face any consequences for what he had done to her.

We proved him wrong. When I need to smile, all I do is think about the moment Jace smashed that motherfucker's head into his desk. Blood and teeth everywhere. So much screaming. Fuck, it was magnificent. Jace promised the bastard he'd suffer far worse if he ever came near Tori again.

Tori did recover and she returned home to Jace. They bought a modest place right outside town and began to plan their future.

Yesterday was far more than a wedding in the park. It was proof that we've all come full circle. Jace and Tori are married. I've been given a chance to be Jace's best friend again. I'm now a dependable brother to my amazing sister.

This is the way things should have ended up all along.

An urgent canine whine jolts me out of my daydream. McClane's scarred nose nudges my hand.

"I didn't forget about you, pal." I scratch the sleek fur behind his ears and he turns to me with a look that could be called a smile, if dogs had the ability to smile. I believe this one really does smile. He's Jace's dog and he's smarter than some of the people I've come across. He had been a stray and his battle wounds hint he might have been used in a fighting pit. He's an excellent hiking companion, always trotting along right by my side.

I would estimate we've traveled about three circuitous miles through the unmarked flatland east of town before pausing to take a break on a boulder, the same one I recall stumbling across as a kid. Finding that big rock in exactly the same spot and knowing it's been doing nothing but baking under the sun year after year feels signifi-cant. Like I ought to be moved by the evidence that some shit stays the same no matter what else is going on.

If Jace were around, he could definitely put that thought into better words. Tori says he's writing again, that he's almost done with the first draft of his book. Imagine writing an entire book. I can hardly sit still long enough to tap out three lines of text.

The dog is happy now that he's getting some of my attention and I check the position of the sun. I don't wear a watch and I've long refused to be cemented to my phone, although these days I'm trying to stay in touch more because my sister gets upset when I don't answer. I think I left the phone in my truck, which was parked at the edge of Old Country Road before we took this long walk. But I'm good at reading the sky and I don't need a digital clock to tell me that it's after four in the afternoon.

This means it's time to head back. I've got plans that need to be kept.

McClane thumps his tail when I pour water into the cap of a

thermos and push it in front of his nose. He laps up the contents in about three seconds and I fill it again.

When I remember tonight's plans, my thoughts swerve to a different place.

Among yesterday's wedding guests was my old football coach, Drew Toledo. There's kind of a rough backstory between us but I find no value in nursing ancient grudges and I made it a point to visit him the first time I returned to Arcana. The guy's got terminal cancer and his wife is married to another man now. He lives alone, or at least he was living alone until recently.

"Colt, you probably heard my daughter Susanna is in town for a while. I know she'd love to see you. Why don't you come over for dinner tomorrow?"

Yeah, I already knew that Susanna Toledo had temporarily moved back here from San Antonio to care for her dying father. Tori mentioned it, said she even tried to prod Susanna into coming to the wedding. My sister's voice leaked some curiosity, like she was wondering what my reaction would be to hearing Susanna's name.

On the outside, I didn't have one. I changed the subject.

If Tori had questions, she didn't ask them. To this day she doesn't know everything that happened me and Susanna. Neither does Jace. They thought I was just dicking around in the way I always dicked around.

Whatever.

Sure as hell doesn't matter now.

Still, I couldn't force myself to pass up this chance when my old coach threw the idea out there. I even offered to bring pizza. As for the restless tightening in my gut today, that shouldn't be nerves but it is. Susanna and I haven't seen each other or spoken in ten years.

Her dad says she's a scientist. She's probably got some scientist boyfriend awaiting her return to San Antonio. I can just picture him. He couldn't complete an hour of hard labor to save his life, but he drives a ninety thousand dollar car, reads physics textbooks for fun and slips Einstein quotes into everyday conversation.

He's a fucking tool, this boyfriend of hers, and I already hate his imaginary ass even though I just invented him ten seconds ago.

When I snort out loud, the dog's head whips around to stare at me. I wouldn't say it's hot today but the sky is clear and it's warm enough. Maybe warm enough for the sun to fry what few brain cells are still rattling around in my head. I mean, here I sit, getting all jealous of some dude who might not exist while feeling anxious about seeing a girl who probably hasn't given me a second thought since high school. It's kind of a sad sack way to spend time.

Back in the day, Susanna and I burned for each other like crazy. But anyone could have guessed that we weren't built to last. We were always too different.

I don't know when my right hand strayed down to the keychain hanging from my belt loop but I feel the pad of my thumb absently graze a recognizable shape, an old piece of metal that's become worn and scratched through all our travels together. Jace's sharp eyes caught sight of it recently and he was shocked. He asked if it's the same one I used to have and with a nod I confirmed that it was. He might have been waiting for an explanation but Jace knows I don't hand out information I don't feel like handing out so he let it go. Even my sister has never heard the story behind the good luck charm that I've kept close at hand all these years.

McClane's ears twitch when I get to my feet after screwing the thermos cap back on. "You ready for the trip back? Come on, double time." I snap my fingers and take off at a brisk trot.

The dog matches my steps, glad for the exertion. That's what I love about dogs, this one in particular. He's just happy to go with the flow. We cover the flat miles in record time and I open the passenger door, whistling to McClane to jump inside. I'm dusty and sweaty and in need of a shower before I can be considered presentable.

There's not a lot of activity on the Arcana streets today. Jace and Tori's wedding was probably the highlight of the year. This is a small town that looks to have gotten smaller since my youth. It's true that outside interest has spiked since NFL champion Jace Zielinski decided to move back here, but many of the downtown buildings are still in need of a facelift and there are fewer retail establishments than there once was. Jace and Tori are hoping to change that and their optimism knows no limits. To them, Arcana is, was and will always be home.

For me, it's not as simple. This is where I grew up and when I'm here, I'm glad to be back on familiar ground. I just can't imagine ever sticking around permanently. In three weeks when Jace and Tori return from their honeymoon and reclaim custody of McClane, I plan to be on my way. I'll be back again to visit. Everyone I care about is in Arcana. I just won't ever live here again.

With one finger, I slide the steering wheel into a right turn on Tumbleweed Lane. When Gloria Zielinski died she left strict instructions in her will. Her house was to be left in equal shares to three people.

Her grandson, Jace.

And Tori.

And me.

My sister and I were the kids next door and Gloria always treated us like spare grandchildren. I spent countless nights on Gloria's couch when I didn't feel like returning to my own house. I was served endless meals at Gloria's kitchen table because my mother rarely stayed up to date on the grocery shopping. Gloria was heartbroken over what happened between the three of us.

There was probably a creative legal way around the terms of her will but Jace was determined to honor his grandmother's wishes and did not challenge the will or attempt to sell the property. Gloria left no explanation for her decision but she must have been holding out hope even after all this time. Hope that somehow the three of us could be salvaged. Or maybe she had some kind of uncanny ability to predict the future. In any case, right here in this little house is where Tori and Jace reconnected after so many years apart. They have their own home now and this house sits empty most of the time, awaiting my sporadic visits.

McClane leaps through the front door the second I crack it open. He claims his favorite spot on the living room sofa, performs a noisy yawn and drops his broad jaw into his paws. By the time I'm finished adding some food to his empty bowl, he's breathing deeply with his eyes closed.

I sure wish I had the talent to nap on demand like that, even if it wouldn't come in handy right now because I've got other things to do. Following a quick shower, I'm standing in the middle of the guest bedroom and emptying the contents of my duffel bag in search of something decent to wear. I'm not a stylish dresser and the small mountain of denim, flannel and faded t-shirts would never win a wardrobe competition. Finally, I select a pair of jeans that look slightly newer than the others and pull on a plain blue shirt over a white tee. I roll the sleeves above my elbows and hope the wrinkles will sort themselves out since I don't own an iron.

Back in the living room, McClane is in the middle of a happy dream. His tail wags and he laps up invisible treats while stretched across the entire sofa.

"I'll be back," I tell him on my way to the door.

His ears perk up but he remains asleep. He's not the kind of dog who chews things up or throws a tantrum when he's alone so I'm not worried about Gloria's house getting ripped apart. I'll always think of it as Gloria's house, no matter how long she's gone. She was on my mind a lot yesterday as I watched Jace and Tori exchange their vows. Gloria would have given anything to see their wedding. Jace seemed sure that somehow Gloria had a front row seat from the mystical unknown. I like to think that's true.

All the energy spent hiking and showering and brooding over my outfit choice has swallowed a lot of time and I'm now in danger of being late.

Damn.

I should have called in the order to Giorgio's ahead of time.

I also should have shaved, a fact that occurs to me when I catch a glimpse of my face in the mirror. For yesterday's wedding I was clean shaven but overall I have kind of an on again/off again relationship with the razor. Sometimes I quit shaving for months on end and sprout a mismatched reddish beard that always becomes annoying sooner or later. Right now I just look kind of sloppy but there's no time to do anything about that.

With a grunt, I steer my truck down Tumbleweed Lane and wonder why I'm giving myself a complex. I never spend more than three seconds fretting over my appearance and it's unlikely that Susanna Toledo is going to shut the door in my face if I show up with a day of beard growth. Honestly, I never have any trouble turning the heads of women whether I want to or not. Most of the time, I don't want to.

Sex tends to come with strings and expectations attached. I've turned down many promising fucks when reading between the lines sets off alarm bells, hints that there's hope of a *relationship*. I'm terrible at those and I hate being the reason for anyone's tears. Yet I feel no envy when I see happy couples like Jace and Tori. I can't imagine being like them.

"Fuck." Now I'm rolling past Giorgio's Pizzeria and I can see there's a line of people stretching out the door. There's no way I'll make it to Toledo's house by six and because I don't collect phone numbers I can't even call to warn that I'm going to be late.

As luck would have it, I catch a break when the owner spots me waiting in line and walks over for a chat. Steve Giorgio catered the wedding yesterday and thanks to the fact that his restaurant is a favorite of football star Jace Zielinski, business has been booming. He's known me since I was a kid and must be eager to give out favors in gratitude to Jace because he pulls me inside the restaurant and insists on handing over free pizzas.

Normally I don't accept favors with grace but I can make an exception today. Steve Giorgio nods with a smile when I mumble a heap of awkward thank yous. On my way out the door I stuff two twenties into the tip jar by the front register.

Pulling up to Coach Toledo's house shouldn't feel weird. This isn't my first visit.

It's just the first visit in a long time where I'll be coming face to face with the girl I once loved more than I should have.

I dig my phone out of the glove box. The battery is at two percent and the time is eighteen minutes past six.

With two hot pizza boxes balanced on one palm, I glance up at the easternmost window on the second floor and wonder if Susanna stays in her old room. This neighborhood isn't a central location and there was rarely a reason for me to pass this way when walking was the only means of local transportation. Somehow I would often find myself on this street anyway, pausing there on the sidewalk I just stepped across, staring up at a window belonging to a girl who made me feel all kinds of problematic things.

For a second those days melt into this moment. Then I blink and suddenly it seems like I'm thinking about shit that happened to someone else two lifetimes ago. Memories are funny like that. Now and then they tumble over themselves and fuck with your head.

One finger presses the cracked plastic doorbell and a tuneless chime moans inside the walls. I don't count the passing seconds but they feel endless. I'm on the verge of pressing the ugly doorbell again when the knob turns and the door swings open.

Susanna Toledo never considered herself beautiful and she was always wrong.

She'd be even more wrong now.

The glasses she always wore are missing, as is the single loose ponytail that used to trail halfway down her back. Her hair is a rich dark brown, slightly wavy, and falls just past her shoulders. She's wearing makeup but not a lot and she's uneasy, flattening her palms on her slim hips as we appraise each other wordlessly for longer than a heartbeat.

"I'm late," I say because someone has to say something.

"I know," she replies.

It occurs to me that the words we've just spoken to each other are packed with more meaning than they seem to be.

Her clear green eyes are impossible to read when they fasten to mine. Susanna has never flinched from looking anyone in the eye and she still doesn't.

I can feel a smile breaking free. "Nice to see you again, Susanna."

Her lips part and then close just as swiftly.

She doesn't return the sentiment but she does step back from the doorway in a sign that I'm allowed to come in.

3

SUSANNA

Originally, I chose a dress, one that I assumed had been packed away into my storage unit and was surprised to discover at the bottom of my largest suitcase. The dress, with a bright turquoise bodice and floral printed skirt, had been a gift from my mother two birthdays ago, part of her enduring but well meaning effort to install fashion sense in her unwilling only daughter.

The dress is not one I would have decided to purchase but I can grudgingly admit that my mother has good taste and the style does suit me. I don't have an outstanding figure. I'm too thin in the important places and my breasts don't quite fill a B cup. Yet I'm pleased with the reflection in the bathroom vanity and even apply a dash of lip gloss with touches of eyeliner and mascara. My glasses have been replaced with contacts for the evening and my hair shines. I am my own harshest critic and even I think I look damn good.

Following one final mirror appraisal, I slip on a pair of black flats and dash downstairs to the kitchen to toss the large garden salad I'd prepared to serve with dinner. It's a colorful bowl of iceberg lettuce, grape tomatoes and slivers of shaved carrots. The salad makes up for an earlier baking mishap, the evidence of which still sits atop the stove and is responsible for a faintly lingering acrid odor that hasn't quite been extinguished despite the open windows.

Satisfied with the salad, I shake a bottle of Italian dressing. It's just too bad I forgot to replace the cap when I removed the safety seal. Dressing lands everywhere, including on the skirt of my dress.

"SHIT!"

"Susie?" My father's anxious voice drifts from the living room.

"I'm fine, Dad." Gritting my teeth, I run a checkered dishtowel under the tap and dab at the vinegar-scented splotch. The effort is pointless. I toss the dishtowel in the direction of the apron sink. The thing has the nerve to bounce off the surface and fall to the floor with a splat.

"What happened?" My dad stands in the doorway and observes the scene with dismay.

"It's nothing, no big deal." I swoop down to retrieve the dropped dishcloth and use it to remove oily salad dressing from my hands. "I just need to run upstairs and change."

This makes my father unhappy. Since he woke up this morning he's been watching the clock in anticipation of our dinner guest. "But Colt will be here any minute."

"I know that," I mutter before trudging upstairs. I don't have another surprise dress squirrelled away in my luggage. The best I can do is a pair of dark jeans and a black v-neck top that's been laundered a few too many times but still looks respectable. Somehow the tangy aroma of salad dressing still clings to me so I spritz a few fragrant pumps of honeysuckle perfume and gallop back down the stairs.

Apparently, I shouldn't have rushed. Though it's a quarter after six there's still no sign of Colt. My father has returned to his armchair but keeps glancing at the wall clock with a frown.

Growing up as the daughter of a football coach is probably similar to being reared by a drill sergeant. I was raised to believe in early rising, resolute determination and fanatical punctuality. While I was never required to run laps or kicked off a practice field, my dad's ideals were ingrained in me since I could walk. Even now the thought of arriving to a meeting or an appointment thirty seconds late is enough to send my heart racing.

My father stares at the clock. I fold the napkins on the dining room table. The table is a chic dark wood colossus designed to seat fourteen people, but I can't remember an occasion that filled less than half the available seats. My mother declined to take the table with her when she left. I don't know why my father has kept it.

The three place settings look somewhat sad and lonely amid all the empty space. For the fifth time I straighten the blue linen placemats and struggle with the cork in a bottle of red wine found in my dad's largely untouched liquor cabinet.

He eyes me from his armchair. "I'm not sure Colt drinks wine."

The cork releases with a pop. "I drink wine, Dad."

"You do?"

"Sometimes."

Once or twice a year. I set the bottle down on the table.

My father is still watching. "I think that bottle came from Eddie."

"Eddie?"

"Eddie Moldano. Used to be part owner of that Ford dealership in Plainsfield. He moved to Idaho a couple of years back."

"Oh." I remember Eddie's son, Tony, from high school. He was a football player. He was also an asshole.

"Yeah," my dad nods. "I remember for sure now. Eddie gave me that bottle. It was a gift the year we won State."

I say nothing and consider the placement of the glass salad bowl. A pivotal year, that state championship season. Jace Zielinski was a second string player full of untapped potential until the quarterback spot opened up. A spot that was originally reserved for his best friend, Colt Malene.

The salad bowl gets relocated from the center of the table to a spot closer to the head.

I step back from the table and survey my work. There's no centerpiece. I should have found a centerpiece. A flower arrangement perhaps or a candle display.

All at once I'm annoyed.

Annoyed with myself for fretting over a simple dinner.

Annoyed with my father for extending the invitation to Colt in the first place.

And most of all I'm annoyed with Colt. For being late. For returning to Arcana.

For existing.

No, that's not true. I wouldn't be in such a state if I didn't really want to see him.

I *do* want to see him.

It's all I've been able to think about.

The doorbell rings and I freeze.

My dad tries to rise from his chair and erupts into a coughing fit.

"Are you okay?" I ask him as he hacks into his elbow and turns red in the face. He waves at me and points to the door.

I've seen no recent pictures of Colt. In an era where people record every meal and milestone for the world to see, Colt has no social media profile at all. When I open the door I'm not expecting to find the teenage boy I remember so clearly. Indeed, that's not who I find at all.

He's bigger, brawnier. His eyes are as blue as ever and match the color of his simple button down shirt.

He's also completely, jaw droppingly gorgeous.

I thought I'd lost the taste for rugged tough guys, instead trending toward polished academic types. The instant pull of attraction now zooming through every muscle in my body betrays the truth. At one glance, it's clear that Colt, with his rough, unshaven appearance and blunt stare, has nothing in common with the men who would usually prompt me to look twice.

It's also clear that no one else has ever, or will ever, have the effect on me that he does.

"I'm late," he says casually, two pizza boxes balanced on the palm of one large hand.

"I know." This sounds rude.

But he smiles. "Nice to see you again, Susanna."

Politeness is not a virtue I struggle with, but I've devolved in an instant. I've returned to the gawky, infatuated teenage girl I used to be. Without responding to him, I step back and retreat to the dining room.

My dad has recovered from his cough and makes up for my lack of obvious enthusiasm by fawning all over Colt. He pumps Colt's free hand and greets him with delight, as if they didn't just see each other yesterday at the wedding. He slaps Colt on the back and steers him to the table with a huge grin on his face.

It's all a little surreal, considering.

Colt sets down the pizza and flips open the lid of the top box. My dad rapid fires questions and Colt answers courteously, if monosyllabically.

"Did Jace and Tori leave for their honeymoon already?"

"Yup."

"Wasn't that a fabulous wedding yesterday?"

"Sure."

I've already poured myself a glass of wine and gulped a large mouthful. My dad beams at me.

"Doesn't my Susie look stunning?"

I nearly spit wine all over the damask tablecloth.

Colt's head swivels in my direction. He's thoughtful as he looks me up and down. My cheeks catch fire.

"Yes," Colt says, quite matter-of-factly and adds nothing else. He takes a seat and seizes two slices of pizza from the open box. Before I can offer him some wine, he notices the filtered water pitcher on the table and fills his glass.

My dad eases into the cushioned chair at the head of the table. He gestures to the salad bowl. "Susie did an excellent job with the salad. Don't you think so?"

Colt is amused. He takes a large helping of salad and then his eyes skim over me with a smirk. I ball my fists in my lap, trying not to squirm in my chair. One glance from him can still do this to me. There was always something magnetic about Colt but the years have added a raw, brute sexiness. I force my gaze away from his lips and refuse to imagine how it would feel to kiss him, to touch him, to be underneath him.

My fingers clench around the stem of the wine glass. Thank goodness I'm not strong. The thing might have shattered in my hand.

"Why don't you have some salad, Dad?" Without awaiting an answer, I take my father's empty plate and fill it with pizza and salad, including a generous portion of grape tomatoes because they are among his favorites. He picks up the tiniest bite of lettuce, nibbles at the edges.

Colt pays careful attention as I serve my father. Then he proceeds to shovel food into his mouth with the speed of a caveman.

He's not a talker, this adult version of Colt. He'll respond to direct questions but his answers are short and he doesn't elaborate. I don't get the impression he hates being here, but neither is he thrilled. He's cautious, unreadable. I can't even guess what he's thinking.

"Susie is a scientist," my father announces and from the lack of surprise on Colt's face I get the feeling he's heard this news before. Maybe more than once. He wipes his mouth with a napkin and settles back in his chair.

"That's nice," says Colt.

"She's extremely successful," my dad insists.

I swallow a bite of pizza. I'm beginning to feel like a five-year-old being paraded around by a swaggering helicopter parent. "Actually, I'm a chemical engineer. I used to work for a pharmaceutical company."

"Sounds interesting," Colt says, although his tone implies boredom.

"*Used* to work?" My father is staring at me now. "You love your job. Aren't you planning to go back?"

"Yes, of course." My bottom lip tends to tremble when I lie so I flatten my mouth into a thin line.

Colt notices. He raises an eyebrow.

"She's is in charge of an entire floor of scientists," my father boasts.

Colt nods.

My dad takes that as a cue to continue bragging. "And she's been earning six figures since she graduated from college."

Oh god.

This is mortifying.

"No kidding," Colt says and while he keeps his voice even, I could swear he's on the verge of rolling his eyes.

"Sure," says my dad. "She's one of the best scientists in the country."

That isn't even close to true and this time Colt can't contain a snort of laughter. He shakes his head and empties a packet of parmesan cheese on his pizza.

True, my father's praise is cringeworthy. Yet I can't help but feel defensive.

I grab the wine bottle and top off my glass. "So, what do you do again, Colt? I heard you're an itinerant builder of custom housing or something."

He shrugs. "If that's what you've heard then why did you ask?"

"Because I was curious about where you actually live."

"Usually close to whatever job site I'm working at."

"How unconventional," I mutter and instantly wish I'd said nothing because the comment sounds condescending.

Colt agrees.

He delivers a flat glare. "I don't know what you mean by that, Susanna."

"Well, don't you ever want to settle down in one place and have a real home?"

He doesn't hesitate. "No, I do not."

We stare at each other. He thinks I'm being a bitch. Maybe I am. Maybe we both are.

I pick up a pizza slice and bite off a large section, partially to stop my mouth from running.

My father looks back and forth with confusion, like he can sense the tension but is unsure why.

I'm not real clear on the reason myself.

Colt crosses his arms and observes me chewing in silence, as if he knows the act will unnerve me.

Which it does.

"Is that what *you* want?" he asks me when I'm still chewing after thirty seconds. "To settle down and have a real home?"

The enormous bite of pizza doesn't go down easily. I'm forced to take a big sip of wine before answering. "I do have a real home."

But I don't, not really.

The thought has never occurred to me before but the sale on my condo was finalized last week. I have every intention of remaining here to care for my father but I'm also painfully aware that's a task unlikely to extend past the summer. I'm not sure what I'll do when he's gone. I've been deliberately refusing to consider my next move. The idea of remaining in this big house alone is ghastly. And Arcana isn't exactly brimming with job opportunities that would suit me. It's possible to argue that right now I'm about as rootless as Colt.

Colt's mocking blue eyes are no longer boring into me. Instead, he's gazing around, looking at the photos on the wall and perhaps noticing that my parents' wedding picture remains prominently displayed. His focus shifts back to my dad, who is currently pushing grape tomatoes back and forth on his plate and making a sour face.

Right now, I'm wondering if Colt is recalling the good times, when Drew Toledo was his devoted coach and mentor.

Or the bad times, when Drew Toledo became his worst enemy.

In any case, he certainly had no obligation to come here tonight and suffer through an awkward meal. Colt might be a little rough around the edges but I'm not exactly bursting with social graces either.

I should do better, be nicer.

"I bet you get to see a lot of interesting sights," I say, trying to sound interested and cordial. "I mean, since your work takes you to so many different places."

It takes Colt a few seconds to realize that I'm speaking to him. He takes his time trying to decide if I'm being sarcastic and then decides that I'm not.

"You could say that." He shifts in his chair, drums his fingers on the table and swivels his head toward the door. He gives the impression that having a prolonged conversation is not something he is used to doing. Or enjoys. This seems strange, considering that once upon a time, Colt Malene was the most fun loving, extroverted guy I've ever known.

But I also remember when he changed.

Abruptly.

Irrevocably.

I suppose we both did. In different ways.

After a long moment of silence that sends me wracking my brain for something else to say, Colt finally clears his throat. "In fact, I helped Jace map out a route for the honeymoon."

I nod, relieved to have a topic to seize on. "That's great. I heard he bought an RV for the trip."

"He did. He surprised Tori with it."

The thought of Jace and Tori's romantic honeymoon adventure is a nice one. Some love stories do work out after all. Some dreams come true in the end.

My dad jumps back into the conversation and asks Colt if there has been any more trouble with tabloid stalkers. Colt shakes his head and says he expects the press has lost interest now that Jace has left town. My dad sighs and I can read him well enough to know when he's growing wistful. He's still in disbelief that Jace chose early retirement, turning his back on a successful NFL career that would have made him a legend.

"Remember that thirty yard pass he threw in the fourth quarter?" My dad stabs his fork into the tomato that's been shuffled back and forth across his plate. He's rehashing Jace's winning Super Bowl game. Again. If he was thinking clearly, he'd probably realize that football might be a touchy subject at this particular gathering. After all, Colt's dream, the one thing he ever truly wanted and worked for, was to be a pro quarterback.

Colt, however, seems unbothered by the subject. A smile even shoots across his face, stealing my breath for a second. No other man on earth has this talent, to kickstart my heart with the most casual of smiles. Colt Malene's smile dredges up too many memories. Of him. Of us.

"I remember," Colt says, sounding nothing but proud of his best friend.

Colt and Jace. Jace and Colt.

They were infamous best friends, the lords of Arcana High. Close as any brothers. Everyone knew them, or wished they did. By the time they faced each other as rivals on a high school football field, their friendship was already badly damaged. That was the night of a brutal confrontation, of a hollow victory, of understanding that I hadn't done the right thing after all.

I'd done the opposite.

Just when I was hoping my father would have the sense to move on from the topic of football, he studies Colt and says something that shouldn't be said. "You had such incredible talent. You should be in the middle of your own NFL career."

I can feel my mouth pull into a wince. Everyone sitting in this room knows the reason why Colt stopped playing football. Or *should* know. Lately my father's mind isn't nearly as sharp. I suppose it's possible he's forgotten.

"Colt Malene will never get fucking near a football field again."

Colt returns my father's stare. I'm expecting to see anger but there is none. I'm not sure what his blank expression means.

"Things just didn't work out that way," Colt says without a hint of malice and calmly takes another slice of pizza.

I rise to my feet a little too suddenly. The chair tips over.

"There are cookies," I announce. "Chocolate chip."

My dad abandons his torture of the grape tomatoes and sets his fork down. "The ones you made this afternoon? You said you burned them."

"Just a little."

"I thought you threw them away."

"I didn't." Only because I forgot. They are still sitting on a flat silver cookie sheet on the counter and might be edible if one doesn't mind scraping a blackened layer off the bottom.

My dad frowns. Then brightens. "You know something? There's a twenty dollar bill that's been burning a hole in my pocket." To prove this, he stands, slowly extracts his billfold from khaki pants that hang from his withered frame, and drops a single bill on the table. "Why don't you two go out and get some ice cream from that new place that just opened?"

His suggestion is full of eagerness. This thrills him, sending us out on a pseudo-date as if we're a couple of teenagers. This is something he never would have done back when we actually *were* teenagers.

Colt looks at me. I look at him.

"Get me a pint of butter pecan," my dad adds. He carefully lowers himself back into his chair. "I've been craving it all day."

These days it's rare to hear that he's craving anything. Despite my best efforts to coax food into his mouth, my dad eats like a bird and a little less each day. I'll happily get him his butter pecan ice cream if that's what he wants.

"I can go myself." I pick up the chair. "It'll give you two a chance to visit more."

"I can drive." Colt stands up too. "Anyway, my truck is blocking your driveway."

"You don't mind moving it, do you?"

"No. But you shouldn't get behind the wheel after guzzling half a bottle of wine."

I don't appreciate the comment. Since Colt's arrival, I've had exactly two glasses, not 'half a bottle'. And Colt is hardly one to be handing out lectures on alcohol consumption. Back in his Arcana High heyday, he had a reputation for drinking like a frat boy on perpetual spring break. He once barreled his mother's car into a stop sign while plastered off his ass.

But instead of arguing, I smile at him. "All right, Colt. You drive."

Colt doesn't make a move to pluck the twenty off the table so I do it instead, not because I need the cash but because my dad's feelings might be hurt if I don't. Colt reaches the front door first and holds it open for me.

My father, still at the table, waves at us gaily.

"Take your time," he urges, clearly pleased to see us leaving together, side by side. I wonder if Colt finds this moment as bizarre as I do.

A gentle spring twilight has settled but the darkness brings a slight chill to the air and I debate running back inside for a sweater. But no, we won't be gone long. It's a short drive to downtown Arcana and back.

The vehicle that partially blocks the driveway is a washed-out orange pickup.

"Montana plates," I notice with some surprise. That must be where he spends at least some of his time.

Colt unlocks the passenger side door the old fashioned way, with a long silver key. "Yup," is all he says and then walks over to the driver's side with his head down.

The interior of Colt's truck is clean and instantly I think of Christmas, courtesy of the pine scented air freshener dangling from the rearview mirror. There are no other personal objects in sight; no random receipts or empty soda cups. The windshield is free of smudges and bug splatter. I'm still buckling my seatbelt when Colt jumps behind the wheel and fires up the engine. But he doesn't drive off, not yet. He turns my way and gives me a long, searching look.

Again, a long dormant piece of my soul quivers.

Maybe he wants to say something, perhaps something important that he couldn't say earlier while we were regarding each other with mutual wariness across the dining room table.

"Colt..." I hear the breathy longing in my voice, the lost years and regrets. Then I don't know what else to say so I bite the corner of my lip and wait.

He's still staring. "I can't drive until you close the door."

I blink.

And then I realize that the passenger door still hangs wide open.

"Right." Feeling like an idiot, I reach over and yank it closed.

Colt immediately rolls away from the curb. He drives slowly down the street and takes care to use his blinker before making a left. He looks straight ahead, eyes fixed on the road. My own eyes keep sliding over for a peek at his profile. He is classic, square jawed, chiseled perfection. I can't think of a single celebrity who could outshine him.

But surely he's aware of his appeal. He must have battalions of horny women falling at his feet. He doesn't need to catch me drooling.

I force myself to turn away and stare at the passing houses. All the windows in Colt's truck are open. Gooseflesh erupts on my bare arms. I always did get cold too easily. I couldn't imagine living in a place like Montana.

"The new ice cream parlor is three doors down from Giorgio's," I tell him, in case he didn't know.

"Yeah, I've seen it."

I rub my arms, partly for warmth and partly due to anxiety. "I really want to thank you for coming to dinner tonight. It means a lot to him, seeing you again."

Downtown Arcana has seen some recent improvements but still looks a little anemic. Colt swings his truck into a narrow parking lot that has just been repaved. He backs into an empty space and cuts the engine. He doesn't make a move to leave the truck right away and neither do I.

Colt finally sighs. "How is he doing? I mean *really* doing?"

"Dying." The word still accompanies shockwaves of dread. I have to swallow hard before continuing. "He keeps losing weight. The cancer's deep in his bones now. The doctor doesn't know how much more time he has left."

Colt nods and it's clear the news is expected but still troubles him. "And you're planning to stay in town?"

"Yes. But he doesn't know that my leave of absence from work was denied and I quit. It's fine. I can always find another job. But I sold my condo in San Antonio and I don't plan to go back. I'll stay here in Arcana until...well, for now."

I didn't mean to be so revealing. Colt is silent, although I have no doubt he's listened to every word. The prolonged silence is not uncomfortable, although I do wish he'd say something.

My hand strays to the door handle. "If you prefer, you can wait here while I go inside for the ice cream. Did you know that Hannah Graff owns the place?"

Not that it matters now, but back in high school Colt used to date Hannah Graff's younger sister, Brynna. Arcana is small enough where these connections are never surprising.

Colt runs a hand over his jaw. "Didn't know that. But I did hear she married Aiden Rios."

"Yes. He used to be a cop in Plainsfield but he just joined the Arcana PD."

He nods. "Talked to Aiden yesterday. He was hired to help work security at the wedding."

My hand remains frozen to the door handle. "So is strawberry still your favorite flavor?"

His fleeting smile shakes my senses, proof that Colt Malene still has the power to unravel me whenever he wants to.

"Susanna Toledo and her perfect memory," he says. "Yeah, I still like strawberry."

I shiver and crack the door open. "I'll be right back."

"Wait." Colt swiftly unbuttons his shirt and shrugs out of it. He tosses the shirt in my lap and I gawk, thunderstruck, at the way his impressive muscles stretch the material of a basic white tee.

"What's this for?"

"You're cold." He begins fiddling with the radio.

The shirt is soft and still holds the warmth of his skin. It smells of soap with the tint of spiced aftershave and I drape it over my shoulders. "Thanks."

Colt continues messing with the radio. Anyone else would be pulling out a phone right now to connect to the digital world. Not Colt. I haven't seen him glance at his phone at all this evening and once he finds a radio station that plays old country ballads, he appears content to lean back in his seat and enjoy the music.

Feeling out of sorts, I exit his truck and make the short walk over to the ice cream parlor. Hannah is training a new employee, a red-faced teenage boy who takes his job very seriously and prepares my order with extreme care. Hannah greets me warmly and asks after my dad. She was two grades ahead of me in school and I always liked her far better than her snotty younger sister.

I don't want to discuss death and cancer anymore tonight so I lie to Hannah. I tell her that my father is doing well and yes, of course I will tell him she said hello.

Hannah quickly rings up my order and insists on extending a friends and family discount. That's what happens when you are the coach's daughter in a small town. Drew Toledo remains an extremely popular Arcana resident, the man who brought the state title home and coached the legendary Jace Zielinski. Two years ago, his health demanded an early retirement and the high school has had trouble keeping his position filled, resorting to a rotating roster of temporary replacements.

Stepping out of Hannah's ice cream shop and into the small, familiar world of downtown Arcana summons a nostalgic tenderness for the town I couldn't wait to leave and yet still think of as home. I suppose I won't have any reason to visit ever again once my dad is gone.

I hate when such thoughts creep up on me.

A sudden breeze carries with it a distinct chill and I pull Colt's shirt closed. Wearing his shirt shouldn't feel like such an act of intimacy. If I'd experienced passion more recently then I probably wouldn't be on the verge of swooning over a silly shirt. I can't help the fact that the most intensely sensual moments of my life happened many years ago and included Colt.

He waits in the exact same position in the driver's seat while Johnny Cash's hypnotic voice drifts through the open windows and promises to walk the line. Colt doesn't notice me until I open the passenger door and that's when I realize his eyes had been closed.

"You got your ice cream?" he asks. I've noticed that his words now have more of a country twang than they used to.

"Yes." I climb into the truck and manage to bump my head on the frame. "I got butter pecan, strawberry and -"

"Vanilla," he finishes, proving I'm not the only one with a good memory. Vanilla has always been my favorite. He looks me over. "How hard did you hit your head?"

I rub at the tender spot on my forehead and grumble, "I'll survive. But I'm living proof that time doesn't erase clumsiness."

Colt chuckles, a low timbre that yields a fluttering sensation in my belly.

Johnny Cash finishes singing. The next song is one I don't recognize. Colt waits until my seatbelt is buckled before driving away. The paper bag containing the ice cream rustles in my hand and I relax my tight grip. Being close to Colt, being alone with Colt, shouldn't make me anxious. He glances over when I clear my throat.

"You're staying in town the whole time Jace and Tori are gone?"

"Yeah. I have a break between jobs. Besides, someone needed to take care of McClane."

"That's Jace's dog, right?"

"Hell of a dog. But I don't think he knows he's a dog."

"Maybe that's because he has a man's name."

"True. Jace named him after the main character from *Die Hard*."

I have to admit I'm entertained by the thought of Colt rearranging his plans to look after his best friend's pet.

"Susanna." Suddenly he's very serious. He pauses at a stop sign and shifts in the driver's seat, a hint that something important is on his mind.

I realize I'm holding my breath, waiting to hear what comes next. "Yes?"

The truck rolls forward. "I've been thinking...."

I wait. And wait.

Colt moves his hands high on the steering wheel and I wonder if he's changed his mind about whatever he intended to share. One more turn and we'll be back on my street.

"You've been thinking about what, Colt?"

"You're right about your dad. I know how much it means to him when I come around. But more than that, I know he really wants to see us hanging out together."

Us.

The word bounces around in my head in an exciting way, even if that's not what Colt meant.

"I know he enjoyed having dinner with you tonight. Again, thank you for coming. You didn't have to do that and I'm grateful."

Colt pulls up in front of my house. No one has turned the carriage lights on but the living room window shutters are open. I wonder if my father is watching us right now.

"I'll be in town for three weeks," Colt says. Even in the darkness the heat of his gaze is piercing. Yet he speaks slowly, measuring the words before unleashing them. "I don't have any plans other than dog sitting. Let's make him happy."

"What do you mean?"

"We could see more of each other. For his sake. I mean, if you're up for it."

"You really want to do that?"

"Wouldn't have asked if I didn't."

A sudden head rush leaves me speechless for a few seconds and I chew my lip while Colt waits.

"Colt, I don't mean to sound unappreciative. But we both know why there's no love lost between you and my father. Why would you go out of your way to make him happy?"

He thinks about the question for so long I'm afraid he's offended. He taps his fingers on the steering wheel and then directs a very long, frank stare my way before responding.

"I'm not proud of every choice I've made. I think he knows how that feels and he doesn't have much time left to make up for it. So, what do you say, Susanna? Can you stand the sight of me hanging around for a little while?"

I swallow and order my heart to quit pounding. "Yes, I can stand the sight of you."

"Good." He nods and promptly hops out of the truck.

Colt keeps his head down on the walk to the front door. I feel like

I should fill the silence with something meaningful but I have no idea what to say.

My dad is waiting in his armchair with a grin full of joy. "Welcome back, kids."

I hold up the bag. "I've got your butter pecan right here."

The three of us reclaim our seats at the absurdly long dining room table and he tries. He really does. He brings the pink plastic spoon to his mouth again and again, attempting to slurp some rapidly melting ice cream through dry lips. He's not very successful, though the light never fades from his face as he watches me. He watches Colt nearly as much.

How I wish there was a way to rewind time, to the days that seem so long ago, when he was the vigorous, invincible Coach Toledo, when my mother remained part of our family, when I was certain that there couldn't possibly be a better man in all of Texas than my dad, when the complexity and sorrow of the future was not even a shadow.

Colt is slightly more talkative over dessert. He supplies more details about Tori and Jace's trip. He's seen all the places they are going. The Grand Canyon. Yellowstone. Glacier National Park. I've seen none of them. I'm not a traveler, not adventurous, never have been. I enjoy the comforts of home in my pajamas. It seems Colt and I are more different than ever.

The overhead lighting in the dining room affords an excellent view of Colt's impressive physique. The boy positively bursts with strapping muscle and I struggle to focus my eyes elsewhere.

Before long, my father yawns and then grimaces. He's in pain much of the time and rarely agrees to take the medication that would help him manage it.

Colt is perceptive enough to catch on and stands. "I should get going. The dog needs to be let out."

He ignores my protests that I'll clear the table myself and conveys all the dirty dishes to the kitchen sink. When he returns, his keys are already in his hand and he looks straight at me.

"What time should I come by to pick you up tomorrow, Susanna?"

"Uh...tomorrow..." I'm sure that I should already know what he's talking about.

Colt seems to agree that I should already know what he means. "We're going out tomorrow night, aren't we?"

"Oh! Yes. We're going out. I'm going out with you tomorrow." I haven't ingested a drop of wine since those first two glasses and yet somehow I still manage to sound drunk.

Colt waits. He lifts an eyebrow. "So what time is good?"

"I don't know. Five. Six. You pick." It just keeps getting worse. I've turned into a babbling imbecile.

"She'll be ready at six," my dad says, plainly delighted.

I have no better suggestions and so I agree. "I'll be ready at six."

Colt twirls his keys. "I'll be here at six."

He's reached the door by the time I find my voice again.

"Bye!"

He turns. Stares. "Bye."

It's only when I hear his truck vroom to life and take off that I realize I'm still wearing his shirt.

"Well." My dad pushes back from the table. "How nice to see you two spending time together."

"Yes." I don't really know what else to say.

Colt has recognized that my father desperately wants to atone for the past. All he's doing is trying to ease a dying man's conscience. Tomorrow night isn't technically a date. I need to keep this in mind.

"Hey Susie, do you know where my iPad is?"

I look up to find my dad is searching the cracks in the couch cushions.

"I saw it charging on the kitchen counter. If you want to go to your room I'll bring it to you in a minute."

He nods and rubs a hand over his sagging jaw. "Okay. I was going to watch the Astros game before bed. Maybe I'll be tired enough to sleep tonight."

"Do you want to try the pain meds again?"

"Nah. Makes me feel like I'm underwater."

I don't know what difference that makes when he's just going to bed anyway. "All right, Daddy."

His tender smile is a reminder that he was once a very handsome man. "I'm really glad to know you'll be going out and having fun. I worry about that. I worry that you don't get to have any fun.

"Please don't worry about me. I'm not missing anything."

"Good night, Susie."

His steps down the hall are slow and careful. I hear the water running in the bathroom and then a handful of coughs. I feel the need to rush over and tap on the door to ask if he's all right, but he tends to get annoyed when I do that. Instead, I go to the kitchen and find that Colt managed to conduct a vigorous cleaning campaign though he was in here for less than a minute. All that's left for me to do is switch on the dishwasher and dispose of the unfortunate batch of cookies that were cut too thinly from the tube of cookie dough and then thoughtlessly placed on the lowest rack of the oven. They didn't stand a chance.

I didn't stand a chance either, not from the day I met Colt Malene. He was my first major crush, my first kiss, my first and only love. And my first and only heartbreak. That turbulent history must have influenced the person I am now, for better or for worse.

The iPad is sitting on the counter and I unplug the charger. I haven't heard my dad emerge from the bathroom so I hug the device to my chest and wait.

Colt's offhand comment about my perfect memory returns to bother me. I wouldn't say my memory is technically perfect but a near photographic recall of words on a page has always made life easier.

On the flip side, long ago events and conversations haunt me with persistent clarity. Perhaps my memories of Colt shouldn't remain in the foreground but they do, even now.

All of them, good and bad.

From the very beginning.

4

COLT, AGE 14

I hate sitting around if there might be something better to do, but the air outside feels like hot soup and I have no money so I'm stuck here on the living room couch with Tori and Jace. We're watching *Jurassic Park*. The original, not one of the dumb ass sequels. We're not bothering anyone but along comes my mother, staggering and scowling like the sight of us fucks up her day.

"Get out of here," she slurs, waving her arms around so that she looks like a broken bird. "It's summer. Go get some fresh air!"

That's code for *'get the hell out of the house'*, which is bullshit because we never hang out here. If we're not at the pool or riding a bus to the mall then we're over at Jace's. The only reason we're not at Jace's today is because this afternoon Gloria is hosting her craft club and she and her friends like to show off their latest couch doilies in peace. Gloria is Jace's grandmother and she's the only adult I know who isn't pissed off ninety percent of the time.

"Go on!" My mother shoos us off the couch like we're stray cats. She runs the back of her hand across her mouth and smears pink lip gloss all over her left cheek. She's been in a crappy mood all week thanks to her dipshit boyfriend. Out of nowhere he packed up and moved to Missouri to go live with his ex-wife.

Jace is already heading for the door and Tori hisses something obscene under her breath but I try a different tactic. I smile at my mother and try to sound polite.

"Hey Mom, could we have some cash please?" I'm hoping that she's eager enough to get rid of us that she'll part with a few bucks.

"Go earn your own money!" she shrieks and there go her arms, pinwheeling around again. "I don't have any!"

Well, that's a crock of shit because I know she cashed a big child support check this week and I heard her blabbing on the phone about how she won five hundred bucks on a scratch off lottery ticket.

Tori glares at our mother and mutters, "Let's get out of here. She's totally shitfaced."

That's true. And it's also true that there's usually a man to blame when my mother gets drunk in the daylight, but I feel kind of bad when I see that her eyes are all red and puffy. Even if my mother is a self centered jerk, I still hate seeing her cry.

"Are you okay?" I ask her and the look she throws my way is creepy, like I'm a stranger she doesn't want to be introduced to.

"Leave me the fuck alone," she snaps and then starts staggering down the hall. "All of you!"

That's about all my sister can take. Tori darts outside and slams the door behind her. Jace glances at me with sympathy and follows. He knows all about dickhead parents. He's got two of his own.

When I catch up to Tori and Jace they're all the way at the end of the street. Tori plops right down in the shade of the willow tree that sits on the Morrisons' corner property. Kathy Morrison is a good friend of Gloria's and I know we won't get yelled at for sitting in her front yard for a few minutes.

Tori moves her hair out of her face and from the way her mouth pulls down I know what she's going to say before she says it. "Are you seriously not coming to Dad's again this weekend?"

I don't hesitate. "Nope."

"He's going to be upset."

The fuck he will. Sometimes I don't know if Tori enjoys lying to herself or if she's just trying to turn her wishes into reality. Tori wishes that Eric Malene was really my father and she wishes that I felt like his son.

Neither of things will ever be true.

Every time my dad comes by the same thing happens. His face lights up when he sees Tori and she goes running into his arms while he laughs and says something dumb like, *"There's my princess!"* At some point he gets around to noticing that I'm in the area and he'll nod in my direction with a *"Hi there, Colt,"* kind of flat greeting.

Really, I shouldn't have rocked the boat. I know damn well he's always shelled out gobs of child support without complaint. He's the one who makes sure that we have a house to live in and buys me all the football gear I need.

Eric Malene calls me his son. I call him my dad. We've never talked about the messy details.

Not until recently.

A few months back I was at his place and he was hassling me after getting an earful from my mother about how I was running wild and picking fights and being a dick to my history teacher, and blah fuckitty blah. Eric Malene sat me down and started off with this obnoxious lecture about how when he was my age he knew how to keep his head down and show respect. I should learn how to do the same. But because I was in a crappy mood that day I blurted out words that should never have been said.

"What the fuck do you care anyway? You're not even my real dad."

He froze and his throat bobbed and right then I felt like worse than shit. I knew I'd really hurt his feelings. In another minute I would have apologized and been sincere about it. In fact, I was just about to. But he stood up and ran out of the room without another word.

We haven't really talked much since then and when I started saying that I didn't feel like coming around on weekends anymore he didn't argue. If he'd argued then I probably would have changed my mind. But if he hasn't brought it up yet then he's not going to. As for my mother, she doesn't give a rat's ass where I spend the weekends as long as the child support checks keep flowing and she gets to party her stupid head off.

I don't know who my real father is. I just know it's not Eric Malene.

The only story I know is the same one everyone else in town has heard. Shortly after Tori was born, Eric Malene was deployed with his National Guard unit. The next time he saw his wife, her belly was swollen with some other guy's kid. That kid was me. They didn't stay together for very long after I was born but Eric Malene's name is listed on my birth certificate even though that's biologically impossible. He also assumed legal and financial responsibility for me, which was completely honorable and not something he was required to do. We should have had an important conversation a long time ago but now I've blown it and I don't know how to fix that.

I've never had the guts to ask my mother about my real dad. I'm not sure she even knows who he is. I'm also not sure I want to hear the fucker's name even if she does know.

Tori sighs and quits trying to persuade me to go with her this weekend. I saw her duffel bag sitting in the hallway earlier, all packed and ready to go. I know she can't wait to get out of here for a few days. Lately, she and my mother have been butting heads even more than usual.

It's barely noon and there's a lot of time to kill. We can't really sit under the Morrisons' tree for the next four hours. But without any money, there's not much to do in town except for the public pool and Tori refuses to go there. In fact, she's being real stubborn and grumpy about it. When I try to get her to change her mind she finally yells that she can't go swimming because she has her period, which is a fact that I could have cheerfully avoided hearing about until I die, but I guess the fault is mine for being pushy.

Poor Jace doesn't know where the hell to look when Tori screams the word PERIOD and I feel kind of sorry for him. Jace doesn't have any sisters and even though he's around Tori all the time he doesn't know how sisters can get, all moody and screeching about their periods for no good reason. It's just him and Gloria in the house next door and that's the way it's been ever since Jace's dad dumped him there right after his mother split. Jace doesn't ever talk about his mother and doesn't really talk about his father either, except to complain when the man crashes into town and gives everyone a headache.

He's a real class act, Jace's dad. Always giving Jace a hard time about football, which Jace doesn't care much about, and making a drunken ass out of himself all over town. He's visiting now and he must have been out getting trashed last night because he was passed out in the front seat of his truck this morning. I was eating breakfast at the kitchen table when I watched him fall out of the driver's side door, crawl over to our front lawn and then stand up to take an endless piss at the base of the half dead pecan tree. I can't explain why he'd choose our yard to piss in instead of his own, other than that's just the kind of guy he is.

Jace's dad actually makes my own dad seem like Superman. But I still don't want to go to his house this weekend.

Tori stands up and grumbles that we should just go to the pool without her but I can't do that. At school, she usually sticks with her own friends, but outside of school and especially in the summer she always prefers to hang out with me and Jace. And I'd never ditch my sister. Not even when she acts like a bossy pain because she thinks being one year older means that she gets to be in charge for eternity.

Jace has been pretty quiet. I think he's still recovering from hearing about pools and periods. But now he joins the conversation and says it's too bad we don't have any money. If we did, we could take the bus to Plainsfield and catch the new zombie movie he's been dying to see. He hates asking his grandmother for money because she never has much to spare. His dad doesn't even pay child support. But mine does. And I'm aware that my mother extracted more from him than usual this month because she made up a story that I lost all my football gear and she had to replace it. I could let him know she's lying but that would cause more problems than it's worth. They already hate each other and neither of them are especially fond of me either.

But if my mother can make shit up in order to scam money on my behalf, then I should be entitled to some of it. She might be passed out by now and even if she's not, I could probably sneak in and get to her purse, which always hangs on a hook in the hallway.

When I mention this to Tori, she gets anxious. I know what she's thinking, that I'm going to get caught and then our mom will start threatening to ship me off to military school again. This is a fairly new thing but it's not especially scary, even though I'm sure military school would require infinite pushups and running through forests at four a.m. No, it's not scary because Janna Malene doesn't have enough parental interest to glance at our report cards, let alone shop high and low for some fictional military school that nobody can afford.

"I won't get caught," I tell Tori and she continues to look doubtful.

"Just be careful," she says, a little primly, like I'm a clumsy three-year-old.

"I will."

"I mean it, Colt."

I turn around so she doesn't notice when I roll my eyes. "Be right back."

The Morrisons's wooden gate is unlocked and they won't mind if I cut through their backyard. Tori always thinks she needs to be the one to take care of me. She has no idea how much I actually look out for her. Like last spring when Micah Grant spread a lie that she'd touched his dick under the bleachers during gym class. Everyone knows Micah's a complete bullshit artist but some of those assholes at school like gossip as much as they like making girls feel shitty so they harassed Tori until she couldn't take it anymore and ran out of school so nobody could see her cry.

I don't especially like fighting but I'll do it when I have to. And when some lying sack of shit makes my sister cry, then I have to.

Jace was there, always willing to have my back, when I seized Micah by the collar of his polo shirt and stuffed his head into the dirtiest toilet in the boys' room. I gave Micah a simple choice. He could either admit to the whole school that he's a big fat fucking liar or he could look forward to getting the living shit kicked out of him every single day until we all graduate from high school. Micah cried and pissed his pants and caved completely. Then Jace and I went out for tacos. We never told Tori why Micah decided to apologize and admit the truth.

Four hopped fences later I'm in my own backyard and it's a sorry sight. Next door, Gloria's backyard is a paradise of lush grass and flowers and a fenced in vegetable garden. My backyard, on the other hand, looks like a toxic waste dump. Now and then my mother yells at me to cut the grass but there's not much grass to cut. Just a prickly collection of weeds and rocks and dirt and pieces of broken patio furniture.

Going through the front door is not an option. The hinges are so noisy that opening it would be like yelling 'Hello, I'm here!' through a bullhorn. The window in my bedroom is always unlocked but it's right next to my mother's room. However, Tori's window lock is broken and her room is on the other side of the hall so there's less of a chance I'll be heard.

Just as I'm congratulating myself for moving in complete silence, my left foot kicks one of the painted rocks sitting on Tori's desk. It crashes to the floor as loudly as a gunshot but at least it didn't break. The rock looks like one of Gloria's projects so Tori would have a fit if anything happened to it. Gloria is always giving us stuff. Dinner and homemade birthday cakes and funky little craft items like the ones that are all over her house. Tori and I don't have a grandmother that we hear from more than once a year so having Gloria next door has always meant the world to us.

For a few seconds I remain crouched on top of Tori's desk, waiting for the sound of my mother's footsteps. I'm fast as hell and can be back on the other side of the window and sprinting across the yard to leap the fence before she can turn the doorknob.

Half a minute passes and there's no sound from the hallway. This should be a piece of cake. About eight feet to the right of Tori's bedroom door is the mounted hook rail where my mom's bubblegum pink purse always hangs.

And there it is, right where it should be. Her bulging purple wallet is right on top and I swiftly pluck out two twenties from the sea of bills. She'll never miss it. She'll just think she spent too much on fake nails or something.

I'm about to retreat the way I came in when I freeze at the sound of a man's voice. Then there's laughter. My mother's laughter. This isn't a big house and immediately I know the noise comes from right around the corner in the living room.

"I heard you lost your job again," my mother says.

"Fuck you."

I know that voice too, low and hoarse. That's Jace's dad. Among the things Jace hates the most in this world is the fact that he shares the same name as his father.

There's the sound of glasses clinking together as liquor gets poured into them.

"Good thing I don't depend on you for child support, Jace."

He grunts. "You got lucky. Eric's enough of a pussy to pay for some brat that's not his."

"Yeah, Eric's a lot of things but at least he's no deadbeat drunk. Even your wife got smart enough to take off and never look back."

He's angry now. "Why do you always have to be such a fucking bitch?"

She laughs. "No, I'm the bitch you've never been able to *stop* fucking. Have another shot."

There's a crash, the sound of glass breaking. My breath stalls and my muscles tighten. My mom and Jace's dad never hang out. I'm still confused by the words I overheard but this needs to be put on hold for now. Whatever is happening in there doesn't sound good. She's drunk. He's drunk. Despite my issues with my mother, I'll kill any motherfucker that tries to slap her around.

"So we're gonna play rough today, are we?" My mother's voice has changed to something that makes my skin crawl. "Do it, you bastard."

Next comes a distinct thud and the tearing of fabric, followed by a smothered scream.

That's all I need to hear.

I barrel into the living room, ready for war.

What I find is worse than any violence.

SO MUCH FUCKING WORSE!

My mother lies on her back on the brown carpet. Her shirt is torn down the middle, her skirt is shoved up over her hips and Jace's dad, naked from the waist down, pushes himself between her wide open legs.

"Yeah, oh yeah." She moves underneath him with her tits exposed, clearly having a good time. "Your cock is still the best I've ever had, Jace."

He groans.

I'm frozen.

I'm sick.

The room spins.

"Fucking hate you," growls Jace's dad but he doesn't look like he hates her at all.

Thrust. Thrust. Thrust.

"Hate you more," my mother says but she's smiling.

She stretches her arms up and makes all kinds of noise as they bounce around on the floor together.

Jace Zielinski, not the one who's my best friend, but a different Jace Zielinski, shudders and throws his head back. His eyes snap open.

Eyes that are bright blue. Eyes like mine.

Maybe he saw me in that instant or maybe he didn't.

I don't ever want to know.

Somehow, I've rediscovered the ability to move and I'm running down the hall, dashing across Tori's room and diving out the open window to land on my knees in the dirt. There's a flash of pain when my palm scrapes on a sharp rock but this is nothing. I've staggered all the way to the far side of the backyard when I realize I'm going to puke. Right now. I'm going to puke *right fucking now*. I end up vomiting into gnarly patch of purple sage beside the trash cans and I'm gasping, gagging, unable to take a solid breath.

They all grew up together, my folks and Jace's dad, because that's the kind of small everyone-in-your-business place Arcana is. I knew this and never thought much of it because they're not friends as far as I could tell but they've always known each other.

Always.

"Good thing I don't depend on you for child support."

I don't even remember when I found out that my last name doesn't really belong to me, that my sister is my half sister, that my dad isn't actually my dad, that my mother tells lies and keeps secrets.

"I'm the bitch you've never been able to stop fucking."

Moaning and groaning and naked bodies and the stench of the cheap malt liquor that was spilled all over the floor.

No.

NO.

NO!!!!

Can't think about it, won't fucking think about it.

I can almost hear the click deep in my brain, a switch being flipped.

Refusing to look behind me, I run the back of my hand across my mouth to wipe away strings of saliva. The cereal eaten hours earlier is now a gummy lump in the bushes. The two twenties I stole from my mother's purse remain clenched in my fist.

Slowly, I relax my hand and smooth out the wrinkled bills before folding them in half and stuffing them in my back pocket. Then I start hopping fences back to Tori and Jace.

The two of them are still huddled together underneath the willow tree, deep in conversation. Jace says something that makes Tori laugh.

In a heartbeat, I know I can never tell them what just happened. They'd be upset. Really upset.

My sister likes to act tough in order to hide the fact that she really does get hurt easily. This would hurt her. A lot.

As for Jace, he already struggles with abandonment issues while his relationship with his father is uneasy at best. This would hurt him too.

My best friend notices my arrival first. "You all right, man?" He's concerned, my best friend.

My best friend.

Jace *is* my best friend. He has been since the long ago day when Tori and I discovered him sitting sadly in Gloria's front yard, friendless and alone.

Today I saw and heard things that might change everything.

Everything we know about who we are.

Everything about the little world of Arcana and the past and the future.

I can't let that happen. We need to stay as we are right now, the three of us. No matter what, we'll always have each other. That will never change.

Today I have the power to protect them both and I will.

Forcing a smile, I make a show of waving the cash in the air. "Mission was a success. Now let's go. I'm freaking starving."

We decide to get lunch at Dave's Tacos before taking the bus to Plainsfield. The interior looks as plain as the school cafeteria but the food is both cheap and excellent and there's no limit on how many hot sauce packets you are allowed to have.

Maybe I shouldn't have an appetite at all after what happened, but I wasn't lying when I said I was starving. In fact, I'm so busy stuffing my face that I don't notice when Coach Toledo strolls in and Jace has to poke me in the arm to get my attention.

Drew Toledo is a strapping bear of a man with the loudest voice in the county. We could often hear him belting out orders to the Arcana High varsity players from two blocks away on the middle school athletic field. Everyone says he's tough but the guy sure gets results. Arcana High suffered a long losing streak before he came onboard last year. He whipped up the team into such solid shape there was talk of a state championship but they had to settle for a county title. Still, the future of the Arcana High football program looks bright now that we've once again got a coach who knows how to win. It's been almost twenty years since Arcana went to State and everyone is hungry for another opportunity.

In the fall I'll be starting Arcana High and I'm hell bent on playing quarterback for Coach Toledo. I'll get that state championship the town is craving. No one wants it more than I do.

Toledo is at the counter, yakking with Dave himself. My eyes are so intent on my future coach that at first I don't even see the girl. When I do see her, I take a long second look.

She stands completely still with her head up as she silently observes her father carrying on with Dave. She's taller than most girls, wears a blue and white Save The Whales t-shirt with cracked lettering and her brown hair hangs down her back in a messy ponytail. There are chunky orange flip flops on her feet and her face is overpowered by large black-framed glasses. It's clear she could turn a lot of heads if she chose to and it's equally clear she does not choose to. We've never met but I already know her name. She's Susanna Toledo, the coach's daughter.

Dave notices her standing there and pauses long enough to reach for the tower of fountain cups beside the register. He hands a cup to Susanna and she responds with a smile before scooting over to the drink machine to fill her cup with ice and Dr. Pepper.

Meanwhile, Coach Toledo has been hogging the counter for so long that there are now five people in line behind him. He says something that makes Dave honk with laughter and then he pays for his food over Dave's protests. Coach's head swivels around in search of his daughter and he notices us sitting in the back booth beside the windows. To my surprise, he grins. Then he claps a hand on Susanna's shoulder and steers her in our direction.

Most of the other tables are occupied and interested heads turn in our direction when Coach booms, "Glad to see two of my future players enjoying the summer." He doesn't miss a beat before nudging his daughter. "Susie, these two boys sitting here will be wearing Arcana High colors in the fall."

Team tryouts are next month. There's no guarantee either me or Jace will be playing in the upcoming season.

Susanna calmly sips her soda and nods.

Tori, annoyed at being overlooked, raises her hand. "I'm sitting here too in case anyone cares."

Susanna practically chokes on her straw as she snorts with laughter. She shoots my sister an approving grin. "Hi, Tori."

"Hi, Susanna. Thanks again for giving the Junior Honor Society a tour of the high school."

"No problem. Let me know if you want to meet up again before school starts. Dad, this is Tori Malene."

Coach is pleased. "Malene. You must be Colt's sister."

Tori coughs. "Among other things."

Coach's attention has been caught by Dave, who has his order all bagged up and ready to go. He tells Susanna that he needs a minute to have a quick chat with Mr. and Mrs. Salenger, who both teach at Arcana High and just happened to walk through the door.

"But you stay here and hang out with the kids," says Coach Toledo and I think I hear a sigh come from Susanna. Coach has a few more words for us before moving on. "Really looking forward to seeing what you boys can do at tryouts."

He's technically speaking to both me and Jace but he's staring directly at me. It's true that I had a great season last year on the junior squad and there's talk I might get to start on the varsity team in the fall, but I don't want to get my hopes up or seem like I'm full of myself.

"Yes, sir," I say in my most respectful voice.

Coach grins and leaves Susanna behind.

She's got her straw in her mouth again. Judging by the look on her face, I bet she'd rather just take off but doesn't want to disobey her father.

"Susanna, sit." Tori scoots over and pats the empty space beside her. She waits until Susanna slides into the booth and then jerks a thumb in my direction. "This joker across the table is my brother, Colt. That's Jace right next to him."

Susanna assesses each of us in turn. "I've heard of you guys."

Jace and I exchange a glance and I wonder whether to be excited or worried. Susanna's a year ahead of us in school and it would be interesting to know that the Arcana High girls are looking forward to our arrival in the fall. "What have you heard?"

"That you crash parties and waste perfectly good soda."

That makes me laugh. "Guilty, on both counts."

It's not unusual for me to drag Jace off to some high school bonfire that neither of us have been invited to. A few times we've narrowly missed getting our asses kicked because I have a habit of shooting my mouth off but it's all in good fun. And on the last day of middle school the two of us, along with Rafe Hempstead and a couple of other guys, mopped the main corridor with gallons of orange soda right before the first bell. Everyone's shoes stuck to the floor and there was a hilarious amount of anger. It's nice to know that story reached the high school. I kind of feel like a celebrity.

My sister, however, is looking less than pleased. Sometimes she has no sense of humor. My earliest memories are of Tori dragging me around by the arm while howling about whatever it is I did wrong.

"What else have you heard about me?" I ask Susanna because I don't care if Tori wants to pout.

Susanna is thoughtful now. "My dad believes you're the best prospect coming up from the middle school." Then she remembers Jace is at the table too. "Uh, both of you, that is."

Jace probably knows that's not completely true but he won't mind. I expect he'll drop football altogether one of these days. He's much happier with his head in a book or scribbling one of the monster stories he likes to write. Mostly he plays ball to hang out with me and keep his dad from complaining.

Just that brief thought of Jace's father is enough to send me back to the living room.

"I'm the bitch you've never been able to stop fucking."

My mouth goes dry and my vision swims.

Susanna sits up straight and her eyes widen. "Are you bleeding?" She's looking down at the table.

I look down at the table too. There's red liquid seeping between my fingers.

"No."

I've crushed a hot sauce packet. Jace passes a stack of napkins to me and I wonder how much I look like a first grader with bad table manners as I mop hot sauce from my fingers.

"How old are you?" Jace asks Susanna and she looks a little startled at the suddenness of the question but that's just how Jace is, forever collecting details about people and then filing them away for future use.

"I'm fourteen," Susanna says. "I should be in your class but I skipped a grade."

Tori twirls her hair around one finger and kind of chuckles. "That's funny. I'm older than you but you're a year ahead of me in school."

I know she doesn't actually think this is funny at all. It's a sore subject, the fact that our mom held her back from starting school so that we could go at the same time. I think this bothers Tori now more than it used to.

Susanna is surprised. "You and your brother are fifteen?"

Tori answers for all of us. "I'm fifteen. Colt is fourteen. Jace will be fifteen in a few months."

Susanna is even more surprised. "I thought you and Colt were twins."

That makes sense. Susanna hasn't lived here for long. The gossip over my origins must not have reached her.

Tori shakes her head. "Nope. I'm the oldest. I get to share a birthday with my little brother but we're a year apart." She grabs her empty cup and starts to climb out of the booth. "I'm getting a refill."

Coach Toledo has settled down at a table to socialize with the Salengers. The guy really likes to talk.

Susanna checks out her dad's location and I wonder if she's wishing he would wrap things up so she could escape. Meanwhile, Tori has found someone of her own to socialize with by the salsa bar. Hatch Bianco is the captain of the Arcana High soccer team and even though the soccer team has a long history of sucking ass, this doesn't seem to matter to my sister, who belts out a fake laugh over whatever garbage Hatch just said to her. She's flirting, which is gross, but there's no law against standing at the salsa bar and telling jokes so I can't say a thing.

When I'm done stewing over the idea that I'll need to get used to pricks like Hatch checking out my sister, I notice that Susanna is watching me. She keeps staring even when I stare right back at her.

And you know what?

I kind of like that.

Susanna wants to look at me and doesn't feel the need to hide the fact that she's looking. Girls will usually blush and squirm and become engrossed in their phones when you lock eyes with them but she doesn't. I bet I could ask her a question on any subject and she'd give me a direct answer. Plus, it's really starting to sink in that this girl sitting across the table is far cuter than any other girl I can think of off the top of my head.

I glance over at Jace to see if he's thinking the same thing but he's distracted. Actually, he's leaning halfway out of the booth and glaring daggers at the salsa bar where Tori is still talking to that tool who probably eats soccer balls for breakfast. Jace looks as anxious as a mother hen and he's obviously straining to hear what's being said while he squeezes a brown napkin in his right hand. That's how you know your best friend is the shit; when he's every bit as protective of your sister as you are.

Too much time has passed since anyone at the table has said a word so I blurt out the first thing I can think of.

"I guess you're pretty damn smart," I say to Susanna. "You'd have to be to skip a grade."

She doesn't seem to think the comment is weird. "Yes."

"I'm not. Smart, I mean. Tori's smart. Jace is smart. But I'm lucky to scrape by with C's."

Jace flinches at the sound of his name. He's got a confused look on his face and I think he forgot we were here. "Huh?"

"Nothing." I elbow him. "Go back to daydreaming."

He stands and tosses the balled up napkin on the table. "Gotta hit the rest room."

Jace walks in the direction of the bathrooms but his eyes are so cemented on Tori and Soccer Creep that he ends up colliding with Coach Toledo's chair. He mumbles an apology and moves on.

"There are a lot of different ways to be smart," Susanna says. "It doesn't always have to do with books and school."

I've never heard anyone say this before. "You think so?"

"Of course." She gets animated all of a sudden and starts talking more rapidly. "My dad has a friend who can fix anything with an engine but he dropped out of school in the tenth grade. And at my last school there was a guy our age who won a citywide art competition, beating out all the professionally trained adults. From what I hear, you've got a lot of talent on the football field. That means something, Colt. I couldn't do what you do."

I can't remember listening to this closely to anyone. This girl makes me wish we were somewhere else, somewhere private and quiet. Not because I want to mess around with her, although I sure wouldn't say no to that. I'd be happy just to hear what else she thinks about.

Susanna has been honest and I want to be honest back.

"I'm nervous about the team tryouts," I tell her. "I haven't even admitted this to Jace or Tori but I've had trouble sleeping for weeks. I'm worried that I won't impress your dad. I'm worried I'll fail to make the team."

Susanna considers my confession in silence. Then she plucks out a silver chain necklace that was hiding beneath her shirt and pulls it over her head. There are a handful of charms clumped together at the bottom and I watch as she opens the clasp, selects one and slides it off. The necklace is returned to its place around her neck but she extends the hand holding the small silver object. "Here. This will bring you luck."

When I unfold my fingers, she deposits the charm neatly in my palm. The feel of her fingertips grazing my skin produces a shiver that's not at all unpleasant. She must feel something too because she freezes and her breath catches before she yanks her hand away.

Our eyes meet and a warm sensation spreads through my chest. Susanna drops her eyes first and I notice the sudden flush in her cheeks. I look at the silver object in my hand. It's only about an inch long and in the shape of the letter U.

"It's a horseshoe," she explains. "They have always been considered good luck. I found it at a gift shop when my folks took me to visit Santa Fe a couple of years ago. I wore it when I competed in the county Science Olympiad."

"And you won?"

"Twice." She smiles, showing her braces. Yeah, she's cute as hell. She's not a girl who will smear gobs of makeup on her face and fuss with her hair constantly.

My heart thumps.

"You sure you want to give it up then? What if you need to win another science competition?"

"I don't. I want to give it to you," she says with finality and if I argue anymore then I might insult her.

I feel a little off balance. Girls don't make me nervous, never have. I have no trouble talking to them and I've even kissed a few without losing my head.

Susanna, I can tell, would be different.

I believe I could lose my head over her.

"Thank you." With care, I store the charm in the back pocket of my shorts.

"Susie!" Coach Toledo has abruptly decided it's time to leave. He stands at the door with three bags of food in his hand and beckons to his daughter.

Susanna now seems reluctant to slide out of the booth. When she's on her feet we lock eyes again. She bites her lip. The unfamiliar warmth in my chest spreads.

"I guess I'll see you around?" My words come out like a question although there's no doubt since Arcana High is not a big place. What I wanted to say is that I *hope* I see her, that I *want* to see her, that meeting her is the best thing that's happened to me in a while.

A quick smile flares across her face. "I'm sure of it, Colt."

If she wasn't the daughter of Coach Toledo, I'd surely find the nerve to ask for her number or suggest that we ought to hang out soon. But she *is* Coach Toledo's daughter and I can't afford to piss him off. While I'm still mulling over this unfortunate piece of reality she hurries over to her father and I'm left alone, watching the way her ponytail swings when she takes one final look over her shoulder before rushing out the door.

Jace returns from the bathroom and he's glad when I suggest that we ought to drag Tori away from Soccer Creep and get moving in order to catch the next bus to Plainsfield.

The zombie movie isn't really my thing but there are some cool battle scenes and the theater is nicely air conditioned so it's not a bad way to spend the afternoon. Jace thinks the movie rocked and now he has all kinds of plot ideas for the story he's working on. On the bus ride back to Arcana, he and Tori are in the middle of a serious discussion about whether zombies can be cured of their taste for brains and if they can have crushes on people.

"Hey, what's that?" Jace notices that I'm holding the silver horseshoe. I'd been half listening to their conversation while letting my mind wander back to the moment when Susanna gave it to me. If I tell them the story they'd both be interested to hear it but somehow I want to keep that information to myself.

"Just a good luck charm." I stuff it back into my pocket. I don't really want to go home. If I go home then I might have flashbacks to what I saw this afternoon.

We return to Tumbleweed Lane just in time to see my dad pulling up to the curb. Tori shouts that she's just got to grab her bag and she dashes through the front door. Eric Malene stays in the truck. He waves to me and waits for a few seconds to see if I'll wave back. When I don't, he turns his head.

I exhale too loudly and it sounds like a sigh. Jace hears and taps my shoulder in solidarity. I don't need to look at his face to know that he feels bad for me. His situation sucks just as much as mine does. It just sucks in a different way. I'll never be glad his parents didn't feel like being parents and shoved him off on Gloria because being happy about that would make me a real dipshit of a friend. But I'm grateful that he's here, grateful that he lives right next door and understands when I'm in a crappy mood and can't talk about why. Nobody's a better friend than Jace.

Tori swings through the door like she's escaping from prison and makes one last try at dragging me along. She's disappointed when I shake my head and tell her to go without me. After flinging her duffel bag into the back of our dad's pickup, she jumps into the passenger seat and I watch as the two of them launch right into a happy conversation as they drive away. My mom is nowhere in sight.

But Gloria is. She's been watching from the front door of her house and now she comes outside. She's wearing a very Gloria-type outfit that looks like a flowing blanket shot through with every shade of purple.

Jace reads something in his grandmother's expression and his shoulders wilt slightly. "Dad left already, didn't he?"

Gloria's eyes are filled with love but also sadness. "Yes, he did. He was sorry he didn't get to say goodbye, but he received a call about a possible job offer and had to leave immediately. He wanted you to know that he loves you and promises he will visit as soon as he can."

That's probably bullshit. For Jace's dad, 'soon' might be six months from now. Gloria's in a tough position, trying to salvage her grandson's hurt feelings while pretending her only son isn't a worthless fucker.

Jace lowers his head and I can imagine the conflict warring inside his head. He can't stand his dad but still wants to be loved by him. I can relate.

"Boys." Gloria's faded blue eyes shine with tears but she has a tender smile ready for us. "I just finished a giant batch of gingersnap cookies for the church bake sale and I need some taste testers. How about a snack?"

I clap my hands together. "You know me. I'm always hungry."

Gloria tilts her head and gazes at me with affection. "Yes, I do know you, Colt."

"I could eat," Jace says slowly and while I can still hear the hurt in his voice, I know he won't let it keep him down for long.

We follow Gloria back to the house and I glance next door at the house where I've lived since I was born and would prefer to never see again. "Is it okay if I crash here tonight?"

I've probably stayed at Jace's house a thousand times over the years and I know I don't need to give a reason. The reason is that I just can't look at my own mother right now. And with Tori gone for the weekend, the prospect of being alone in the house with my mother is making me want to add to that pile of vomit I created in the sagebrush hours earlier.

"Of course." Gloria answers before Jace does. She holds the screen door open and peers up at me because, like Jace, I'm now quite a bit taller than her. I wonder if this strikes her as strange, that these little kids she's known since birth are now people she needs to crane her neck to see. But she's old enough to have watched a lot of people grow up so I guess she's used to it.

"You're always welcome here," Gloria says and those aren't just words to her. Gloria's not phony about anything. Whenever I walk into her house I feel like I belong there more than anywhere else.

Later, after we've eaten far too many cookies, devoured the hamburgers Gloria cooked for dinner and played video games until we got tired, I'm lying atop the covers on the foldout sofa in the living room and rolling a silver horseshoe charm between my fingers as the flat surface of the dark ceiling stares down at me.

My mind keeps threatening to replay scenes that shouldn't be burned into my memory but refuse to leave. If I try hard enough, maybe I can keep pushing them down, beneath layers and layers of better memories.

My thumb traces blunt edges of metal and the act is soothing. At the base of the U is a fixed extension in the shape of a hollow circle and this is how Susanna was able to thread it onto a necklace that was kept close to her heart.

"I want to give it to you."

With this echo in my mind, the night becomes much more friendly and I'm no longer haunted by horrors I'd much rather forget. Instead, the sun is shining and I'm back in the booth at Dave's and she's there with me, proving that if I work at it, I can erase that disgusting piece of today, replacing the void with thoughts of the girl I met.

Her name repeats in a comforting loop inside my head.

Susanna. Susanna. Susanna.

The first hints of sleep begin to crowd the edges of my thoughts and I have more faith that my dreams won't be terrible. I have Susanna's good luck charm in my hand and Susanna's smile in my head. That's enough to carry me through for now.

Till the next time I see her.

5

SUSANNA

When Colt arrives one minute before six p.m., I've been ready for two hours and I'm wearing a dress, the one I meant to show off at dinner last night. Thanks to some internet sleuthing, a liberal application of baking soda and two strain-treated wash cycles, no trace of the salad dressing encounter remains.

All the trouble was worthwhile when I answer the door. Colt is not quick enough to stop his eyes from sweeping up and down my body.

It seems we're even. I'm not fast enough to tighten my jaw before it drops. Colt wears a black short sleeve shirt that does a spectacular job of featuring his powerful arms even as they hang casually at his sides. He hasn't shaved again and his dark jeans appear comfortably broken in. He looks insanely excellent.

He nods to me in greeting. "I'm not late today."

I nod back. "Good."

"Nice dress."

"It's the only one I have."

He shrugs. "Okay."

I can't think of a single appropriate response.

A wrinkle appears between his brows. Perhaps he's wondering why he has condemned himself to hours of hopelessly awkward conversations like this one.

"Colt!"

At least this particular exchange is put out of its misery by my father. He pumps Colt's hand. He snaps a photo of Colt and me standing close together. His hopeful smile is brighter than a one hundred watt bulb. His excitement seems a bit excessive. Is he under the impression that Colt and I are going to elope tonight?

I push my arms into a thin black cardigan. "Dad, I left you a salad and a plain bowl of pasta in the fridge."

"I promise I'll eat it," he says with good cheer and I'm encouraged to believe that just might be true. He's been in a superior mood all day and obligingly finished an entire bowl of oatmeal.

Colt and I find ourselves enthusiastically pushed out the front door with no plan as to what to do next.

I clear my throat. "I thought it might be nice to escape the watchful eyes of Arcana for an evening."

Colt looks to the curb where his truck is parked. "How's that?"

"Well, there are only so many places to go in town and there's always a shadow from high school yesteryear lingering around every corner."

He's standing so close. I'm five foot ten but the top of my head barely reaches his chin and his jaw moves as he considers the suggestion. There's nothing fair about how outrageously sexy he is. "Sounds like you have a plan in mind."

"The mall in Plainsfield is still around. How about dinner and a movie? My treat."

"Dinner and a movie," he repeats. "Let's go."

Colt ignores my offer to drive and proceeds straight to his truck, opening the passenger door in one swift move. Silent macho vibes roll off him in aftershave-spiced waves as he assumes I'll cooperate with being ushered inside before he casually walks around to the other side to climb behind the wheel.

And I do cooperate. Not only do I suspect my father is watching from a window but I'm keenly aware of something important.

Just by showing up, Colt has done me one hell of a favor. It's a favor I'll never be able to repay.

Tonight he keeps the windows of the truck rolled up, perhaps because he remembers how I shivered the night before. The radio plays a subdued hum of mournful country music at low volume.

"I forgot to return your shirt to you last night. It's in the dryer. I washed it this afternoon. I can give it to you later."

He accelerates at the freeway entrance. "Fine."

The center of town was left behind before we veered toward the freeway. Dense neighborhood grids give way to rural properties set far back from the road. Other parts of the state have sustained an explosion of residential development but that trend has yet to spread to this corner of western Texas.

While trying to sort out my nervous energy, the skinny strap of my handbag has become laced around my fingers. After yesterday's dinner I have a slightly better sense of Colt Malene. I understand he does not feel compelled to spark conversation. If I'm bothered by the silence then I need to be the one to break it.

"So did you do anything fun today?" The perkiness in my voice is despicably phony. I am not a perky person.

Neither is Colt. He studies the road. "Not really. Fixed some things at Gloria's house. Picked up two truckloads of wood for the shed I plan to build for Jace and Tori." He glances at me. "What did you do?"

"Laundry. House cleaning." I lack the imagination to make this sound interesting.

Colt has nothing to add. I run my palms over the crisply ironed material of my dress.

On one hand, the years roll away and I'm back to being a shy teenager, secretly infatuated with the hottest, rowdiest football player in school.

One thump of my heart later and I remember where I really am;

sitting beside an enigmatic grown man who has no clue how much he's been on my mind for the last ten years.

I've always deeply regretted my role in the way things ended. For us. And, ultimately, for him.

The Plainsfield Mall was once a prime destination for teens within a forty mile radius and it has seen better days. Some of the big box department stores are now vacant and the declining appeal of indoor shopping malls has shuttered many of the smaller stores. Our dining options are limited to either the food court or a sports bar and grill so we choose the latter. The four mounted screens above the bar are all tuned to a baseball game and I'm glad it's not the season for football. I've seen more than enough football in my life.

The restaurant is not busy tonight. We're nearly alone in a sea of shiny dark wood tables and knobby chairs with most of the customers preferring to sit at the bar. A waiter introduces himself as Javier and swiftly returns with our drinks. Colt hardly glances at the menu before ordering a bacon double cheeseburger with sweet potato fries.

"Grilled chicken sandwich with a side of fresh fruit," I tell Javier and he gladly runs off to relay our order to the kitchen.

Colt sits with his elbows on the table. The table is small. Colt's arms are not. He's gazing over at the bar and I wonder if he's watching the cute young blonde who stands behind the counter, laughing as she fills a row of shot glasses with whiskey. But then she moves away to the right and his eyes don't travel with her.

"Who are you rooting for?" I ask him because his attention seems to be drawn to the game.

"Nobody." He leans back in his chair and returns his focus to me. "I never really did have the patience to follow baseball."

I wish I'd ordered an appetizer. Diving into a plate of nachos would give us something to do besides stare at each other and squirm. I'm used to using my phone as a way to escape social interactions but I can't very well do that in this situation, when we're the only two people at the table and Colt is looking directly at me.

"How did you get that scar?" I point to a five inch line that stretches along his left forearm.

He doesn't even glance down. "Occupational hazard. Someone got reckless and left a steel rod where they shouldn't have. Turned a simple fall into a trip to the ER for twenty-two stitches."

"Ouch."

He shrugs. "Part of the job."

The conversation dies.

A three run homer ignites the crowd inside the mounted television sets. A man at the bar claps his hands and hoots.

Strange, but for all the time Colt and I spent together, all the nights we talked for endless hours, all the ways we nearly had sex but never crossed that bridge, we never had this, whatever *this* is.

"Are we on a date, Colt?" I blurt out.

The abrupt question has amused him. He smirks. "Do you want to be on a date?"

I huff out an annoyed breath. "Don't do that. Don't answer my question with a question."

"Sure, we're on a date, Susanna. I thought that was clear."

"It wasn't clear."

"Well, now it is."

I have no reason to be so pleased but I feel as if an invisible wall has been broken. I think we will be able to relax now, both of us.

Javier returns with our food. Colt politely requests hot sauce and this makes me smile because Colt has always drowned his food in hot sauce. This is one of the very first things I ever learned about him.

His sudden question catches me completely off guard. "What happened to your boyfriend?"

"What are you talking about?"

"I figured you must have one. So where is he?"

"Did my dad tell you I had a boyfriend?"

He wags a finger. "Don't answer my question with a question."

I roll my eyes. "You're funny. Throwing my own words back at me."

"Still waiting for an answer."

"I guess I *did* have a boyfriend."

"You guess? You don't know?"

"I've outgrown the boyfriend label. Seems juvenile at this point."

"Huh. So how did he fuck things up?"

"You don't have to be so crude."

"Sorry." Colt pops a fry into his mouth. "So how did he fuck things up?"

With my fork I push a tomato slice from my grilled chicken sandwich. "Nate was all right."

"How long did you stick with him?"

"A year."

"Must have been serious."

"It wasn't serious at all."

Colt waits for me to explain. And curiously, I don't mind explaining.

"I think we just got used to each other. Comfortable. But it wasn't an intense relationship, not ever. We got together maybe once a week, if that. He had work and I had work. We were never one of those crazy-for-you couples. We never even had..." I bite off the word that nearly came out of my mouth and finish with a different one. "Chemistry. We never had chemistry."

"Got it." Colt nods gravely. "His dick couldn't get the job done."

Many things about Colt have changed and some haven't. He remains bizarrely perceptive. And he has a knack for expressing himself in the most mortifyingly frank way imaginable.

Yet he has pricked a nerve.

"Nate's anatomy works just fine," I grumble.

Colt laughs. Loudly. Two men at the bar glance over at our table.

I kick him lightly under the table. This has become equal parts embarrassing and exciting. "Control yourself or I will spend the rest of our date ignoring you and binging the latest season of *The Crown*."

He's still chuckling. "The what?"

"Not important. Behave."

"Okay." He decides to whisper. "I'm sorry."

"You are not. But somehow you succeed at being simultaneously charming and exasperating. Let's drop it and have a nice meal."

He stuffs half his hamburger in his mouth. And he winks at me.

This is potentially dangerous. I could like him. Very easily and far too much for my own good. We've been down that road before.

I'm hungry enough to overlook the rubbery texture of the over-cooked grilled chicken patty. Colt polishes off his hamburger in roughly ninety seconds, which is rather a mesmerizing feat. I couldn't eat that fast even if it was my job. He slows his pace, chewing one sweet potato fry at a time, while I succeed in choking down two thirds of my sandwich. I take a sip of my raspberry tea, which has the honor of being the tastiest part of my meal.

"Colt, can I tell you something?"

He wipes his mouth with a napkin and gives me his full attention. "Absolutely."

I take a deep breath. "Last week I received a text from Nate. He wanted me to hear the news of his engagement from him. He always said he didn't ever want to get married and now he's marrying some girl he just met six weeks ago at a wine bar."

Colt is pissed on my behalf. "What a prick. That must suck."

I shake my head. "Actually, it doesn't suck. I thought it would but I truly don't care very much. We've been finished for ages, before I even decided to move back home. In theory, Nate and I were perfect together. He was good looking, we worked in the same field and had similar taste in entertainment. I should have been crazy about him but I wasn't, not even in the beginning, not ever. Anyway, I don't miss him."

Colt takes his time before commenting. He appears to check out the score of the game, nods his head and then turns back, examining my face for a long moment. "We can't help it when we want someone. And we can't help it when we don't."

"I suppose that's the crux of the matter. I didn't want him." Feeling slightly lightheaded, I take a deep breath. "I'm unloading all my personal baggage on you. Forgive me."

"I don't mind." He crosses his arms over his chest, leans back in his chair. "Damn powerful thing when it is there."

"What is?"

"You called it chemistry."

"What would you call it?"

"Fucking."

I can feel my face reddening. "I'm not talking about sex. It's completely possible to have relationships without ever having sex."

He stiffens. His blue eyes flare. "Shit."

I look around, searching for the problem. "What's the matter?"

He hesitates, clamps his lips shut.

"Spit it out," I order him. "Or I'll think the worst."

"Might be better that way."

"I'll take my chances."

"You've never done it, have you, Susanna?"

He can't possibly mean what I think he means. He must be referring to something else. "Done what?"

"You've never fucked anyone."

Seconds pass and I'm still too stunned to speak. Colt's level of insight is rather terrifying. He's like a wise mystic with an appalling trash mouth.

When I do manage to speak, my voice croaks. "That's both private and irrelevant."

He frowns. "I didn't mean it as an insult."

"I'm not insulted." I'm really not. Insulted is the wrong word. My pride might be a little wounded but then again, I dropped too many hints. Colt managed to put the right pieces together.

Anyway, he's correct.

In technical terms, I'm a twenty-seven-year-old virgin. I doubt many people can make the same claim.

Hooray for me!

Colt is still frowning. He pushes his plate away and sighs. "All right, confession time. It's only fair."

"What is it you want to confess?"

He doesn't beat around the bush. "I haven't had sex at all in over four years."

I want to laugh. "YOU? Seriously?"

He's amused by my disbelief. "Seriously."

"Forgive my skepticism. It's just that I very clearly remember the way you used to be in high school."

"And how was I?"

"Promiscuous. Very."

Colt falls silent.

Damn.

I had no right to say that.

And now I want to swallow my dinner plate.

Perhaps that will stop me from saying anything else inappropriately revealing and/or offensive.

"Colt, I'm really sorry. Please forgive me for that last inexcusable remark."

Now he's puzzled. "Why? You've always told the truth, Susanna. I'd expect no less now." Then he winces and shifts in his chair. "Anyway, you're right. I started early. Too early. I'm not proud of myself for that."

I feel an urge to reach across the table, to touch his hand. If I had more courage, then perhaps I would. In high school, Colt's reputation was notorious. And earned. Yet he always had a rotten home life and a lack of role models so he searched for attention elsewhere. I know that better than anyone. Back then I was the only one he confided his secrets to.

He watches my inner struggle and then laughs lightly through his nose. "Don't look so tragic. I swear you didn't hurt my feelings."

"Good to know." I chew my lower lip.

Colt cocks his head. "Something else on your mind?"

"Maybe."

He grins and uses my words against me once more. "Spit it out."

"I'm just a little curious about why you've been alone for so long. I doubt you have any trouble attracting women."

"Hell no."

"Arrogant," I accuse, although now I'm smiling.

"Accurate," he shoots back and he's grinning too. His grin fades. "I got used to keeping my distance. And I'm no good at playing games."

"What does that mean?"

"It means there's nothing permanent about me, Susanna. I'm not a guy who sticks around. There's no point in making promises that I can't keep."

"I see." And I do. But something about the offhand nature of his revelation saddens me and I blow out a sigh. "You said you don't stay in one place. Makes sense that you wouldn't be searching for a relationship."

He lets the comment stand unchallenged and it's impossible to guess what he's thinking. I dislike the sense that he's got me all figured out while I haven't a clue what's going on in his head.

Pushing my chair back, I raise my hand to hail Javier for the check. He pounces and tries to talk us into ordering dessert. The options are bread pudding and lemon cake. I don't feel tempted to take my chances on either, so I settle for one of the after dinner peppermints offered with the check.

Colt grabs the check first and refuses to accept the card I try to push in his direction. He slaps some cash into Javier's hand and tells him to keep the change. Then he's halfway to the door before I can even rise from my chair. At least he waits at the exit. In gallant fashion, he even holds the heavy wooden door open.

The spring evening is clear with a soft breeze. The lights of the movie theater beckon only a hundred yards away and cutting through the half empty parking lot will be quick.

"What movie do you want to see?" I ask him.

He crunches on a peppermint. "No idea what's playing."

"Well, what kind of movies do you enjoy these days?"

He squints in the direction of the digital showtime schedule above the ticket counter. "You choose," he says, sounding like he couldn't care less.

That's not the answer I was looking for. Since Colt offers no input, I wind up selecting a western flick that starts in ten minutes. This time he's unable to stop me from shoving my card through the ticket window and purchasing two tickets.

The movie is short at an hour and twenty minutes. The hero, a leader of a band of stagecoach-robbing ruffians, reminds me of Colt. An insufferable outlaw version of Colt, which isn't hard to imagine. There's a dash of romance in the subplot when the hero runs into an old flame, who happens to be the daughter of a local sheriff.

The ending is a downer.

Just when the hero is poised to abandon his old life of looting stagecoaches and gunslinging in order to live peacefully with his lady love, their frontier town is invaded by violent gangsters. She is killed while shielding a group of children in the midst of a raging gun battle. The hero weeps at her grave and then swears to the sky that he'll never love again before he boards a train bound for the west coast. The end.

As the picture fades amid orchestral strains of somber music, I turn to Colt, who hasn't moved since he sat down.

"That's what you get for letting me pick the movie," I tease.

He doesn't answer.

The reason he doesn't answer is because he's sound asleep, head tilted back in the reclining chair while breathing evenly through his mouth.

The music keeps playing.

The credits keep rolling.

Colt keeps sleeping.

When the house lights begin to brighten, I heave a sigh and leave the theater. I need to use the restroom. I'll worry about waking my date up when I get back.

Moments later, as I examine my face in the bathroom mirror, I'm wondering what Colt sees when he looks at me. In high school, I never spent much time deliberating my appearance in the mirror. I thought the lines of my face were too sharp, my body too skinny. I wasn't hideous but neither was I much of a step above ordinary. Boys didn't gawk when I walked by. My own mother made her disapproval clear as she constantly tried to fix me.

"Susanna, maybe if you wear your hair down..."

"Susanna, maybe you could try one of these cute skirts..."

After dinner I had pulled my hair back with a plastic clip. I release the clasp and fluff the thick brown waves that fall past my shoulders. Instead of my serious reflection, I see the smile of the boy who used to make my knees weak and my heart race. He was the only boy with that talent, the only boy who made me feel like I could be seen as something more than the coach's nerdy daughter. I loved him then, with a level of desperate passion I've never felt since.

And he never knew.

By the time I was ready to tell him, everything had gone wrong.

Dismissing the haze of regret over things that can't be fixed and are likely forgotten by everyone but me, I snap a paper towel from the silver dispenser and dry my hands. After flinging open the door to the restroom, I nearly collide with a wide awake Colt Malene.

"There you are," he says, as if he's perplexed over how I could have wandered away right under his nose.

"The movie's over." Sidestepping him, I march straight down the hall, through the lobby and to the exit.

Colt keeps up just fine and says nothing until we are halfway across the parking lot.

"You seem pissed, Susanna."

"You seem sleepy, Colt."

"Nope, I had a nice nap in the theater."

I stop walking. The urge to stomp my foot is nearly irresistible. "We didn't have to see that movie! Or any movie."

"You wanted to see a movie. I didn't want to argue."

"Well, stop trying to be agreeable. Instead, be straightforward."

"Okay. I hate going to the movies."

"Since when?"

"I don't know. I haven't been to the movies in years. What difference does it make?"

"You could have said so. I don't always love going to the movies anymore either. Too often the plots are convoluted, derivative or just uninspiring."

With that, I resume walking and I walk fast.

Colt falls into step beside me.

His truck remains parked in a distant part of the lot and the lot has mostly emptied out. Only the lighting of the yellow overhead lamps saves the moonless dark night from being creepy as our footsteps echo on the pavement.

"I'm not angry," I assure him as he unlocks the passenger door of his truck.

He opens the door, spins his keys around his right forefinger and stares at me. Whatever he sees causes him to quit spinning his keys and take a step closer. We are now mere inches apart. The shadows of the night hide his expression but even if we stood in broad daylight I doubt I'd be able to read him accurately. Colt reaches his keyless left hand to my face and with slow deliberation pushes a section of loose hair behind my ear. His fingertips graze my cheekbone. He tips his head forward and touches his forehead to mine.

"Yes, you are," he whispers.

The rush of desire is out of my control, slamming into my senses with the grace of an earthquake. I suspect Colt knows this. He knows that I want him more than ever. He retains a powerful hold over me that has never been replicated, even if the years have only enhanced our differences.

I want him anyway. He's the one who said we can't help who we want. He's right.

My arms have already begun to circle him. But Colt abruptly breaks contact and walks away. He climbs behind the wheel and shuts the door while I'm still reeling, a torrent of confused emotions leaving me to weakly lean against the truck for a moment while he waits inside with the engine running.

Maybe he's trying to prove that he's in complete control of the situation. Or maybe he doesn't want to kiss me at all.

I don't know. All I do know is that I can't stand around outside Colt's truck all night.

He watches with patience as I buckle my seatbelt and primly clutch my purse in my lap.

"Take me home please."

"Just about to." Colt shifts into drive, cool and composed as can be while my heart batters itself against the walls of my chest.

I switch the radio on and flip the station to something other than country music. Colt gives no sign he notices. Before long we're back on the freeway, rocketing back to Arcana.

Finally, he lowers the volume on the radio. "So, you hate movies."

"I didn't say I hated movies. *You* said you hated movies."

He snorts. "That's not really the point I was getting at."

"By all means, elaborate."

He doesn't elaborate. He says nothing at all. Miles pass in silence with only the faint gurgle of a Madonna marathon from the radio.

Soon enough, we're closing in on Arcana. The roadside monotony is broken by a brightly lit billboard of a tractor with a smiling cartoon face, an advertisement for a large company specializing in farming equipment. There aren't many farms in this area but they must find some value in keeping the billboard up because it's been there for ages. The first time I saw it was from the backseat of my dad's truck as we drove into Arcana for the first time. My folks had been intermittently arguing since we left Dallas and my mother was fretting over the fact that we'd lost sight of the moving van. My dad glanced at me in the rearview mirror and grinned with a roll of his eyes, the two of us sharing a private joke as we often did at my mother's expense. Then I glanced out the window and noticed the passing tractor billboard. I wondered uneasily if Arcana would prove to be an easier place to make friends.

"I was just trying to ask what you like to do." Colt's voice jars me back to the current moment and I need a few seconds to catch up.

When I don't respond immediately, he looks over at me. "You said you weren't a movie fan. So how do you like to spend your time?"

I can't remember when I was last asked that question. I have to give it a moment of thought.

"I'm always reading. I do enjoy a lot of nonfiction but lately I've started gravitating toward romance. I tend to reread the classics again and again. Right now I'm halfway through *East of Eden* for the fourth time. While I'm not a huge fan of movies, I do love documentaries and historical dramas. My idea of a spectacular Saturday night is curling up on the couch in my pajamas with a thick book and a bowl of lightly salted kettle corn."

He nods, says nothing.

"All in all," I shrug, "I'm still a specialist in the most anti-social hobbies. What about you, Colt? What do you like to do?"

"Chop wood. Haul rocks. Also very anti-social."

"What else?"

"Hiking. Camping. Fishing. With a decent set of tools in my hands I can build anything. If I stay inside the same four walls for too long I start feeling like I'm locked in a cage."

"Sounds like we don't have much in common."

"That's not exactly a newsflash, Susanna. We never had anything in common."

He doesn't mean the observation to sound harsh. I can't explain why it cuts me just the same.

My fingers tug nervously on the soft edge of my cardigan. "This is weird, isn't it?"

He cuts another inscrutable glance my way. "What is?"

"Being on a date when we never had one in high school."

This time his expression is obvious. He is honestly surprised. "What are you talking about? We hung out almost every night that summer."

That summer.

Our summer.

I always think of it as the last summer, the last *real* summer. When days were free of obligations, there were endless hours to daydream and my heart had yet to suffer its first beating.

"That's because I snuck out of my bedroom window almost every night," I remind him and chew the corner of my lip as I weigh how to crack his somewhat stoic shell. "Being together like this doesn't feel at all odd to you after all these years?"

He chooses not to answer the question.

Instead, he exits the freeway, rolls down the concrete ramp and pauses at the stop light. Then he turns his head, slowly looks me up and down and allows the hot need in his voice to betray him. "You are still so fucking beautiful."

I swallow hard. "Pull over please."

The traffic light changes to green. He eases off the brake and moves forward. We're not far outside of town but aside from a long abandoned bread factory and scattered residences on large circles of acreage, there's not much around.

"Colt." My tone sharpens into a demand. "Pull over."

He slows down.

"NOW!" I shout and he brakes hard. The seatbelt keeps me from flopping forward and I shoot a glare in his direction but he's not even looking at me.

Within two seconds I'm unbuckled and I've bolted from the truck. This stretch of the two lane road is dark, used mainly for shortcuts by locals trying to circumvent the more modern main roads. The shoulder is filled with jagged rocks and I grit my teeth when my ankle rolls after a couple of steps but I keep walking. I don't even know where I'm going or why. I just couldn't sit beside him in that truck for another second or I would have erupted.

All at once, everything has caught up to me.

My father is dying.

My father is dying and I'm alone.

My father is dying and I'm alone and I have no plans for the future.

My father is dying and I'm alone and I have no plans for the future and seeing Colt Malene again reminds me of things I've never been able to forget, feelings I've never recovered from.

His truck inches along behind me and then pulls over to the side. The headlights remain on and a vehicle door closes.

"You planning to walk back to town?" he calls.

I whirl around and march right over to where he waits beside his truck.

Thanks to the illumination from the headlights, I can see that

Colt appears mildly interested in this turn of events but nothing more.

I get right in his face. I jab a finger into his rock hard chest. "You can't do that."

"What the hell did I do?"

Words spill out in a tidal wave. "One minute you're charming and the next you're saying something completely outrageous. You're so bored that you fall asleep on our date and then you have the nerve to touch my hair before telling me I'm beautiful. You can't do that, Colt. You can't do any of that!" My arms flail around to make my point. And my point makes me sound like a raving lunatic.

Colt must think so too. He decides it's wiser not to argue. "Sorry."

"You don't have to be sorry. Just be...I don't know." I push my hands through my hair, sigh loudly and then stand next to him with my back against the frame of his truck. I cross my arms and my elbow bumps his. "I sound insane, don't I?"

"No. Well, a little."

I cough into the crook of my arm. "I'm a mess right now, Colt. I know that. This little outburst of mine is not your fault at all. But it's still maddening how I have no idea what you're going to say or do from one minute to the next."

And then, once again, he shocks me.

Colt changes position so that we're face to face. He cups my chin in his big hands and brushes his lips over mine. My response is instant, like a lit match that touches kerosene. My arms clutch his shoulders. Our tongues meet and a low groan rasps out of his throat. He's no longer gentle and I don't want him to be. He seizes me around the waist and crushes my body to his. Colt was always an incredible kisser. He kisses me now with abandon and I love it; the rough scrape of his unshaven face and the invasion of his tongue. His hands roam everywhere; under my sweater, over my breasts, up my skirt. He can't hide how hard he is and he doesn't try. His hips grind into mine to make his intentions clear.

I've already decided he can have whatever he wants. I would welcome the distraction. Lately my days have been filled with sadness and regret. Let them be filled with something else, even for a little while. That's all it will be, a little while.

Colt won't stay. He's already said that. He never stays. But tonight I don't care. Tonight I can have him and I'll take what I can get.

We break for air and he moves his head, sucking hard at my neck. He lifts me and my knees give way, opening for him. He groans again, louder this time, and sets me down. He's no longer kissing me. He's pulling away.

"This wasn't supposed to happen." He tries to back up, breathing hard.

"But it did happen." I won't let him go. I kiss his jaw, his neck. I tilt my head back to look up into his eyes. "I want to be with you."

Even in this light I can see the flicker in his expression and I realize my mistake. My own words echo back to me and I remember when I said the same thing to him once before under different circumstances, the meaning not at all the same as my meaning right now.

"Tonight, I mean," I correct myself. "I want to be with you tonight. Let's go to your place."

I'm not thinking about the fact that I can't possibly stay out all night. I'm not thinking clearly at all.

But Colt is thinking clearly and his message is firm. "We shouldn't."

"Please." I hate myself when I hear the pleading in my voice.

He shakes his head and carefully peels me away. "No, honey."

"We both want to."

"Susanna."

Angry tears gather and threaten to fall. "Don't say my name as if I'm some child that you're scolding."

He does it anyway. "Susanna, you don't really want to come home with me."

"Because you're not a guy who sticks around?"

"That's part of it."

"But not the only reason."

"No."

"Do I have to beg for an explanation?"

"It's not a good idea."

"Why?"

He sighs.

"Why, Colt?"

He closes in and backs me against the truck with one thick arm propped on either side.

"You're asking me to take you to bed when you know exactly what will happen."

"Naturally." I stare him down in defiance.

"All right." He roughly shoves the skirt of my dress all the way up. "If I take you home then these…" He deftly slides one finger into my panties and tugs. "Will be coming off and I'll fuck you. I'll fuck you hard and more than once until you can't catch your breath and you'll love every second. But I can't promise you more. I can't promise you forever. You won't be able to handle that. You're the type that is going to want forever. And tomorrow you'll hate me. You'll hate me for what I took from you."

With a suddenness that makes me gasp, he pops the elastic of my panties against my skin and withdraws. The fabric of my skirt flutters back down to cover my body.

Colt might be right. He might see me more clearly than I see myself.

But right now I don't want him to be right and I have a choice to make. For once I'll be bold. He watches while I reach under my dress and push my panties over my hips and down my legs, stepping out of them.

"There." I fling my satin black underwear at his chest. "They came off and I seem to be handling myself just fine."

He catches my panties and exhales thickly. Rakes a hand through his short hair. He expected me to back off and I haven't.

I feel a sense of triumph, knowing that he didn't see this coming and doesn't know what to do now that the tables have been turned.

Then he nods to himself and raises his head, gazing at me with raw lust.

He crushes my panties in his fist. "Then get in the fucking truck."

Colt doesn't wait to see if I will obey his order. He's fast as hell and has already circled to the other side, jumping behind the wheel before I even get around to opening the passenger door. He doesn't look at me once while navigating the dark roads leading to the meager lights of our sleepy hometown. I have no idea what he did with my panties.

Hugging my arms around myself, I stare down at the shadows playing on the floral pattern on my dress. It's possible that I really don't know what I'm doing, that being with Colt has dredged up too many old passions and sent me into a tailspin. This, combined with the lonely, miserable monotony of my current situation has twisted into a perfect storm that was unleashed the instant I felt ignited by his touch. It's also possible that tomorrow I'll regret being foolish and impulsive, especially because I'm never foolish and impulsive.

Except when I get near Colt.

He was my lone teenage rebellion. Now I'm turning him into my lone rebellion in adulthood, however short-lived it will be.

This should bother me.

I'm not paying attention to our location but when Colt stops, I finally look up to see that we are not where I expected to be.

"This is my house." All the lights are on and the living room shutters are open.

He says nothing and shuts the truck off.

"Colt, why are we at my house?"

He jumps out and then leans back inside to deliver a humiliating blow. "Because it's time for you to go home."

There's a sudden bitter taste in my mouth. "Is this revenge? Is that it?"

After all, I did reject him at a very critical moment. This is not a subject that's come up yet.

The sound he makes is almost, but not quite, a laugh. "No. Now get out of there. Your dad's watching."

He's right. There's a shadow at the living room window. I hadn't realized my father would be waiting up for me. This just adds to my misery.

Colt waits for me on the sidewalk and reaches for my hand as we proceed up the brick-paved path to the front door. But he's not trying to hold hands. No, he's just pushing my discarded panties into my palm. Hoping that the darkness hides my mortification, I stuff them into the side pocket of my handbag.

We proceed in silence until we're standing in the pool of light blazing from the wrought iron lantern above the front door. It's a tossup whether I'm more furious at myself for behaving badly or with Colt for his mixed signals.

Colt, meanwhile, has now become inexplicably cheerful. "Good night, Susanna. I had a great time."

I can feel my eyes narrowing. Then I realize he's putting on an act in case my father is listening. This leaves me feeling more at a loss than ever. Why is he willing to go to such lengths to bring comfort to a man who treated him so horribly?

Or to a girl who broke his heart.

In reality, Colt owes us nothing. Nothing at all.

Sorrow and a deluge of unwelcome memories steals every ounce of my fight. The bitter taste in my mouth remains and I'm finding it difficult to look him in the eye. I drop my head to gaze down at the toes of my black ballet flats and croak out, "Good night, Colt."

I don't expect to feel a hand on my face but there's Colt, tipping my chin up and leaning in for a brief, chaste kiss.

He waits right there on the front step until I'm safely inside with the door closed behind me.

"Oh hey, Susie." My father blinks at me from his armchair and looks around. "Must have fallen asleep here. Did you have a nice evening?"

I know he wasn't asleep but I let him pretend. And I do some pretending of my own. "I'm glad you got some rest. And yes, I had a lovely evening."

He smiles. He allows me to help him up and escort him down the hall to his room. Earlier, I noticed that his skin was beginning to take on the strange cast of possible jaundice. Tomorrow I will call the doctor for advice.

With my dad settled, I'm free to seek the sanctuary of my own bedroom. Sometimes I get anxious about being so far away at night in this big house. I'm not a light sleeper and should my father suffer a fall or other emergency in the middle of the night I'm not sure I'd hear him cry out. Last week I joined an online forum for caregivers of terminally ill family members and there was a thread that mentioned the use of baby monitors. It's a good solution, even if the idea of installing an infant monitor to hear to my father's nightly movements is horribly depressing.

A nice hot shower feels like the right antidote to my mood. I adjust the water temperature as high as I can stand it. Tonight's events replay in my head and I'm cringing as I inhale the steam. I try to guess what Colt thinks of me right now and can't.

There was always a curious contradiction that came with being in Colt's world. Most people around here thought of him as the careless and unruly boy who could do anything with a football but had little promise off the field.

With me, he was different.

He was genuine and he was sweet and he was vulnerable. Yet even then I worried over him. At the back of my mind lived the fear that despite all the hours we spent sharing our most intimate details and clandestine thoughts, Colt Malene might always be just out of reach. When he changed into a callous stranger I was left with an agonizing puzzle.

Maybe I hadn't known the real Colt after all.

Or maybe I was to blame for what became of him, for why he deserted the sport he loved, for why he quit school, for why he became cold and cruel and finally disappeared.

A terrible thought, that I might have been the one to push him over the edge, that the boy I'd loved was also the one I'd helped destroy.

6

COLT

Tori and Jace are at the Grand Canyon. My sister just sent me a photo of them wearing sunglasses at the South Rim with their arms around each other. Their smiles are authentically brilliant and with the pastel backdrop of the world famous landmark, the picture checks all the boxes of a perfect shot.

Tori writes that they plan to spend two nights at a nearby campground and then they'll drive north. She wants to know how I'm keeping busy back here in their absence. And she wants photos of McClane.

As a photography subject, McClane could use some work. We go out back and I try to catch a photo of him sniffing around in the small fruit orchard. He lifts his leg and pisses on a peach tree with his giant pink tongue halfway out of his mouth and a gleam in his beady eyes that seems to say, '*Haha, loser. Caption this!*'

Then I try to snap a shot of him pausing thoughtfully by the rose bushes, but he jumps up and starts chasing a butterfly. I do get a picture of him leaping into the air and decide it's good enough to send.

Tori responds with a smiley face. I'm hoping she's in such a state of honeymoon bliss that she doesn't repeat her first question. No such luck.

What have you been up to?

I've said nothing to her about Susanna and since I'm unsure if Susanna ever wants to see me again after last night's disaster, I'm not going to touch that topic now.

I'm still mulling over how to give my sister an answer that won't raise more questions when she starts typing again. I wait for the three dots to dissolve into a new message.

Rochelle knows you're staying in town. She and Carrie would love to hear from you.

Rochelle is my stepmother. She's only got nine years on me and didn't marry Eric Malene until I was in high school so I've always had some trouble thinking of her in terms of that word. Plus, there's the whole inescapable fact that her husband wasn't really my father and I suppose there could be a technical argument against calling her my stepmother at all. However, she thinks of herself as my stepmother and Rochelle is really an outstanding person so I don't mind.

Carrie is her ten-year-old daughter. Carrie was only a toddler when Eric died. She calls me her brother. Again, I don't mind.

I'll check in with Rochelle.

This is good enough to satisfy Tori.

Next, she relays a message from Jace. Jace bought me a gift shop souvenir, a keychain with a full color engraving of the Grand Canyon. He knows I like keychains.

Tori's last message is an order. She says McClane and I need to take care of each other. I'm glad she and Jace are having such a fabulous time.

And now I can return to doing what I was doing before Tori messaged me.

Which is sink into the nearest chair and brood over how epically I managed to fuck up last night's date with Susanna.

The thing is, my intentions were noble. The other night while I was sitting at their huge dining room table and looking at all the empty chairs, I was struck by the sadness of it all. Coach Toledo is dying. His daughter spends her days providing round the clock care with the miserable awareness of how it will end. I already know there's no one else they can turn to, no other family.

What happened ten years ago is done. At this stage I feel no wrath towards my old coach and even if I did, a dying man deserves some peace. I made Susanna an offer to hang around for the next three weeks because I knew it would make her dad happy and because she could probably use some time away from the daily death watch. Susanna has always idolized her father and watching his life slowly ebb away has got to be killing her.

I really do want to help. For a lot of years I did a shitty job when it comes to being supportive of the people I care about. Lately I've turned a corner. I can be a friend. I can be *her* friend. There doesn't need to be any more to it than that.

But there is.

No matter how much I try to deny it.

I've always been intensely drawn to Susanna. In high school she was nothing like the other girls I hung around with. Yet none of those other girls ever jumpstarted my heart the way she did.

Never before and never since have I wanted anyone else the way I wanted her.

Years ago, when everything in my life blew up in my face, I felt like I was being smothered from the inside. In order to cope, I got used to shoving my feelings way down into some undiscoverable internal cave. That's where I sent my feelings for Susanna. But they never died, those feelings. They were just dimmed and muted.

Now some of those feelings are back.

We seem to have lost the easy magic of just being in each other's company. Maybe that just comes with the territory of adulthood. We're not the same people anymore.

I want her anyway and I can't help that. What I *can* do is demonstrate some self control.

At least I thought I could. My efforts turned out to be pretty crappy. In the end, I nearly gave in. How could I say no when she clung to my neck and pleaded for more? I kissed her. I touched her. I said things to her that are making me cringe today.

Then I refused her offer and took her home. And Susanna, humiliated and angry, asked if I was acting out of revenge.

Fuck.

It kills me she thinks that. I always promised Susanna that she could trust me. That's still true.

It's also true that the more I try to be virtuous and polite, the less successful I am.

The dog gets curious about what I'm doing over here, hunched on a chair with my elbows on my knees. He sits at my feet and cocks his head.

"What should I do, McClane?"

McClane barks at me twice with sharp impatience.

"You're right." I scratch the dog's ears. "I'm a dumbass. Instead of sitting around like a useless turd I should go over there and apologize."

He receives a biscuit in gratitude for his good advice. I leave him napping on the couch and drive over to Susanna's house.

My truck convulses and nearly stalls at a stop sign. The thing is a constant work in progress. Anyone might assume that I can't afford better than this lumbering Ford relic that's been around longer than I have but they'd be wrong. I've reached a point where I'm skilled enough to command a decent paycheck and I live with bare simplicity. By now there's over two hundred grand accumulated in a Missoula bank account that can be drawn on anytime. I could go to the nearest auto lot today and pick out their shiniest piece of inventory. But I like this old truck and therefore I'll keep this old truck.

Pulling up to the curb prompts another flashback to last night. What happened was my fault. I tried to play it cool, to act like the sight of Susanna Toledo doesn't send me reeling. I failed. She might just shut the door in my face today. I'm definitely feeling the anxiety when I ring the bell.

However, Susanna doesn't shut the door in my face. She's not even home. Drew Toledo is slow to answer the door but he invites me right

in. Susanna is at the grocery store and he was just watching a baseball game. That's the thing about baseball season; there's always
some kind of game on. I don't follow the sport at all but I don't want
to be rude so I take a seat on the couch and fake some interest. Half
an inning later, I notice when he takes the last sip of his glass of water
and I offer to get him more. At first Coach starts to get out of his chair,
determined to get it himself, but then he changes his mind and nods.

"Thanks. I'm a little winded today."

He's putting on a brave face. Jace checks in on him all the time.
Jace is the one who let me know that the cancer is now deep in his
lungs. It is, of course, inoperable.

That other night I watched Susanna worrying over how to get her
father to eat. With the glass of water in hand, I attempt to add a
snack, a slice of bread. He shakes his head with some amusement and
resumes watching the Texas Rangers clobber the New York Yankees.

Susanna walks through the front door when I'm in the middle of
showing off Jace and Tori's Grand Canyon photo. She must have
noticed my truck sitting outside before coming in so she isn't shocked
to find me on her living room couch. I thought she might be angry
but no, she's not angry either. I like the way she's dressed; casual tight
black pants with a long navy blue shirt that falls from her right shoulder. Her hair is pulled into its classic ponytail and today she wears
her glasses. There are faint circles under her eyes. She's still gorgeous,
maybe even more today than yesterday, and that's saying a lot.

"Hi." I stand up and cross the room to take the brown bag of
groceries from her arms.

She hands the bag over willingly. "Hi."

I carry the bag to the kitchen counter and set it down. "Is there
more?"

"In my trunk, yes."

On my way to the door I pass within inches of her. "I'll get it."

She lowers her eyes and nods.

The remaining three bags in the trunk of her Acura are easy to
deliver in one trip. Susanna moves quickly to unpack the contents.
She doesn't look up so she doesn't notice how I stand eight feet away,

admiring her in silence. There's a slight flush on her cheeks and once she tiredly swipes a hand across her forehead. The impulse to sweep her into my arms nearly gets the best of me.

Meanwhile, Coach scolds the pitcher on the screen for throwing a wild pitch.

Susanna pulls out the last food item, a cluster of celery held together with a red rubber band, and stores it in the fridge.

Now there's nothing left for her to do and she finally looks my way. She starts to speak, stops, and starts again. "Have you been here long?"

"Not long, no."

She folds her arms across her body, chews on the corner of her lip.

"There you go," Coach cheers when the pitcher throws a strike. He coughs, grimaces, and then tenses as if hit with a tremor of pain.

Susanna is immediately anxious. "Do you want your pills, Dad?"

"No, Susie. Told you I'm not taking those."

She sighs.

I clear my throat. "Susanna, if your dad can spare you, I was hoping you might agree to come out for a little while. I want you to meet a friend of mine."

While she's still figuring out how to respond to this, Coach becomes lively. "Go on, both of you. Have fun. Don't hang around here just to watch an old man cough." He stares eagerly at his daughter. "Susie, I'd be happy if you went with Colt. I was just going to take a nap anyway."

Her mouth presses into a vague smile. "All right, Daddy. Call me if you need anything."

She's quiet when I lead her out to my truck. She's still quiet when I start driving but the tension isn't difficult to sense, even for an insensitive blockhead like me.

No big deal. I can wait until she's ready to talk. I'm just glad she isn't furious with me.

"Oh." She sits up straight and peers out the window. "It's your old neighborhood."

I switch off the engine. "Gloria's house is the only one that looks pretty much the same."

She's still looking out the window. "So where is this friend of yours?"

"Inside the house. Come on. He's waiting."

This is a slight exaggeration since McClane has no sense of time and has no idea I'll be showing up with a visitor but that doesn't matter.

He's off the couch, tail whipping around like a propeller, by the time I get the door open. He pays special attention to Susanna, wiggling with excitement over the surprise of this brand new friend, and he closes his eyes in ecstasy when she crouches down to pet his broad head.

"What a handsome boy you are," she says and McClane is in love.

Grabbing a handful of biscuits from the pantry, I lead the party outside so McClane can show off his tricks. On my command he sits, he rolls over and he shakes hands. Each time he receives a crunchy biscuit and each time he also glances at Susanna to make sure she's watching.

"Good job," she claps with a huge grin and I can almost hear my own heart turning to mush at the sight of her smile.

Once the treats are gone, McClane goes exploring in the yard. The day is beautiful with a cloudless robin's egg sky and the scent of newly cut grass in the mild air.

Susanna and I stand side by side on the patio and watch the dog stick his face into a batch of zinnias and then sneeze three times in a row. He backs away, regarding the flowers with indignation.

When I look at Susanna she's no longer smiling and she's not watching the dog anymore either. She's staring absently at an empty corner of the yard and her shoulders sag.

"He had a bad night last night," she says.

I'm aware she's not talking about McClane.

"What happened?"

"He couldn't sleep. He says he can't breathe when he lays down.

He kept pacing the house and I was afraid he was going to fall so I stayed awake too."

"You must be tired."

"A little. His doctor already gave me the hospice care number. I hadn't been able to find the nerve to call yet. Soon enough he'll be in such bad shape that I won't be able to leave him alone."

"I'm so sorry, Susanna." Feeling an unstoppable need to comfort her, I reach out and touch her shoulder. She doesn't flinch or move away. "I know how close you two have always been."

"No." She shakes her head. "My dad and I actually haven't been close for a long time. Once I went away to college I hardly visited and when my folks split that was just one more excuse to stay away."

I don't want her to see that I'm stunned to hear this. Susanna worshipped her dad. To my knowledge, the only thing they ever fought over was me. But that alone wouldn't have broken their bond. Susanna obeyed his demands to cut me loose and everyone moved on. At least, that's what I always thought. Something else had to have happened, something that I won't force her to talk about now.

She inhales raggedly, exhales slowly. "We all expect to outlive our parents. I guess it's fair to say that's what we *hope* for because otherwise we die young. But I took time for granted, thinking next time I'll do this or that. But next time might never come. He's only fifty-three. There should be more time, don't you think?"

I'm helpless as I agree with her. "Yes, there should be."

"Maybe it would never be enough."

"Maybe not."

She's hurting so much right now and I can't stand it. I move behind her and slip my arms around her waist. She doesn't resist at all. She leans back slightly against my chest and allows me to hold her more securely.

A spring breeze flutters the fresh green leaves of the fruit trees. McClane discovers an object of interest in the dense carpet of grass and attempts to dig it out. Then he abruptly gets bored, cracks a wide yawn and trots over to the shade to stretch out on his belly with a happy sigh.

Susanna breathes out a small wheeze of laughter. "I am spectacularly embarrassed about last night."

"Nah, don't be." I raise my chin high enough to prop it on top of her head. Her hair smells like cherry blossoms. "I'm the one who made the first move."

"And then I threw myself at you."

"But you have no idea what it took to turn you down."

She swivels around so that we're facing each other now. My arms remain around her and she doesn't move away.

Susanna peers up at me and her long lashes flutter behind her glasses. "Are we going to be really honest with each other now?"

"We should be. I'm no good at the alternative."

This brings a fleeting smile. Then she grows serious.

"Colt, I haven't said this to you yet, but I am so incredibly happy to see you again."

"I'm incredibly happy to see you too. And I'm trying really hard not to be a bad guy."

She moves her arms and hooks them over my shoulders, presses closer and whispers, "You've never been a bad guy."

I'm focused on her lips now. Soft, slightly parted and inches away. It goes without saying that I'm already hard as fuck. She must feel that. Just like I can feel the way her breathing is fast and her heart pounds.

We've already decided we're going to be honest.

Now it's my turn to be completely honest with her.

"You know I want you, Susanna. Even so, I don't regret leaving you at your front door and walking away instead of the alternative. I just wish I'd gone about it differently. I should have let you know how much you've been on my mind all these years. I should have been able to treat you with more respect."

She thinks about that and rests her cheek against my shoulder. "You never treated me with disrespect. Not last night or any other time. I've thought about you so much, wondered about you so much. I'm aware that we're very different. Different from each other and different from the kids we were back then. And I want you too, Colt. But I already told you that."

I'm imagining it all; carrying her inside, undressing her in a frenzy and taking her the way she really wants me to. The way *I* really want to. I might even feel tempted to remain here in Arcana for longer than I originally planned to stay.

But in the end, I would still leave. That's the problem. I'd grow restless and she'd be disappointed. I'm not built for the kind of life Susanna Toledo deserves.

Even knowing all of that with absolute certainty, I can't make myself push her away.

She moves and lightly kisses my neck. I sift my fingers through her hair, slowly pulling out the elastic band.

No, I don't have the willpower to keep her at arm's length.

And maybe we can't have everything, but we can have something.

My free hand slips under her shirt, touching the warm skin of her lower back. She breathes sharply and moves her head, angling for a kiss. She gets my tongue. Her answering sexy moan is an invitation to kiss her harder. She moves her hands down my back, eager to touch and to be touched. My own hands roam everywhere. Her right knee hooks over my hip. We're on the verge of dry humping in the backyard and I'm about fucking ready to bust through the zipper on my pants.

She trembles when I reach between her legs. I'm stroking her, enjoying the way she quivers when my fingers graze a sensitive spot. "Let's go inside."

She looks up, blinks. "Really?"

"Yes." I sweep her hair aside to whisper a fact into her ear. "We can make each other feel good without going too far."

She nods and breaks into a smile of mischief. "I remember."

"And you want to?"

"Badly."

I do end up carrying her, lifting her with ease. McClane pops his head up, curious about what new game we're playing, but then he looks away and returns to contemplating the tree leaves.

Whenever I'm staying here I sleep in the guest bedroom at the end of the hall. This is where we're going. Susanna giggles while holding onto my neck and I grin because it's clear she's enjoying this gesture. She quits giggling when I set her down on the bed and she's kneeling as she faces me with an uncertain expression.

I take the lead and pull my shirt over my head. My ego enjoys the way her eyes widen as she greedily surveys my muscled chest.

"My god, you're hot," she says and then rolls her eyes when she sees the look on my face. "Now quit smirking."

I don't quit smirking at all. "Only if you give me something else to do with my mouth."

She glances down at herself and clucks her tongue. "I looked far cuter last night. You should have taken advantage of me then."

"You look hot as shit today." Without hesitating, I drop my pants. "And I'm ready to take advantage of you now."

Again, her eyes flicker down. I'm still wearing my boxers but there's no way to disguise the truth. I'm pitching a tent the size of Mount Everest.

Susanna exhales slowly. I wonder if I should back off a little until I'm sure what she's in the mood for. We won't be fucking, at least not in the traditional sense. Last night she admitted that she's never had sex at all. I can't help but admire her for that. Susanna was always very candid about the fact that I was the first guy she ever kissed, the first guy she ever messed around with. That was a long time ago and I assume she's done a few things since then, but she might be out of practice.

That's fine. I'm out of practice too. I'm now realizing I should have kissed her again before yanking my pants down. I can do better than this.

"Come here, honey." Gently, I reach out and hold her face in my hands. My thumbs brush softly over her cheeks. She really is exquisite.

I lean in gradually, tenderly. Our lips meet, my arms circle her and she relaxes. Aside from her, I was never a huge fan of kissing, always in a hurry to get to the next step. Kissing Susanna was different and still is. I'm confident I could kiss her for hours on end and still want more.

She's the one to break the kiss. But that's because she wants to take her shirt off. Underneath she's wearing only a white cotton tank top with no bra and the way I can see her tits through the fabric drives me instantly crazy.

Susanna watches as I finish kicking my pants away. With a shy grin, she slowly pushes her own pants down over her hips. Her panties are white and immediately I'm aching to put my mouth all over them. Her body is absolutely fucking perfect. Thanks to some bullshit her mother told her, Susanna always used to put herself down, believing she was too awkwardly thin and too tall. She's neither. Every inch of her is flawless.

This time when I kiss her the mood grows feverish. She pulls me onto the bed and I roll on top of her, careful not to crush her with my weight while my dick throbs and begs to be set free. This is torture but it's the sweetest kind of torture.

"You're so amazing," she breathes between kisses and I shove the straps of her tank top away so I can use my mouth on her tits, sucking at one nipple and then the other. Her tits are small and perfect and I'm crazy for the way they feel in my mouth.

She moans and she whispers my name. She wraps her legs around me and moves her body while I lose my mind.

"Fuck," I hiss when I realize that somehow my boxers are down and I'm close, so close, *dangerously fucking close* as I grind and push, the only barrier a little piece of white cotton that could be history in half a second but won't be, at least not today.

Because I made a promise, to Susanna and to myself.

I roll over to my back and take her with me. She cooperates, moving to a straddle position, making no objection when I lift her thin tank top over her head so that I can feel more of her skin. We're sitting up, face to face, her knees over my hips, only those flimsy cotton panties separating us in any way. Susanna wants more kissing and I'm glad to oblige. Her palms rest on my shoulders and I hold her in place with one arm around her back. My other hand reaches down between us to touch her, lightly at first, over her panties.

She loves this and starts moving in rhythm, clutching me and whimpering as my tongue demands her mouth and my hand demands the rest of her. My thumb slides past a line of elastic, notes with satisfaction the slipperiness found within and nudges inside her, just enough to give her what she needs. I roll my thumb in a slow circle, teasing her, delivering the right mix of friction and play. It's hot and it's dirty but it's not too far. It's something we've done before.

In another minute she's going wild, unable to continue kissing as she rides my hand and comes hard.

"Oh my god, Colt. Fuck, oh, fuck!"

Holy hell that does it for me, always has, hearing dirty words from her mouth and feeling her quake as she gets off.

I have to grit my teeth and think of unsexy things such as wood piles and highway signs in order to avoid exploding too soon.

Just as she's winding down, sighing with pleasure and ready to collapse in my arms, another wave hits her and she comes again.

For my part, I'm feeling rather smug and I'm also thinking I deserve some kind of endurance trophy for holding out this long.

My reward comes when Susanna reaches down to take me in her palm.

"No one has ever made me feel the way you do," she says, still breathless as her soft hand torments the stiff length of my cock.

I'm almost there already and could easily reach the brink with her hand on me. Susanna has another plan. She pushes a palm to my chest to indicate that I should lie back. I watch and push my fingers through her hair as she kisses her way down my chest. She goes lower. She meets my eager cock with her mouth and that's it. I'm fucking done for.

In another moment I would have erupted no matter what but then I look down and see her sweet lips sliding up and down my dick and the world tilts sideways.

"Susanna," I gasp out, not wanting to rudely come in her mouth with no warning. "Back up, baby. I'm just about there."

She stops, gazes up at me from behind her glasses with an adorable level of wide-eyed innocence, finally understands what I mean, and decides she wants to finish sucking me off anyway.

She's glorious, this girl.

Afterwards, I waste no time gathering her into my arms and she lays her head down on my chest. We're both spent and mildly sweaty and it's more intimate than anything else I've had in a lot of years, since the last time I touched her. The little things make her so happy, like when I reach for a blanket and cover her with it.

Susanna really is exhausted and she sleeps for a little while as the afternoon deepens and the shadows lengthen. She's hungry when she wakes and I offer to whip up some French toast, which is something I'm an unofficial expert at making.

We eat at Gloria Zielinski's worn but cozy kitchen table where I gobbled up a thousand meals as a kid. Susanna notices all the cross stitch art and trinkets everywhere and wants to hear more about Gloria, who she remembers clearly but never spent much time with.

I'm happy enough to talk about Gloria but I also feel a guilty twinge of sadness for failing to appreciate her while she was alive. She tried to keep track of me. Sometimes the Christmas cards and random packages of homemade baked goods sent by her would reach wherever I was. The most I ever did in return was drop a card in the mail now and then. I didn't call. I didn't visit. I should have. What's more, I'm reminded of what Susanna said, how we all take for granted that the future will hold more opportunities, more chances to do what's right.

But the truth is, none of us are guaranteed that there will be a next time.

Susanna takes pity on McClane, who has been patiently waiting for handouts. She throws him a bite of French toast and laughs when he snaps it right out of the air. Then her attention shifts to me because I'm holding my palm open in the middle of the table. I want her to see what I just retrieved from my key ring.

She stares in shock. "I can't believe you still have that. I thought you must have thrown it away."

"Never. It goes everywhere I go."

For a few seconds she's at a loss for words. Then her expression changes to curiosity. I have no doubt she remembers the day we met. She remembers everything. "Does it bring you luck?"

I close my fingers around the charm that hangs from my keychain and wink at her. "I feel pretty lucky today."

She bites her lip and blushes, definitely flashing back to our fun times in the bedroom. I wasn't just referring to that. I'm lucky to be here with her.

Susanna checks her phone and her face falls. "Damn, I didn't realize it was this late. I need to go. My dad seemed kind of shaky today. He shouldn't be alone for too long."

McClane is unhappy to see his new crush departing. He follows us to the door and pitifully offers his paw as Susanna gives him one final pat on the head.

"Don't worry," I tell the dog. "I'll be back soon."

I could swear he understood every word. He sits down, temporarily appeased.

At Susanna's house, Coach is sound asleep in his armchair. I watch from the doorway as she quietly tiptoes to his side, removes the silver tablet that is about to fall out of his lap, and covers him with a fuzzy yellow blanket that had slipped to the floor.

Susanna stands up and stares at her father for a moment. From this standpoint it's clear how frail he is, how much weight and muscle mass he's lost. His head is tilted back with his mouth open and without the animation of his cheerful smile, his face is drawn and pale.

I feel like I'm seeing too much, judging too harshly. I look away.

Susanna joins me at the door and I motion that we ought to step outside so we don't wake up her dad. She nods, taking my hand, and I carefully close the door behind me.

Outside, the sun still presides over a peaceful late afternoon and it's hard to believe the shadow of death is so nearby. Now that she's back home and confronted by her responsibilities, Susanna has grown noticeably tense and sad.

"Thank you for the French toast," she says, bravely managing to smile. "You'll have to tell me your secret. Mine always comes out soggy and tasteless."

"Use thicker bread. And add a touch of vanilla." I'm gazing past her now, at the house. Coach has been sick for a couple of years and he must have been unable to perform basic maintenance for quite some time. Those things can add up; chipped paint, loose roof tiles, warped door frames.

I can fix all that. I can fix all that and more.

When I suggest this to Susanna, she cheers up. "Just yesterday I was thinking about hiring a handyman."

"I'm handy. And I'm a man."

"Of course, I would pay you for your time."

"No way," I scoff.

"What's your going rate? I'll match it."

"Not taking your money, Susanna. It's a favor."

"Very well. I'll just bake you some cookies then."

"Shit, there's no need to threaten me."

She laughs. Then she throws her arms around my neck and hugs me hard.

I hug her back. I inhale deeply and again smell cherry blossoms. "I'll be here tomorrow. Does nine a.m. work?"

"Yes." She steps back and then sort of laughs to herself.

I raise an eyebrow. "What?"

"I was just thinking about something."

"Are you going to share or should I try to read your mind?"

Her hand grazes my cheek. "Chemistry."

I remember our conversation from last night. "We've always had it."

She drops her hand and tilts her head. "I had a wonderful day with you, Colt."

I pull her close. "Then kiss me."

We don't get all graphic here in the front yard in broad daylight, but our kiss is no casual peck either. I drop one final kiss on her forehead, reluctant to leave her, but unable to think up an excuse to stick around.

"See you tomorrow. Make me a list of the small repairs that need to be done."

"I still plan to pay you somehow."

I start walking backwards toward my truck. "We'll work something out."

Susanna touches her fingers to her lips with a dreamy look on her face and I'm not sure she realizes she's even doing it.

Funny, but I've watched her make the same move before. It's a core memory and I'm thinking about it even after she returns to her house and closes the door.

Then I raise my eyes to look at a curtained second floor window.

My memory is nowhere near as impressive as Susanna's, but there are some things I won't forget, not as long as I live.

Like the sight of a girl standing in her bedroom window and touching her lips with a smile, right after receiving her first kiss.

7

SUSANNA, AGE 15

My mother is eight inches shorter than me and her boobs are two cup sizes larger. It makes sense that I wouldn't fit into her dress but that didn't stop her from pulling the thing from the bowels of her closet and stuffing me into it. She frets over the fact that she didn't get alterations done but ultimately decides the fit is just fine when it most certainly is not.

I've seen pictures of the time she wore this dress to her own homecoming dance when she was my age. It looked fabulous on her perky cheerleader body, however it's not nearly as impressive on me. All this shiny blue satin and sequins (*gag, actual sequins!*) just screams that I'm drowning in some kind of sad cosplay fail.

Tagging along with my parents to the Arcana High homecoming dance isn't my idea of a great time. I don't have a date, but I do have plenty of studying and I need to begin finalizing plans for next month's science fair project. My dad expressed a little sympathy and usually he's one to speak up in my defense but he's preoccupied now that the season is underway.

Arcana is a place that acts as if the fate of the world hinges on whether the high school football team wins. Yet I cheer as hard as anyone else in the stands on the home team side and hold my breath during every touchdown pass because for my dad, leading his team to victory means the world.

"Susanna, your hair," scolds my mother while we walk through the school parking lot.

She throws me an unhappy look before taking my father's arm and I pat my head self-consciously. On the short drive over here, I plucked out a few of the bobby pins that have been stabbing my scalp since this afternoon's visit to the salon. Judging by her expression, the elaborate twist that's been torturing me since then has suffered a visible defeat.

I don't know why it matters. No one will be looking at me. Even if I were drop dead gorgeous, which I definitely am not, Drew Toledo is both formidable and a protective father. In some ways that makes things easier for me than they are for other girls and in other ways it makes things harder. Mostly I'm treated with polite deference by the school's male population and I'm likely to spend my years at Arcana High without being kissed once. Such is life.

My dad turns and winks at me with a broad grin and I stop fussing with my hair. He couldn't care less about hair and makeup and dresses. He hangs my report cards on the fridge and always wants to know what I'm studying. It's a comfort to know that at least one of my parents values my real accomplishments rather than searching for ones I'll never have.

One final hiss from my mother. "Smile!"

The gym erupts into applause as my folks glide in like the king and queen of Arcana, awkwardly trailed by the bespectacled and blue sequined grand duchess. Last night's homecoming game was a resounding victory, with Arcana crushing rival Bredon High by a score of forty-two to ten.

Thankfully, I already have an assignment to keep me busy here. The Honor Society is helping with refreshments and I'm glad to have something to do. The dance, like any high school dance, is rather a chaotic collection of loud music, junk food and bickering teenagers.

Gloria Zielinski oversees the food tables and ensures that no one adds vodka to the rows of drink cups. This happened last year and the result was a bunch of bombed ninth graders who vomited red fruit punch and potato chips all over the dance floor.

"Susanna," says Gloria with true delight. "You look beautiful, honey."

I don't agree at all but Gloria is nice so I smile and thank her and ask how I can help. I am sent to the kitchen to retrieve more napkins, which is where I nearly crash into Tori Malene, who carries a tray of chocolate cupcakes.

"Whoa." She pivots and avoids disaster. Then she looks me up and down and blinks.

"Not a word about the dress," I warn because I know Tori well enough to understand there's no need to be phony. "It belonged to my mother."

"Vintage. Cool."

"Not really. It's been given the opportunity to torment me after biding its time in a plastic bag for over twenty years."

Tori grins. "Is that why it's so shiny?"

"Hush or I'll cut you with my sequins."

She laughs and moves on. Seeing Tori makes me think of her brother but I wouldn't dare ask about him. Anyone within earshot would wonder why and I'd hate for word to get back to him. I'm sure he's around somewhere. He's on the homecoming court and I've heard he's bringing Brynna Graff to the dance. Brynna is pretty and bubbly and probably shares a similar IQ to cotton candy.

Mean. Mean. Mean.

Usually I'm not so unkind, not even in my head. Where Brynna's concerned I'm chalking it up to old fashioned jealousy.

After returning with the napkins, the sight of Jace Zielinski gets my attention. He's not on the dance floor or huddling with his teammates while planning to make trouble later. He's leaning against the wall nearest to the locker room entrance and nodding along to whatever his English teacher, Mr. Salenger, is saying to him.

Jace is definitely easy on the eyes but that's not why I'm watching him. My only interest in Jace is the knowledge is that if he's within view, then his best friend is sure to be nearby. Apparently, that's not the case today because after three more songs, Jace remains best friend-less.

In a way, I'm glad. I have little desire to be seen in all my blue sequined glory. With every passing minute my discomfort rises. I should have worn something under the dress. The bodice is supremely itchy but if I make a move then it might seem like I'm scratching my boobs and my boobs have enough problems right now. They are currently adrift in a sea of heavily padded cotton to keep the neckline from drooping down to my navel.

My parents are making the rounds on opposite sides of the room. My father appears to be reenacting a play by play of yesterday's game to an eager audience of faculty and chaperones, while my mother cackles with a squad of her friends, mothers of my classmates, many of whom she's known since her own days attending this high school. They both appear happy and relaxed and attractive and no one would guess how often they yell terrible words at each other. Life at home always get a little worse after every failed fertility treatment and following last month's negative result, my mother told him that she didn't want to try anymore and no, she wouldn't consider adoption either. She's closing in on age forty and she's changed her mind about wanting to start over with a new baby.

For my dad, who still holds out hope for the big family he's always wanted, the news was a blow. He growled that she is selfish. She shouted that he is callous. He took a long walk, slamming the front door. She cried. I've heard my parents arguing hundreds of times and this was the first occasion I can remember feeling more sympathy for her than for him. On the top shelf of my dad's closet he keeps a collection of sports jerseys in different childhood sizes, all intended for a son he's probably never going to have. He wouldn't want me to know that and so I pretend that I don't.

Now I can see Brynna Graff on the dance floor but she's not with her date so I breathe out a sigh of relief. Instead, she's with Dodson Kemp and the way they've got their arms wrapped around each other doesn't exactly look innocent.

After an hour, the refreshments are running low and there's no reason for so many of us to be standing around back here. Gloria makes a gallant effort to push us into the social maelstrom but some of the other Honor Society members mumble excuses and break for the exits.

Tori, apparently, has also had enough of the homecoming dance. She hugs Gloria, says she'll be over for her piano lesson tomorrow and tells me to say hello to my fairy godmother.

"What?" I've been scanning the dancing couples and I'm puzzled by her comment.

"In that dress you remind me of Cinderella at the ball. In a good way," she adds hastily.

I gaze down past all the satin shininess. "Well, no one would mistake these black flats for glass slippers." I refused to wear heels tonight, another source of unhappiness for my mother. Not only are heels uncomfortable but *sheesh*, one thing I do not need to add is height. At two inches shy of six feet, I'm not exactly headed for the record books, but I am one of the tallest girls in the school.

"See ya." Tori waves and marches right through the crowded gym.

Jace is now talking to some of the football players and his head whips around to watch her go. It's not the first time I've noticed the way he stares at her with hungry intensity and I wonder if Tori has any idea that her brother's best friend is smitten with her.

Sadly, I did not inherit the social talents of either of my parents. I don't want to dance and I don't see anyone I'd like to talk to. All I want to do is exchange this ill fitting eyesore of a dress for my pajamas and curl up with my math book. My folks, however, have a long history of never being the first ones to leave any party. I'm sure my dad would drive me home if I asked but my mother would find out and problems would ensue. She'll be annoyed if he leaves and more annoyed to hear that I'd rather be studying at home instead of participating in normal teenage traditions like loitering in a smelly gymnasium until my temples throb from the pounding music while gossiping with my peers about who is currently screwing who.

After some deliberating, I decide to approach my mother. I'll let her know that I'd prefer to go elsewhere and hang out with friends. She won't be pleased but she'll likely ask fewer questions.

"We're going to go get some pizza," I tell her. "And I've got a ride home."

Her lips purse. Then she declares, "The homecoming court will be taking the stage soon."

Which is...not interesting to me at all.

I try to look like I'm in a hurry. "They're waiting for me outside."

"They?"

"Yes. My friends."

My father would demand to know names. If they were names he didn't approve of then he would object.

But my mother has either lost interest or she is just pleased that I'm discarding my nerd crown for a little while. She shrugs. "Be home by eleven."

I maintain a straight face. "I will. I promise."

My house is a twenty minute brisk walk from the school. I'll be home eons before eleven.

Now that I have an escape route, I waste no time using it. While hurrying toward the double door exit I overhear a smattering of laughter. When I look over, I see a crew of sophomore girls staring at me while bubbling over with giggles. It's pretty clear that the sight of me running for the door in my outdated fairy tale getup has inspired some hilarity. Though I'm the most brutal critic of my own appearance, I won't tolerate being the butt of someone's joke. I stop in my tracks, raise my chin and glare at the girls, a silent dare to repeat their comments to my face.

Every one of them backs off, fidgeting and pulling out their phones. I knew they would. While I'm not one of the most confidently popular girls in school, neither are they. I am the coach's daughter and I am the president of the Honor Society. Even with sequins dripping in my wake, I'm no one's fool.

The cool night air is liberating after the stuffy collision of perfumes inside the gym. A bunch of my classmates, all juniors, are piling into two pickup trucks, likely heading for one of the remote party spots on the outskirts of town. I don't expect to be invited and I'm not.

Now that I'm free of maternal scrutiny, I pull every single unwanted bobby pin from my hair and throw the pile of them into a nearby overflowing trash can. My hair falls everywhere in soft waves and I wish I had a scrunchie to pull it into a comfortable ponytail. I settle for tucking it behind my ears.

I'm certain to attract some notice if I linger here for long. There's no shortage of busybodies in Arcana and I'd rather avoid being a topic of conversation.

This will mean cutting across the dim athletic fields and sticking to side streets on the walk home. While the football field remains lit for tonight's festivities, the adjacent grassy fields that host the less popular sports are dark. It doesn't occur to me until I've left all the homecoming dance commotion behind that I'm alone and it's dark and I would be smart to feel nervous.

Furthermore, realizing that I *should* be nervous succeeds in actually making me nervous. The tiny can of pepper spray given to me by my dad is not in my possession.

Tires squeal in the distance and a chorus of voices howl a noise that can be roughly translated as 'WOOHOO!' A loud thud comes from the vicinity of the soccer field and the low rumble of male laughter ricochets. I'm watching when a shadowy knot appears in the hazy glow cast by the field lights. The knot separates into individual figures who shove each other and hurl obscenities. I count five of them, all boys. The last boy, the one who walks a few paces behind the rest as if he thinks there's nothing worth rushing toward, is the one who steals my breath.

I'd know him anywhere.

Colt Malene.

Even the silent whisper of his name brings chills.

He's been my constant crush ever since that summer afternoon when I met him over a year ago. I'd heard his name before, but he was a year behind me in school and I had never really taken a good look at him. Once I did take a look, I didn't want to look anywhere else.

It's not as if there are no other hot guys at Arcana High. There are plenty. But Colt is more than just another cute football player. Something about him keeps me up at night, turns my fantasies wild. We don't run in the same circles, not at all. His approach to academics is lazy and he's the life of every party, or so I'm told. A lot of girls are crazy about him and I suppose I'm just one more. But I tell myself they don't see the same things in him that I see.

Of course, he has no clue about what goes through my mind.

He always smiles at me in the hall and he's just as polite to me as the rest of my dad's players. He gets invited to dinner at our house sometimes and I've heard my father lament Colt's rotten home life. In spite of Colt's poor grades and penchant for low level trouble, my father likes him very much. He thinks Colt is the hardest worker on the team, and perhaps the most talented on a team filled with athletic talent. Colt reminds my father of himself, before he got his act together, earned a university football scholarship and turned that into a coaching career. But he believes Colt can go a whole lot further in the sport than he ever did.

Sometimes I wonder if my father sees his players as stand ins for the sons he wishes he had. Colt would be at the top of that list.

Colt is no longer following his friends. One of them, Rafe Hempstead I think, turns and calls his name but Colt has stopped in the middle of the field and stares up at the sky.

"Fuck the dance," Colt grumbles.

The other boys shrug and return to the gym.

I haven't moved. Colt stops looking at the sky and looks directly at where I'm standing twenty yards away.

"What are you doing out here?"

"Escaping. How did you even see me?"

"I have superior vision. And your dress kind of glows in the dark."

"As absurd as this dress is, I don't think that's true."

He's already on his way over here and now I can see that he was wearing a tie but it's been undone and hangs loose around his neck.

In the next second he steps into the shadows and I can hardly see him at all by the time he stops right in front of me.

"You didn't answer my question."

"You mean about why I'm out here? I'm walking home."

"Alone?" He sounds alarmed.

"It's not far."

"I'll walk with you."

I couldn't be more thrilled if he'd just asked me to the prom.

But Colt interprets my silence as something else and becomes unsure. "Is that okay, Susanna? If I walk you home?"

"Yes. But don't you need to get back to the dance? I assume you have homecoming court obligations."

"Nah, not into that stupid shit. Anyway, the seniors always win homecoming court."

"What about your date?"

"Brynna?" He laughs. "She's always looking for a better option. Last time I saw her, she's already found it."

He's close enough for me to smell the soap he uses; a clean, sharp scent that makes me think of the forest.

"Thank you," I say, more stiffly than I'd like. "If you want to walk me home, I'd very much appreciate the company."

Colt doesn't seem to mind that I speak as if I'm seventy years old. He suggests we keep cutting through the field. There's a hole in the fence on the far side and from there we can easily access the maze of Arcana's residential streets.

"What were you guys doing in the bleachers?" I ask him once we're on our way. I wish I'd brought a sweater. This dress is far from warm and the bite of autumn is in the air.

"Eh, just messing around," he says, somewhat cautiously.

"Have you been drinking?"

"A little. But I'm not drunk." He pauses. "Don't tell your dad."

"Colt, I would never."

We've reached the chain link fence that marks the edge of school property. Colt knows precisely where the fence gap is and he checks it for obstructions before motioning me through. On the other side is a regular neighborhood, complete with street lamps that allow me to see better.

Colt waits, ready to assist if I stumble over the rocks and trash that litter the other side of the fence. This is a popular place for kids to go hide when they're cutting class and they tend to do a rotten job of cleaning up after themselves. I'm happy to find the sidewalk without making a fool of myself.

Colt walks on the curbside and nudges me. "I was watching when you walked in with your folks."

"Awesome. I look ridiculous."

"No, you look extremely pretty. But you seem uncomfortable."

Colt Malene called me pretty.

I try not to pass out.

"The dress isn't my style. I'm not built for the spotlight. I don't belong there."

"Why not? Just look down your nose at all those worthless pricks and say, 'I own this shit and I own all of you.'"

"You have a way with words. But I don't own anyone. And I don't own this shit either."

Colt howls with delight. "She curses! I can't believe it."

"Shows what you know." I toss my hair. "I curse all the time."

"Cool. Say something else. Say fucker."

"I'm not a parrot," I mumble and throw him a sideways glance. "Fucker."

He claps. "That a girl."

"Just so we're clear, I wasn't really calling *you* a fucker."

"Didn't think you were. So how come you didn't want to stay at the dance?"

"I'd rather be at home. Besides, I have studying to do. I have a big calculus exam on Tuesday."

Instead of scoffing, Colt actually looks impressed. He asks me what other classes I'm taking and says he has heard that I am ranked first in the junior class. I'm a little shocked that he would have heard such a thing at all but then I remember how much my father likes to brag about my grades. Colt must have heard it from him.

Anyway, Colt has some successes of his own worth bragging about.

"You played a great game yesterday," I tell him. He didn't start in the game against Bredon. He was brought in during the third quarter when first string quarterback Greg McGinnis sprained his ankle. Colt threw a gorgeous twenty yard touchdown pass and ran a second touchdown into the end zone.

"I like knowing that you're watching." He lowers his head as he says this, almost like the confession makes him feel nervous.

"Well, I like *you*."

WHO SAID THAT?

Me.

I said that.

Shit.

"I mean, you're a fantastic football player. And you're a nice guy. You'd have to be, to walk me home and all."

It takes guts to risk a glance in his direction. He's still looking down at the sidewalk but I think he's smiling now.

"So..." He draws out the word. "I never really see you with anyone."

"Well, I'm not a complete loser. I do have a few friends."

"That's not what I meant. I never see you hanging around anyone special."

"You mean like a boyfriend."

"That is what I mean."

I can't explain Colt's effect on me, but his presence is like a truth serum.

I take a deep breath and put it all out there. "I'm not really allowed to date. My mother would probably be thrilled if I had a boyfriend but my dad is a different story. He wants me to keep my grades up and he thinks high school relationships are nothing but a distraction. Anyway, it's irrelevant because no one is asking."

"Come on, I don't believe that."

"It's true. I've never even been kissed."

Colt doesn't laugh or tease me. He becomes very quiet. In fact, we cover half a block in silence. A car rolls down the street and I recognize the driver as a senior who is in my calculus class. But he's kind of a loner, wears his headphones and sketches in the margins of his notebook all the time. He glances at us but doesn't stop and I doubt he finds anything interesting about the fact that Colt and I are walking together after dark. He won't mention it to anyone.

The temperature has dropped and I cross my arms to keep from shivering.

Colt glances over. "If I had a jacket, I'd give it to you."

I rub my arms. "It's not exactly freezing out. I'm just a wimp."

"Hey." Colt stops walking and so I do too. Slowly, he extends his arm and drapes it over my shoulders. "Does this help?"

I'm no longer chilled. Now I'm on fire.

"Yes," I whisper, wondering what he would think if I huddled closer.

Colt peers into my eyes. We're so close and it's not close enough. Being this close is like being teased with a delicious taste of something too expensive for me to afford.

There are stories about Colt. He drinks a lot. He flirts endlessly. And the things he's been known to do in plain sight at parties with a variety of girls makes me blush just thinking about them.

Even if everything I've ever heard is true, I'm not judging him. I'm really not.

But it's still intimidating to know that I could never compete with all the experiences he's already had. In many ways, Colt will always be out of my league.

Colt keeps his arm around me as we resume walking. I can't imagine what my father would say if he saw us like this. I doubt he'd be pleased. For this I feel a little guilty but then for some reason I picture all those little sports jerseys in his closet and all of a sudden I feel less guilty.

We're about to turn the corner and arrive on my street. The dance won't be anywhere near finished. This means no one else will be home for hours.

"That's my house over there." I point.

He nods. "I know."

Of course he does. He's been here plenty of times before.

Once when he was invited for dinner his mother showed up with him. She's very beautiful, his mother. She was a couple of years behind my own mother at Arcana High but they knew each other from cheerleading. During dinner Janna Malene drained an entire bottle of wine on her own, announced that it's a good thing her son is good at sports because he's too stupid to do anything else, and then put her hand on my father's leg when she thought no one else could see. He tactfully edged away from her and acted like nothing had happened. Colt, who is usually brash and talkative, barely spoke a word during that evening.

No one thought to leave the carriage lights on and the front yard is very dark. The front door can be opened with a keypad code and Colt keeps his arm around me as I punch in the numbers.

"Do you want to come in?" The question sounds so timid. I really do want to be alone with him. I've thought about it, dreamed about it. But now I'm suffering a mild panic attack over the idea that he might say yes.

The deadbolt clicks open and I turn the knob. Colt has still not answered my question. He also doesn't drop his arm from my shoulders.

Finally, he inhales deeply and then sighs. "You have a lot of studying to do, don't you?"

The relief flooding through me is inexplicable. "I have that calculus test next week. I really do need to study for it."

With his other hand, he begins searching for something in his back pocket. With the front door cracked open, the hallway light spills out and allows me to see what he's now holding.

"You want this back now?" he asks. "Might help you on your test."

I can feel my jaw drop. He's holding the good luck charm I gave him the day we met. Now and then I've wondered if he threw it away or lost it. Obviously not. There it sits in his palm, attached to a split keyring.

"It got me through the team tryouts," he says. "I make sure to have it on me for every game I play."

My shock begins to wear off. "Then you need to keep it. I told you I wanted you to have it."

He grins and returns the thing to his pocket. Then his grin fades into a more serious expression.

"I should let you get your studying done."

Strange, the mix of relief and disappointment. "Okay."

He draws another deep breath. "But can I kiss you first?"

Colt seems hopeful, almost shy. This is at odds with everything I've heard about him. But it fits with everything I've long suspected.

I swallow. "Yes. I'd like to kiss you."

His smile has the power to knock the breath out of me. It's a miracle that I can remain standing as Colt shifts position, facing me and circling one arm around my waist while his other hand gently slides over the back of my neck.

He pulls me in slowly. My eagerness mixes with anxiety. After all, Colt knows his way around. But me? I'm not even sure if I'm supposed to hold my breath. And my glasses...should I take them off? At least my braces have been gone since the summer.

Colt closes his eyes. I do the same. The first kiss is simple and innocent, just the softness of his lips on mine. My arms relax and wrap around his shoulders, marveling over the discovery of hard muscle. All the anxiety melts away and I melt with it. What was I worried about? Kissing is easy. At least, kissing *him* is easy. Colt is slow to use his tongue but when he does, I respond swiftly with my own. He makes a low noise in the back of his throat and holds me tighter, kisses me harder. I can taste whatever alcohol he was drinking under the bleachers but I like the taste.

He pulls back first and my eyes fly open. His are still closed.

With reluctance, I drop my arms and take a step back. "Thank you for walking me home."

Now he opens his eyes. And smiles again. "You better get an A on that math test."

"I'll try." I will. I always do. I just don't want to brag. "Good night."

I cross the threshold and stand in the foyer, my hand on the inside doorknob. Colt is already heading down the front path. I'm about to close the door when he suddenly spins around.

"Susanna, will you let me know if things ever change?"

"What things?"

"Your dad's dating rules."

My heart skips. "Why?"

"You said no one has asked you out. But I would be asking."

There can't be another boy like this in town. Or anywhere else in the world. "I will definitely let you know, Colt."

"Till next time." He raises a hand in farewell but he remains where he is, just watching, waiting to make sure I'm safely closed inside my house.

I finally close the door and flip the lock. I'm not sure how I'm going to study tonight. Or sleep. My adrenaline is through the roof. In the coming days I'll be reliving every second of that walk home.

Sprinting to the stairs, I take them two at a time and I don't stop running until I'm in my bedroom. Flipping on my desk lamp, I examine my face in the mirror above my desk. I see a girl who has just been kissed. And I smile.

I'm floating on air as I wander over to the single window in my room. It's unlikely that I'll catch a glimpse of Colt. He's probably long gone. My fingers stray to my lips, trying to recapture the sensation of being kissed. But I look down and there he is, at the end of the walkway, hands stuffed in his pockets while he stares right at my bedroom window. I suspect that right now if I repeat my invitation to come inside then he would. I'm about to fling open the window and do just that when he suddenly turns and disappears into the night.

My forehead touches the glass window pane. I echo his words in a whisper.

"Till next time."

8

COLT

There's no chance to knock before the door swings open. My little sister stands there with her hands on her hips. "You're early."

"That's because I knew you'd be waiting."

Carrie giggles and runs to me with a hug. I'm always taken aback by just how delighted she is to see me every time I show up. Makes me feel a ton of regret that I wasn't a part of her life until last year. I can't do much about the pile of regrets that litter my past. All I can do is make an effort to do better when I'm here.

Carrie drags me into the house and chatters excitedly about our plans today. I was feeling at a loss over how to entertain a ten-year-old girl for an entire afternoon but when I mentioned this to Susanna she suggested taking Carrie out to lunch and to the shopping mall. Sounds simple, but I'm not sure I would have thought of it on my own.

"Colt." Rochelle Malene approaches me with open arms and her hug is every bit as enthusiastic as Carrie's. Then she takes a step back and smiles up at me. "You have no idea how much she's been looking forward to spending an afternoon with her brother."

Carrie performs a cartwheel in the living room. "Colt, can we go to The Grounder for lunch? They serve popcorn instead of breadsticks."

"Sure."

Carrie does another cartwheel.

Rochelle laughs. She asks me if I would like a cup of iced tea before we leave and I think the polite thing to do is say yes so I do the polite thing.

Carrie looks on with some impatience as her mother presents me with a tall glass filled with ice and sweet tea. There's a slice of lemon on the rim and a sprig of mint floating at the top. I appreciate the presentation even if it is kind of wasted on a guy who's been known to drink out of old tin cans.

Rochelle takes a seat at the table and from the way she looks at me expectantly I realize I'm being invited to do the same.

"So," says my stepmother as she folds her manicured hands in front of her, "have you been enjoying your stay in Arcana?"

I gulp down a mouthful of tea. "I've been keeping busy."

This is a bad time to think of being naked with Susanna. It's not like I rip off her clothes every time we meet but we do find plenty of opportunities to fool around. By now she and I could co-author a book entitled '*All The Ways To Come Without Really Fucking*'.

Shit, it'd be a bestseller.

There's been a long list of odd jobs to do around her house and I typically spend a couple of hours a day chipping away at those tasks. Sometimes I also keep Coach Toledo company if Susanna has a lot of errands to run. She stopped trying to throw money at me after the first couple of days when she finally understood that I could never be talked into accepting any. She was beginning to feel restless without a job so she has taken a part time position tutoring college students online. This gives her something to do with the flexibility of staying home. Sometimes we go out to eat or else I pick up takeout so we can have dinner with her dad, who is doing no better but no worse either.

We have an unspoken agreement not to bring up ancient history. Every time I look at my old football coach as he withers toward his final months I'm reminded that life is too brief to stew over the past.

We also haven't talked about what'll happen when Tori and Jace's honeymoon is over. Since last year I've been committed to working on a project way up north along a remote segment of the Judith River. It won't be possible to dash all the way back to Texas on weekends. In fact, when I'm on a job like that I typically don't stray too far from the site until the work is done. And in this case the work is not expected to be done until mid October.

In a way, I've become hungry to escape the humdrum surroundings of small town Arcana.

In a bigger way I'm already agonizing over the thought of leaving the girl who stole my heart the first time she smiled at me and has unintentionally kept it ever since.

I can't stay. And yet I hate the idea of leaving.

I never planned for this, never planned for her.

In order avoid answering more questions, I ask a few of my own. Rochelle glows when she mentions her boyfriend and it's good to see her happy. Rochelle only recently began dating again. Eric Malene has been dead for almost eight years but photos of him are hung all over the house and while Rochelle has good reason to keep his memory alive for Carrie's sake, anyone can see she remains heart-broken by the loss. I suppose Eric Malene was the love of her life and she'll never completely get over the unfairness of his death at such a young age.

And where was I when I heard the news that the only father I'd ever known had suffered a fatal heart attack on his last cross country trucking run?

I remember it clearly. I wasn't quite twenty and had just returned from a month of being completely off the grid along the Idaho/Wyoming border. Cell signals can be sketchy that far from civilization so I didn't bother to look at my phone for weeks. A tearful voicemail from Tori was waiting with the news. I'd missed the funeral. All I could do was send some lame flower bouquet to Rochelle along with a sympathy card.

That wasn't nearly good enough.

"Tori and Jace come home next week, right?" Rochelle asks me.

I confirm with a nod. "They're expecting to be back on Friday."

"Can we go now?" Carrie waits until my tea glass is nearly drained before asking the question. She bounces on her toes and seems ready to haul me right out of the chair.

I grin at her. "Sure, we can go." I look to Rochelle. "What time do you want me to bring her home?"

Rochelle shrugs. "I'll leave that up to you."

"You have my number if you want to know where we're at."

She takes the empty tea glass and winks at me. "I trust you, Colt."

"Come on." Carrie drags me out the door and makes a beeline for my truck.

On the drive over here, I was stressing over how to amuse a kid her age. While I've seen Carrie a number of times by now, it's always at an event with a ton of other people, like Jace and Tori's wedding. This afternoon I'm on my own and I'd hate to disappoint her.

It turns out I worried for nothing. Carrie is ecstatic just to be in my company and she talks up a storm, telling me everything there is to know about her dance classes and her friends and her pet bunny rabbits.

She wants macaroni and cheese for lunch but then dislikes the cheese after one taste so I order her a second meal of a hamburger with fries.

Carrie chews happily on a fry. "If you lived in Texas then we could have lunch together like this all the time."

"I'll be back to visit," I promise her. "We'll have lunch again then."

She swirls the end of another fry in a puddle of ketchup. "Colt, why do you move around so much?"

"Don't you ever want to settle down in one place and have a real home?"

When Susanna asked me the question that first night at dinner I was annoyed. I'm not annoyed now. I'm actually thinking it over.

"I don't know," I admit to Carrie.

An adult would never have been satisfied with this answer but my little sister thinks it's good enough. She nods and takes a big bite of her hamburger.

Next we go to the mall because Carrie wants some new nail polish. Since her nails are already painted bright pink I assume she's allowed to have it and she's excited when I allow her to pile a bunch of colorful bottles in a small plastic basket. Carrie is looking at a carousel stocked with plastic jewelry and I'm standing in line to pay for a lifetime supply of nail polish, which is something I never expected to find myself doing, when I spot a rack of graphic tees and the lettering on one of them says *The Book Did It Better*. I choose a pink one.

"Since when do you wear pink shirts?" Carrie asks me, somewhat doubtfully, after we leave the store. I hadn't realized she was watching me at the checkout counter.

"A friend of mine is a big time reader. I thought she'd like it."

Carrie pounces. "Who?"

"Her name is Susanna."

"Who is she?"

I am unprepared for a way to explain Susanna. "She's, ah, she's someone I've been spending time with."

"What does that mean?"

"It means we're friends."

"She's your girlfriend?"

"Not exactly."

"But you *want* her to be your girlfriend." Carrie nods with certainty and then leaps to the next question. "Where did you meet her?"

"We knew each other in high school. Look, there's a frozen lemonade stand."

But Carrie is not easily distracted when she's really interested in a subject. "Wow. And you've loved her all this time. You must have. It's just like Tori and Jace."

"Not like Tori and Jace at all."

"Are you getting married?"

I wonder if my face is getting red. "No, Carrie. Susanna and I are not getting married."

"Is she pretty? I bet she's pretty. Why can't I meet her?"

"She's all the way in Arcana."

"Arcana's not that far. We can go right now. Anyway, I want to see McClane. Please, Colt. Please!"

I don't have the heart to say no to her. Besides, Arcana will be an easy drive from here. Sure, I'll have to double back in a few hours to bring Carrie home but I never mind being on the road.

Carrie has more Susanna-related questions. She knows who Coach Toledo is. She's met him before, most recently at Tori and Jace's wedding. She asks to see a photo of Susanna and is stunned when I don't have one.

"Not even on your phone?" she presses.

"Nope."

"Hmm." Obviously, she disapproves.

Carrie becomes very energetic once we reach the outer limits of Arcana. This is her father's hometown. This is where her parents were happy together. This is where she lived for the first couple of years of her life, until her widowed mother decided to move closer to her own parents for support.

She cranes her neck, looking out the window. "I heard a bad story about Arcana once. There was a murder somewhere around here."

"Many years ago," I assure her. "He's long gone."

I don't add that I went to school with the grandson of the convicted murderer. In fact, Rafe Hempstead was a friend of mine. People always gave him shit over his family history and he'd act like it didn't bother him to be tagged with the nickname 'Killer', but he wasn't made of stone. I know the mean spirited taunting got to him and it was never fair. None of us are responsible for the fucked up things that were done by other people before we were born.

Carrie and I decide to go see McClane first. Predictably, he is over the moon to receive a surprise visit. Carrie asks if we can bring him with us to Susanna's and since I've brought the dog over there before I'm hoping it will be all right.

Susanna had said that Paul Elkins would be stopping by in the morning to go over some legal paperwork with her father. Judging by the pained look on her face, I assume the legal issues have to do with Coach Toledo's will.

When we pull up to the house, Paul's gold Cadillac is nowhere in sight. McClane bounds out of the truck and right to the front door with Carrie galloping right behind him. Carrie's already pressing the doorbell before I can call out a warning to wait because I know that Coach often gets tired enough to nap in the afternoon.

Within seconds the door swings open and McClane expresses his love for Susanna by trying to knock her to the ground.

She staggers back but laughs.

"McClane!" I snap my fingers and the dog immediately sits. Jace has him trained but sometimes his excitement wins over.

Susanna notices my little sister. "Hi, Carrie. I was really hoping I'd get a chance to meet you." She opens the door wider as a signal for all of us to step inside.

"Behave," I warn McClane. His left ear twitches before he trots into the living room.

Susanna has just finished one of her online tutoring sessions and her dad blinks at us groggily from where he's sprawled in his armchair beneath a warm blanket, but he denies that he was sleeping. In any case, he seems delighted with the unexpected company.

Carrie makes herself at home on the couch beside McClane, who assumes that every household hosts ninety-pound dogs on the furniture. Susanna, as always, manages to be casually stunning in an unbuttoned plaid shirt over a black tank top and grey yoga pants that wouldn't be nearly this sexy on anyone else.

"Hope we're not bothering you," I say.

She shakes her head. Her hair is down today. She wears her glasses and no makeup. She takes my arm. "Not at all."

Carrie asks Susanna if she wants a manicure. Susanna, who wears her nails short and unpainted, smiles and says she would love one. While Carrie runs out to the truck to grab the bag of nail polish and Coach fusses with the television remote, I slide my hand up Susanna's back.

"Got any plans later?" I lightly massage her neck.

She leans into my touch. "No plans. Only laundry."

"How about I come back after I drop Carrie off? Maybe we can get food and go for a drive out to the crater or something."

She shoots a glance my way. "Or something."

My imagination runs wild.

"Susie." Coach smacks the plastic remote against the side of his armchair. "This thing won't work."

She sighs and leaves my side. "I'm sure it just needs new batteries, Dad. I'll take care of it."

There's always a cringeworthy quality attached to seeing Susanna deal with the basic needs of her formerly imposing father. If just watching the two of them makes me sad and uncomfortable, I can't even imagine how she feels.

Carrie returns with the nail polish and also announces that it's time for Susanna to receive her gift.

Feeling a little sheepish with everyone's eyes on me, I hand the folded t-shirt to Susanna. "It's not a big deal. Just something I thought you'd like."

"Try it on!" Carrie insists.

Susanna shrugs right out of her plaid shirt and pulls the tee on right over her tank top. Her smile is priceless. "What do you think?"

On impulse, I hold my phone up and press a button. "Beautiful."

Her hands are on her hips. "Did you just snap a photo of me?"

"Sure did."

We exchange a look. There's plenty of heat packed into that look.

Carrie, who can be a little bossy at times, hauls Susanna over to the dining room table and they spend some minutes debating the virtues of different nail polish colors.

I take a seat on the couch beside a suddenly sleepy McClane. Coach Toledo asks me who I like for next year's Super Bowl. Football season is months away from starting and I have no idea who looks good. In recent years the only time I've paid any attention at all to football is when I'm following Jace's progress. Now that Jace has quit the NFL I don't especially care who is winning. But Coach is waiting for an answer so I say the Arizona Cardinals and he nods, impressed with my insight.

Susanna and Carrie giggle a lot together and Susanna ends up with bright purple nails. By now the day is starting to get long and I want to be responsible about getting Carrie back to her mother so I break the news that it's time to go. Carrie hugs Susanna as if she's leaving her best friend and McClane is sound asleep on the living room couch. He cracks an eye but doesn't move when I explain how we need to leave.

"I don't mind if he stays." Susanna sits on the sofa and pats the dog's head. "You can just pick him up later."

McClane likes that idea. He falls right back to sleep.

"I really like Susanna," Carrie confides once we're back in the truck.

I flip the sun visor down. "I like her too."

Carrie keeps looking at me and I get the feeling she wants to say more. Finally, she does.

"She'll miss you when you leave."

"Did she say that?"

"No. But I can tell. She kept looking over at you. And every time she said your name she smiled."

There's no way to explain to a ten-year-old the complicated nature of adult relationships. Anyway, I'd be a poor instructor. Relationships aren't something I know much about.

"Why don't you find something on the radio?" I suggest. "Otherwise I'll switch the channel to country music and I know you don't like that."

The sun is low in the sky when we return to Carrie's neighborhood and a bunch of kids are out playing a game of kickball in the street. It's good to see that even in this digital age some traditions survive.

The house smells like oregano and basil. Rochelle asks me if I want to stay for dinner but I tactfully decline. Carrie receives permission to go out and play with the other kids until dinner is ready.

"I had fun today, Colt." She hugs me around the waist and squeezes with all her might.

I ruffle her curls. "I'm glad. Thanks for hanging out with me."

"You'll visit again, right?"

"Of course. I'll be back this way in the fall."

Carrie nods and then goes tearing outside to join the fun.

"That little girl is your biggest fan," Rochelle comments while using a fluffy pink feather duster on the wall of family photos.

"I think you've got that backwards. I'm her biggest fan."

She laughs. When we met, I was a sullen teenager who hardly acknowledged her and was barely on speaking terms with her husband. She must have forgiven me for that.

Among the sea of photos is a framed picture of Eric Malene with me and Tori, taken when we were kids. I don't remember who took the picture but I do recognize the densely forested campground in the Ozark mountains. We spent a whole week there the summer after Tori and I finished the fifth grade. We fished and we hiked and we ate over a campfire every evening. In the photo, Tori and I are smiling as Eric props a large, steady hand on each of our shoulders.

I had a great time on that trip. And I'm reminded that despite what happened in the years to come, I did inherit some things from the man I called Dad.

My name. A love of the outdoors. An appreciation of country music.

If he were here, I'd thank him for all of that.

"He talked about you often." Rochelle has noticed the way I'm staring at a childhood moment in time.

"Did he?" I'm surprised to hear this.

She sets down her feather duster and joins me. "He was sorry, Colt. He knew he'd let you down. He deeply regretted that and he even went looking for you after you left home."

Well, I wasn't easy to find. Anyway, in those days I was stewing in so much anger and self blame that I wouldn't have listened to whatever he had to say.

"Does she know?" I ask Rochelle.

I don't believe I need to articulate exactly what I mean about the complicated mystery surrounding my paternity. Rochelle looks quickly at the door to make sure Carrie hasn't returned.

"No," Rochelle admits. "I haven't found a way to explain it to her. But even if she did know, it would make no difference. You're her brother. Always."

That's nice to hear. Knowing Rochelle and Carrie, it's absolutely true.

I give my stepmother a quick hug. "You take care."

"You too, Colt. Don't be a stranger."

"I won't."

Carrie has abandoned the kickball game and she stands on the front lawn across the street chatting excitedly as a group of kids appear to hang on her every word. She doesn't see me exit her house and I don't want to interrupt her time with her friends.

Before I drive away, I take a quick look at my phone, which is not something I do regularly. For a number of minutes I remain where I am as sunset advances.

I'm staring at a photo, the one I took of Susanna this afternoon.

9

SUSANNA

The phone rings and it's my mother calling.

Colt is downstairs waiting so I don't have much time to talk right now. Besides, my mood is rather grim tonight. All day I've been unable to escape a sense of imminent misery.

He's leaving tomorrow. Tonight we are having dinner with Tori and Jace, who only arrived home from their honeymoon two days ago.

Then Colt and I will say goodnight.

And tomorrow he'll be gone.

I understood the stakes from the beginning. I have not begged him to stay. Nor will I.

"Hi, Mom."

"Hi, sweetheart. I just wanted to check in with you."

The sharp edges of my mother's personality have softened considerably since her remarriage. She's happy with Keith. They travel often and he absolutely adores her.

She and my dad never relaxed into one of those friendly post-divorce couples. She doesn't still carry a torch for him the way he does for her. But she always wants updates on his health and I know she's sorry over the state of things. Her sigh is full of distress when I tell her the news. Nothing more can be medically done. All we can do is make him comfortable in the time he has left.

She asks if there is anything she can do and of course there isn't but it's nice to know she cares. She's actually pleased when I explain that I need to cut the call short because I have plans for dinner. I make no mention of Colt's name. I'm certain she remembers everything and I don't have the energy to open up that door right now. I promise to call her next week.

Downstairs, Colt waits in the living room with my father. At first, neither of them notices me on the landing. Colt is seated on the far side of the couch, leaning forward, elbows on his knees as he listens intently to my father.

It's a scene out of the past and yet it's wrong.

Because in the past, Colt is sixteen and my father is healthy.

But I do recall with crystal clarity looking down at the two of them, the dedicated coach and his most promising player, with a range of emotions while they occupied these same poses, unaware of anything but their conversation with each other.

"There's nothing wrong with cutting loose sometimes to party with your buddies or get wild with some cute girl at a party. But stay focused, pay attention in class and keep your eye on the prize."

"Yes, sir."

"The team's counting on you, son. I'm counting on you."

"I'd never let you down, Coach."

Back then, I knew better than to interrupt them. If they did notice me, my father would likely toss over a glance of impatience if his train of thought had been broken. Colt might risk a quick smile if he was sure his coach wouldn't notice.

There had been an incident, a few weeks after the homecoming dance.

Nolan Bart, a player known for his lackluster talent on the field and his belligerent attitude off the field, was furious after being benched for three games straight. He was overheard bragging in the locker room that he had a plan all worked out. *"Wait till I fuck the brains right out of Toledo's uptight, prissy bitch daughter. See how the bastard likes that."*

The following day, Nolan was kicked off the team. What's more, he was stuck skulking through the halls of Arcana High with one hell of a shiner, courtesy of Colt. While my dad didn't approve of fighting, especially in the middle of the season, he was pleased to hear that Colt felt compelled to defend my honor. My father smiled as he discussed the fight over the dinner table and even boasted that he'd talked the principal out of charging Colt with any punishment. He considered Colt's actions to be a mark of loyalty toward him, having little to do with me, an incidental player in their macho melodrama.

However, I heard that in his next locker room speech Coach Toledo laid down the law to every single member of the team so there would be no future confusion.

"My daughter is off limits. Now and forever."

Mere seconds have elapsed as this yesteryear baggage streaks through my memories.

I'm still on the landing and Colt notices me first. Now he doesn't bother to hide his smile. He immediately stands up and watches me proceed down the remaining steps.

"Ready to go?" I ask him, a cheery brightness in my voice that doesn't match my heart.

My dad winces as he heaves himself out of his chair but then he holds his hand out with a grin. "Safe travels to you, Colt. I hope you find your way back here again to see us real soon."

Colt's work commitments will last until mid autumn. In calendar terms, that isn't forever. Yet when I appraise my father and note the way pain and exhaustion have begun to overcome his every move, I can't help but feel bleak about looking ahead.

"Yes, sir," replies Colt, gently pumping my dad's hand.

"I won't be gone long, Dad." I deposit a kiss on a shrunken cheek. "Call me if you need anything."

He accepts my help to resettle into his armchair. "Tell Mr. and Mrs. Zielinski I said hello."

"Will do."

Colt takes my hand and I wait until we're on the other side of the front door to heave out a long sigh.

He examines me with concern. "You okay?"

I kiss him quickly on the lips. "I'm fine."

On the drive over to Tori and Jace's place, I ask him what he and my dad were talking about in the living room.

"Your father's familiar with Montana. He's done some big game hunting in the Marshall Wilderness."

"I didn't know that."

"Yup, back in his college years. Once he had to run for his life after clipping the shoulder of a fully grown bull elk."

Colt grins and flips the steering wheel with one hand in order to make a sharp right hand turn. The lurch deep in my chest is courtesy of my aching heart. God, I'm going to miss him.

"I haven't heard that story."

"I'm sure your dad would be glad to tell you about it."

My fingers silently twist a leather handbag strap. "I'll ask."

Tori and Jace's home sits on a modest parcel of flat acreage and it's marvelous. Even from the outside, it's all cozy farmhouse style with tasteful country accents. A spring wreath hangs on the door and a pair of wooden rocking chairs occupy the shaded wide front porch. Colt points out the red barn-style shed he just finished building out back. The interior aesthetic is even more charming with an old fashioned stone fireplace in the front room, rustic wood furniture and lovingly displayed photos. This is a home for holiday gatherings and family and comfort. The vibe contrasts sharply with the empty rooms and lonely echoes of my own house.

Despite only arriving home from their long trip the day before yesterday, Tori and Jace have whipped up an impressive dinner of tender pot roast with glazed vegetables, homemade rosemary rolls and loaded baked potatoes. The two of them are the adorable essence of newlywed bliss and sit very close together as we dine on the back patio.

Tori slides her arm through her husband's and nods to her brother. "Colt, no wonder you love it so much, being out there in the endless wild. There was one morning in Wyoming when we woke up with the sun and watched the first light hit the mountains and I was speechless. I've never seen anything so beautiful."

"I have." Jace, who'd been staring at his wife, leans in for a kiss.

Tori obliges and they stare into each other's eyes for a sweet moment.

McClane is overjoyed to be back on his home turf with his people. In between chasing long-eared jackrabbits and tasting random lumpy objects in the deep fenced yard, he trots over for a reassuring scratch behind the ears.

"But I am happy to be home." Tori grins and tosses McClane a bite of meat. She gives Colt a fond smile. "So it's Montana next, right? To work with your friend's construction company? I know that's where you often spend the summer."

"Yup. My buddy Jimmy's got a knack for finding the best crew around. Just no nonsense people who work hard and mind their own business."

"Will you be in one of the places we visited?"

"No, but the Judith River is an underrated piece of the world. It's almost a crime to be building anything on that pristine ground."

There's a current of anticipation in his voice, reminding me that Colt is now a wanderer at heart. He can't wait to return to the middle of nowhere with minimal human interaction. He'll never be bound to Arcana or anywhere else.

Tori hangs on her brother's words but when I look up from pushing vegetables around my plate, I catch Jace eyeing me with sympathy. The Jace Zielinski who lives most clearly in my memory is not what he would eventually become; the surly quarterback who mowed down the opposition with frightening determination. No, I remember him as a thoughtful boy filled with creative dreams. And even if his best friend has told him nothing about us, Jace likely understands the situation anyway. He knows Colt and I are something other than old friends.

I just hope he can't hear my heart cracking out here on his patio.

The sky darkens and the spring evening is filled with a honeyed warmth and the growing buzz of emerging insects. Jace serves coffee and lemon scones that he proudly baked from scratch.

"These are amazing." I'm genuinely impressed. "Seriously, I'm jealous. I can't seem to successfully bake a sheet of premade cookie dough."

Tori now sits in her husband's lap and gives me a smile. "I'll force him to bake another batch and we'll bring them when we stop by this week."

I smile back at her. "That would be wonderful."

We'd already covered the topic of my father's status. There's no way to sugarcoat hospice care but I tried to sound upbeat anyway. I'm sure I fooled no one.

It's barely eight p.m. when Colt yawns and says we should get going. He's early to bed, early to rise nowadays and tomorrow he plans to be up exceptionally early to get a jump on the morning traffic.

Jace gives me an awkward hug before Tori envelopes me in a much softer hug. She promises to kidnap me for lunch one day soon. Then she throws her arms around her brother and forces him to swear that he'll call at least once a week.

Jace and Colt's farewell is more subdued. Colt murmurs something to his best friend and Jace nods and says of course he will.

Tori and Jace wave to us from their front porch as we pull away.

I return their wave and lean into the headrest. "That was nice. Thank you for bringing me."

Colt glances in the rearview mirror one last time. "They were meant to be, that's for sure."

I'd rather not envy Tori and Jace. They earned the life they are sharing. But I do envy them just the same.

He touches my knee. "It's early. Where do you want to go?"

I want to go to bed with him. I want to get him undressed and taste his skin and hear him groan out loud when I stroke him.

But then letting go will only be harder.

The long, flat shape of Arcana High looms a mile ahead.

"Let's park in the school lot. Then you can walk me home."

He's surprised, maybe a little disappointed. "You got it."

Aside from a fellow battered pickup that probably belongs to a member of the janitorial staff, there are no other vehicles in sight. I suppose we are trespassing, but Colt seems unconcerned. The exterior lights are blazing but the classrooms are all dark. So is the football field. Easter was this past Sunday and the schools are in the middle of a short break.

I have not set foot on the grounds of Arcana High since my graduation. The school is centrally located in town and I pass by it all the time yet I always avoid looking too closely, lest nostalgia, both sweet and bitter, comes flooding back. The way it's flooding back now.

"The place looks smaller." I reach for Colt's hand. "Don't you think so?"

He considers the idea and then shrugs. "It looks exactly the same to me."

"I often think about the night of the homecoming dance. You walked me home and gave me my first kiss."

"I remember."

"I was nervous."

"I was more nervous."

"I doubt that. I'll miss you, Colt." There I go, blurting out the truth without meaning to.

We have reached the fence gap on the perimeter of the athletic fields, where generations of Arcana youth have cut through. He leads the way to make sure there's no glass or debris. He slides an arm over my shoulders and we walk for more than a block in total silence. With Colt, silence is not uncomfortable. I can be silent with him more easily than I can talk to just about anyone else. Still, every step we take is another grain of sand through the hourglass. Our time is running out.

"Susanna, I can stay for a few days longer."

"A few days," I echo and then shake my head. "You should go tomorrow, like you planned."

"That's not what you want."

"No, but you were right. "

"About what?"

I need to face him to say this. We've reached a corner and a street-light flickers nearby.

"You were right about me. You told me that one night wouldn't have been enough. And that's true. For me it's true. One night would *not* have been enough. A hundred nights wouldn't have been enough. I would have wished for forever. You saw through me and you were right."

He lowers his head and exhales deeply. He's feeling guilty and miserable, which is the last thing I want.

I pick up his hand, kissing the knuckles.

"Colt, you've made the last few weeks bearable. You gave me romance and friendship during an awful period when I wasn't expecting either one. I've thought about you constantly over the last ten years and I'm so glad we had this time together."

"Damnit, Susanna." He gruffly pulls me close. "I'll miss you too."

I'll cry in another second. That's likely inevitable but I don't want him to see my tears. I'll save them for later, when I'm alone. Instead of crying, I kiss him. We wrap our arms around one another and kiss with the slow leisure of a couple who have all the time in the world instead of only a few moments. I can feel him, how hard he is, and I desire so much more. It's him I'll be thinking of later when I let my own hand stray between my legs in search of relief.

Even proceeding at a snail's pace brings us to my front door eventually. I kiss his lips, curl an arm around his neck, breathe him in.

"Till next time," I whisper.

He lets me go with reluctance. "What was that?"

"Just repeating something you said to me once."

Colt plants a final kiss on my forehead. "We'll see each other again."

Maybe.

Maybe not.

Colt isn't a man who can be kept, not by me and probably not by anyone else. I will cry later and likely tomorrow too. Even knowing that, I wouldn't change him.

He is, unapologetically, Colt.

As he should be.

"Goodbye, Colt."

With a smile, he says, as I knew he would, "Till next time."

Now I need to slip inside the house and shut the door or I'll abandon propriety and cling to him with no shame.

With my hand over my mouth, I stand in the dark entryway until I'm sure I've heard his retreating footsteps. At least my father has gone to bed already, which saves me from faking a smile.

I never meant to fall in love with Colt Malene. I wasn't supposed to. I've done it anyway.

Again.

I couldn't help it, then or now.

10

COLT, AGE 16

I need to see her or I'm going to fucking explode.

Jace knows nothing because I've admitted nothing. He just thinks it's weird when I ask to get dropped off at the high school.

"Someone's got to put this shit away before it's missed." I'm gesturing to the archery equipment that we borrowed without permission.

He pulls in and parks. "I'll help you. That way you don't have to walk back."

I glance at a gleaming black pickup a few spots away. "Nah, I'm gonna work out afterwards anyway."

My best friend cocks an eyebrow. He has a nose for bullshit. Especially my bullshit. "Really? You're going to pump iron after a three hour hike in the heat?"

I shrug. "Got to stay competitive."

Jace's suspicion changes to sympathy and he ducks his head. He knows I have a good reason for spending every spare minute with the weight bench.

I was primed to take the starting quarterback position for Arcana High this season before my mother decided she needs to marry her asshole insurance salesman boyfriend and drag us fifty miles away to Bredon. The wedding is at the end of the summer and I think the house goes on the market tomorrow. I still don't know how to deal with this. I've lived in Arcana my whole life. Starting a new school is shitty enough but now I've got to prove myself to a new team. And not just any new team. A damn good team that happens to be our biggest county rival. They've already got one of the best quarterbacks in the state so I'm confronted with a mighty task of trying to carve out a spot somehow.

But I don't see any way out of this move to Bredon so all I can do is make the best of a crappy situation. Coach Toledo has generously offered to let me live at his house. Of course, he wouldn't do that if he knew everything, but that's not why I had to say no. I can't leave my sister on her own to handle a new town and a new school. Besides, Tori and our mom get along about as well as Batman and The Joker. Without me around, she'd have no one on her side. Gloria invited us both to stay with her in order to finish high school, but she's been on my mother's very long and very petty shit list for years so that's not happening.

When the news first broke, I thought there was a chance our dad would come through. We're not on great terms but he adores Tori and he couldn't very well invite her to live with him without inviting me as well. Maybe he's just too busy with his new wife and future kid to care. At any rate, if Eric Malene hasn't made the offer by now then he's not going to.

Jace gives up. "Don't push yourself too hard."

With a snort I flex my arm and repeat my best piece of advice. "If you're not willing to push yourself till it hurts then you're not doing life right."

Jace grins. "See ya later, shithead."

"Adios, fucker." I jump out of the truck and seize the archery crap from the back. He waves before he pulls away. I don't wave back because my arms are full. I won't really see him later. He'll be off somewhere with my sister.

I've had more than a month to get used to the news and it still hits me with the force of an atomic bomb at times. One day, out of nowhere, the two of them sat me down in Gloria's living room and they're like, *"Guess what, Colt? We're boyfriend and girlfriend now!"*

I thought I was hallucinating. I kept muttering, *'What the fuck?'* and craning my neck in search of a camera, sure that I was being screwed with in some elaborate and rather disgusting prank.

But no, Tori and Jace watched me with pale-faced anxiety and then joined hands before turning their lovesick eyes on each other.

That's when I knew they were for real.

My sister and my best friend.

Fucking hell.

Never once did I suspect they would get together.

My first instinct was to puke.

My second instinct was to smash Jace's nose with my fist.

Luckily, I did neither of those things as my brain struggled to catch up. They tried to explain, as if there's any reason on earth why I might want to hear about how much fun they have touching each other. I'd rather eat the locker room urinal cake than think about the two of them doing...

AAGHHH!!!!!

Nope, I still can't even complete the thought without blowing chunks.

Even so, I have to admit that it's pretty clear they're not just messing around.

That's right, Jace and Tori are in love. Like head over heels, completely wild for each other in a way that's impossible to miss.

And I'm sincerely trying get over my disgust. I want to be happy for them. Of all the guys in Arcana, Jace is the best. He's honest and smart and he doesn't treat girls like cheap toys. If your sister simply must have a boyfriend, then he's the one you'd pick.

But....

He's *Jace.* He's like family. And Tori is my only sister.

I don't know anyone who wants to think about their family members groping each other and I don't want to think about it either.

I've always assumed that she thought of him as a brother and vice versa.

Apparently not.

I must have missed some important clues along the way because these days they can't be in the same room for eight seconds without smiling like idiots in between sucking face. This will take some more time, but I'll learn to live with it. I guess I have to. There's no other alternative.

The archery equipment isn't heavy but it is bulky. I've just wrestled the whole mess to the top step of Arcana High when the door swings open.

"I saw you coming," Susanna says and props the door open against her back. She crosses her arms and tilts her head, analyzing me as she always does.

But today things are different. She's nervous. She's blushing. She even shivers when I intentionally brush against her as I cross the threshold.

Yet Susanna holds her ground when I pause inches from her face and look her in the eye. Her breath catches and her lips press together.

Oh yeah, she's thinking about it. She's thinking about last night.

So am I.

No matter how hard I try, I haven't been able to think about much else.

The rumble of men's voices echo from a distant part of the building.

I nod toward the noise. "Who's here?"

We're inches apart. Some loose strands of hair have escaped from her careless ponytail to frame her face. I'd brush them aside if my hands weren't full of the stupid archery equipment. I'm freaking *dying* to kiss her.

She swivels to peer into the dim recesses of the school and her ponytail slaps me in the face. Her hair smells like fruity, like berries. She wears a pale pink sweatshirt and black shorts. I'm a huge fan of the shorts. They are tight and high cut and show off an excellent view of her long legs.

With a sigh, she turns back. "My dad. The rest of the coaching staff. The district athletic director. Along with the biggest booster sponsors. They're in the cafeteria wringing their collective hands over next season."

Understandable, since last year's graduation class took a lot of talent with it. And once I'm gone, they'll be officially short a quarterback. Coach Toledo would be even more upset if he knew that Jace is tossing around the thought of quitting the team. I hope I talked Jace out of that bad idea over lunch. The team needs him. And football is a whole lot more important to Jace than he realizes. He'll be hurting when me and Tori aren't at his side next year. I hate to think of him all lost and lonely without the team to lean on.

"Here." Susanna tries to pluck an archery target out of my arms. "I can take some of that."

No, she won't. I sidestep her because I'm totally the kind of pig who won't ever let a girl carry his gear. "I got it. Let's take a walk to the equipment room."

The murmuring voices escalate and then break into laughter. Susanna glances down the corridor but falls into step right beside me. The empty halls echo with our footsteps. Funny how the high school manages to smell like dirty socks even when it's practically empty. I wait until we're around the corner before speaking again.

"You didn't say hello."

She bumps me with her elbow. "Hello."

"I meant at Dave's."

She nods. "I know what you meant."

Jace and I were sitting in Dave's Tacos and stuffing our faces when Susanna strolled in. It's true that she didn't say hello but then again, neither did I. I just kind of froze and stared at her as she grabbed her takeout bags and then ran out of the building. She drove away in her dad's pickup truck. The reason why I ordered Jace to take off was because I noticed that same truck in the high school parking lot and I hoped Susanna would be around. Jace knows something is up. He's no dummy and he was already clued in thanks to the way I fell all over myself the second I spotted Susanna. Usually, I don't hesitate to tell Jace all the dirty news when it comes to girls but this is different.

She is different. I can't go shooting my mouth off where she's concerned.

Anyway, I don't feel bad about keeping secrets from my best friend because he never found the time to mention that he's always had the hots for my sister.

So there. I can have secrets too.

My secret is that I'm crazy about the coach's daughter.

Neither of us meant for this to happen. Sure, we had that one epic kiss last fall and we're in the habit of flirting when no one is watching, but there were plenty of reasons to keep ourselves in check. Susanna's time has always been consumed with studying her head off, being the president of everything at school and trying to meet her father's high expectations. Meanwhile, I didn't want to piss off the man who's been my role model since I started Arcana High. Susanna is everything to him and he's incredibly protective of her. Plus, Coach Toledo trusts me. I know what it's like to be caught off guard by someone you trust. So, I got used to smothering all the complicated feelings I had for his daughter and looked elsewhere for fun.

But between the upcoming move to Bredon and the Jace Loves Tori bombshell, I've been spinning. None of these other dipshits around here are the sort you want to spill your guts to. Jace and Tori have always been my people but now that they're preoccupied with each other. I felt like I needed to confide in someone else or I'd run through the streets screaming.

One day I screwed up the nerve to call Susanna. She was glad to hear from me, happy to talk and be a friend. And I can tell this girl anything, shit I've never said out loud before. I can tell her about my dad and about how I've always felt like an unwanted reject. I can tell her about how I choked out my guts in the sagebrush after catching my mother getting drilled by Jace's father one afternoon. I can tell her the awful things I heard them say to one another and what I'm afraid it all might mean.

She listens. She doesn't care what I can do on the field or how many other girls I've messed around with or that I sit on the top tier of the Arcana High social scene. She likes to hear what's on my mind and she's willing to tell me what's on hers. Her intelligence can be downright intimidating but in a good way. When we're alone and I'm listening to her talk, suddenly I want to be a whole lot more than some shit-for-brains meathead who can throw a ball but can barely pass algebra. I want to be worth her time.

Maybe we were kidding ourselves to believe for a minute that we wouldn't do more than hang out all alone under the stars and confess our deepest thoughts.

Maybe I always knew that I wouldn't be able to keep my hands to myself indefinitely.

Last night she planned to sleep over at a friend's house and had the use of her mom's car. We took a drive out beyond the meteor crater, where I used to camp out with Jace and Tori all the time as kids in search of adventure. We were pointing out the names of the lights in the sky while we sprawled on a scratchy wool picnic blanket she'd dragged out from the trunk of the car. Neither of us looked at our phones once and when a shooting star burned itself out on a long streak across the inky blackness I reached for her hand. That might sound like a real junior high level move. It wasn't, not with her. My heart sped up when she laced her fingers through mine and she shifted position, staring at me in her usual direct way while I waited to hear whatever it was she wanted to say.

"Colt, I need to tell you something."

"I'm listening."

"I want to be with you. I always have."

She'll never understand what she did to me with those words.

I don't even completely understand it.

All I know is that moment on the picnic blanket will be seared into my memory as infinitely as the stars above us are branded in their distant orbits. And what I did next came naturally. I brought my other hand around to gently cup the back of her neck and I kissed her.

Kissing a girl you've been wanting forever and truly care about is unlike anything else. It's pure fucking magic.

We didn't stop at kissing. In fact, we came damn close to doing everything there is to do. Susanna was as into it as I was and she was eager for more. But I had to back off because I didn't have any rubbers. And because I managed to keep my wits enough to realize she deserves much better than an impulsive moment on a prickly old blanket. Susanna is special. We're not just going to hook up and then say, *'So I'll see you around or whatever.'* No fucking chance of that.

I just hope she's not having second thoughts today. I'm sure not. But she went running out of Dave's with her head down and not a word spoken so now I'm wondering.

"You looked like you were busy," she explains after a long moment of silence as I wait to hear why she dashed out of Dave's.

"Why would you think that? I was just shooting the shit with Jace."

Susanna stops walking and fires a rather pointed look my way. "Jace looks mighty pretty in a bikini."

Ah, crap.

Somehow I totally forgot that Brynna Graff was lurking at our table and trying to strike up a stupid conversation when Susanna breezed through the door. Brynna hasn't really been on my radar for quite a while and I was never wild about her in the first place but Arcana High is a small enough place for gossip to stick when it comes to who has a history of hooking up. I'm ashamed to know that Susanna likely, probably, almost definitely, has heard an earful about my exploits. If I could change that then I would but I can't.

While I'm getting all red in the face and trying to piece together a response, she huffs out a sigh and looks up at the ceiling.

"Oh my god, forget I said that please. I do try to stifle my jealous stalker urges when I see you talking to another girl."

"You have jealous stalker urges?" I can't help but smile at the idea. She shrugs. "A few."

I can understand. I fucking hate the idea of another guy looking at her and getting ideas. I really don't know how half the panting pricks at Arcana High aren't chasing her. The fact that she's Coach Toledo's daughter has something to do with that. Nobody wants to get on his bad side, not even guys who aren't on the team. Plus, guys can be assholes about being with a girl who is ten times smarter than they are. They don't like getting shown up or something. Not me. I love the fact that she's crazy smart. Another thing I love is that she's totally unaware of just how hot she is.

We're steps away from the door that leads down to the basement. Susanna takes the lead and shoves the door open, clearing the way for me to escort the archery junk downstairs. She switches the light on and follows me into the vast graveyard where outdated gym gear and shabby drama club sets go to die. The equipment cage is still open because that's how I left it.

Susanna watches from outside the cage while I take care to return everything to its original position. The lock has been busted for ages so the best I can do is close the latch and rewrap a length of wire around the door, which won't deter anyone but it's better than nothing.

At this point I've become a little sweaty and that's part of the reason why I pull my shirt over my head. The rest of the reason has to do with the way Susanna hungrily checks me out.

I know I'm smirking. "Hey, that sweatshirt you're wearing looks a little warm. Feel free to remove it."

She fights a smile. She loses. "I'm not getting naked in the Arcana High basement."

I circle around her. "We could go to the locker room instead."

"Colt." She acts like she's going to shove me with exasperation but I'm ready for this. I seize her wrist with one hand and slide the other around her waist. She allows me to back her into the nearest wall and breathes out a soft noise of pleasure when I fasten my mouth to hers.

Kissing Susanna is a different kind of experience. I tend to lose track of all else but the heat of her body and the taste of her tongue. She trembles when I touch her, like just getting close sends her into sensory overload. This thing between us is electric, combustible.

I've never wanted anyone this much before and I've never been so worried about fucking it up somehow.

Her long legs climb up to wrap around my waist. I'm ready to rupture through the seam of my shorts. My fingers explore the smooth skin of her belly, travel lower to find the snap of her shorts, and flick it open.

She loves this. She groans into my mouth and wraps her legs around me more tightly. I wish we were alone, really alone, in a place where we could have each other and take our time about it. Susanna moves her mouth to suck hard at my neck. I push my hand all the way up her shirt. Her bra is unhooked with ease.

FUCK.

If I don't back off right now, then I won't be able to back off at all.

"Colt," she breathes in my ear. "I think about you constantly."

This is the kind of talk that puts the squeeze on my heart.

I kiss her lips and pull back to stare into her eyes. She's flushed, breathing hard, and her ponytail has been wrecked. But she looks at me with green-eyed directness.

"Did you mean what you said last night?" I ask her.

Her brow furrows ever so slightly. She thinks the question is odd. "Of course. I mean everything I say to you."

I don't doubt that. There's always been a straightforward decency about Susanna that isn't easily found. This girl is one of a kind.

And she wants to be mine.

I know I could be a lot better than I am. Susanna believes this too, that there's more to me than football and partying. It's true that I'm not as much of a brain as my sister or even Jace, but I could do better in school for sure. For years I've been just scraping by doing the bare minimum because I can get away with it.

"You really want to be with me, baby?"

She answers without hesitation. "Yes."

I skim my knuckle along the delicate ridge of her cheekbone. "You can trust me, Susanna."

It's the truth. I'm no angel but I'd never *ever* do wrong by her.

"Of course I can." She says this like it's a foregone conclusion but then she sucks in her lower lip and shifts her eyes.

"What's the matter?"

She runs her palms over my shoulders, lingering over the swell of the muscles I've worked on for countless hours in the gym. "You told me you've never had a real girlfriend."

I shrug. "So? You said you've never had a boyfriend."

The look on her face becomes adorably shy. "Is that what I should call you?"

"I hope you do."

Her forehead touches mine. "It's so unfair that you're leaving now."

"Bredon isn't that far. I've been saving for years to get a car and I've almost got enough for something that will actually start when you flip the ignition. In the meantime, I can catch rides with Jace because he'll be going back and forth a lot. And there's always the bus, which is workable even with changing routes three times."

She disconnects from me just long enough to push her glasses up her nose. She smiles. "And my mom will let me borrow her car on weekends. I know she will."

"What about your dad?"

Her smile wavers. "He doesn't really let me drive his truck outside town."

"We need to tell him about us. I don't want him thinking we've been sneaking around."

"But we *have* been sneaking around. Whenever we're together, my parents either think I'm off at a friend's house or they assume I'm asleep in my bed."

"Yeah well, before we were just hanging out and talking. Then last night happened. And now I'm your boyfriend." I'm really starting to like the way that sounds.

She does too. She flashes a smile and then becomes serious. "Colt, my dad tends to rule with an iron fist."

"I'm aware. But your dad likes me. He even invited me to move in."

"That's because he doesn't know you've been kissing his daughter. And when he finds out-"

I put an end to her objections with another kiss. She lets me. But then she pushes a hand on my chest and arches an eyebrow.

"I've heard him talking you up to Cassavetes."

"The Bredon High coach?"

She nods. "He's been doing everything in his power to make sure you get a spot on the team. He's doing that even while knowing Bredon is our strongest competition and adding you to their roster will only make them even tougher to beat."

I'm touched. I really am. My own dad would never go to so much trouble for me.

Her face twists into a frown. "Look, I know my father. He'll see this as a betrayal that happened right under his nose. He'll be angry but not at me. He'll be angry at you. He could really mess things up for you, Colt."

"He wouldn't do that."

She's not so sure. "He holds grudges. Trust me."

I'm a little shocked to hear Susanna talk about her father this way. As far as I know, she's always believed her dad hung the moon.

"So I take it you want to keep this a secret?"

She chews her lip again, becomes apologetic. "Just for now, just until you move. Once the Bredon coaches see what you're really made of, nothing my dad can say would make any difference."

I understand her point. I really do. It's probably the wisest course of action and the move to Bredon is coming up real fast so we're not talking about a lot of time. I still don't like it.

An unpleasant thought crosses my mind.

I reach out and tip her chin up. "You're not ashamed of me, are you?"

She rolls her eyes. "Oh, please."

"What?"

"Look at you."

"I can't. There's no mirror down here."

"You're obscenely gorgeous, Colt. And you're funny and you're authentic and every time I'm with you I feel like I'm on fire. No, I could never be ashamed of being with you. I can't wait to tell the whole world."

That's what I like to hear.

I grin at her. "All right. If you think it's best, we'll keep this quiet until I make the move to Bredon. I won't even tell Tori and Jace. But after that, all bets are off."

"How so?"

"I'm gonna climb the fucking Arcana water tower and scream the news to the whole town that my girlfriend is Susanna Toledo."

She giggles. "You'll get arrested."

"Worth it." I kiss her neck. "And everyone can suck on their jealousy."

Her legs are back up around my waist. I'm kissing her neck harder, impatient to leave my mark yet knowing that I shouldn't.

"I'd do anything for you, Susanna." I slide my hands low, finding the back pockets of her shorts and pushing inside. "Just tell me what you want."

She squirms to get as close as possible, her shorts now wide open, and I know she feels me, every fucking stiff inch. Her eyes close and her breath is a shudder. "*You* are what I want. I want to do everything with you, Colt."

She's going to kill me talking like that but I know I asked for it.

No, I can wait.

I'm not going to screw her in the high school basement or on some itchy blanket in the dirt. We won't have sex at all until we're in the clear and everyone knows about us. If Coach Toledo still wants to have a fit, then so be it. Nobody can stop us. Susanna and I are in this for the long haul.

But right now, I have to let go. Carefully, I hook her bra and look away when she zips her shorts.

She needs to get back upstairs before her dad starts wondering where she's gone.

I tug on her hand. "Meet me tonight?"

"Come over. My parents have a dinner party to go to. They'll probably be gone from seven until midnight."

Being alone in the house with Susanna for hours on end?

Fuck, that sounds like paradise.

It also sounds like a good opportunity to break the promise I just made to myself.

"How about if I show up at your back door at eight? We'll find something to do."

"Counting the hours." She hugs me and I receive one last happy kiss before she dashes up the stairs.

I hang around in the basement for a few minutes in case anyone's around up there on the ground floor. For the first time, the move to Bredon doesn't feel like a doomsday countdown. I'm up to the challenge of proving myself. I can work ten times harder than I've been working. Coach Toledo has tried to get me thinking about playing college ball, especially because it's the only path to the pros. He's careful not to promise the stars because everyone knows the NFL is a distant longshot, but he believes in me.

More importantly, Susanna believes in me.

She's only got another year of high school left and she'll be going to college for sure. I'll be graduating a year later and then maybe I can play ball at whatever college she's at.

It's not an impossible idea, not at all.

With Susanna beside me, I don't think anything is impossible.

Now there are voices in the hallway above, all men. I pick out Coach Toledo's deep chuckle after a comment is made that I don't hear. I do hear the next comment, although I can't place the voice.

"You really think that Zielinski kid's got possibilities?"

"He's undisciplined," says Coach Toledo, "but he's got the natural talent. He just needs a hell of a push."

"Then push him."

"Oh, you better fucking believe I will," replies Coach.

They move on and I can't hear what's said next. I wonder if Susanna is with them. She hasn't mentioned anything about her dad's plans to replace me with my best friend so she must not know.

I shouldn't be upset. I'm leaving. The team needs a quarterback. And Coach is right about Jace. He's not real devoted to football but he could be great if he wanted to be. I should probably give him a heads up that he plays a big role in the team's future plans but somehow I don't want to. That just makes it all too real. And if I'm being honest, I should admit that I'm still a little sore at him for forgetting to declare that he's always had a thing for my sister.

Everything is changing and it's all changing so quickly.

My mom is marrying an insurance salesman.

I'm moving away.

Tori and Jace are in love.

And I finally have Susanna.

This is what I'll concentrate on.

Susanna.

Whenever I have the urge to punch a wall and wish for everything to go back to the way it was, I'll just think of her.

I'll think of her and be glad that things don't stay the same.

11

SUSANNA

Summer has never bothered me before. However, this latest heatwave put a bullseye on Texas and right now the month of July feels like purgatory.

What's worse, soaring triple digit temps are killing central air units all over the place, including the one at my house. Every box fan I could dig up has been strategically positioned in my father's room in an effort to keep him cool as he wheezes beneath a thin sheet. Meanwhile, I'm reduced to fanning myself with an old People magazine on the living room sofa while awaiting the verdict from the technician who is here assessing the air conditioner.

Jace Zielinski deserves the credit for finding a company even willing to take the job. It seems every air conditioning company within seventy miles is working around the clock to service the massive number of failing units amid dangerously high temps. But after one phone call from the ex-NFL Super Bowl champ, the owner of Badger Cooling and Heating fell all over himself to give us a same day appointment. I'd feel guilty about exploiting that celebrity connection if I was less desperate to make my father's last days as comfortable as possible. His hospice care nurse asked if we might consider respite care in one of their facilities but I know he doesn't want to be moved. He isn't always alert and sometimes he fades into a half-conscious bout of sobbing, but he has repeatedly expressed a wish to die here at home.

He'll get his wish. And I know he'll be getting it soon.

My arm has grown tired of fanning the magazine and it gets tossed to the coffee table. There are piles of magazines there, most of them filled with glossy pages depicting the latest frivolous celebrity news. They all belong to my mother. She arrived two days ago with a suitcase and the determined resolve to stay for as long as necessary.

I did not expect this move from her. I nearly cried with relief when she showed up.

Even with Tori and Jace stopping by three or four times a week and local friends like Paul Elkins checking in with regularity, I was feeling terribly lonely and drained. I longed for more family, for siblings and relatives that I don't have and for time to move backwards, even a couple of months to the days when my dad could easily communicate and didn't require twenty-four-hour-a-day constant care.

Nobody prepares you for this.

I suppose it's impossible to understand what it's like, being the caregiver to a terminally ill loved one unless you've done it yourself. There's the ever present odor of sickness and the relentless worry that you're not doing enough, that you could always be doing more. And there is always *always* the constant terror of the inescapable end. There's the fear that you'll be guiltily relieved when death finally does come and the horror that this thought even crossed your mind.

The creak of a man's weight on a ladder broadcasts the emergence of the technician from the attic. After peeking in on my sleeping father, I walk down the hall to see what the verdict is.

"Compressor needs to be replaced." The man wears a name tag that says Nick and he wipes his flushed face with a red bandana. "I called the office and they're trucking the part out here as we speak. It'll take me a few hours to get it done but you'll have cold air blowing again by nine p.m."

"Thank you," I breathe, pleased that at least one problem is going to be solved before the day's end. "I really appreciate the quick service. How much will I owe you?"

Nick stores the bandana in the front pocket of his beige company shirt and grins. "It's paid for, courtesy of Jace Zielinski."

My mouth falls open. "That's got to be at least a thousand dollars.
"

He shrugs. "Closer to two. No matter. I'm told he insisted."

Now I really do feel guilty. I never expected Jace to cover the cost of repairing our air conditioner for crying out loud.

Nick excuses himself. It's time for his meal break. The part should be here by the time he returns and he promises to get right to work.

No sooner has he walked out the door when my phone buzzes. Tori is outside. She always texts rather than ringing the doorbell out of fear she'll disturb my dad.

I find her just beyond the front door. Jace is out by the curb beside the Badger company truck, agreeably posing for a series of selfies with a very excited Nick.

Tori looks up from her phone and smiles. "I ran into your mom in town today. She was walking past the office so I dashed out to say hello."

I shut the door behind me. "She met a friend for a lunch date at the diner. She was planning to visit a few other friends as well but she'll be back by this evening."

Tori nods and absently rubs her belly. "She says she's staying here."

"Yes. She and her husband agreed that this is where she needs to be right now. My parents' divorce was not a friendly one. I was surprised when she showed up."

"She wants to be here for you," Tori says and gently squeezes my arm. She's become a good friend over the past three months. Back in high school we were friendly but not close. I always liked her, always thought she was one of the better people populating Arcana High. After she and Colt moved to Bredon I didn't see her anymore.

"How's the property business?" I ask her. She operates as an independent realtor inside the law office of Paul Elkins.

She waves a hand. "It's all good. Sales are booming."

"Look at you," I marvel. "You're starting to show."

She beams and touches her stomach again. "I know. I'm out of the first trimester now. This is actually the first time I'm wearing a maternity shirt."

"You look adorable. I'd invite you indoors but I think it's hotter in there than it is out here."

She glances behind her. Nick is in the throes of pretending to toss a long pass while talking a mile a minute. Jace listens politely. "Didn't they fix the air conditioning?"

"Waiting on a part. It'll be fixed by tonight. I need to thank Jace for using his famous athlete status for good. Although I do wish he'd let me pay for the work."

"He wants to help you, Susanna. And he's determined to make good on his promise."

"To who? My dad?"

She shakes her head. "No."

"I don't understand."

"To Colt."

The air still leaves my lungs whenever her brother's name is spoken. "What?"

"Before Colt left, he made Jace promise to look out for you. Jace takes his promises seriously."

I swallow, exhale, try to look casual, realize I'm failing. "How is Colt?"

She tilts her head. "He talks to you. I know he does."

"Now and then." I look away so she can't read my face.

Colt and I suffer from the same affliction; we are awful at long distance phone conversations. Besides, he's located in such a remote area that reception isn't great. Once every week or two he takes a drive to the nearest small town in order to buy supplies and touch base with a phone call. I try to make my daily life sound more cheerful than it really is. Colt responds more tentatively than he normally would.

I don't admit how desperately I miss him, how I can never get to sleep at night until I imagine the comfort of his arms around me. To do so would be unfair.

Jace extricates himself from his superfan and Nick drives away in his work truck, presumably to investigate Arcana's dining options.

Jace's eyes are on Tori as he joins us. He slides a strong arm around her shoulders. Jace Zielinski always gazes at his wife with amazement, as if he just knows he's the luckiest man on two legs. Their child is due in January.

He gets embarrassed when I thank him. He declares it's no big deal, that he owes his high school coach far more than a silly air conditioning repair. He's very understanding when I tell him that my dad isn't awake for visitors right now.

"Maybe next time," he says.

I nod, trying to think of something optimistic to say.

On his last visit, Jace's former coach became confused about who he is. I was warned that this would happen and yet it was disconcerting. For ten years, from Jace's state championship win in high school through his meteoric rise in pro football, his name has been the one my father says the most.

And yet Jace has now been forgotten. At one point my father mistook Jace for Colt.

I'm sorry to see them leave. Being around Tori and Jace means being close to something special. It means being close to happiness.

My father is awake when I look in on him again. His mood is rather grumpy and he wants to know who took his television away. Last week he demanded the immediate removal of the mounted screen.

"The shadows are looking at me, Susie. I don't want them looking at me."

I promise him I'll put the television back tomorrow. I'll need help to hang it again.

After some coaxing, he agrees to drink a fruit smoothie. I need to hold the glass and bend the flexible straw to his lips but he does manage to drink half the glass before turning his head and saying he doesn't want anymore. I set the glass on his nightstand in case he changes his mind. He sleeps again, his mouth open, his breathing labored.

Before long, Nick returns with the necessary part. The heat in the attic must be unbearable but Nick still whistles while he works.

Thanks to the whir of six different box fans, my father's room is the most tolerable place to be. I settle into a chair that has been relocated from the living room. It's my father's favorite chair and I curl my legs up, sinking into the buttery leather that has become worn in patches after countless hours of watching sports or napping.

My mother texts to ask what I would like for dinner. She can pick up pizza from Giorgio's if that sounds good. Sure, I tell her. Pizza really does sound good.

It's the thought of pizza that sends my mind back to Colt, back to an early spring evening when I opened the front door and faced a man I no longer knew and yet have never quit dreaming about no matter how many years we are apart.

"Susie."

I'd been drifting, not quite asleep and not entirely awake and now I find my father is watching me. His green eyes were once the same as mine but now they have dimmed into a non color. They are focused on me with urgency and I tense, leaning forward.

"What is it, Daddy? Are you in pain?"

A vague shake of the head, a blink of those penetrating eyes, and a slow tear that rolls down a sunken cheek. "Do you forgive me, Susie?"

He could be talking about anything. "Of course I do," I assure him.

But he frowns, frustrated that I don't grasp his meaning. "For Colt. Do you forgive me for Colt?"

"I despise you now. And I'll despise you always."

Yes, I said that once. At the time I assumed people could be divided so neatly into good and bad. Nobody is all of one and none of the other.

"Daddy, I forgave you for that a long time ago."

He shuts his eyes and falls asleep again, floating among his ravaged memories and hopefully finding the pleasant ones instead of the unpleasant.

I'm tucking the sheet around him when I hear my mother arrive home. I never expected to be under the same roof again with both my parents.

She's opening the pizza box in the middle of the dining room table when I find her. She looks closely at my face and becomes anxious.

"Did something happen?"

I don't want to tell her what he said. I'll only start to cry. "No, he's sleeping."

She pushes her brassy hair to the side and makes a face. "It's so stuffy in here."

"The air conditioning should be fixed within a few hours."

"That's good." The heels of her stylish sandals clack on the tile when she briskly ventures to the kitchen for plates and napkins. She also returns with two glasses and a bottle of wine.

"I've been wanting to try this merlot. It's from a wine-of-the-month club Keith signed up for." She uncorks the bottle expertly, fills the glasses and promptly chooses the seat that was her usual place when this was her table.

I take a sip. "It's good."

She pushes the pizza box at me. "Eat. Peppers and mushrooms, your favorite. I don't think I've seen you eat more than twice since I arrived."

"I haven't been very hungry." Nonetheless, I accept two slices of pizza and deposit them on my plate, aware that I'm being observed with maternal eagerness.

My mother looks satisfied and takes another sip of her wine before plucking a slice of pizza for herself. "I was talking to Keith on the phone while I waited for the pizza. He sends you his love."

This must be a strange situation for him, watching his wife run to the bedside of her dying ex. "I'm glad he had no issues with you coming here."

Her eyebrows rise and she sets her glass down. "Keith understands that I had a family long before I met him. I am here for you, Susanna, but I'm also here for your father. He should be surrounded by people who love him."

I can't hide my astonishment. "You still love him? I mean, I remember how it was with you two. The fights, the anger, the tears. I always thought the divorce must have been a relief after so many battle scarred years."

Her lips press together and she plays with a section of her hair. She looks to the framed photo on the wall, the one of her first wedding day, and she sighs before turning her attention back to me.

"Your dad and I really did love each other very much. I know sometimes it didn't seem that way. In the early years we were so happy. But slowly we stopped listening to each other while picking away at all the little things and finally reached a point where we just couldn't live together anymore. I'm sure we would have split up earlier if not for you. I was raised as the child of divorce and I wanted better for my daughter." She swallows and stares down at her lap. "I'm afraid that I was always too hard on you, Susanna. I was so very wrong for trying to turn you into something different rather than appreciating you for who you are. And I deeply regret all the unhappiness you saw and heard."

We should have had this conversation long ago. What a difference it would have made. "Are you happy now, Mom?"

She lifts her head. "Very. My only sorrow is that I don't get to see you nearly as much as I'd like." She brightens. "Keith and I were talking about taking another trip to Hawaii next year. We would love for you to join us. While Keith is off golfing we can hit the spa together. And you have to try parasailing. I admit, I was skeptical but Keith talked me into it. When you're in the air you can imagine exactly how a bird feels."

She's forgotten that I'm terrified of heights. And next year feels so very far away. But I would hate to discourage her when we're finally connecting. "That all sounds wonderful."

There's a distinct click overhead and then cool air begins blowing through the vent once more. Nick cheers from the attic and climbs down the ladder to confirm the good news. The air conditioner has been resurrected.

The next time my father wakes up he is both moderately cheerful and lucid. He wants his face shaved. I'm about to tell him that tomorrow I'll call his favorite barbershop to request another house call when my mother volunteers to do it herself.

I watch them from the doorway of the room they used to share. She leans over him, her hair tickling his forehead as she uses the razor on his gaunt face with extreme care.

"Kelly," he says, and his voice becomes stronger than it's been in a while, "how is it you've only grown more beautiful?"

She swishes the lathered razor in a bowl of water and for a second I'm sure she's going to cry. Then she bends her mouth into a smile and assures him that he will always be the most handsome man she's ever met.

I suppose if your parents have the power to surprise you then anything is possible.

All the while, I remain in the doorway and don't say a word.

I can't.

I'm too busy memorizing everything about this moment.

12

COLT

Murphy is deaf in one ear and there's little proof his good ear is much better.

"Murph! We're packing it in."

Nothing.

The man selects another long board from the stack of reclaimed hardwood being used for the flooring and nudges it into position.

"Hey." I resort to hopscotching over the unfinished floor and poking him in the shoulder.

"Shit!" He rocks backwards and nearly falls over before scowling up at me.

"We're out of here now," I tell him.

"Could have just said so without scaring the shit out of me," he grumbles but he starts getting his tools together.

I don't let anyone leave tools on site. I've been burned doing that before. If there are thieves around, they will still find you even forty miles from the nearest two stoplight town, just local dickheads looking to score a quick dishonest buck rather than work themselves. Materials, on the other hand, can't be easily toted around in a toolbox but the heavy stuff rarely suffers as a target anyway.

Leaving Murphy to his bellyaching, I go outside to toss my gear in my truck. The ribbon of blue known as the Judith River shimmers in the summer sun and I spend a few seconds appreciating the view. I wouldn't call it majestic, especially not after some of the other places I've seen, but it does score plenty of points for tranquility.

The cluster of homes we're building right now are for a large extended family who intend to chuck the New York City life, literally exchanging that concrete world for greener pastures. The floor plans were designed to capture maximum light during the hard winters and materials are environmentally conscious. When this area is finished, we'll be moving on to the other side of the valley for a very similar project. Those buyers are coming from San Francisco and they are vineyard owners who plan to start a bee farm, which doesn't seem suitable for these parts. I bet they have no idea what they're doing, but that's not my problem.

I build things. Once the things are built, I'm no longer interested in them.

I'm watching as a pair of curlews step gracefully along the river bank and then skim the surface of the water with their long beaks. The breeze picks up and the birds gets spooked at the same time and fly away. Despite the calendar date, the temperature feels like Arcana in March. There's no doubt it *can* get hot here but it's not hot right now. All the scorching heat has been delivered to Texas. Jace tells me they've been baking beneath triple digits for the last week. If I could shift this cool breeze in that direction then I would.

At least once a day I think about leaving. It's agony to think about how far away Susanna is while knowing how much she's hurting in the final weeks of her father's life. Family emergencies are not unheard of among the crew and the owner is a friend. He would understand if I needed to run off for a week or two. Susanna's too proud to ask when I'm coming back but I hear all the unsaid things in the long pauses during short conversations. Those are the moments when I wish I could be an everyday kind of guy; one who wants to live at the same address all year, toss steaks on the backyard grill for dinner and make family plans.

"One night would not have been enough. A hundred nights wouldn't have been enough. I would have wished for forever."

Jace is exactly that kind of guy. He traded in being the king of the NFL for being the king of Arcana and he's ecstatic about it. Now he and Tori are pregnant and he's even more ecstatic about that.

Jace and Tori have not asked exactly what happened with Susanna when I was in town this past spring. I'm sure they've figured it out anyway, or at least the basics.

Jimmy Greco, the company owner, hails me with a wave from the flatbed that huffed its way out here this morning to deliver another stack of reclaimed wood. I'm in the middle of tossing around the idea of collaring him for a quick talk about the situation back home when he drives away.

Most of the crew has already taken off in separate directions for the day. This is not a social bunch, which is usually my preference. I don't want to be dragged to the nearest drinking hole to fuck with billiards or get smiled at by women. My partying days began when I was too young and were filled with extremes. Maybe that's why I got sick of it all by the time I turned twenty.

Or maybe I'm just an asshole.

That's also likely.

Murphy finally gets his act together and carries his shit out here. Due to a childhood lawnmower accident, he limps noticeably and now he hobbles over to his car while I check the tarps that have been stretched across the unfinished roofs. Murphy doesn't hear me when I shout a goodbye. Every day he makes the forty mile drive back and forth to his trailer in the town of Grainedge. I'm aware that he damn near drinks his weight in liquor each night but he's had an unhappy life after losing his wife to breast cancer a few years back and what he chooses to do with his own time is none of my business.

Daylight is disappearing fast. At this point I usually retreat to my rented two room cabin ten miles away in the opposite direction of town. I'll heat up some canned garbage on the stove because I haven't been to the store lately and it's all I've got left, then maybe I'll practice wood carving techniques or shuffle cards or jerk off until I get drowsy, which will be early.

But today I'm not doing that just yet.

I'm going to follow Murphy's car to Grainedge in order to maximize my phone reception. I'm going to call Susanna. Just the idea of hearing her voice makes my heart pound faster.

Murphy drives slowly and I catch up to him quickly. He gets visibly pissed off over the way I'm riding his rear bumper and starts flipping the bird around but this is mildly entertaining so I keep doing it.

Once I hit the outskirts of Grainedge, I give Murphy a break and pull over. Then I open up my glove box and realize I left my phone back at the cabin this morning.

"FUCK." I punch the glove box closed. I'm an honest to god failure at cell phone protocol.

My fingers drum the steering wheel.

I check the time.

I could double back to the cabin, retrieve my phone, which may or not be charged, and then try again. But I don't know what time it will be when I finally get through. Susanna's up at odd hours and snatches sleep when she can. Even with her mother there to help her now and the hospice nurse checking in every day, she's got her hands full. I don't want to risk waking her if she's actually managing to get some rest.

I make a different plan.

I zoom back to the cabin, grab the phone from where I left it on the sink counter, and drive until I'm sure I'm in a place where the call won't get dropped after eight seconds.

And then I call my sister.

She answers the phone after one ring. "Hey. I wasn't expecting to hear from you today."

Jace's voice murmurs in the background. I have faith that Tori will know the answer to the question I need to ask so I just blurt it out.

"Tor, does she want me there right now?"

Tori isn't puzzled by the question and doesn't need me to explain. "Yes. She won't admit it. But I know she does."

"Okay. Don't tell her I'm coming."

"I wouldn't."

"See you soon, big sister."

"Drive safe, little brother."

Next, I call Jimmy Greco and explain that I'm needed at home. I'm not sure for how long. As of right now this project is ahead of schedule so I'm hoping that fact will soften the blow. I promise to work like a demon when I return.

"Colt, it's not a problem," he cuts in while I'm still talking. "You do what you need to do."

I'm keyed up as hell and I'd like to leave right now. Common sense tells me to wait until the morning. After a long day of back breaking labor I need to catch a few hours of sleep so I don't nod off and slam into a tree.

The cabin feels lonelier than usual but that's been my state of mind on and off ever since leaving Arcana.

No, ever since leaving Susanna.

I think about her all the time. I dream about her. I jerk off to memories of her.

I fucking *miss* her.

Those feelings are as strong now as they were three months ago on the day I left.

Then why don't I ever tell her so?

That's not important now. What's important is that Susanna is trying to get through an extremely painful time. And I trust my sister. If Tori says that Susanna wants me around right now, then I'm going. Susanna can lean on me all she needs to.

There are a few things I'm good at and a lot of things I'm *not* good at. But I like to think that I've redeemed myself a little, that ever since Jace Zielinski found the gruff loner who used to be his best friend and asked for help, I've been able to come through.

Just like I'll come through now. For Susanna.

But I'm still enough of a prick that I can't fall asleep until I put my hand on my dick and pretend it's her mouth. One skill that comes with solitary living is that I've got beating my meat down to a fucking science. In my head, getting sucked off isn't enough right now. I want to be inside her and this is where I finish after the Susanna in my fantasy trembles and curses her way to a climax.

Falling sleep is easy once I've exhausted myself and my eyes pop open promptly at five a.m. Twenty minutes later I'm showered, packed and out the door. I thought about flying but I've never been on a plane in my entire life and this feels like a bad day to break tradition.

The drive is unremarkable. I don't stop often and I make good time, although I'm not stupid about it. When I feel my eyes starting to get heavy, I pull way off the road and catch some sleep in my truck.

It's just after six p.m. the following day when I roll into Arcana. The heat has not let up one bit. Since the air conditioning in this battered old box doesn't work exceptionally well, I've been keeping the windows rolled down. Returning to Arcana is no longer the stark memory jolt that it used to be after I spent a decade avoiding this part of the world completely. Now when I spot the high school and Dave's Tacos and Paul Elkins's office I'm just glad to be back.

Still, when I close in on Susanna's street I catch a case of nerves. I probably should have called and warned her that I was on my way. That's what a normal person would do, not cross half the country and just show up without a word.

After all, Tori might have been wrong.

It's possible that Susanna has so much on her plate that she'd rather not deal with all the complications that come with seeing me.

I park at the curb and stare at her house. I should have least brought her something; flowers or cookies or whatever.

Too late now.

I'm empty handed as I cross the paved walkway and reach the door. I rap my knuckles three times on the wood and wait. The knob twists and I hold my breath.

Susanna's mother gapes at me. Her mouth literally hangs open in shock.

"Ma'am." I clear my throat. "I don't know if you remember me but-"

"I remember you, Colt," she says. A smile breaks and she calls over her shoulder. "Susanna, you have a visitor."

"What visitor?" Susanna asks and her mother opens the door all the way.

Susanna is wearing the t-shirt I gave her. Her hair is down. Her glasses are on. She's barefoot. Exhaustion and grief are written on her face and still she's a vision.

She is also truly stunned to see me. For a second I'm afraid this might have been the wrong move. But then a soft cry leaves her lips and she runs straight into my arms.

"Colt!" She hugs me forcefully. "I can't believe it's you!"

She turns her face and I kiss her without holding back, vaguely aware that her mother is still watching. I kiss her again and hug her back every bit as tightly, even lifting her off the ground a little.

Susanna pulls me into the house. She laughs about my beard. I'd completely forgotten that she's never seen me with one. When I'm out on a job I don't bother to shave and after three months the thick growth on my jaw is pretty much filled in.

We look in on Coach Toledo and I try to hide my shock. Three months ago, he was visibly ill but still functioning. Since then, he has wasted away to skin and bones. He sleeps, unaware that he is being watched as his body noisily struggles to draw each breath. Susanna's mother checks his pulse and kisses his forehead.

Susanna has said that her parents have not been on friendly terms at all since their divorce so it's surprising to see her dad being cared for so tenderly by his ex-wife. I suppose there's no end to the complexities between two people who share a long history.

As we move to the living room, Susanna clings to me and I keep my arm around her. We take a seat on the couch and I pull her into my lap. With a sigh, she rests her cheek on my shoulder. She grows quiet as I sift my fingers through her hair. Susanna doesn't seem to care what motivated me to make the trip. For her, it's enough that I've come.

Her mother joins us only long enough to announce that she has some errands to run. She smiles at the sight of her daughter being cradled in my lap but also seems mystified. No wonder, considering her memories of my name might not be all that pleasant. In any case, she's kind enough to give us a few moments of privacy.

Susanna waits until her mother is gone. She burrows closer and runs her hand over my chest like she's trying to ensure I'm real.

"I'm so glad you're here," she whispers.

I should have known she'd feel this way. I should have come sooner.

13

SUSANNA

I'm in the kitchen transferring a foil-covered plate of lemon scones to a plastic container when my mother shuffles this way in search of coffee.

She rubs the back of her neck and winces at the stiffness. "Is Colt asleep?"

"Yes." In fact, he's asleep in my bed. We've agreed that someone should always be with my dad out of fear he might die alone. Colt stayed up with him from midnight until six a.m. and then we switched places. Since his arrival a week ago, Colt has been here the whole time, leaving on only a couple of occasions to dash to the store in order to buy something we need.

"I just brewed a new batch of coffee." I hold out the container of scones. "Have some. Tori dropped these off earlier."

"She made them?"

"No. Jace did."

"Wow. Never thought I'd be eating pastries baked by a Super Bowl champion." She takes two scones and drops them on a plate.

"Tori says she and Jace plan to come by later after she gets off work."

"That's nice." My mother pours a cup of coffee. "I forget. When is her baby due?"

"January. The nurse is still here, right?"

"She's with him right now. I told her I'd be back soon. I just needed a short break." My mother slides gracefully into a tall kitchen chair and pats the chair beside her. "Come here. You look like you're going to fall over."

"I'm not," I assure her but dutifully take a seat.

My mother nibbles at a scone. I've never seen so much gray in her hair before. She's always been obsessive about covering it. The lines around her eyes are more pronounced and she hasn't bothered about makeup today. Observing my mother's vulnerability combined with her steadfast devotion provokes a wave of tenderness.

"I love you, Mom."

She drops her scone and stares at me. I'm not sure I've said that before, not since I was a small child.

"I love you too, Susanna."

Mothers and daughters should say such things in ordinary conversation but lately I've been a basket case and my tears come so easily. I don't want to cry now so I concentrate on sipping coffee until the urge to cry passes.

My mother is already onto a different topic. "You didn't tell me about Colt. Did you think I wouldn't approve?"

"That's not true. I mentioned how I'd seen him in the spring when he visited."

She snorts through her nose. "Rather an incomplete summary."

"I didn't know what to say. Not to be cliché but...it's complicated."

"All right." She shrugs, now smirking. "I'll let you off the hook. But not before stating that the boy has sure grown up nicely."

Now I'm the one who snorts. "I can't argue with that."

She wants some fresh air and I don't blame her. Even the oppressive heat is better than the suffocating sadness inside my father's room. He has stopped taking food and water. He is unconscious most of the time. It won't be long.

"Are you coming outside?" she asks before exiting the kitchen.

"No, you go ahead."

Once she's gone, I pour a fresh cup of coffee and carry it upstairs.

Colt is stretched out on my bed, sound asleep, wearing only a pair of black boxers. I have no intention of waking him. I'm only here to leave the coffee beside the bed on the painted white nightstand, part of the bedroom set I received as a Christmas gift when I was twelve.

However, I'm only human and I can't seem to leave without taking the time to brazenly admire Colt's muscled body. He sleeps atop the covers. The dusting of hair on his arms and legs matches the light brown color on his head. His beard is more of a reddish shade. His skin shows the effects of working outside and the muscles sculpting his arms and chest shows that he works very hard. He is perfection. I've never seen a sexier man.

We've been keeping things very PG since he's been back. Kissing. Cuddling. No more than that. But even in the midst of grief, I *ache* for him.

Colt cracks one blue eye open.

I smile, hoping he didn't catch me gawking at his body. "Go back to sleep. There's a cup of coffee waiting for you when you wake up."

"Wait." He yawns, rolls to his back.

My eyes flicker down. He's aroused. And he sees that I've noticed.

"Come here." He reaches for me, a smug grin tilting his lips.

"The door is open."

"Shut it."

Suddenly I feel giddy, lightheaded. I close the door anyway. I even lock it.

Colt props an arm behind his head and drowsily watches me climb on the bed. "Closer," he demands.

"If I come any closer, I'll be sitting on top of you."

"I know."

I'm wearing a pair of nylon shorts and a blue tee that I sometimes sleep in. Not exactly prime seduction material. Colt doesn't seem to mind. He grows impatient with my tentative approach and seizes my hips, sliding me forward until I feel him between my legs.

"I was dreaming about you." His hair is tousled, his eyes partially closed. He pushes his hands under my shirt.

I arch my back and roll my hips. "I think you're still half asleep."

"Maybe." He sits up and finds my mouth.

For a few heated minutes our tongues play and our hands roam. We kiss and grind and drive each other crazy. I want so much more. He does too.

But the hospice nurse will be leaving any minute. I need to go back downstairs.

When he senses that I'm pulling away, Colt leans back and stares into my eyes. "How are things this morning?"

"The same. We're waiting and watching."

"I'm sorry, baby."

I wrap my arms around him and hug tightly, drawing comfort from his warmth and strength. No matter how often I tell him how thrilled I am to have him here, I know the words are inadequate.

After one more kiss we disentangle our bodies.

Colt is wide awake now. He hops off the bed, strolls to the door and says, "Gonna go shower and jerk off." His right eyebrow peaks. "Want to watch?"

That's Colt; tenderly sensitive one minute and filthy the next. I love him for it.

"I do want to watch. But I need to get downstairs."

He casually rubs the massive bulge in his boxers and kisses the air.

I can't stop giggling. "I beg you not to walk into the hallway like that. You may accidentally terrorize my mother."

Colt swipes a pair of jeans from his suitcase and pulls them on before yanking the door open.

I listen to the bathroom door close and roll back on the bed with a groan.

For years I wondered what was wrong with me. Why couldn't I have satisfying adult sexual experiences like everyone else? My fantasies were much better than reality. I didn't have sex because I didn't want to. In the olden days I suppose I would have been called *frigid*. Colt was the only person who has ever made me feel differently. I've always been worried I'd never find that intense physical connection with anyone else. I don't believe I ever will.

The shower is running when I pass by the hallway bathroom. Downstairs, I find my mother wearing a grim expression and listening as Tanya, the hospice nurse, speaks to her quietly in the living room.

All good feelings evaporate and my heart lurches.

They both notice me at the same time and Tanya is quick to offer reassurance that my father is as comfortable as he can be. His breathing remains labored but that will not be improving. Tanya pats my mother's arm and shoulders a boxy tote bag covered with Disney princesses.

"You have the number to call if you need it," she says.

My mother presses a palm to her head. "Yes, we do. Thank you."

"I'm off for the next two days. David will be the nurse who comes in the meantime. I'll see you on Friday."

I suspect Tanya does not believe my father will still be alive on Friday.

She turns her compassionate smile on us and departs. I don't know how anyone can do a job like hers every day and not sink into a state of perpetual despair.

There are two chairs at my father's bedside. My mother and I each claim one. He inhales raggedly, exhales with a whistling wheeze. A few seconds pass and the sounds are repeated. The three of us are sitting there, a lost family growing more lost by the hour, when Colt joins us.

He stands behind my chair and lays a warm hand on my shoulder. The scent of his soap fills the room. Bending my head to the side, my cheek brushes the back of his hand.

Colt is not one to dissect the past out loud, particularly the unpleasant parts. But I have no doubt he remembers everything and it's somehow fitting that he's here in my father's last hours. He was not to blame for what happened to our family, but the story includes him and so it also belongs to him.

"Where's my Susie?" Drew Toledo asks this question clearly, though his eyes remain closed.

My had reaches for his. "I'm right here, Daddy."

He struggles through another breath and smiles gently, still without lifting his eyelids. I wonder if he is thinking of me as a care-free little girl, when he would ask the same question and I would rush into his arms with joy, or if he sees me as I am now, an imperfect woman holding back her tears.

Perhaps it doesn't matter. Either way, I'm still his child.

My mother is very tired and I urge her to get some rest. She has been sleeping on a pullout sofa in the room that has always served as my father's office. When I pointed out that she could have chosen the guest bedroom on the second floor, she smiled and said she'd rather remain downstairs to be closer to my dad.

A pile of my childhood books sits on a nearby table. I've been keeping them in here to read out loud. My dad was always partial to Shel Silverstein's poems. We used to laugh over them together.

Colt decides to take a trip to the supermarket and pick up some groceries. The fridge is filled with casseroles and pasta salads gifted by well meaning neighbors and my father's former students but we're running out of milk and eggs. Colt, as expected, shakes his head when I try to give him money.

"I'll be right back." He kisses me softly, pauses for a long look at my father, and then lowers his head with a sigh before leaving.

For a few minutes I listen to my father breathe. I'm not imagining the erratic pace of his breathing, or that the efforts grow further apart.

I select *Where The Sidewalk Ends* from the book pile. "I bet you'd like to hear some of your favorite poems."

He doesn't answer of course. I have no way of knowing if he can even hear me, but I like to think my voice is a comfort.

Colt returns while I'm still reading out loud. He's brought me vanilla ice cream and the sympathy of everyone he ran into. Hannah Graff and her husband. Paul Elkins. Steve Giorgio. They all made Colt promise to let me know that my father is very loved in this town.

When Jace and Tori arrive, my mother is still asleep. Tori has brought me a bouquet of sunflowers. I wonder who told her they are my favorite flower. The sight of them in a jar of water on the dining room table does succeed in adding a little cheer.

Before they leave, Jace pulls Colt aside and I'm sure he doesn't mean for me to hear his incomplete request to his best friend. "Call me when..."

Colt nods with understanding and squeezes his shoulder. "I will."

Dinner is a reheated dish of beef stew, courtesy of Namra Aref from across the street. She and her husband moved here from Austin with their three boys last year.

My mother joins me at the dining room table while Colt looks in on my father and returns to report that he's awake and would like a drink of water. By the time I bring the glass in there, my father has once more retreated into unconsciousness. I leave the glass on top of the dresser.

We're going to keep the same shifts as last night. I trudge to bed at midnight, opt against changing my clothes and fall asleep almost instantly.

I'm not dreaming. I've sunk into an empty void and this is where I am when Colt's deep voice brings me back.

"Susanna."

He's sitting on the edge of my bed. The room remains dark but the first wisps of dawn have begun to slip through the shutter cracks. Something is wrong and I do not want to hear what it is. I reach for Colt and try to pull him down on the bed with me. He comes willingly, nestling his strong body against my tired one. He slides my shirt down, kisses my bare shoulder, and whispers in my ear.

"Wake up, honey. He'll be leaving us very soon."

I've had many months to prepare for this. It wasn't enough.

As I listen to my father gasp out his last breath I'm thinking of echoes. A life can be summed up in the echoes of what's been done and said and what should never have been done or said.

At the end, none of it can be changed but holding onto bitterness would be pointless and cruel.

"I love you, Daddy. Please don't worry. I'm really not angry anymore. And I'll miss you always."

14

SUSANNA, AGE 16

I'll probably never find out who told, not that it would make a difference.

My father thunders upstairs without warning and demands to know what the hell is going on with Colt Malene. He doesn't even wait for my answer before he begins throwing out all kinds of accusations.

He calls me a liar. He calls me a thief. He screams that I'm throwing my life away just because I'm hot for a boy who couldn't possibly give a damn about me.

Drew Toledo has always been known for being strict and exacting, yet he rarely loses his temper. He doesn't have to. His players are motivated by respect rather than fear and they are aware that he rewards loyalty.

The sight of my father in the midst of a volcanic eruption is an uncommon one. And he has never turned his anger on me.

I try to explain.

I try to apologize.

I try to defend myself, and I try to defend Colt.

We never set out to deceive him. I'm sorry that I've been sneaking out. Colt and I really care about each other. All we want is to be together.

And he likes Colt. He always has. This should not be a problem.

But he won't listen.

He's already made up his mind. He snatches my phone and leaves, nearly colliding with my bewildered mother, who has arrived home in the middle of this chaos with shopping bags roped over her arms.

"You'd better damn well stay put," my father warns me before slamming the front door so hard the house shakes.

I don't need to be told where he's going. He's going to find Colt and he's taken my phone to make sure I don't send out a warning.

Colt was supposed to attend his mother's wedding today. And then, since I planned to be busy writing a paper on the Russian Revolution, he intended to hang out with his friends afterwards. I'm not even sure where he is right now.

My very alarmed mother drags me to the couch. In between a lot of crying and hiccupping, I manage to spill the main bullet points.

"How did he find out?" she asks, almost like she's asking herself that question instead of asking me.

"Wait, you *knew*?"

She gives me a tight smile. "I'm not blind, Susanna. I know when my daughter is in love. I didn't know who you were seeing, but I could tell you were happy. So I thought I'd wait for you to come to us."

Fresh tears erupt and I choke on them. "I'm so sorry, Mom. I didn't mean to sneak out and to lie. You should have seen the way Daddy looked at me."

She wraps me in a hug. "Everything will be okay."

She doesn't sound sure.

"What'll he do to Colt?" I whisper.

She pats my back. "Your father has his faults. But he is not a violent man."

That doesn't really answer my question. Colt doesn't have parents who will look out for him. And no one would be foolish enough to want my father as an enemy.

I take a breath. "Someone told him that I was stealing condoms from the Arcana Drugstore. And he believed it. I wasn't, I swear. I don't know who saw me, but I was in there one day and I was just... looking at them. I didn't steal any."

She sighs but she's not angry. "Have you and Colt been, um, intimate already?"

I hug my arms around my body, mortification beginning to seep in. Sex is not a subject my mother and I have discussed at all since I got my period three years ago. Frankly, there has been no reason to. "We haven't had sex."

I'm telling the truth. Colt and I have not had sex. We've just done many (MANY!) other things that I'd rather not describe to my mother.

Less than fifteen minutes later, my father's truck screeches to a halt out front.

My mother glances at me with some uncertainty and I realize she doesn't know what to expect when my father comes through the door.

Neither do I. I want to throw up.

He's still furious. I can tell from the flush in his cheeks and the way he refuses to look me in the eye. He tosses his keys angrily on the coffee table.

"That's it. He knows it's over."

I jump off the couch and get right in his face. "What did you do, Daddy?"

He glares. "I let Colt Malene know that he has no fucking place in your life."

"You have no right!"

"Don't give me that shit. I'm your father. The kid's no good."

"I don't understand. You tried to invite him to move in here so he could stay on the team. Clearly you didn't think he was that awful if you wanted him in our home."

"I assumed there wouldn't be a problem, that he would never..." He flails an arm, unable to complete the sentence. His jaw hardens. "Look, I've seen the kind of girls he goes for."

"What kind is that?"

He shifts his weight. "Don't be dense, Susie. Cheerleaders, the popular girls, the prettiest ones."

I get it now. I need to swallow painfully before saying the words out loud. "You didn't believe Colt Malene would want to look twice at me."

My father's eyes flare for a second. He's shocked that I read his mind. His mouth starts to form words but lies aren't really his style. His shoulders slump and his irate expression changes to a puzzled one. "No, I sure as hell didn't."

"Drew, don't." Even my mother is stunned as she rises from the couch. The three of us stand in an awkward triangle and she holds up her hands in a defensive pose, trying to fend off the swift and irreconcilable fracturing of her family.

My chest is tight. I would have been less astonished to hear the admission come from my mother. She's always regarded me with a confused version of hope that if she instructed me how to apply makeup correctly and wear heels without rolling my ankle that I would transition into the poised glamour queen she thought she should have spawned.

But my dad?

I thought I knew where I stood with him.

From an early age I dove headfirst into racking up accomplishments in part to make up for the fact that there was only one of me. If he couldn't have the full house of boys that he's always dreamed of, then I'd at least make him proud of his only daughter.

And I assumed that I had.

I must have been wrong. It's now clear that he sees me as nothing more than a silly girl who is too awkward and uninteresting to attract much attention. He was sure he could install his star player in the bedroom next door and that Colt wouldn't be tempted in the least. Nothing about me impresses my father, not really.

I raise my chin and for the first time in my life I openly defy him. "There's nothing you can do to stop me from seeing Colt."

My father's eyes grow cold and something about the steely look within ignites a spark of fear. "Oh yeah? Think again. Your boyfriend won't want to play this charade anymore when I make another call to the Bredon High coach. I can make sure Colt Malene will never get fucking near a football field again."

It's the cruelest thing he's said yet. He knows better than anyone how dedicated Colt is to football, how much it would crush him to have that opportunity taken away.

"You can't do that," I complain, aware that this objection is futile. "You can't do that to him!"

He crosses his thickly muscled arms. "I will if you try to keep seeing him."

"You fucking asshole," I swear.

The words just slipped out. My father is startled for a second, but then icy resolve returns and he wags a finger.

"Don't you test me, little girl."

"Don't you threaten me, old man."

He hisses with disgust. "This is what hanging around that punk has done to you. You forget how to respect your own father."

"Well, it's too bad you didn't have the sons you wanted instead. They might have given you the respect you'll never again receive from me!"

It's a terrible thing to say. I know that. But he said terrible things first and now we can't stop ourselves.

My father is on the verge of exploding. His face is nearly crimson as he fires back. "Yeah, it is too bad! Because right now I'm thinking that a son would have caused me a lot less trouble than this ungrateful bitch of a daughter."

I cough out a bitter laugh. "Well, you're stuck with me, Dad. No sons, only me. That's not my fault. Blame your useless dick for failing to deliver."

He lunges, grabbing a fistful of my shirt as I yelp and try to twist away. I can smell the fumes of the lone beer he always drinks with dinner and I feel the savage pressure of his fingers on my skin. My father has never hit me, not once. I think he might hit me now. In a way, I want him to. I want to have a reason to hate him forever.

"DREW!" My mother shrieks and dives in the middle, savagely chopping at his hand, trying to force him to let go.

And he does let go.

He releases me and takes a big step back. It's clear from the look on his face that he knows he's gone too far.

My mother stands between us, breathing fire and shielding me with her petite body.

Remorse has now set in and my father collapses into his armchair with his head in his hands.

"Go upstairs, sweetheart." My mother uses a gentle tone that I haven't heard since I was very small. She escorts me to the staircase. "It'll be all right."

I have little choice but to go to my room. The alternative is to run through the front door and as bad as things are at the moment, I understand that move will only make them worse.

But I leave my bedroom door open a crack. And I listen to every word of the argument that rages downstairs.

Their roles have changed and now it's my mother who puts up a fight in my defense. "I don't give a crap what your so-called sources said. Susanna would never steal anything."

"Next you'll say she'd never sneak out either."

"She's a teenager! She's bound to make some mistakes and she should be allowed to. She's always bent over backwards in search of your approval and it's high time she pushed back a little."

"She'll ruin her reputation and make a fool out of herself."

"*Reputation?* What year do you think this is for god's sake?"

"She understands nothing. That little shit is a brainless party animal. He's just using her and she's letting him."

"Oh, give me a break. I know Colt too and he's a decent enough kid. And you underestimate Susanna. I trust her judgment."

"I don't."

My mother huffs out a noise of pure exasperation. "You're willing to destroy your relationship with your daughter because she dated a boy without begging for your permission?"

"It's about respect! That girl has none."

"Bullshit. She's not one of your goddamn football players."

"Don't you cross me on this, Kelly."

"Go to hell, Drew."

A door slams.

My father curses.

I shut my bedroom door, curl up in a ball in the middle of my mattress and cry myself to sleep.

A soft hand on my head awakens me and I'm surprised to see both the morning light and my mother's sorrowful face. She doesn't shy away from the terrible news.

"Colt was in an accident last night. He's okay," she assures me when I gasp and bolt upright. "Apparently after your father confronted him, he drove his mother's car and crashed it into a stop sign. No one was hurt but he'd been drinking and he will face consequences for that. He was arrested. Gloria Zielinski bailed him out this morning."

All of yesterday's emotions come rushing back and I can hardly breathe through my tears. "What will happen to him?"

"I don't know. I suppose he will be charged with drunk driving."

"But Daddy can talk to Chief Radcliff. He's done it before when one of his players gets in trouble. You said no one was hurt."

She winces. "Your father won't lift a finger to help Colt."

"Maybe he will."

"Susanna, I've already asked. He sees this incident as proof that his worst suspicions about Colt were correct. He won't budge."

I grew up thinking of my mother as the petulant ruler of the household, always getting her way. Never before did I realize how much more complicated things really are.

"I'll ask him." I tighten my ponytail and look to her for hope. "Maybe he'll do it for me."

She's doubtful but doesn't discourage me. "Dry your tears first. You know he doesn't like tears. Speak to him calmly."

"I will." I swing my legs over the side of the bed.

My mother leaves the room and I take my time in the bathroom, washing my face and blotting it with a soft towel. My forehead remains blotchy and the angry set to my jaw is difficult to relax. I change to a blue and white sundress worn only once to a sweet sixteen party last spring. A desperate move, made in the hopes that if I look pretty, perhaps he'll be more sympathetic.

He's on the back patio, calmly drinking a glass of orange juice and scrolling through his phone. I pause at the back door and turn to see my mother right behind me. She gives me a nod of support and I take a deep breath before stepping out onto the patio.

"Hi, Daddy."

He lowers his phone immediately and breaks into a pleased smile. I can see now that there are deep pockets under his eyes, like maybe he didn't sleep at all last night. "Good morning, Susie."

He watches, almost nervously, as I sink into a cushioned patio chair. I cross my legs at the ankles and fold my hands in my lap. My mother remains where she is in the doorway.

"Daddy, I'm sorry about yesterday."

He leans forward eagerly. "Oh honey, I'm sorry too. I'm so ashamed of losing my temper that way. Susie, you know how much I love you."

I thought I did.

"I just can't stand the thought of you getting hurt," he says with such earnestness that I know he believes this to be true and so it justifies whatever he does.

But I can't argue with him, not with Colt's fate on the line.

"I heard about Colt's accident."

My father's expression becomes wary and he leans back in his chair. "And you shouldn't be surprised. I'm not."

"Please help him. You can talk to Radcliff. I understand that Colt messed up but-"

"He could have killed someone. What if you'd been in that car with him?"

"I wasn't. And he won't do it again. He's just having a tough time right now. You know his home life is awful. He's moving to a new town. He needs to start over with a new team."

My father shakes his head. "Nah, he can forget about playing now. No chance Cassavetes is going to play someone with a record."

"You can talk to him."

"I cannot and will not order another coach to play a criminal on his team. Anyway, why the hell would I do that?"

"For me."

He crosses his arms, appraises me with shrewdness. "I haven't changed my mind. You're not seeing him anymore."

My fingernails dig into my palms. Getting angry will do no good. "Will you help Colt if I promise to break things off with him?"

He sighs. He stares moodily at a far corner of the yard and thinks. "I'm not telling Cassavetes to play him."

Maybe that wouldn't matter. Colt is capable of proving himself if given the chance. "Just don't tell him not to. And talk to Radcliff."

My father looks me over carefully. "How can I trust you, Susie? You've been lying to me for a while."

Over in the doorway, my mother sighs noisily and shakes her head, clearly getting pissed off. My father ignores her.

"I promise I will tell Colt that we're through. He's moving in two weeks anyway. That will be the end of it." Saying those words makes me nauseous.

"You don't need to see him again to say that."

"I do need to see him!"

"You can call to break it off."

"That won't be good enough. He'll know you're pulling the strings. I'll do it, Daddy. I'll break up with him, but I need to do it in person. And you need to talk to Radcliff and see what he can do about minimizing Colt's charges."

He considers the idea for so long that I'm sure he'll scoff and refuse.

Finally, he nods at me. "You'll tell him today."

I swallow a sob. "It's early. He's probably at home. I'll go tell him right now."

"Fine." He digs his keys out of his back pocket and tosses them to me. "If you're not back here in half an hour I'm coming to find you."

I manage to keep my tears in check until I've returned to the house. My mother follows and tries to comfort me but I can't concentrate on anything she's saying. After grabbing my wallet and flipflops I run out and take off in my dad's pickup truck. Hanging from the rearview mirror is an engraved ornament that says World's Best Coach with my father's name underneath. It was a gift from some of his players at his last school. With a savage pull, I rip it off the mirror and throw it out the window.

It's not even nine a.m. I could have called to ask Colt if he's at home but my phone privileges have been suspended. Colt's mother is supposed to be on her honeymoon in Vegas but his car accident might have changed her plans.

There are no cars parked outside at Colt's house. A realtor sign in the front yard has been knocked over. The place has an eerie, desolate feel to it as I ring the doorbell. Even if Colt's not awake, Tori must be here.

A full minute of silence elapses. I ring the doorbell twice more and knock loudly. If I don't see him now, I don't know when I'll get another chance.

Then the door is jerked open and I find myself face to face with a very battered Colt.

He's an absolute wreck and I hear myself gasp. His jaw is visibly bruised and he has a black eye. There's also some vague discoloration on his torso, like he's taken a beating.

He gives me a pained smile. "Guess I've looked better."

Overcome with emotion, I throw my arms around him and he returns the fierce hug, lifting me against his body. He's wearing only a pair of loose gym shorts and he smells like Irish Spring soap and his hair is wet from a recent shower. My own body responds hungrily to the feel of him.

"Colt, I'm so sorry. My father...."

"I know." He kisses me, again and again. "It's not your fault."

I run my fingers over his jaw. He winces. "What happened? This can't be from the accident."

"It's not. That was hardly a fender bender."

A horrifying thought crosses my mind. "Oh my god, did my father do this to you?"

"No." He shakes his head and closes his eyes with a grimace, like he's trying to blot out a memory. "I got into it with Jace last night."

"You fought with *Jace*?" That's the last thing I expected him to say. Colt and Jace don't fight, at least not with each other.

He glances at the house next door, where Jace lives with his grandmother. He frowns and puts an arm around me. "Let's go inside."

The living room is another shock. Moving boxes are strewn everywhere, many of them toppled with the contents spilled all over the floor. There's a broken table, shattered glass. I don't need anyone to tell me this where the violent brawl between two best friends happened.

Colt takes my hand and steers me toward his bedroom, which is tiny. His bed is neatly made and covered with a gray fleece blanket. He sits down on the edge and keeps his head down as I sit beside him.

"Where's Tori?"

"No idea. Probably off with him."

"Jace?"

He nods.

"Colt." I touch his shoulder in the hopes he'll look at me. "Why on earth were you fighting with Jace?"

He rubs his eyes and sighs. "It was after your dad showed up and made a scene. Jace and Tori came running out half dressed, obviously just after they'd finished screwing each other, and I kind of lost my shit. Fuck, I said some things I shouldn't have said. I guess I didn't realize how pissed I was at him. And then I heard that your dad plans to make him the quarterback and I don't know, I just went nuts."

I kiss his shoulder. "You guys will work it out. You've been best friends forever."

His face falls as he remembers something else. "Tori admitted that our dad asked her to live with him so she could finish high school here. But he said I wasn't part of the deal. He doesn't want me in his house. And then when Jace and I started trading blows, she took his side. She actually picked up a piece of furniture and hit me with it. My own sister."

This is an even tougher piece of information to digest. Tori has always been devoted to her brother and I cannot picture her doing that at all. How horrible the whole fight must have been for all of them.

"Anyway," he continues, "everything just boiled over and I took off in my mom's car even though I'd been drinking. I just couldn't take it anymore, always being known as a good for nothing piece of shit." His voice cracks and he buries his face in his hands. "Susanna, nobody thinks I'm worth much."

His pain cuts right through the center of my soul.

"I do." I brush my lips over the smooth skin of his shoulder again. And again. "I think the world of you. You're everything, Colt."

He lifts his head and kisses me.

My mission evaporates with the touch of his lips.

I don't care what I promised my father. Let Drew Toledo rage and scream. He can't control me. He can't control *us*. Nobody can break what Colt and I have.

When Colt drops his shorts, I kiss him more urgently.

When he eases me back on the bed, I let him.

"We could leave this fucking place," Colt says between heated kisses. "We could go anywhere and leave all this shit behind."

There's still a sensible part of my brain that works and it's screeching at me. We're both minors and we don't have the resources to last more than a few weeks on our own.

A shudder of dread rolls through my belly as I recall my father's hateful words. He's ready to destroy Colt just for the crime of touching me. The consequences would be far harsher if I ran away.

But I say nothing and return Colt's kisses just as ravenously. I pull him as close as possible and feel him, hard and insistent, against my belly.

If we have sex right now, then I won't be able to handle walking away from him.

If we *don't* have sex right now, then I'll be cursed to look back on this moment forever and wish we had.

"It's you and me," he whispers. "As long as we have each other we don't need anyone else."

"It's you and me," I whisper back.

My panties are pulled down and then off. My legs open for him.

We're doing this and we're going to be careless, *very* careless.

I might even get pregnant.

Maybe that's what I want, to go home and tell my father how I'm having Colt Malene's baby and there's nothing he can do about it. Maybe I want to see how that news destroys him after the way he's treated us both.

But my mother, who despite her flaws also has high hopes for me, would also be hurt. She doesn't deserve to be hurt.

All my dreams of college and beyond would be over. I'd struggle to finish high school and then be lucky to land a job at the Arcana Drugstore. Colt would have to forget about football or a chance at any kind of meaningful future.

If I turn on my father right now, he'll make Colt's life a living hell.

Everyone would suffer.

Colt most of all.

"I love you, Susanna," he breathes into my neck. "I love you so much. I'd never hurt you."

My knees bend up and my legs open wider. I'm ready to do this. I *am* doing this.

And then I know that I can't.

I love you too, Colt. And I HAVE to hurt you.

"Stop." I push on his chest and he reacts instantly, rolling off the bed and yanking his shorts back up.

I cover myself in a hurry while Colt looks away. When he turns his head again, he's full of apologies.

"I'm so sorry. Fucking hell, my head's not right today. I didn't mean to be pushy. I'd never do that, never try to take something from you that you weren't ready for. Please believe me."

Of course I believe him. Colt has always been supremely considerate when it comes to seeking my consent. I nod my head and he breathes with relief.

He sits down at my side and I touch his hand one more time before breaking his heart.

"Colt, I can't see you anymore."

He flinches. The look on his face is terrible to see. "You don't mean that."

"Yes I do. The new school year starts soon and you'll be fifty miles away. I'll be taking so many difficult classes and I need to concentrate if I want to be valedictorian and...."

I've lost track of what I'm saying. Colt has already stood up and walked away, facing the opposite wall.

"I never thought you were a coward, Susanna."

"You don't understand."

He whirls around, blue eyes blazing. "Yes, I do! I'm no genius like you but I'm not fucking stupid either."

"I know that!"

"Then why are you sitting there coughing up bullshit about your class schedule instead of admitting that your father is making threats?"

I should have realized he would see through me. "He'll destroy you, Colt."

"Yeah? Let the fucker do his worst."

"No! You have a chance right now. You can start over and you can still play football. You can still have everything you want."

He crosses the small room and drops to his knees at my feet. "I don't care about any of that as long as I have you."

But he's the one who just admitted how he's not thinking clearly today. He's reeling after the fight with Tori and Jace. He's devastated by the news that the only father he's ever known doesn't want him around. He's facing an uncertain future in a new place and now matters are even more complicated after last night's accident. Colt can still get back on track and he still has a lot to lose. I'm doing my best to make sure he doesn't lose everything.

Even if my own heart breaks into a million pieces.

"But you don't have me," I tell him and stand up. "You can't. It hurts now but you'll get over that. I know you will. I really do believe in you, Colt. No matter what else has happened, please remember that I have meant every word I've said to you."

He doesn't cry. He doesn't yell or argue. He just remains where he is on the floor with his head down, defeated.

"Till next time," I whisper and then, with my tears flowing freely and my heart gravely damaged, I leave him there.

Both of my parents are waiting when I arrive home. The air is tense, my mother's posture is stiff, and I know they were yelling at each other again while I was gone.

"It's done." I return my father's keys. "Colt and I are officially finished."

"Susanna." My mother tries to hug me but I move away because there's still critical business to discuss.

I glare at the man who has always been my hero and never will be again. "Now you keep up your end of the bargain."

He nods. "I always keep my word, Susie."

"And now you understand that I keep mine. You are my father and nothing can change that. But I'll never forgive you for this, Daddy. I despise you now. And I'll despise you always."

He blinks. His chin quivers. "That's fine," he says but he coughs on the words.

Instead of allowing my mother to comfort me, I retreat to my bedroom where I can cry alone.

15

COLT

On the day of Andrew Toledo's funeral, clouds move in and the temperature drops by fifteen degrees, almost like the heavens decided to have pity so that his mourners wouldn't suffer beneath the blazing sun.

Susanna confirmed that her father was raised Catholic, although he hadn't been to a church in many years. She had discussed his funeral wishes with him and knew he preferred a simple graveside ceremony. She has decided to deliver the eulogy herself.

Despite the clouds, rain is not expected. The former Arcana High football coach has kept his popularity over time and scores of his colleagues, friends and former high school football players have shown up to honor him. Many of them are known to me by name, or at least are familiar by sight, and a few are openly dabbing tears from their eyes.

My own eyes are dry. Because my feelings for my old coach are complex.

I remember all the praise and encouragement he went out of his way to heap on me when I wasn't really receiving praise and encouragement anywhere else.

And I remember how he discarded me with no notice when I

broke a cardinal rule and fell for his daughter. I don't blame him for being protective of Susanna. My track record wasn't exactly the greatest. But the things he said out loud were the worst things I'd ever thought about myself and that was a hell of a hit to take at age sixteen when my life was already going up in smoke.

Ten years ago, I would have spit on Drew Toledo's grave.

Now, however, I've grown up enough to understand that people are flawed. I had no difficulty giving him the forgiveness he craved. And I don't hate him, not even a little bit. I just won't be crying today.

My arm has remained around Susanna as the mourners all straggle across the grass. She looks to me and I squeeze her shoulder to signal that I'm all about her right now. She hasn't cried much either. She's had time to get used to the fact that this day was coming.

Susanna's mother, who used to be Kelly Toledo and is now Kelly Stratton, holds the arm of her current husband and stares down at the casket that has been painted the same shade of blue represented in the Arcana High colors.

Tori and Jace are standing right behind us. They've taken charge of handling the food for the funeral since everyone has been invited to Susanna's house after the ceremony. I think it's weird that people are in the mood to eat after burying someone, but I guess that's how it's always been done.

When the group has grown to a considerable size and people are starting to look around for clues as to when someone is going to get on with things, Susanna takes a deep breath and steps forward.

"Andrew Ricardo Toledo lived many different roles. He was a beloved football coach, a steadfast colleague, a loyal friend. To me, he was and always will be, my dad. And I will always be his Susie…"

She speaks clearly with her head up and doesn't once glance at the notecards in her hand. She keeps the eulogy short, acknowledging her mother and sharing a couple of sweet childhood anecdotes about her father. When she's finished speaking, she turns and Tori hands her a single red rose. Susanna bends down to gently leave the rose on her father's casket and whispers, "I love you, Daddy."

She raises her head and does not cry. Others in attendance sniff through their tears. People handle grief in all different ways.

Following a signal from Susanna, Paul's granddaughter Nina moves just beyond the line of mourners waiting to pay their respects. She begins singing *Amazing Grace*.

Susanna and her mother embrace for a long time. Jace pulls me aside to say that the catering truck is on its way to the house. He and Tori are offering to meet it there to start setting up. He has been very affected by the death of a man he always thought very highly of and his eyes are red. Drew Toledo, after all, was a big driving force behind Jace's meteoric rise to football greatness. Even with his father's persistence, Jace would have either left the sport or been content to sit on the sidelines as second string if not for the way he was aggressively pushed by Toledo to fill the quarterback gap.

Funny how things work out. Reminds me of what Susanna said moments ago; one person can mean many different things to a variety of people.

I've been holding Susanna's keys in my pocket and I hand them over to Jace so he can get inside the house.

Before leaving, he studies me. "You all right? You've been quiet."

Jace knows I'm no blabbermouth but I catch his meaning. He can tell when I've got a lot on my mind. The past. The present. *Susanna.* I'll be leaving again the day after tomorrow.

I nod to reassure my best friend. "I'll see you back at the house."

Susanna will be stuck here for a little while, receiving condolences from a bunch of people she hardly knows. She's far more gracious than I would be. I doubt I'd have the patience to accept endless handshakes and keep a pleasant look on my face just after losing someone I love. I hope I'm never put to that terrible test.

Once every couple of minutes, Susanna looks around and seems comforted to locate me waiting in the same place, a solid ten yards from everyone else with my hands in my pockets.

When she's heard the last person say, "So sorry about your father," she heads right over to me. We link hands and walk silently across the immaculate grass toward the lot where my truck is parked while I rummage through my brain in search of proper and meaningful words to say to her at a time like this.

"Good thing there was a break in the heat wave," I finally say when we're inside the truck. Not exactly meaningful.

She buckles her seatbelt. "Yes, it's surprisingly pleasant out."

I start the ignition, shift to drive, then switch back to park. "Your eulogy would have made him proud."

Susanna pats my knee. "Thank you for sticking around for the funeral."

I cover her hand with mine. "I want to be here."

She leans back into the seat cushion and rolls her head to the side so she can stare at me. The sadness in her eyes burns a hole right through my core. I lift my hand to gently stroke her face. She closes her eyes, quivers, kisses my palm.

And just like that, my dick jerks to life, demanding to know where the party is. Because I'm an animal and I suck.

I lean over to kiss her quickly. Then I face forward and begin driving back to her house before I do or say something gross.

We might be the last ones to arrive at Susanna's house. There are cars and lifted pickup trucks stacked up and down the street, some of them blocking driveways, which must thrill the neighbors. Jace and Tori have successfully worked with the caterers to get the food all laid out and when we enter through the front door there's a sea of people cramming stuffed mushrooms and cheese squares into their faces.

Susanna is the one everyone wants to talk to. I feel bad that I can do nothing to stem the tide of tearful people trying to corner her in order to share their memories.

"The years he coached me were the best of my life."

"No one had faith in me like Coach Toledo did."

"Every year he dressed as Santa at the faculty Christmas party."

Susanna keeps smiling, although I know she's got to be getting hungry. This morning she was so nervous about delivering the eulogy that she wouldn't eat any breakfast. At least I can fix her a plate since it might be awhile before she can extricate herself from the crowd.

On the way to the refreshment table, people keep saying hello to me and it's a real blast from the past because many of them I haven't seen in a decade. I spot Jace and Tori in the living room having a conversation with Mr. Salenger, who still teaches English at the high school. His wife used to teach in the science department and is now Principal Salenger.

"Colt Malene! How the hell have you been?" A hand claps on my shoulder and I'm face to face with a prematurely balding Micah Grant. I remember him best as the kid who needed his head shoved in a toilet after he spread around a lie that my sister touched his dick under the bleachers.

There's only so much phony bullshit I can tolerate so I knock his hand away and point beyond the living room. "Toilet's that way."

I don't wait around to hear what else he has to say because I don't give a fuck.

After filling a plate with fancy chicken wings, miscellaneous pastry things and wedges of colorful cheese, I carry it all over to Susanna. I have to cut through the line of people waiting to talk to her but that's all right.

Her face brightens when she sees me coming. "How did you know I was starving?"

"Let's take a seat." I steer her toward the only empty chair in sight. Jace rented a pile of white folding chairs like the ones used at his wedding a few months back and he set them up all over the place. It was a good move and I wouldn't have thought of it.

I appoint myself as Susanna's guard, making sure she gets a few minutes to eat in peace without being bothered. I know everyone here wants to talk about the loss of Coach Toledo, but this day has been toughest for Susanna and she's the one I care about.

Eventually, I need to quit glaring at people like a weirdo and allow them to have access to Susanna. She hugs me around the waist before returning to her hostess duties.

For a little while I watch my sister as she circulates throughout the room while keeping her hand on her slightly swollen belly. As a local realtor and Arcana resident, Tori is a lot more familiar with these people and has been making the rounds, pausing to speak to just about everyone.

Except Micah Grant. She walks right past him. Good. Fuck that guy.

Jace is slightly more social than I am, which isn't saying much, but I decide to join his conversation with Paul Elkins. They're discussing a contract for a piece of commercial property and they do their best to include me, but the effort is wasted. Anyway, it's stuffy in the house and I'm not contributing anything so I excuse myself.

On the way to the back door, I pass a giant photo of Coach Toledo that has been blown up to poster size and propped on a wooden easel. In the photo, he's wearing the school colors and he's grinning. I'm told the picture was taken about five minutes after Arcana High won the state championship the year Jace led the team. I wasn't at the game so I'll have to assume this story is accurate.

Not many people have figured out a path to the backyard, but among them is Susanna's mother. She sits on an ornate stone bench on the far side of the yard and in her hands is a framed photograph. She seems to be thoroughly absorbed in a moment of reflection and I have no intention of disturbing her, however she notices that I'm standing around and looks at me expectantly.

She's hugging the picture to her chest when I cross the distance between us. "It's so crowded in there. I needed some fresh air. I guess you had the same idea."

"Yeah, the stench of perfume and heavy aftershave is thick enough to choke on. I met your husband earlier."

"Oh yes? I suppose I shouldn't have left him alone to be subjected to awkward conversations with strangers."

"He seems nice."

"He is." She holds the picture frame away and I can now see it's the wedding photo that usually hangs on the living room wall. She gazes at the photo and sighs. "We were so young, so absurdly in love."

I stuff my hands into the pockets of the black suit I borrowed from Jace. "I'm really sorry for your loss."

She nods and the photo wilts in her hand. "I suppose this looks strange, the sight of me sitting out here with a wedding photo from my failed marriage."

"No." Not after seeing them together in his final days. I think they were married for about twenty years. That's not something you can just extinguish.

But I'm not sure she heard me respond. She's lost in thought and staring at a row of bottlebrush along the opposite wall.

"I heard it said once that every marriage is a country unto itself, with a unique history and customs. Marriage is hard. Keith is nothing like Drew. Keith and I are very compatible. Drew and I couldn't even agree on what to have for dinner. I did love him, even when times were bad, which was too often. Still, we should not have stayed together for so long."

She looks past me and smiles. I turn to see what's going on. She's caught a glimpse of Susanna inside the house.

"But I got her out of the deal," Kelly says, still watching her daughter, "so I'm not complaining."

My eyes are now glued to Susanna. Her black dress is simple yet does good work in capturing my interest thanks to the way it hugs her body. Her glasses are on, her hair is pulled back into a casual bun and her sexy librarian vibe is really doing things to me.

"She is something else," I say and then realize I'm openly drooling over Susanna right in front of her mother.

Luckily, Kelly doesn't seem to notice. "Thank you for being so good to her, Colt. I keep trying to find a way to tell you that I was always sorry about what happened when you were kids."

"It's in the past." I shrug. "It's over."

She touches the surface of the bench she's sitting on. "This was a Mother's Day gift from Drew the year we moved here. It used to sit in the shade of an apple tree and the apple tree is gone now but the bench remains." She stands up. "Will you do me a favor? Will you put this picture back where it belongs? Keith has been extraordinarily understanding but I don't want him to see me walking around with the photo of my first wedding."

I reach for the picture frame. "You got it."

A growl of distant thunder warns that rain might be on the way after all. Once Susanna's mother is out of sight, I return to the house via the side door. The kitchen is only occupied by two of the catering staff but they're too preoccupied to notice when I stick the wedding photo in a drawer where it will be safe until I can get it back on the wall without a huge audience.

An hour later, a light rain begins to fall and somehow people regard this as a cue to leave. Properly fed and satisfied that they have honored Coach Toledo, they exit in small packs. Before long, the only ones left are Jace and Tori. Even Susanna's mother and stepfather have left.

Jace and I fold up the chairs while Tori takes stock of the long refreshment table and begins consolidating the leftovers. There are *a lot* of leftovers.

"Maybe I went overboard," my sister muses and covers a tray of stuffed mushrooms with aluminum foil.

With a toothpick, I pick up something that looks like a tiny biscuit stuffed with pink paste. "What is this?"

"It's a crab puff. Eat it."

"I hate seafood."

Tori goes into bossy mode and props her hands on her hips. "Don't be a brat."

I pop the crab puff into my mouth. "You win. It's not bad."

Tori smirks. Then she nods to Susanna. "Rochelle wanted you to know that she and Carrie are thinking of you. They would have been here if Carrie didn't have a cold."

Susanna smiles. Her bun has come loose and her hair cascades over her shoulders. "I saw the flower arrangement she sent. It was kind of her. I'll be sure to send her a note." She tilts her head and her smile grows wistful as she gazes at Tori. "How are you feeling? I've been meaning to ask."

Tori pats her belly. "Ever since leaving the first semester behind I am fabulously pregnant with energy."

I decide to swipe another crab puff. Those suckers are addictive. "So if it's a boy, will you be naming him Jace Zielinski, The Fourth?"

"No!" shouts Jace, who has just finished stacking the rental chairs. He joins us and lovingly touches his wife's stomach. "Our child deserves his own name."

Growing up, Jace was always conflicted over his name. He wanted to honor his Polish immigrant grandfather, the original Jacek Zielinski, yet despised having the same name as his own deadbeat father.

Tori smiles up at him and they kiss and it's all very cute. When I look away, I discover that while I watched Tori and Jace, Susanna's eyes have been focused on me.

Tori covers another tray. "What should we do with all this food?"

"I can bring some it some of it across the street," Susanna says. "The Arefs have three growing boys and they have many friends so that house is always filled with hungry kids. Last week Namra joked that they'd probably eat the kitchen table if it tasted better."

"I'll do it." I grab the three nearest trays and head for the door.

The rain is still coming down in light sheets and I hope I'm not ruining Jace's suit by getting it wet. The house across the street is a one story brick home and Namra Aref answers the door. Since leaving the funeral, she's changed to a set of blue scrubs for her shift at the hospital. Sounds of incoherent adolescent shouting echoes from somewhere within and with a roll of her eyes she states that there is currently a very intense video game competition happening in the basement. She expects the participants will appreciate being fed.

"Tell Susanna she's in our thoughts."

"Will do," I promise and return to the other side of the street.

Jace and Tori don't stick around for much longer. My sister makes me swear to stop by before skipping town again and Jace snorts out a chuckle when I ask if I ought to get his suit dry cleaned.

"Nah, keep it for all I care. Last time I wore that thing was at some bullshit awards ceremony."

Tori raises an eyebrow. "Was that bullshit awards ceremony when you won the Heisman Trophy?"

He grins and balances half a dozen food trays on his right hand. "Something like that."

The two of them are stopping by the newly built Arcana Community Center with the remaining food. The senior citizens who congregate there on weekdays for checkers and socializing will no doubt get a kick out of a visit from Arcana's most famous son.

Once they are gone, it strikes me that for the very first time ever, Susanna and I are alone in her house. She's mystified when I visit the kitchen and return with her parents' wedding photo.

"Did someone try to take a souvenir?"

"Your mother." I carefully hang the picture on the wall where it belongs. "I found her outside alone with this in her hands. She didn't want anyone to see her with it."

Susanna comes closer to look at the picture, which is hung right at eye level. Drew Toledo is standing behind his new bride with his arms around her waist. They are both beaming with joy, likely assuming that their happiness would last forever.

Susanna looks away from the picture. She folds her arms over her body and scrunches up her face. "I don't like being here. Just feels weird right now."

I start massaging her shoulders, which are tight with tension. "We could go stay at Gloria's house tonight."

She relaxes at my touch. "Really?"

"Sure. It's empty and all the utilities are on."

She really likes this idea. "Give me five minutes. I'll change and pack a bag."

I don't have to pack a bag. I've only brought one bag with me, a tattered army surplus duffel that's lost its strap. But I'd rather get out of this suit so I perform a quick wardrobe change, instantly feeling more comfortable in a t-shirt and jeans. Susanna returns with an overnight bag after exchanging her dress for a pair of black shorts and a blue button down shirt that looks very familiar.

"You loaned it to me the night we went for ice cream and I kept forgetting to give it back to you." She zips her bag closed. "So I adopted it."

"Looks better on you anyway."

Susanna has already spent time at Gloria's house during my last

Arcana visit but she's no less charmed as she gives herself a tour of the living room.

"I love this picture," she says, pointing to one of Gloria and Jacek that must have been taken shortly after they were married. She moves on to admire some of the cross stitch projects decorating the walls in random places and pauses over a photo of an unsmiling teenage boy wearing a blue cap and gown.

"This is him, isn't it?" she says.

"Yup."

Jace and Tori brought much of Gloria's framed photo collection to their house. They did not, however, bring along any pictures of Jace's dad. The blue eyes of that other Jace Zielinksi glare out across the decades, like he's demanding to know who the hell we think we are to be staring at him.

Susanna touches my arm. "You never told Jace, did you? About what you saw and heard that day?"

"No."

"And you didn't tell Tori either?"

I shake my head. I'm about to inform Susanna that she's the only one I've ever told about the day I saw my mother fucking Jace's dad, but then I remember this isn't one hundred percent true. Someone else once received an earful about what I saw and heard.

That, however, is not a memory I'm willing to touch right now.

Susanna might be a mind reader. "And I'm aware that you don't talk to your mother at all."

"Nope." I was relieved as hell when she didn't show up to Tori's wedding.

Susanna senses that I'd rather abandon the topic and asks no more questions. Anyway, she wants to go out back and watch the sunset.

"It's raining," I remind her.

She takes my hand and pulls me toward the back door. "Then we'll watch the rain."

Susanna is easy to please. She's happy to drag a wicker sofa under the shallow patio roof and snuggle close as we watch the grey light fade. I should show her where to find real sunsets and scenery that would blow her mind if she'd be willing to travel, but Susanna, by her own definition, is a complete homebody. She's happy when I haul her out of her chair and into my lap.

"I like this house." She nuzzles my neck. "My house felt empty and unhappy even when I was a kid."

I slide my hand up her back. "Gloria's house was always my refuge. Mine and Tori's."

I glance at the beige slope of the neighboring rooftop, flash to a harrowing scene on the carpet, and immediately bury the images.

Susanna shifts in my lap. It's impossible *not* to get hard when she's this close. It's even more impossible when she kisses the side of my neck and runs her palm over my chest. The light is nearly gone. The rainclouds blot out the moon. No one can see us even through the back chain link fence.

My fingers locate the top button of the shirt she's wearing and flick it open. The next button follows. Her breath catches when I reach into her shirt to feel the firm, sweet shape of her tits over her bra. I love this part, how she dissolves in my arms and shudders out a moan.

The rest of these silly shirt buttons need to go. I can make that happen quickly and I do.

Susanna's getting really worked up in a hurry and she starts squirming around.

"Colt," she whispers, "no one has ever made me feel like you do. Not even close."

I want to hear more because I like the dirty side of her. "What does that mean?"

She's found my cock. She traces the rigid shape and now I'm the one hissing out a moan.

"It means you are the only one who's ever been able to make me come. It means when I want to make myself come, you're what I think about."

Well, *fuck me.*

That's got to be the hottest goddamn thing I ever heard.

But then she stands up, waits until I'm standing with her, and outdoes herself with a simple statement that's laced with erotic promises.

"Let's go to bed."

Hell, you won't hear me complaining about the fact that it's only eight p.m. To bed we will go.

Susanna giggles when I grab her up and carry her into the house. We make it as far as the hallway beyond the living room before I'm overcome by the need to get her clothes off. I've hardly touched her since I've been back in town because trying to get her naked in the middle of her father's last days seemed like a shitty move.

But tonight, she's the one who's asking so I'm ready to quit being a gentleman.

We crash into a wall while our mouths are locked together and her long legs tangle around my waist. Her shirt is wide open, then off, and her tits are mine, all fucking mine. I hold them in my hands over her lacy black bra and she pulls at my jeans. She wants the zipper down and I help that happen. My shirt isn't doing anyone any good and I get rid of that too. It's music, the way she groans and trembles when my hands go exploring. Next, I want her shorts gone and she lowers her legs to let me push them all the way down.

"I want to feel you," she breathes between hot kisses as she stands there in only her panties and bra. "All of you."

I shove my jeans all the way off and my cock tries to bust through my boxers when I press against her. "You'll feel me all right."

She's so ready she might rub one out right here in the hallway but I want better than that. I want to see her on her back and at my mercy.

The guest bedroom is only ten feet away. I slide my hands over her sexy, tight ass and lift her up. Susanna kisses my face, my neck, and a fleeting pang hits me when I remember that soon I'll have to leave her again.

But right now we're here and we're going to enjoy this.

The lights in the room are on and they will stay on. A jerk of my wrist unhooks her bra and the thing is history by the time we hit the bed. I always enjoy teasing her with my hand and my tongue but we're both in too much of a frenzy right now. We've been missing each other too badly and this, combined with the day's emotions, has lit a fuse. Together we're a powder keg on the verge of exploding.

I don't need to worry about her panties; she pulls them off before I get a chance to. She wants me on top of her and I'm glad to cooperate. Our next kiss is almost ferocious and then I suck her tits, which only gets her more riled up. She opens her legs and it's beyond a triumph to feel her naked and writhing underneath me, this brilliant girl who excites me to no end and has been the first and only owner of my heart.

"Don't stop," she begs. "Please don't stop this time."

I don't make a plan or think twice.

Susanna will have what she wants. I want it too, right here, tonight, just like this.

I'm free of my boxers one second and ready to slide into her the next. I'm trying to go slow, pausing when I hear a sharp gasp. Susanna's eyes are shut and I hope to god I'm not hurting her. She opens her legs wider and I feel her muscles relax as she gets used to me. She rocks her hips now. She urges me deeper inside.

I am unprepared for this, not just the fucking feel good mania of sex but the intensity of finally having what I've always desired more than anything. *Her.* The moment, so many years in the making, is consuming. I can think of nothing but the primal impulse steering every thrust.

I'm no longer moving slowly. She wanted everything and that's what I'm giving her.

Susanna stiffens and buries her face in my neck, crying out as she comes. The tremors hit her hard and it's too much for me. I'm going over the edge.

There should be a voice of reason shouting at me, and at her, but it doesn't matter because neither of us are listening.

Driving into her with one last powerful push sends me hurtling into oblivion. I'm coming so fucking hard I might snap in two.

Susanna whispers my name as I finish releasing inside of her and

I refuse to be fucking sorry at all. My heart still threatens to pound right out of my chest and I'm ready to collapse. I roll to my side rather than risk crushing her with my weight.

She curls closer to me and I kiss her gently before collecting her in my arms. I hope she feels how fast my heart thuds. I hope she knows it beats for her.

I might feel guilty tomorrow. And even more guilty the next day, when I'll be leaving.

But right now, as I hold Susanna in my arms and listen as she breathes a sigh of bliss, I'm nothing but happy.

16

SUSANNA

Colt wants to get takeout food from Dave's Tacos. "Come on, it's my last night in town."

Hearing the words spoken out loud is like having a boulder dropped on my head. I won't mention this. He'll only feel bad and I suspect he already feels bad. "Sounds good."

He grins at me and leans in for a kiss.

The sky remains cloudy but this has brought much needed relief from the heat. Colt suggests taking a quick hike in the barren area east of town. I'm not much of a hiker but this is a favorite pastime of his so I'll try.

Dave's has no drive thru so we need to go inside to order. Dave himself is nowhere in sight and the counter is being staffed by kids who likely attend Arcana High. I'm relieved to see that I don't know anyone here. People mean well, however I'm not in the mood to be approached for more, *"I'm so sorry about your wonderful father,"* sympathy.

As we wait for our order number to be called, Colt nods to an unoccupied table along the back wall. "Should we claim our table?"

"No, let's just eat in the truck."

"That table is where we met."

"I remember." It was a summer afternoon, not unlike this one. Today might even be the anniversary.

Colt hears something in my tone and looks at me funny.

"Number eighty-six," calls the girl behind the counter. She holds out a bag of food with a smile.

I'm actually not very hungry. I sip my soda while Colt polishes off three tacos and then drives out of town. He steers with one hand and reaches over to touch my bare knee. He's wearing sunglasses and his expression is unclear.

We've both been walking on eggshells all day. He was awake early and performing some minor maintenance on his truck while letting me sleep late. When I did finally wake up, groggy and still tired, he sweetly made me coffee and French toast. Later, we paid a visit to Jace and Tori. Now we are eating tacos and going for a hike.

And tomorrow, he'll be gone again. He's leaving early, before dawn.

We haven't talked about last night. I'm not sure I want to. I would probably cry or plead with him to stay and I shouldn't do either. We shared an impulsive but beautiful moment and I do not regret the fact that we made love.

I'm just having trouble hiding the fact that I'm *in* love. I'm completely, wildly, hopelessly in love with Colt Malene.

Colt veers off the road. "Jace and I used to spend a ton of time out here."

I get the feeling he's trying very hard to make conversation. The flat landscape is pocked with rocks and scrubby brush. Arcana sits in the rearview mirror. "I don't think I've ever been out here."

He glances at me. "Is that right?"

"Yes. Won't it be muddy after yesterday's rain?"

"Nah. It would take more than some drizzling to really soften this ground."

He clears his throat. I sip my soda. The truck rolls to a stop.

Colt yanks his keys out of the ignition and stares down at his lap as he tries to sort something out. "Susanna…"

I open the passenger door. "Let's go for a walk."

Colt is right. The ground is damp but not muddy. There's no one else out here except for the small creatures that shake the bushes and sometimes skitter away in a panic when we pass too close.

The land all looks the same to me but Colt leads the way to a large flat boulder. "This is where I often used to sit and contemplate the meaning of life," he jokes.

I hope this means we are taking a break. My stamina leaves a lot to be desired.

Colt doesn't join me immediately when I sit down. He gazes out at the horizon. He toys with his keys. He kicks at a loose rock. He takes a deep breath.

"I heard you talking to Tori about listing your dad's house."

"Paul Elkins confirmed that everything has been left to me. I never really loved that house and I don't think there's anything left for me in Arcana."

Not without you here.

I manage to choke off the words before they are heard. I choose new words. "It will take me some time to clean the place out and get it ready for sale. Tori says she'll help with the real estate listing."

He nods. "And after that?"

I shrug my shoulders. "I don't know. My college roommate lives in Phoenix. She sent me some job leads."

He manages to grin. "I could find my way to Phoenix."

I pull my knees up. I chew my lower lip.

Don't ask. Don't ask. DON'T ASK!!!

I ask anyway.

"How often?"

"What?"

"How often would you visit, Colt?"

He's thinking and his brow creases. "Don't know. As often as I could."

It's not a terrible thing to say and he's being truthful. Colt doesn't stay in one place and so Colt doesn't make promises. He can't know that I'm one breath away from crying.

Colt will think I'm getting all weepy because we finally had sex but that's not the reason at all. Since his return I've received a taste of how it would be to share my life with him. And yes, I want more. I'd jump at the chance, any chance, to be with him all the time. I would follow him anywhere.

But that offer was not made. And never will be.

I'm too transparent. Colt is too perceptive.

"You're pissed at me," he says with a sad sigh.

"No, I'm really not."

He drops to his knees, tips my chin up and looks into my eyes. "Yes, you are," he whispers and I hear the echo of another scene, the aftermath of our disastrous movie theater date.

Perhaps it's fortunate that I cried so much in recent months while my father was dying. Even as the dead weight of sadness threatens to engulf me, I have no tears left at this time.

I back away from him, ever so slightly. "I don't know what to say right now, Colt. I'm so grateful to you. Thank you for being here during this awful time."

"Grateful," he repeats, dropping his hand, plainly displeased by my choice of words.

"Yes, grateful."

"What's really on your mind, Susanna?"

"It doesn't matter."

"The hell it doesn't. When did you stop telling the truth?"

"I suppose a broken heart interferes with my honesty."

He flinches and his blue eyes cloud. "Am I breaking your heart?"

"No."

Yes.

He stands and walks a few paces away. He's looking at the horizon again.

My knees crack when I get to my feet. "It hurts to see you go. I'm sorry."

"Why are you sorry?"

"I'm trying not to be unfair. I always knew you'd be leaving again."

He whirls around and holds out his hands in a helpless way. "What do you want me to do, honey? Tell me."

I want him to stay. Or take me with him.

Colt is waiting for my answer.

For a second, I consider giving him the real one. But he is the one who said from the beginning that he could not give me forever. I have no right to demand it from him now.

"I want you to get some sleep tonight," I say. "You have a long drive and you're leaving early."

He just stares at me. He's still staring when I start walking. I walk right past him, keeping my head up as I march all the way to the truck in the distance. When I'm almost there I hear his footsteps behind me. He's moving fast now and he reaches the passenger door before I do. I climb in without a word.

I've left my overnight bag at Gloria's house. I don't want to go back there now to get it. Colt gives no sign that he understands when I tell him I'll get Tori to return the bag to me. I'll wait until Colt leaves and tell her I forgot it there.

The bulky shape of Arcana High passes by my window.

"You really want to be with me, baby?"

"Yes."

How easy that seemed back then, to confess the truth out loud. I had yet to learn some excruciating lessons.

Colt rolls to a stop in front of my house. It's a home that would probably be loved by a large family who could fill all the rooms with laughter but for now it's just a sad and empty place.

Colt's hand lands on my thigh. "Let's not leave things like this."

I know he's desperate for a smile, for a little piece of reassurance. My hand squeezes his, only for a second, before letting go.

"We'll see each other again."

He'll remember how he said that to me last time. It turned out to be true. I don't know if it's true again.

I was wrong to think that my tears were finished. Tears, it seems, are infinite and there are always more waiting. Before Colt becomes aware of this, I leap out of his truck and run to the front door. Only when I'm standing on the other side do I surrender to the pressure of those tears.

And Colt?

He sits outside in his truck for a long time without moving but eventually he does drive away.

17

SUSANNA, AGE 17

O n the ride to school, my father asks me if I've finished writing my valedictory speech yet.

"Almost." I haven't actually started yet.

He turns into the parking lot and it's possible he suspects the truth. "I'm sure it'll be great. Don't be nervous, Susie."

"I'm not."

Graduation is two weeks from tomorrow. Today is the last day of school and I've already taken the AP exams. I expect to score highly and earn college credit. After today, all I have left are two finals. Then there's Graduation and high school will be over.

My dad glances at me and swings the truck into his usual prime parking spot. "I was talking to Eddie Moldano and he extended an invite to come down this weekend and get first pick of the fleet of used cars that are coming his way. What do you think?"

"Thanks, but I won't really need a car on campus and I can keep borrowing Mom's until I leave in a few months."

He deflates a little. "Let me know if you change your mind."

"Will do." I hop out of the truck before he can add anything else.

Stretching across the front entrance of Arcana High is a colossal banner that says, in obnoxiously huge letters, TEXAS STATE FOOT-BALL CHAMPIONS. It's been hanging there since last fall and has begun to look a bit weathered around the edges. I bet if it falls or breaks it will be replaced immediately. The whole town has been on an adrenaline high ever since winning the title and the name Jace Zielinski is now spoken everywhere with awe.

The hallways of the school are filled with ecstatic teenagers signing yearbooks and taking selfies and making summer plans. A couple of them greet me by name and I nod without stopping to talk.

The only emotion I feel over finishing high school is relief that I will no longer need to walk these halls under the watchful eye of Coach Toledo. I've earned a full scholarship to Rice University and in three short months I'll be leaving Arcana behind.

Life at home is not spectacular. My parents have not grown friendlier to one another. The main difference since last summer is that the noisy arguing has stopped and been replaced with a glacial silence. The unhappiness within that house feels like a living thing, a malicious unseen family member that feeds off our misery.

The last day of school is a short one. When the final bell rings, a chorus of cheers erupt and people spill out in every direction. I won't be waiting around for my father to conclude his meeting with the director of the athletic department. They have big plans for next year, thanks to Jace.

"Susanna!" A blue and white yearbook is shoved in my face. "Sign my yearbook!"

The girl's name is Ashley and I hardly know her. She was briefly a member of the Student Council but stopped showing up to meetings after the first two weeks of school. I sign her book anyway.

Have a fantastic summer. Best wishes, Susanna Toledo.

Inspiring stuff.

She snatches her book back without examining what I've written and dashes in another direction. "Robert! Sign my yearbook!"

I left my own yearbook at home on my desk. It's been there since the day I received it and it's still empty of signatures.

I've made arrangements to borrow my mother's car this afternoon, however I'll need to walk home from school first. She did not ask me to explain my plans and I did not volunteer the information. I wouldn't have lied to her if she did ask.

The quickest route home is to cut through the athletic fields and then take the side streets. The cheerleaders are on the field right now. They are not in uniform and appear to be just spontaneously performing. I watch as they form an impressively complex pyramid. Brynna Graff climbs to the top and lifts her arms.

There's a smattering of applause from those who are hanging out on the bleachers.

However, the person who was probably the main intended audience doesn't applaud. He doesn't even look up.

Everything about his hunched posture and unfriendly expression indicates he'd rather just be left alone. Jace Zielinski appears to have no awareness of how many people are watching him. It's a safe bet that he doesn't care.

He's engrossed in a book called American Football Trivia. I wonder if he still dreams of being a writer, a fact his best friend shared with me more than once. Or maybe that's just one more thing that's changed over the last year.

"Jace."

His head snaps up and he seems neither happy or unhappy to see that I'm the one standing in front of him. At least twice a month my dad drags Jace to dinner at our house. He peppers Jace with cheerful questions and tries to push me in the middle, looking from one of us to the other with obvious hope, like he's saying, *'Sure, I took one boy away, Susie, but now I've brought you a new one!'*

I have no problem with Jace. He's just not Colt. And I'm not Tori. The two of us have nothing in common but shared despair over the people we lost.

He dog-ears a page in his book and sets it aside. "What's up, Susanna?"

"I'm taking a drive to Bredon this afternoon."

For a split second he flinches. "What the hell for?"

I swallow hard. "I want to see him."

"Why? He doesn't want to see you."

That hurts to hear. Even if it is true. "You're welcome to come along."

He snorts. That's his answer.

There are rumors about what happened between Jace and Tori. Some say he cheated on her with Brynna Graff. Others insist that Tori got pregnant by some Bredon guy and humiliated Jace. I don't believe any of those stories.

There have been rumors about me too. Me and Colt. People don't find those as interesting. I understand the reason. No one can really picture Colt Malene with the queen of the nerds.

I have not seen Colt since the night of the rivalry game between Bredon High and Arcana High last fall. Bredon High was way behind and Colt, sent into the game to rattle his former best friend, bulldozed right into Jace with a vicious and unnecessary tackle that ended with Colt being ejected from the game. Then Colt threw his helmet and charged off the field. He ignored me when I called his name. He recoiled when I tried to touch him.

Everyone at the game saw, including my father, although he's never mentioned it to me. Thanks to random gossip, I heard that Colt quit the Bredon High team entirely. I can't imagine Colt without football. The only person I've ever known who loves the sport as much as Colt is my father.

Jace has decided the conversation is over. He picks up his book and begins reading again.

I try one more time. "Jace, I know it's none of my business but maybe if you talked to her-"

"It *is* none of your business." He angrily turns a page. "Do what you want."

When I climb down from the bleachers, I see that the cheerleaders on the field have taken an interest in my conversation with Jace. Brynna elbows her friend and laughs in my direction. I flip her off without a care. After all, I no longer go to school here.

At home, my mother has a migraine and still asks no questions when I remind her that I'm borrowing her car. She waves beneath her therapeutic eye mask as she sprawls on the sofa and only asks if I could please pick up an iced latte with almond milk on my way home.

One thing I did not mention to Jace is that I obtained Colt's address from his grandmother. Gloria Zielinksi might have been curious about my intentions when I showed up on her doorstep yesterday but she did not pry and willingly gave me Colt and Tori's address.

Bredon is fifty miles away and I've never driven so far alone. The radio is tuned to a country music station and I leave it on even though I'm not a fan because it makes me think of Colt and the idyllic hours we spent together.

I still miss him so much. The pain is physical at times.

Bredon is not a place I've been to before but I've already mapped out the address. The closer I get, the faster my heart pounds. Colt's cell phone number has not been in service since last fall so I have no way to reach him. This trip might very well be for nothing. Bredon is larger than Arcana and I can't wander around town indefinitely in the hopes of running into him.

Colt's street looks ordinary, his house unremarkable. My hands shake as I ring the doorbell. I store them behind my back and wait.

And I wait.

And I ring the doorbell again.

It's mid afternoon on a weekday. I should not be surprised if no one is home. The thought of leaving a note skates through my mind and is just as quickly discarded. What would I say in the note? After all, Colt knows exactly where to find me if he wants to. The fact that I haven't even glimpsed his shadow since the night of the rivalry game is a big hint that Jace might be correct.

"He doesn't want to see you."

A hundred times, or maybe a thousand, I've reworked our last conversation in my head. In some versions we have sex and then run away together. In other versions I promise to keep seeing him in secret. But in every single one I tell him that I love him. Because I did.

I do. I love him and I should have said so, especially because I'm not sure he ever hears those words from anyone else.

After ten minutes of ringing the doorbell and standing around, I need to accept the fact that no one is at home. This was a foolish mission in the first place.

I trudge back to my mother's car and consider my options. I really don't have any. I could go search for Colt or Tori at Bredon High, but chances are that their last day of school was also today and they are not likely to be hanging around.

Frustrated tears haze my vision as I drive away from Colt's street. I'm not ready to leave Bredon so easily but I promised my mother I'd be back with her iced latte before dinner. The streets of Bredon offer no clues to a solution. I'm in a busier part of town now and a coffee shop up ahead offers refuge. Perhaps if I sit inside for a few minutes then inspiration will strike. Since no better ideas come to mind, I park the car in the first empty spot I see.

"Green tea please," I tell the boy behind the counter.

He looks to be in high school and he shyly smiles when he hands me the hot cup. I wonder if he knows Colt. Before I leave here, I'll ask.

I choose to sit on a black leather sofa overlooking the front windows. There's not an awful lot of sidewalk traffic right now. A woman passes by holding the hand of a small boy. A pair of preteen girls stare down into their phones without watching where they are going.

That's how they bump into Colt.

He looks the same from the outside, perhaps with a few more pounds of added muscle.

He sidesteps the middle schoolers with a roll of his eyes and the girl he's with, a pretty redhead, moves aside to let the younger girls pass. Then she catches up to Colt and slips her arm through his, hugging him. He brushes her off with annoyed scowl. She's hurt and her face scrunches up for a second. Then she lashes out with words that I can't hear but are plainly angry. He tosses her an indifferent glance and walks a few more steps before she catches him again.

They are now only a few feet from the open door of the coffee shop. They are close enough that I can hear their conversation from my seat.

The girl cuts him off and gets in his face. "I'm so tired of being treated like shit!"

Colt glares down at her. "I never promised you a goddamn thing."

She's on the verge of crying. "I thought that after last night…"

"We fucked. So what? Wasn't your first fuck and wasn't mine either. Hell, it wasn't my fiftieth fuck."

Now she does cry. "Why are you like this?"

But Colt is finished with her. He even laughs before he turns his back.

The girl is crushed. She drops her handbag on the sidewalk, sniffs, and texts something on her phone. She looks at Colt but he keeps moving away and doesn't even turn around. She sniffs again and walks in the opposite direction.

My cup of tea remains clenched between my hands as I try to process my shock.

The boy I saw and heard was indisputably Colt Malene.

And yet that brief, heartbreaking glimpse has shown that he is no longer the Colt Malene I knew.

He is now the Colt Malene who brutally severs ties with his best friend, behaves violently on the football field and publicly humiliates a girl who cares for him.

Still, I have an overpowering urge to chase after him, even though I am aware of what would happen next.

Colt would turn at the sound of my voice calling his name. He would glare at me with the same scorn he directed at the redhaired girl. Perhaps he would shout out a cutting insult. And then he would keep walking.

I rise and toss my cup of tea into a trash can. The sharp agony that came swiftly as I watched the scene on the sidewalk has already receded into a dull ache. When I reach the door and look to the right, the direction Colt went, he is no longer in sight.

At least now I know.

Now I know that I will need to find a way to live with the finality of losing the boy I loved.

Now I know that I did him no favors and likely made his life even more bleak.

Now I know that there will not be a next time, not for us.

18

COLT

This isn't cold by my standards, however my stiffening fingers didn't get the memo. I need to pause for a few minutes to flex some feeling into my skin before I do something clumsy, like bang a hammer down on my thumb. Been there, done that. Not pleasant.

"Hey Murph, I'm taking a break."

The man I'm talking to is busy unraveling one of the huge rolls of wool that will be stuffed behind the walls as additional insulation. In my experience, the wool works better than the artificial shit at keeping the draft out and in a place like this, where blizzards and fatal temperature drops are a thing, more insulation is always better.

Murphy doesn't hear me even after I repeat myself. The third guy working with us today is a kid named Joshua who grew up down in Navajo country and plans to join the Marines next year. He's got headphones on but he looks up and nods with a smile when I motion that I'm stepping out for a few minutes.

The best place to warm up is inside my truck. Thanks to a hard frost last night, the ground beneath my boots is rock solid. Winter comes early around here and it's not at all unusual to get clobbered by a thick blanket of snow in the month of October. The forecast expects the skies to stay dry for the next ten days but forecasts have been wrong before. I hope we do get a break because snow or not, this project needs to get wrapped up before the real hard core weather hits.

My truck engine has to be coaxed to life but sounds smooth once it fires up. A Sherpa-lined hoodie over a flannel layer is warm enough but I should have remembered to pack my gloves today instead of leaving them behind at the cabin. Hot air blasts through the vent and I hold my hands out like I'm warming them in front of a campfire.

It doesn't take long for the sting to disappear as the blood in my fingers begins to freely circulate. This should be the last week that we'll be working in unheated conditions. The electricity is expected to be turned on next Wednesday.

Since I'm out here anyway, I decide I may as well eat my lunch. Though the thermos of canned lukewarm minestrone isn't exactly a gourmet meal of dreams, I'm too hungry to care and pour it all down my throat within a minute. Then I wipe my mouth and stare out the window. I've grown kind of sorry to see the new structures we've built cutting into what used to be an unspoiled section of ground, which is kind of a stupid way for a man to feel when he builds homes for a living.

I have no reason to keep sitting in my truck at this point. My hands are no longer stiff and I'm finished eating. Yet I pull my phone out of the glove box. I do this even though there's no reception out here just yet. I don't need to connect. I just want to look a photo.

Susanna smiles at me from a tiny screen and my chest tightens. This is the only photo I have of her, taken at my little sister's insistence, and if it were a physical copy it would be worn and creased by now because I stare at it all the time. She's standing in the living room of her house, having just pulled on the Books Do It Better shirt I impulsively picked up at the mall. Her head is tilted slightly to the side, her arms are crossed, and her smile is self-conscious, clearly not a girl who enjoys posing for the camera. I'm the one who snapped the photo so I know for sure she's looking right at me and if I stare for long enough I can be fooled into the sense that I'm still there, that only eight feet separates us instead of endless miles. Meanwhile, my dick stirs, but that always happens if I think about Susanna too much. The hunger for her is automatic and I can't stop it so I don't even try.

We haven't talked much in the three months since I left. There are days when I'll spend hours trying to think up a good conversation opener. Unfortunately, I can only say so much about building walls and staring at trees. Aside from the guys on the crew, I interact with no one. I wait until I'm on my last can of soup before visiting the market in town and I don't socialize at all. In another time, I probably would have retreated completely and become a long-bearded mountain hermit who frightens people when I stray too close to civilization.

Instead, I still keep one foot in the real world. That's been partially thanks to Tori and Jace but now there's an inner conflict raging that has nothing to do with them. Physically, I'm right here beside the Judith River on the cusp of winter. My head and my heart, however, remain back in Texas with Susanna.

She's not the one who told me she was staying in town. I heard it from Tori that Susanna had decided not to sell her dad's house and had taken a job teaching science at the high school. She had never mentioned any of this as a possibility. When I called Susanna to ask her about it, she simply said, *"Yes, that's true,"* in a distracted way and mumbled that she had things to do but to let her know when I planned to visit Arcana gain. We don't have a great track record when it comes to chatting on the phone but that was weird and abrupt even for her. Our last conversation lasted for less than five minutes and happened two weeks ago. She sighed when I said I'd be delayed at least a few more weeks because this job was running longer.

If Susanna misses me, she doesn't say so.

Maybe I should say it first.

I've always hesitated because I don't even know what we are to each other. Our last night in Arcana didn't end well.

At the same time, if she's found someone else, then she's unwilling to admit that either.

My fist punches the steering wheel before I can think twice. It's the thought of Susanna in some other guy's arms that taps into a savage surge of jealousy. I'm pretty sure such a sight would stop my heart from beating.

The day I'm finished here I'm heading back to Arcana. Susanna and I need to talk, *really* talk.

I switch the engine off. Nothing will get finished or solved by way of me sitting behind the wheel and brooding. I spend far too many hours doing that in my free time.

The afternoon passes quickly because I keep busy. We finish early since the light disappears quickly nowadays. I tell Murphy and Joshua to take off. I'll stick around a few extra minutes and lock up. One by one, I hear other vehicle engines fire to life outside as the rest of the crew heads to whatever temporary homes they've rented.

Although I've got an LED lantern burning, every passing minute darkens the sky another notch and I move quickly, double checking to ensure that everything is locked down and no obvious safety hazards are in sight. This will be a nice place when finished. Some of the luxury items like a pot filler faucet are kind of over the top for my taste but whoever gets to live here should appreciate their luck.

I was three months shy of my eighteenth birthday when I left home, confident that no one would chase me. No one did. All I had was a plastic bag of clothes, a dilapidated pickup I'd bought for peanuts and an unconfirmed job offer I'd applied for online to work construction in North Dakota. I'd lied about my age, figuring I could fake it once I got there. Lucky for me, my new employers were so hard up for labor they didn't care and soon enough I was legal. Since then, I haven't spent more than six months at a time in the same location. I own no furniture, not even a couch, and that is entirely by choice.

Susanna was amazed when I told her I can fit everything I own into the bed of a pickup truck. She left a storage unit full of stuff in San Antonio. I wonder if she plans to go get it now that she's decided to stay in Arcana. Susanna likes to be surrounded by comforts. She likes to be at home in a cushy chair with a book and a blanket. She likes to be in an unchanging home. She's puzzled by the way I live.

"Sounds like we don't have much in common."

"That's not exactly a newsflash, Susanna. We never had anything in common."

One more check of the locks and me and my LED lantern are out of here. My stomach growls as I'm climbing into the truck. There's nothing back at the cabin but a can of pinto beans and half a sleeve of crackers. Now is as good a time as any to drive to town and hit a store. While I'm there I can check my messages. Who knows, maybe some spiritual piece of the universe whispered to Susanna that I was hoping to hear from her today.

I wait until I'm parked in front of a homely local grocery store that doesn't have a great selection but does offer the basics. Then I haul out my phone and see that there are two new contact attempts waiting, both from Jace. One is a text and one is a voicemail. Both say the same thing.

CALL ME ASAP!

Feeling both uneasy and relieved that my phone is properly charged for once, I press a button and wait for the call to go through. He answers on the second ring. He sounds out of breath.

"Hold on," he says in a voice low enough to qualify as a whisper. "Got to go outside."

I can hear a door open and shut and then another door open and shut.

Finally, he says, "Okay, all clear."

"Clear from what?"

"Didn't want Tori to know I'd called you."

"Why the hell not?"

He breathes noisily and avoids the question. He asks one of his own instead. "Weren't you supposed to back in town by now?"

"I was planning on it but thanks to a block of bad weather the work was delayed. Now we won't be finishing until the third week in November."

Jace pauses and I hear what sounds like pacing footsteps. Whatever he wants to say is not coming easy. "Is there any way you can wrap things up sooner and get back here?"

"Why?" Fear zooms through me. "What's going on with Tori?"

"Nothing," he says quickly. "Tori's fine. The reason I have to keep quiet is because she'd be pissed at me if she knew I was making this call."

"I don't get it."

He sighs. "You need to trust me, Colt. Come home."

"Jace, enough of the mystery. If you and Tori are fine, then why the hell do I need to drop everything and run back to Texas?"

"Because of Susanna."

The hair on the back of my neck stands up.

"What about Susanna?"

Jace's sense of honor won't allow him to tell me everything that he's already sworn to keep secret.

But I manage to fill in some of the blanks anyway.

And I can guess the rest.

19

SUSANNA

I waited to take a test.

I waited even though my biological schedule has always been reliable and I could already feel the changes in my body.

Exactly one month after Colt's last day in town, I stood barefoot in the bathroom, arms crossed, shivering with nerves and watching an unmistakable positive sign appear on the pregnancy test sitting on the sink vanity. Immediately I took another one, just in case. The result was the same.

For a few seconds, the wave of joy was untouchable. I've always wanted kids and never believed I'd find someone I wanted to have them with.

Now I'm not only having a baby but I'm having *Colt's* baby.

Our baby.

And even though we never planned for it, I want this baby more than anything.

My first instinct was to grab my phone and call him even though I had not sorted out what I would say. Colt didn't answer, which should have been unsurprising given the fact that he works in such a remote area and cell phone service is spotty at best.

Two days later, he finally called me back, apologizing for the fact he didn't know I'd called. By then I had lost my nerve. I couldn't bring myself to casually blurt out pregnancy news. Anyway, what could he do from so far away? Colt isn't even reachable most of the time.

Weeks went by and I kept planning to tell him tomorrow or the next day or maybe the week after that. I even typed out long letters on my laptop, though I deleted the contents without sending them. I considered firing off an **I'M PREGNANT** text in order to get the whole thing over with.

Weeks stretched into months and I am now in my second trimester and Colt still doesn't know. The truth is, I'm afraid to tell him. I can't predict what Colt Malene will say or do when he finds out I'm pregnant with his child.

"You'll want forever. And I can't give you forever."

Neither of us said a word about using protection when we had sex. That's as much his fault as it is mine. Still, I'm worried he'll think I was trying to trap him. At the time, I was not considering the possibility of getting pregnant. I'd buried my father that day and I was grieving and emotional and I wanted Colt so very much. I *needed* him.

I knew if I told him about the baby he would feel obligated to come right home immediately. He was supposed to back already. He planned to visit Arcana when his current job was finished. The delays extending the project aren't his fault and he has no idea that I'm waiting on pins and needles as my belly grows by the day.

Meanwhile, my vague plans to move out of state took an abrupt U-turn the day I watched two pregnancy tests turn positive. I told Tori I was not going to sell my father's house after all. She was not even slightly sorry to lose the listing. She was thrilled to hear that I wanted to remain in town and I felt guilty for failing to tell her the reason why. I'm carrying her brother's baby. And I know Arcana is the place he already has good reason to return to. Besides, I didn't know where else to go. Arcana is my hometown too. I can think of no better place to raise a child.

Local job prospects in my field are somewhere between flimsy and nonexistent and I wasn't willing to commute far. When I heard the high school was in dire need of a temporary chemistry teacher until a permanent replacement could be found, I called the current principal, Ada Salenger, and asked to be considered. Once a science teacher herself, she was overjoyed that her former student wished to follow in her footsteps. She assisted me in obtaining an emergency teaching certification and within days I found myself standing in front of a class of rambunctious teenagers with the fear I'd bitten off more than I could chew.

To my shock, I've learned that I enjoy teaching. Some of the kids are uncooperative and hostile but others are eager and enthusiastic. The rest fall somewhere in between. There is much more to the job than showing up during school hours. There are lessons to plan and tests to grade and I always offer extra help after school to anyone who wants it. The work has kept me very busy and leaves me with little time to dwell on the looming inevitable reunion with Colt.

"Bye, Ms. Toledo!" Two girls wave at me from the stairwell as I pass through the lobby. They are both in my second period class.

I wave back to my students. Then I pivot and find myself staring at a massive trophy display case. Protected by glass, it's a collage of Arcana High's sporting accomplishments. Naturally, Jace Zielinski is the highlight. There are a variety of photos of him in uniform among his teammates. Most of those photos feature the team that won the state championship, but my eyes are fixated on one that must have been taken his sophomore year. The reason I know this is because he's standing beside his best friend. They are on the sidelines and judging by the crowd in the bleachers, a game must have been in progress. Colt is pointing at the field and saying something to Jace, who honestly looks a little bored. It was the pinnacle of Colt's football days, and only the dawn of Jace's. I would have been sitting somewhere in those bleachers, always watching the same boy and daydreaming that someday he might be mine.

My father is also mentioned in the shrine to Arcana High's athletic dominance. The closeup photo taken the day Arcana High won State is a smaller version of the one displayed at my father's funeral. Beneath it is a shiny new plaque showing the years of his birth and death, along with an acknowledgement of his contribution to the football program.

One of the most difficult things to get used to is just being here in this building without him. I wonder what he would think if he could see me now, teaching at my old high school and hiding the growing evidence of my pregnancy with oversized shirts. He might have been disappointed. After all, I'm not exactly doing much worth bragging about. However, I believe he also would have been overjoyed by the thought of becoming a grandfather. Yes, I know this is true.

The beep of a reminder on my phone jars me back to the present moment. I have an appointment to get to.

There is no obstetrician in town. Even if there was, I probably still would have selected one twenty miles away. I'm not real keen on running into people I know at the doctor's office.

I'm glad when there is no traffic on the freeway because by the time I reach the silvery maze of new medical buildings located half a mile from the Plainsfield Mall, I need to pee like crazy.

"Of course," says the receptionist when I plead for access to the restroom. She motions that I should just go right through the door separating the waiting room from the rest of the place.

I hardly have time to peel down the elastic band of my leggings before Niagara Falls comes cascading out. A much more comfortable minute later, I'm drying my hands and I catch my reflection in the mirror over the sink. I straighten my back and run my hands over the mound beneath a flowing shirt that was intentionally purchased two sizes too large. I'm starting to show. Very soon I will need real maternity clothes. Perhaps I should stop at the mall since I'm already nearby. I smile down at the soft curve of my belly.

"Oh, can you sign in?" The girl at the reception counter hands me the clipboard just as I'm about to return to the waiting room. She's young and she gives me a guilty look. "I was supposed to remind you before you used the restroom that we'll be needing to collect a urinary sample at your appointment."

"No worries." I sign in hastily and reassure her. "I'm sure I'll have more to offer in ten minutes."

She laughs.

Then I return to the waiting room and realize I've miscalculated.
This, evidently, is also the office of Tori's doctor.

There they sit, Tori and Jace, and they are staring right at me with
identical expressions of astonishment.

Tori recovers first. "Susanna, hi." She smiles.

I'm not as talented when it comes to disguising my shock. I hold
my tote sized handbag in front of my stomach and try to look casual
as I take a seat right across from them. "Hello. How are you? How
nice, running into you here. You must be here to see the doctor."

Jace looks at me as if I've sprouted a third arm from my forehead.
Tori nudges him. He raises an eyebrow.

Tori clears her throat. "Yes, we always see Dr. Chavez."

She glances at her husband, who has not shifted his baffled gaze.
He looks carefully at my face and then pointedly looks at my lap,
which is still being shielded by my mercifully large handbag.

Tori runs a hand over her own stomach, which has grown considerably since the last time I saw her over a month ago. I've been
avoiding her. For reasons which I fear are rapidly becoming obvious.

"I'm just here for my annual checkup," I blurt out.

"Oh." Tori nods.

Jace frowns.

It's a plausible explanation. They might even believe me.

"Have you talked to Colt lately?" Jace asks. There's a rather arctic
chill in his tone.

"Just about two weeks ago." I try to sound nonchalant. "Only for a
few minutes."

Tori tosses her husband a warning look. They share a silent
conversation. Jace leans back in his chair and turns his head to brood
over a rack of magazines.

"We need to have lunch soon," Tori suggests. "Or how about if
you come over one night for dinner? I'd like to hear all the latest
Arcana High gossip."

I've turned down at least half a dozen invitations from Tori
already, usually mumbling some excuse about being busy with

teaching chores. Each time I felt horribly guilty and worried I had hurt her feelings. Plus, I would have loved to have a friend to talk to. I've been so alone. Even my mother has no idea about the baby.

I'm saved from responding when Tori's name is called for her appointment. She shoots me a curious but sympathetic look before easing up out of her chair.

"I'll call you," she promises and follows the nurse with Jace on her heels.

Before stepping through the doorway, he peers at me over his shoulder. There's unmistakable suspicion in his dark eyes but he says nothing.

I drop my bag from my lap and exhale. What a complete fool I've been, believing I could keep secrets in small town Arcana. Even if I hadn't run into Tori and Jace, time is running out. Two days ago, I overheard a group of senior girls wondering out loud if I was pregnant or cursed with abysmal fashion sense. The opinion was split.

"Susanna?"

I rise and follow the nurse. She checks my weight, my blood pressure, asks if I might produce a urine sample, but I'm too rattled for now and I shake my head. Dr. Mia Jackson doesn't keep me waiting long. She asks the perfunctory questions, measures my belly and then we get to the exciting part of listening to the heartbeat. I get choked up every time I hear it.

"Strong and steady," Dr. Jackson observes and then helps me sit up on the exam table. "Your weight and measurements are right on target. Do you have any questions, Susanna?"

How do I break the news to a man who won't stay in one place for longer than a season that I'm having his baby?

"No."

She rolls off her latex gloves. "The front desk will make your next appointment for four weeks from now. As always, call if you need anything."

"Thank you, Doctor."

Tori and Jace are not seen or heard as I tiptoe past the other exam rooms. That's a small relief but I'm in a hurry to get out of here now in case they are still with their doctor. I breeze right past the reception desk with a promise to call tomorrow to book my next appointment and then scuttle out the door.

I'm about to turn the corner to catch the elevator when Jace's voice stops me cold.

"Come on, Tori. This is more than just a rumor around town now. She's obviously pregnant."

"Yes, and it's just as obvious that she doesn't want to talk about it yet."

Two more steps and they would have seen me but I right now I'm hidden from view as long as I stay close to the wall.

"You know it's Colt's," Jace says. "He was here in July and they were together."

She sighs. "Maybe he knows."

"Seriously? There's no fucking way he knows."

"Look, we can't interfere. If they ask us for advice that's one thing but they aren't asking and we don't even know for sure what happened between them."

"Uh, they had sex. Now she's having his baby while he's hell and gone in the middle of nowhere with no clue."

"Jace, you can't say anything. Things are complicated between them. They need to sort it out together."

He mutters something unintelligible.

"Promise me," Tori insists. "She'll tell him in her own time."

He grunts. "She'd better hurry. People are already talking."

"Jace, please. Promise you won't tell him."

"Fine. I promise I won't tell him directly."

The ding of the elevator summons them and I can't hear what's said next. I lean against the wall and decide to wait right here until I'm sure they've had enough time to get to the parking lot and drive off. On this appointment I recorded the sound of the baby's heartbeat on my phone. I listen to it now and wonder how much fiercer this overpowering surge of love and tenderness will become by the time my child is born.

I'm very grateful to Tori for attempting discretion on my behalf, but Jace is right.

Too many weeks have gone by and Colt must be told. I can't wait until next month to see if he shows up or not. On the weekends he usually drives to a nearby town to gas up his truck and pick up supplies. I'll message him on Friday with a request to call me when he's in cell phone range.

The time has come for him to hear that like it or not, he's going to be a father.

20

COLT

Under normal circumstances I wouldn't attempt to drive straight through without stopping, but these aren't normal circumstances.

Following my phone call with Jace, I had to call around in search of someone with a solid set of skills who could take my spot on the crew immediately. As much as I need to get back to Arcana, I can't leave Jimmy and the rest of the guys in a lurch. Sweetening the offer with a pot of cash shortened the process and my first choice was a man I'd worked with many times before who'd just finished up one job and was eager for the opportunity to earn some extra money to give his kids a fabulous Christmas. Once that was done, I sped back to the cabin to pack, forced myself to get a few hours of restless sleep and left hours before the sun was planning to rise. Since then, I've only stopped when I had to use the toilet or find something to eat. The one time I pulled into a truck stop with the intention of taking a nap I was way too restless to even keep my eyes shut.

Jace gave his word. He won't raise the alarm that I'm on my way. In fact, I told him to forget we'd talked. I know he hates keeping Tori in the dark so the less information he has the better. This is between me and Susanna.

By the time I hit the Texas state line, I'm really starting to feel like I've been smacked by a bear but I'm too close to take a break now. I barrel into Arcana shortly after one in the afternoon and I'm about to make a turn in the direction of Susanna's house when I realize she's probably not there. It's Friday, a school day. She'll be at the high school.

Some fucker leans on his horn when I make an abrupt U-turn. I hold up my hand as an apology because I don't want to get into it with some random dick over bullshit.

The Arcana High School parking lot is packed and my dumpy pickup is right at home amongst all the other dumpy pickups that belong to the student body. I don't have the patience to search high and low for an empty spot to open up, so I just park in front of the main entrance and jump out.

It's not until I charge through the double entrance doors that I'm hit with a bizarrely dizzy feeling. I think some people call that déjà vu. Or I could just be ready to pass out after a day and a half on the road. Who the hell knows.

"Excuse me. EXCUSE ME!"

In any case, some balding twerp wearing a tie is now chasing me across the lobby.

"SIR!" He clamps a skinny hand on my arm, which is a bad idea, and he has one volume; screaming. "WHAT IS YOUR BUSINESS HERE, SIR?"

"Just looking for someone." I shake him off with ease and break for the stairs.

"CODE FIVE!" He runs away, arms flailing. "WE HAVE A CODE FIVE!"

Not sure what that is, but I think it might be me.

FUCK.

This adventure has not been well thought out. I'm trespassing in a public high school and I don't have the first idea where to find Susanna's classroom. Dimly, I remember that the science labs are on the second floor. I jog up there and stare down a long corridor with endless closed doors. Susanna must be behind one of them.

Since I'm probably already in deep shit, I may as well keep shoveling.

"SUSANNA! SUSANNA, WHERE ARE YOU?"

A door opens, then promptly slams shut. An overhead loudspeaker crackles.

"All students please remain in your classrooms until further notice."

Meanwhile, I'm pausing at each door and peering into the square window. Startled faces look back at me but none of them are the one I'm looking for. In fact, none of them are familiar at all.

Except one.

Mr. Salenger was my English teacher a million years ago and we spoke at Coach Toledo's funeral. His eyes bug out when he recognizes me and he rushes into the hallway.

"Colt, what in heaven's name are you doing?"

"I need to find Susanna Toledo."

He blinks. "This is a school. You can't just walk in here off the street and wander around, yelling your head off."

"Sorry. SUSANNA!"

He hisses and shoves me into his classroom. Then he grabs the phone hanging on the wall beside the door. He must be calling his wife in the principal's office because he's saying that no, there's no Code Five and everything is just fine. Jace Zielinski's best friend just wanted to stop by to pay his old school a visit. No harm done. He gives me a look that says I'd better go along with his story and I understand he's dropping Jace's name on purpose to defuse the situation. The room is full of kids and their ears have now perked up over the mention of the town hero.

"Are you really Jace Zielinski's best friend?"

"Shit, he must be here too!"

"I asked him for his autograph at the gas station last week and he totally gave it to me."

Mr. Salenger motions to the class to settle down. "All right, keep working on your essays for *The Outsiders*. I'll be right back." He beckons that I ought to follow him out the door.

"Tell Jace I said hi," begs some boy from the back row.

"Sure," I promise the unknown kid on my way out.

I shut the door behind me.

And there she is.

Susanna Toledo is standing roughly ten feet away, wearing a white lab coat with her hair pulled back into her typical old school ponytail. She couldn't possibly look more shocked if cats decided to take over planet earth today.

"Colt!"

I nod at her. "Hey, what's up?"

Mr. Salenger walks briskly toward the stairs. "Come on, Colt. Time to leave the building."

Susanna seems like she may be a little angry. She stalks past me with a glare and trails Mr. Salenger. I know he's got a first name but I can't remember it right now so he gets to remain Mr. Salenger.

Since I'm not going to stand around in the hallway by myself, I shadow them. We march down the stairs and to the door, which Mr. Salenger is kind enough to hold open.

"Next time you want to visit," he says to me, "stop in at the office and obtain a visitor's badge."

"No problem." I shake his hand. "Thanks for rescuing my ass from the fire."

He chuckles and leaves us alone. Susanna and I stare at each other on the front step of Arcana High.

Susanna's cheeks are pink. She holds her lab coat closed so I can't get much of a look at her body. "I didn't know you were coming," she says.

"That's cool. I didn't know you were pregnant."

Her shoulders sag. "Jace and Tori told you that?"

"No."

She takes a deep breath and looks around. "I can't do this here."

"All right. Let's go have this fight in the parking lot."

"Colt, I need to get back to my classroom. I have classes to teach. The last bell won't be for another two hours."

"Fine." I twirl my keys around my finger. "I'll be waiting at Gloria's house. You know where it is. Come over when you finish with your classes or whatever."

She starts to speak, clamps her mouth shut, then dashes back into the building.

I get in my truck and drive over to Gloria's house. Maybe we should all start referring to it as something other than 'Gloria's house' but that will be a tough habit to break. I don't believe in ghosts or spirits or any such shit but stepping inside this house has a calming impact on my soul. I bring one bag inside and leave the rest of my garbage in my truck for now.

All the anxious miles on the road have caught up to me and I'm about to collapse. The couch offers a perfect location to do just that. When I sit down, I notice that the front door remains open but that's fine. I want to be able to hear the second Susanna arrives. My keys are still in my hand and I automatically feel for the charm hanging from the split ring. Then I relax into the couch, close my eyes and feel the room recede. I'm sound asleep when the sound of my name reaches into oblivion and pries my eyes open.

Susanna has ditched her white lab coat and she stands in the center of the living room, rubbing her arms as if she's cold, which she can't be because it's not cold at all.

"The door was open," she explains.

I'm trying really hard to wake up properly. This conversation will be important, perhaps the most important one I've ever had. Susanna watches me mutely as I get to my feet.

I spent the whole drive here trying to understand what the hell she's doing. She had to know about the pregnancy for a while and I've only been in Montana, not Mars. Yet she never dropped the slightest clue. The Susanna I once knew was always so up front about what she was thinking. But now I'm stuck travelling fourteen hundred miles in order to drag the truth out of her.

Susanna seems to read my mind. "I'm sorry."

I rub the remnants of sleep out of my eyes and take a long look at her. She starts to move her arms over her belly, like she's trying to hide, but then lets them fall to her sides.

"So I guess congratulations are in order," I say and then instantly wish I hadn't started with sarcasm.

She sighs. "How did you know?"

"Jace said I needed to get home and I figured out why. You should have told me, Susanna."

"I knew you'd come back to town at some point. I wanted to tell you to your face."

I close the distance between us. "Well, here's my face."

She tips her chin up and looks me in the eye. "I'm pregnant, Colt."

"I can see that. When did you find out?"

"The end of August."

"It's almost Halloween for fuck's sake."

"And you were supposed to be back here before now."

"If you'd given me any idea that you were pregnant with my kid then I *would* have been back here. How do you not know that?"

Susanna takes a step back, becomes agitated. "Things get weird when we're apart. We have trouble communicating about anything important. We have trouble talking about anything at all. And I was afraid you'd wonder if I'd done it on purpose, that I seduced you and got pregnant intentionally."

Seduced. That's a good one. That's so fucking hilarious that I start laughing out loud and can't stop.

She fumes. "There's absolutely nothing funny about this."

"Sure there is. You think I'm too dense to understand how babies are made. I don't remember what kind of grade I got in biology but trust me, I've figured out the basics since then."

"We didn't use a condom!"

"Yeah, I remember. I also remember that neither one of us seemed to care that we had no condom. And let me add that you weren't using my dick in any way that I didn't approve of."

"Point taken. Now what?"

"I don't know. Why don't you start by telling me what you want? You've had a couple of months to think about it."

Her expression shutters. "How am I supposed to answer that?"

"The truth would be nice. What do you *want*, Susanna?"

Her lip trembles and she looks down. "I know you didn't ask for this."

"Oh. Should I just leave then?"

Her head snaps up. "I can't stop you."

I throw my arms up in frustration. "What the fuck, Susanna? Why won't you tell me how you feel when it actually fucking matters? Here I am and you won't even say if you want me to stay or go. What would have happened if I hadn't visited Arcana again? Would you have just mailed me a birth announcement?"

"No! You don't exactly have a regular mailing address."

"Look at me!" I shout and she flinches. "We can stand here and trade insults all day or you can just spit out what it is you want from me."

"I WANT YOU TO STAY!" She bursts into tears. "I want you to stay and I want to be with you. But I know I have no right to ask you for anything and so I won't."

"No right?" I'm so stunned that I nearly fall over. "Jesus, you think you have *no right* to ask me to stay?"

She's really crying now and tries to cover her face with her hand. Gently, I pull her hand away. She shakes her head but she's not getting away. I frame her face in my hands and stare deep into her eyes so she understands this is for real.

"Baby, you're the only one who has the right to ask me to stay. You should be asking me for *everything*. And I've got some news; I'm staying whether you want me here or not. You know why? Because my kid's never going to feel unwanted, not like I felt." I tip my head down and press my lips to her forehead. "You're stuck with me, Susanna, so get used to it."

She breaks down and throws her arms around my neck. "I love you, Colt."

Something eternal happens to me when she says this. I hold her close, folding her tenderly in the safety of my arms.

"I love you too."

She turns her head and our mouths collide. We kiss frantically, even as her cheeks remain damp with tears while I'm left reeling in the best way after hearing the words I've always wanted to hear from her.

This cascade of emotion doesn't mean I'm not hard. I am hard as a motherfucker.

She moans into my mouth and rolls my flannel shirt from my shoulders. I have a t-shirt on underneath and she feverishly pulls it up. I reach behind me and haul the stupid thing over my head. Next my hands dive under her shirt, hungry to feel more skin, but I pause over the unmistakable evidence of how her body is already different. The hard bump of her belly is noticeable, especially to me since I'm intimately familiar with every inch of her.

"Are you sure this is okay?" I ask with my hands on her stomach.

"Yes." She laughs and kisses my neck, my jaw, my lips. "More than okay." She opens my jeans, reaches inside.

I should be exhausted but right now my dick has enough energy for everyone in the room and I groan out a curse when Susanna holds me in her hand.

"Colt," she whispers, "please touch me."

Fucking hell, I'm in heaven.

"I'll be careful," I promise as I unhook her bra.

She nips at my ear. "Don't be *too* careful."

I lead her to the guest bedroom and lay her down on the bed. I undress her slowly and inspect the way she's changed. Susanna is now more than gorgeous, more than sexy. The sight of her stirs a frenzy of lust but something else as well. An intense protective instinct merges with an achingly tender one. I get to hold her and fuck her and worship her and love her. What else could I possibly want?

She grows impatient and pulls my boxers down. Her mouth seeks mine and we're kissing when I enter her, slowly, carefully, just like I promised. She groans and spreads her legs wider. No, I won't be *too* careful. But I keep my weight on my arms as I take her and when she urges me to pump harder I'm ready to listen.

"Colt," she gasps and I can tell how close she is to exploding. "I really do love you."

"I love you too, Susanna."

"You feel so fucking good," she cries out as she trembles and now I'm coming too. I spend everything I have inside her and she makes a soft noise of protest when I finally withdraw.

We catch our breath in each other's arms and she shivers with pleasure when my fingers explore her soft skin. I think we might just fall asleep like this even though it's early, but Susanna sighs and kisses my chest.

"What's wrong?" I ask her as I stroke her hair.

She tightens her arms around me. "I know you don't like to talk about the past, but I need to tell you that I've always regretted the way I ended things with you back then. I deserted you, Colt, and I'm so sorry. You didn't have anyone else to love you and I know I bear some responsibility for the way your life fell apart."

I'm disturbed to hear that this is what's on her mind and that she's been beating herself up about garbage that happened ten years ago. I hug her close. "No, honey. That's not how it was. I was messed up. And the reasons why I was messed up had nothing to do with you. I was hurting myself and everyone around me. If you'd stuck around then you would have just been another casualty."

"But what if-"

"Shh." I kiss her. "Let's not talk about that anymore. Doesn't matter."

I know her mind is still turning but she honors my request.

She kisses my chest again. "I'm hungry. Let's order pizza for dinner."

"Okay. Will you marry me?"

She bolts upright, eyes wide. "What did you say?"

She heard me. She just wants to hear me ask again.

That's fine. I'm happy to repeat myself.

"Will you marry me, Susanna?"

She puts her hand to her heart. Her eyes fill with tears. "Yes, Colt. Of course I'll marry you."

21

SUSANNA

When my mother hears that Colt and I are just planning to get married at the nearest courthouse, she's crushed. Her mind had been dancing with visions of a vast reception hall, a designer wedding gown, gourmet food buffets. She and Keith had generously offered to foot the entire cost.

"Susanna, you'll be such a stunning bride and your height will be an advantage when it comes to picking a gown. Let's plan a shopping trip!"

I'm forced to remind her that I'm pregnant and besides, Colt and I just want to get married quietly as soon as possible.

"But you're my only daughter!" she wails over the phone. "I've dreamed of giving you a beautiful wedding since you were a little girl."

Tori and Jace save the day by offering to host a small event at their home. Given Jace's high profile status, this proves to be sufficient to satisfy my mother provided she's given maximum input on my dress. That seems fair to me.

On the morning of my wedding to Colt Malene, I don't wake up to an alarm. Instead, I wake up to the ecstasy of Colt's head between my legs. My panties are still on and I touch his head to let him know how much I love what he's doing as he kisses his way up and down my thighs.

He stops and gazes up at me with his tousled hair and startling blue eyes. I'm still amazed that he's really mine.

Colt sits up on his knees. He's naked. "Good morning, dirty girl. Thought I'd help you out because you were touching yourself in your sleep."

"I was not," I squeak out, embarrassed because I'm sure it's true. My hormones are rioting and I'm wickedly horny all the time. Even when I'm not awake.

He grins. "Yeah, you were. It was hot." He peels my panties away and lowers himself in order to use his tongue on me.

I have no complaints. I sink into the pillow and tremble as Colt's mouth quickly rouses euphoric waves of pleasure. I'm still trembling when he raises his head, pushes my legs open wider and with a smirk of victory, buries himself inside me.

To say we've been enjoying each other in the two weeks since his return is a phenomenal understatement. The sex is constant and mind blowing. Even better is the shared intimacy of spending our days together. I'm absolutely mad about him in every way.

We won't be having a long honeymoon. I've accepted a permanent position at Arcana High and I'm working on obtaining my teaching credentials. A substitute teacher could only be found for three days so Colt and I will be taking a short trip to a quaint bed and breakfast seventy miles away.

Colt's eyes are closed and he moves harder, faster. I love watching him when he comes.

When he's finished he pulls back, appraises me slowly with heat in his eyes, then abruptly jumps out of bed.

"Come on, sleepyhead. Time for some shower fun."

"Stop." I sit up and reach for my robe. "You're naked."

He pauses. "You want to fuck in the shower while fully dressed? Kinky, but okay."

"What I want is for you to cover your dick when there's a possibility you'll run into my mom and stepfather."

"Shit. Forgot they were here." He fishes a pair of shorts out of the dresser and hauls them on in a hurry. "Better? Let's go."

"Sorry, you'll be showering by yourself today. Don't pout. I'll make it up to you tonight."

He shrugs. "I can live with that."

"Good. And Colt?"

"Yeah?"

I tie the satin belt of my robe just above my belly bump. "I can't wait to marry you today."

The way he breaks into a happy smile electrifies my heart.

Colt disappears into the bathroom down the hall so that I can use the one nearest to my bedroom. My mother thinks it's strange that we're staying in my childhood bedroom instead of moving to the master suite downstairs but I doubt I'll ever be able to bring myself to sleep in the room my father died in. Besides, we plan to remake the guest bedroom up here into the nursery and I don't want to be far away from the baby.

Since I've heard nothing from our guests I have to wonder if they are still asleep. There's no hotel in Arcana and my mother absolutely insisted on remaining here so she could oversee my wedding day bridal transformation. Luckily, Keith is an easygoing guy who tends to indulge his wife's whims and he put up no argument about staying in the guest room.

My mother and Keith are not asleep after all. They are downstairs drinking tall glasses of a green substance that must have been produced by the juice presser my mother brings with her everywhere.

"Here she is, our beautiful bride!" My mother celebrates my arrival. She embraces me and touches my belly with reverence. She insists that I sit down in her chair even though there are others. She urges me to drink the green sludge in her glass "because it's good for the baby", then she stands behind my chair and begins fussing with my hair.

My mother reminds her husband that he needs to leave soon to pick up the centerpieces she ordered at a shop in town. After that, he is to go to Jace and Tori's to ensure that all arrangements are proceeding smoothly.

"Of course, sweetheart," he says with an adoring smile that suggests he would cheerfully remove his left arm if she asked him to.

Keith, already fully dressed in a sharp suit, departs soon after on a quest to carry out my mother's bidding. She kisses him on the cheek, smooths the lapel of his suit and advises him to take his blood pressure medication.

I watch them while nibbling the edge of a slice of wheat toast. Inside, I'm marveling over the difference between the volatile way my parents interacted versus the calm relationship my mother shares with Keith.

Thinking this makes me feel guilty and I shift my gaze to the bare spot on the wall. Out of respect for Keith, I've temporarily relocated my parents' wedding photo to a less central spot in the first floor office.

My mother sits down across from me and becomes melancholy. "I wish he was here to see this day."

I understand she's referring to my father. "I do too."

She blinks away tears. "He would be so proud of you. His little Susie is getting married. When I was pregnant, he wanted a son so very badly. Until he held you in his arms for the first time. Did I ever tell you that? He cried when he introduced himself as your daddy. He wanted to carry you everywhere. If he heard you make the smallest noise in the middle of the night he would already be running to your crib before I even managed to sit up. From the beginning, he loved you best. I knew it and never minded. I guess because I loved you best as well."

No, I have never heard that story before.

When I can't suppress a sniffle, she reaches over and holds my hand. "I'm sorry, honey. No sadness today. Let's talk about what we're going to do with your hair."

A moment later, a freshly showered and cleanshaven Colt runs down the stairs. My mother offers to make him some green juice, which he politely declines.

"I haven't seen Janna in forever," she muses in reference to Colt's mother and then chuckles. "Isn't it strange? We would never have guessed in our Arcana High cheerleading days that someday our children would be marrying each other!"

Colt says nothing and carefully pours a cup of coffee. He's been uneasy ever since hearing his mother has decided to attend the wedding. I was in the room when Tori told Colt their mother was living in El Paso now after splitting from her latest husband and was begging for an invitation to the wedding. Colt pointed out she hadn't even bothered to show up to Tori's wedding and he didn't know why she'd take an interest in his. Colt said he didn't care one way or the other if their mother was there because he didn't intend to talk to her anyway.

I have only a little insight into Colt's history with his mother, all based on things he told me years ago. He refuses to say much about her now. I'm hopeful that her presence today is a sign she'd like to repair her relationship with her son.

"Do you want some toast?" I ask him in an attempt to shift the subject away from his mother.

"Nah." He shakes his head. "I should get moving. Still got to pick up my tux."

I wouldn't have been bothered if Colt wished to get married in one of his flannel shirts, but my mother was horrified by the thought and so Colt's rented tux waits at the Plainsfield Mall.

She watches with a pleased smile as Colt bends down to kiss me before leaving.

"Colt, you do have the rings, right?" she asks him.

"Jace does."

"And you need to remember to wear your boutonniere."

He straightens up. "Yeah, I know."

"Mom," I warn. "He's got it."

Colt winks at me and plucks his keys from the hook. I still can't get over the fact he keeps the good luck charm I gave him so long ago.

Once he's gone, my mother pretends to swoon. "Good lord, he is handsome."

I'm gloating when I say, "I know."

She becomes brisk. "Susanna, I wanted to talk to you about something. Keith thinks he can get Colt a position at the bank. There's a branch in Plainsfield so the commute wouldn't be terrible. Once he completes training, Colt could start as a client relations manager."

I nearly snort orange juice through my nose. I can think of few things more entertaining than the idea of Colt working in a bank. "Thank you, I'm sure he would appreciate the offer but that would not be a good fit. Anyway, Colt is working on getting a commercial driver's license and already has a job offer with a trucking company."

She makes a face. "I remember his father was a trucker."

"Yes, Eric Malene was a truck driver." He also suffered a fatal heart attack on the road at a young age but I don't want to think about that.

"He'll be gone a lot," she frets. "He won't be here to take care of you."

The thought has crossed my mind. I can't say the idea of Colt being on the road makes me happy, but it's not like he'll disappear for huge stretches of time. He will be home more often than he's gone. Still, I keep my face carefully neutral. "We'll be fine."

She presses on. "And what will you do when the baby is born?"

"The school knows I'll be working as long as I can and then I'll be on leave through the summer. After that, I'm sure I can find a daycare."

"Well." My mother leans back in her chair, lips pursed. "As long as you have a plan."

Thankfully, she has little time to dwell on Colt's career prospects. There is a wedding today. There is much to do. She declares she has a million and one things to check on and shoos me off to the shower. The next time I see her she's half hysterical because the stylist she booked for my hair and makeup has cancelled at the last minute, which she seems to regard as a cataclysmic disaster.

I want to laugh but wouldn't dare. As I try to calm her down, I text Tori to ask for advice. Tori offers to come over and help and has the idea to also invite Rochelle, Colt's stepmother. Apparently, Rochelle used to compete in beauty pageants so she knows about things like hair and makeup.

Two hours before my wedding ceremony is to begin, I'm pushed into a seat at the dining room table in order to be made over into bridal material. Rochelle expertly applies makeup and curls my hair while Tori, now well into her third trimester, sits nearby and rummages through a huge plastic train case whenever Rochelle requests mascara or an eyelash curler. My mother paces in the background, supplying a steady stream of unnecessary suggestions, and Rochelle's daughter Carrie adorably practices dance moves in the living room.

"She's so excited she hasn't been able to sit still," Rochelle explains with a laugh. "Not only is she getting a fabulous sister-in-law but she's ready to be a proud aunt twice over."

Carrie performs a pirouette. "Do you know yet if it's a boy or a girl, Susanna?"

"Not yet."

"Tori's having a boy."

Tori smiles.

My dress is simple but classy and I have to give my mother credit for excellent taste. The style is a sleeveless v-neck with a little bit of decorative lace on the bodice and a sleek skirt. The alterations were finished at the last minute yesterday due to my expanding belly. My hair has been left down to fall past my shoulders, but Rochelle has worked magic and produced the kind of soft curls I've never been able to achieve with a curling iron.

When my mother sees me wearing my dress and veil, she begins to cry. "Oh, my baby girl! You are stunning."

Rochelle declares that Colt is going to fall over when he sees me. Carrie insists on taking pictures with her mother's phone.

The doorbell rings and my mother rushes out to greet the driver of the limo, a luxury she insisted on to convey me through the streets of Arcana. Carrie wants to see the limo up close and Rochelle chases after her, leaving just me and Tori.

I'm rather surprised to see that her eyes are also bright with tears and she has been standing quietly beside the couch.

"Are you okay?" I ask.

She nods, swipes at her eyes and comes closer. "I'm glad we have this moment alone. There's something I want to tell you." She touches my hand. "Colt hasn't had an easy time in life. And I just wanted to say thank you, Susanna. Thank you for loving my brother, for choosing him, for understanding how wonderful he is."

Now I'm going to start bawling too. "I will do anything to make him happy."

"I know you will. But don't cry or you'll ruin your makeup and I don't want to know what your mother will do to me if I let that happen." She links her arm through mine. "Now let's go get you hitched."

When we reach Tori and Jace's house, I'm amazed. With little advance notice they've gone all out to turn their extensive backyard into an enchanting wedding venue with an impeccable mix of both rustic charm and sophistication. An enormous white tent will be the scene of the reception, but first the ceremony will happen outdoors in front of a small number of guests seated in white chairs on either side of the aisle.

That's where he waits.

He's waiting for me and he's beautiful.

Colt's hands are clasped in front of him and he goes stock-still the instant our eyes meet.

It's a bittersweet moment when my mother walks me down the aisle. She holds my arm tightly and I swear I can smell my father's aftershave for a fleeting instant and then it's gone.

Neither of us are religious and the ceremony is performed by a retired judge who is a friend of Paul Elkins.

I can't shake the feeling that I'm in living in a dream as Colt takes my hands and we say our vows to one another. I know there are many eyes on us and yet they disappear. I'm only aware of him, of the hushed solemnity in his voice and the unwavering promise in his eyes. I'm ready to promise him the same. I've never wanted anyone else.

"I now pronounce you husband and wife."

Colt doesn't wait to kiss me and he holds back nothing, as always.

We've done it. We're married. We have our fairy tale.

The food has been catered by Giorgio's. Paul's granddaughter Nina sings with the live band. Some of my Arcana High colleagues are here. And Colt's mother really did show up. I don't know what Janna Malene's last name is now. She's burned through several husbands since I saw her last. She was always beautiful and still is, though the lines around her mouth have hardened. She has a place at my mother's table and appears to be primarily interested in the nearby open bar.

Colt keeps his arm slung over the back of my chair while we're seated. Neither of us enjoy dancing at all, let alone dancing in public, and I'm realizing now we should have prepared for the inevitability of being lured to the large square piece of flooring that temporarily flattens the grass beneath the tent. When the band begins playing *Are You Gonna Kiss Me Or Not*, I drag Colt with me out to the floor to please the guests and give the photographer something to work with. Colt pulls me close and I rest my head on his shoulder. The flutter in my belly is now much more than just the thrill of being held by him.

"The baby is enjoying the music."

He peers down at me. "It's moving?"

"Yes. Next month's ultrasound should be able to determine if it's a boy or a girl."

He smiles. I rise up on my tiptoes to kiss him.

My husband.

"I'd like to dance with my son."

Colt's mother has materialized out of nowhere. She sways a little bit and her lipstick is wrecked. There's zero warmth in her smile and I feel Colt tense up.

"Of course," I say and step back, even though she's being extremely rude, cutting in on our first dance.

Janna doesn't look at me as she takes my place. Tori and Jace stand by with worried expressions. My mother is also irritated and she pushes Keith toward the floor so that I don't have to stand out here alone.

He's gracious as he holds out his hand. "May I please have this dance with my beautiful stepdaughter?"

"I'd like that. Thank you, Keith."

Colt is visibly uncomfortable as his mother tries to get him to dance with her. It's a very odd moment. She made little effort to speak to him earlier.

"Your mother is beyond thrilled today," Keith says and smiles at his wife, which prompts me to smile at him.

"I know she is. Thank you for everything, Keith."

The music keeps playing but after the next verse, something sets Colt off and he raises his voice.

"Then why the hell did you come here?"

His mother is just as loud. "To see if you'd actually pulled yourself together."

He snorts. "I guess I didn't turn out to be quite as worthless as you thought."

Janna's laughter is the sharp hysteria of a drunk and by this point everyone is watching.

"You don't have to be much of a man to get a girl pregnant. Hell, even your father managed to pull that off." She swivels her head, searching wildly, and then zeroes in on Jace. "A couple of times." She seems to find her own observation hilarious and laughs again.

Jace's face is a thundercloud of anger. Yet somehow I get the feeling he's unsurprised by what she's implying.

"Mom," Tori hisses. "How could you do this today?"

But Janna ignores her daughter. It's my turn to receive the nasty brunt of her attention and she looks me over with contempt. "Good luck to you, Susanna. You'll need it. Because any child of his will undoubtedly break your heart."

"That's enough, Janna!" My own mother has gone into full mama bear mode and she's beyond furious. She seizes the arm of her old high school friend and literally begins dragging her away. "You will NOT ruin my daughter's wedding. GET OUT!"

Jace and Tori follow them. Colt has turned his back. He stalks out of the tent. I catch up to him beyond the strings of lights and the heat lamps. When I reach out to hold him, he lets me.

"I'm so sorry," he whispers, rubbing my back.

"Not your fault," I whisper back, kissing him. "She's horrible."

He breathes deeply, struggling to get control of his emotions. "She always has been. She fucking does shit like this on purpose."

The scene between them reflected a long and ugly history. While there's so much I don't know about Colt's messy relationship with his mother, one thing is clear; Janna despises her own son.

He sighs and buries his face in my hair. His mother has made sure he's in pain on a day that should have been nothing but joy.

I tip my head back so I can see his face. "What happened, Colt?"

I'm not just talking about his mother's dreadful behavior today. Colt quit high school and ran off the first chance he got. He had nothing; no money, no connections, only a desperate wish to escape. Maybe what he really needed to escape from at the time was her.

Rather than answer the question, he prefers to kiss me again. His tongue seeks mine and we dig in this time with more passion. I respond to him as I always do. I want him as badly as ever.

"Let's get out of here," he says, breathing hard and pressing into me urgently. "Let's go now."

"We could leave this fucking place. We could go anywhere and leave all this shit behind."

The chill of a terrible memory can invade with no warning and sometimes the past folds over to blend with the present. I shouldn't be thinking of that moment of anguish. We were about to lose each other then. That is not the case today, the day we've promised to spend our lives together.

I chase away the dread and brush my lips softly over his. "Baby, we can't leave just yet."

He knows this. He relaxes, even smiles and kisses my hand, the one now wearing his wedding ring. I've never cared for diamonds and we exchanged identical titanium bands.

Colt wraps an arm around my waist and we return to the reception together.

Janna Malene is not seen for the rest of the evening. She was plainly drunk so I'm sure she was not allowed to get behind the wheel, but I have faith that she'll be kept away. Still, the damage is done. Colt tries to be gracious and sociable to the guests and little Carrie manages to coax a smile when she tackles him, insistent on dancing with her big brother. Yet I can tell he is distracted, his mind troubled by the hideous things said by his mother.

Today I am extra appreciative of my own mother. She becomes weepy again when I hug her as we say our goodbyes. She stretches up to kiss my cheek and whispers, "Thank you for being my little girl."

"I love you, Mom," I whisper back.

Tori is still distraught and pulls me aside before we leave. "Susanna, please forgive me. I had no idea my mother would pull something like that or I never would have allowed her to be here. Don't listen to anything she says. Is he okay?"

I glance over at Colt. His head is down as he listens to something Jace says and Jace squeezes his shoulder.

"I think so." I wish I could sound more convincing.

Tori looks miserable and that's a shame. She's not responsible for her mother and she has done so much for us.

"Tori, we're sisters now," I say, which cheers her up instantly.

She smiles. "I'm so glad. I wouldn't have picked anyone else for my brother."

Our pregnant bellies bump as we embrace. She's family now, she and Jace. We will all raise our families here in Arcana. Our children will be best friends as well as cousins.

After stopping at the house to change and grab our bags, Colt and I drive straight to the destination of our short honeymoon.

"It's nice to get away," I observe while admiring the cozy décor of our suite. "Even for a few days."

Colt stands in front of the window, facing out. It's been dark for hours and we're in a semi rural area so there are fewer lights to disturb the night sky. He's been quiet since leaving the wedding. Colt isn't known for being a chatterbox, but I'm worried his silence is more ominous right now.

He's still in the exact same place after I pay a quick visit to the bathroom to change into the lacy white nightgown I purchased especially for tonight. I've been feeling more self-conscious about my pregnant body even though Colt insists I'm completely sexy.

The temperature has dropped down to the forties tonight and I shiver as I approach him from behind, wrapping my arms around his waist. I kiss the area between his shoulder blades. He wears a basic white tee and jeans and though he was devastatingly gorgeous in his tuxedo, I prefer this look on him.

Now I kiss the back of his neck and his breathing quickens. He shifts his weight. If I reach lower, I know I'll find a stiff bulge in his pants, which gets me wildly aroused. I pull his shirt up and he swiftly finishes the task by tugging it over his head.

Colt is already unzipping his jeans when he turns around. Then he does a double take at the sight of me in my lingerie and the corners of his mouth slowly tilt up.

I slide my hands over the bare skin of his muscled arms, his strong shoulders. "You like it?"

He seizes my left hand and pointedly rubs my palm over the rigid evidence. No words are necessary.

The bed isn't far. His pants are off before we get there. He lies on his back and steadies me as I straddle him. I was thoughtful enough to shed my panties earlier. There's nothing between us and I'm so ready I'm almost aching. I'm his.

His strong hands seize my bare hips. I'm so turned on I'm already moving in rhythm but he wavers. With one hand remaining in place on my right hip, his left hand skims up my back and grabs a fistful of my hair. My eyes had been closed but now they open and I find him staring at me with piercing intensity.

"Tell me you love me," he orders.

"I do love you."

He pushes inside, just barely. I moan and whimper for more.

"Say it again, Susanna."

"I love you, Colt." I bite my lip and grind back and forth, already on the verge of an orgasm.

He drops his hand and uses it to brace my other hip while slowly allowing me to have the rest of him. Colt moves the straps of my nightgown aside and I ride him with my breasts bare and our eyes locked until I'm overwhelmed by the sensations in my own body and can only give in.

Colt waits until he's sure I'm finished with my own frenzy before clutching my hips and releasing himself inside me. The he cradles me close and we kiss for a long time until he pulls back a little.

"Are you cold?" He strokes my skin.

"A little."

He helps me get settled beneath the fluffy covers and gingerly touches my belly. I place my hand over his. A gentle wave rolls within and I know he can't feel it from the outside yet but soon that will change.

He raises an eyebrow when he hears me giggling. "What's so funny?"

I snuggle into his chest. "I was just wishing I could go back in time and get the word to my teenage self that someday she would get to marry Colt Malene."

There's a smile in his voice. "And what would she have said? The teenage Susanna?"

"Nothing. She would have passed out, delirious from the thrill."

Colt snorts and reaches over to the nightstand to switch off the vintage milk glass lamp.

His sigh sounds contented now and he runs his fingers through my hair. "I love you so much, Susanna."

I kiss him once more. "We're so lucky."

We really are. Perhaps everyone feels this same invincible optimism on their wedding night but in our case it's real. We've earned it.

Colt falls asleep in minutes but I'm more restless, preoccupied with the day's events which were mostly wonderful. The stark exception was the confrontation with Colt's mother, the culmination of a toxic parent/child relationship that must be a story all its own.

And my earlier question, the unanswered one, echoes in my mind.

What happened, Colt?

22

COLT, AGE 17

After working a double shift unloading trucks at the poultry warehouse, I hardly know what day it is by the time I get home and crash in my bed.

I never announced that I was working all night but it's not like anyone will be looking for me. My mom hardly batted an eye when I quit school months ago and her husband Rusty tends to stay out of my shit. Tori wasn't happy, but in the long run I'm sure she's glad that she doesn't need to waste her time getting all bent out of shape worrying over what kind of mess I'm causing at school. That's been a burden on her for way too long and I never realized it. Of all the ways I've screwed up – and there are a lot to choose from – the thing I'm most ashamed of is how I failed my sister.

The way I treated Jace is a close second.

I was already slow walking to the edge of a cliff. The day Susanna dumped me, I fell right the fuck off. After the move to Bredon, I started blocking Jace's calls. I knew he was anxious to set things right after the crappy fight we had but I didn't let him. I was pissed and I was jealous because his football star was rising while mine burned out. The last time I put on a uniform was the rivalry game between Bredon and Arcana. Arcana had a huge lead and by the time the coach threw me into the game I was seeing red. The first chance I got, I took down my best friend with a blunt tackle for no legitimate reason. I'm sure the betrayal hurt him a lot worse than the hit to the grass. Even if I still wanted to play after that night, the Bredon coaches had seen enough from me.

That was the end.

I'd lost my girl. I'd lost my best friend. I'd lost football.

And next I lost my sister.

When Tori broke up with Jace the day after the rivalry game, I was thunderstruck. I never saw that coming at all. In the weeks before their breakup I'd just assumed they were as united as ever. Tori kept chasing me around, desperate to talk. I thought she just wanted to complain about the way I'd treated Jace and so I ignored her. Only thinking of my own misery, I abandoned my own sister when she was in the worst pain of her life, when she suffered a pregnancy scare, when her relationship with the boy she adored was falling apart.

And by the time I overheard their last agonizing confrontation, it was too late. For Tori and Jace. For me and Jace. For me and Tori. From then on, she could hardly stand the sight of me. I didn't blame her.

"There have been a lot of times lately when I needed my brother. Really needed him. But you didn't care. All you've ever cared about is yourself. Now I don't need you anymore."

We still live in the same house but even now, over a year later, we barely speak. I can do that for her, keep my distance. She's busy with her senior year and has a scholarship offer. Her future is bright. Tori was forced to take care of me from the time we were little kids. If I got into trouble, she was blamed. Our mother even held her back from school for a year so she could keep an eye on me. I'll never ever hold my sister back again. That's the only thing I have to offer her.

My head is pounding when I wake up. I shuffle over to the bathroom in search of aspirin and then wander down to the kitchen. A glance at the living room wall clock says it's three in the afternoon. The house feels empty but it's not empty. My mother sits in the kitchen.

She whirls around at the sound of my footsteps and then scowls when she sees it's me.

"I didn't know you were here," she grumbles and puts out her cigarette on the surface of the table. She smells like a hangover and she wears only a thin pink slip.

There's an inch of coffee in the pot and I pour it into a mug even though I know it's leftover from this morning. I don't like coffee much but right now I'll take anything with some caffeine.

"Worked a double shift." I swallow the coffee in one gulp. "Then took a nap."

She's focused on her phone now. I doubt she even heard me.

Between the aspirin and the stale coffee, my stomach isn't happy. A search of the pantry doesn't turn up much that seems appealing. When I find a sleeve of Ritz crackers, I tear them open and stuff six into my mouth. I bring the rest of the crackers to the table with me.

When the chair scrapes the tile, my mother's eyes leave her phone screen. She frowns, apparently annoyed that I've decided to sit down. Too fucking bad. I live here too and I'll sit in a chair if I want.

She puffs on a newly lit cigarette and crosses her legs. Two months ago she was fired from her job in an orthodontist's office. As far as I can tell, she hasn't bothered to search for another one. She goes out often, mostly without Rusty, and finds strangers to chat with on the internet. One day she left her phone lying on the table and I saw messages from some fucker named Brick. Brick was asking 'When do I get to suck on that hot ass of yours? LOL!' That made me kind of throw up in my mouth and I made a vow to never EVER look at her phone again even if it was being shoved right under my nose.

She sighs with loud irritation. I think the sound is supposed to make me run away. I don't run away. I eat three more crackers. I'm so fucking tired of being ignored. I know I'm no prize, but she's my mother. Mothers are supposed to care about you no matter what. They're supposed to be upset when you do things like drop out of high school. Mine just told me that I needed to start chipping in rent and never mentioned school again. She doesn't care about me at all.

I guess that's why I swallow the last cracker and do something I should have done a long time ago.

"Guess what, Mom?"

"What?" She couldn't be more indifferent.

"I saw you."

The statement means nothing to her. She taps out a message on her phone. Maybe she's talking to Brick.

"I SAW YOU, MOM!"

She's no longer indifferent. She lowers her phone and glares. "What the hell are you talking about?"

"I saw you with Jace's dad one afternoon. I was fourteen at the time. You two were…" I can't finish the sentence. For more than three years I've been keeping that memory at bay and it returns with a sick vengeance, twisting my guts and pounding through my head.

"I'm the bitch you've never been able to stop fucking."

Her jaw goes slack. "No, you didn't."

"Want to bet? The floor of our living room on a summer afternoon. You were both drunk. You were laughing at him, saying it's a good thing you don't depend on him for child support."

Her phone falls to the floor.

"What did you mean by that, Mom?"

She gasps and then shuts her eyes. For a second, I see some humanity there and I think she's going to cry and beg for forgiveness. That's not what happens.

Her eyes open and narrow in my direction with scorn. "You had to know you came from somewhere, Colt. The stork didn't deliver you for god's sake."

All this time I've been hoping that maybe it wasn't true, that I'd completely misunderstood.

But no, I'd misunderstood nothing.

She's basically admitting that Jace's father is also my father.

Blood roars through my head and I knock my chair over when I stand up. "Why didn't you ever tell me that I was the son of my best friend's dad?"

"Don't be an idiot. He wanted nothing to do with you. He was always denying it, saying you could have belonged to anyone, but I knew you were his. The truth is, your real dad is a lousy piece of shit who has only ever been good for one thing and doesn't care if you live or die."

It's been a while since I was this close to crying. "Do you have any idea what it did to me, how bad it messed me up, seeing and hearing the two of you like that?"

Her lips press into a thin line. "You're not a little kid. Quit feeling sorry for yourself."

"I *was* a kid until that day. Not too long after that I started fucking around myself. And believe me, I have fucked around so much that my cock has a goddamn fan club."

She stands and slaps me hard in the face. "You're disgusting!" She slaps at me again, harder. "You make me sick, do you know that?"

She can't hit for shit and so the sting of her hand is slight. The words hurt a little more.

I move back a step just in case she feels like lashing out again. "I guess I take after you, don't I?"

She slams her hand down on the table. "I didn't have to keep you! Did you ever think about what that was like for me? Eric can count. He knew you weren't his. And I'd just had a baby. I didn't especially want another one. That's right, I didn't have to keep you, Colt. But I did. Now you do everything in your power to make me regret it."

"Nice. Is that the speech you're going to give when you win Mother of the Year?"

Her laughter is ugly and hostile. "Pathetic. Your sister at least has a brain. Tori will go to college and she'll do something with her life. But you? I expect you'll either O.D. in the gutter or else I'll be visiting you in prison someday. You're just like *him*. Real good looking and strong but otherwise worthless."

I feel like I've been kicked in the stomach. She's never been the most affectionate mother but now I know she sees me as complete trash.

Well, that's fine. I don't think much of her either.

She puts a hand to her mouth, like she finally realizes the impact of saying the things that must have been secretly stewing inside her head for quite some time.

"Colt..." She sniffs, then holds her arms out. "I shouldn't have said all of that."

"Fuck you."

She flinches, then hardens. Her arms drop. The mask is off. There's no point in pretending.

"You're gone the second you turn eighteen," she swears. "I want you out of here."

"Maybe I'll be gone even sooner."

She raises her chin and her eyes are icy. "Believe me, you won't be missed."

"I believe you." No longer willing to listen to any motherly words of wisdom, I leave the kitchen and return to my room.

My headache is fading and I stretch out on the bed to consider my options.

I think I'd rather starve out on the street than stay here for much longer. I have a little bit of cash saved and I've got a truck now. A shitty truck but it's still a truck. With my eighteenth birthday looming, my mother is aware that the child support spigot is about to be turned off. The funny thing is that ever since I quit school, my dad keeps calling. Tori must have given him my new number. I never answer his calls but he always leaves a message. He wants to talk. He wants me to know that his door is always open if I ever need a place to stay. *My dad.* Fat chance I'll call him back. If Eric Malene really cared, he could have invited both Tori *and* me to live with him. Think of all the shit that could have been avoided. I'd still be playing football in Arcana. Tori and Jace would still be together.

And Susanna...

The heartache of saying her name hasn't faded so I don't say her name at all. But if I hadn't been forced to move to fucking Bredon, then maybe I wouldn't have lost her.

She's at some fancy college now. She probably has a high-end dipshit college boyfriend who plans to be the CEO of something stupid. I bet he's a guy her father would approve of.

I reach for the keys on the floor beside my bed. As always, my thumb presses a metal horseshoe shape while my mind flashes back to the day it was given to me. There have been times when I thought about throwing the thing out but couldn't do it. This is all I have of her. This is the only evidence that once there was someone in my life who truly believed in me, who saw my faults and overlooked them, who might have even loved me the way I loved her.

And at least I had that, if only for a little while.

No, I won't throw this out. I'll keep the charm as I wade through life alone because there will never be another Susanna. There's only one and she's no longer mine. I've tried to move on with other girls. It never works. I just end up behaving badly and being the cause of someone's tears.

The three quick raps on my door end my daydreams and I shout, "Fuck off!" because I have no desire to interact with my mother.

But the doorknob turns anyway because I forgot to lock it. Tori walks in and stares at me with a frown.

"Sorry," I tell her. "Didn't know you'd come home. Thought you were Mom."

She shuts the door behind her and faces me with her arms crossed. "What happened now? She's out there carrying on about what an asshole you are."

"I am an asshole. So is she."

Tori drops her arms and takes a step in my direction. "What did she say to you, Colt?"

I can't bring myself to tell her everything, and not because I'm protecting my mother. Tori's life at home is better than mine but that's not saying much. She doesn't need any more stress.

"I told her the truth and she told me the truth."

"What does that mean?"

"Nothing." I roll over so that I don't say too much. In spite of everything, Tori would be furious if she knew the plan was to kick me out of the house in the near future. She'd definitely call our dad and then shit would really hit the fan.

I need to make an escape plan and I need to make it sooner rather than later. The less Tori knows, the better. She'll graduate, go to college, do great things. I swore I'd never again be responsible for holding my sister back. And I won't.

"Colt?" Tori sits on the edge of the bed. "Do you want to talk?"

I do want to talk. More than anything in the world I want to talk to Susanna. But there's no chance that I'll decide to crash into her college world and turn it upside down.

"I'm pretty fucking tired," I tell my sister and fake a yawn. "Could you turn out the light?"

She stays where she is for another minute, then finally sighs and switches the light off before closing the door softly on her way out.

I don't take a nap after all. I make decisions. I'll give it another month. I'll keep working double shifts to pile up more cash and then I'll take off. As to where I'll go, I'll figure that out along the way.

"You won't be missed."

I know I won't be missed. But my mother's wrong about a few things. I refuse to drink and fuck my way to an early grave. I'm done with that shit. And I won't wind up behind bars. Maybe someday my mother will even regret the things she said today.

Probably not. But maybe.

In the meantime, the world's a big place.

And the next time I come this way, I'll be a better man than I am right now.

23

COLT

Christmas hasn't held much meaning for me in many years, but Susanna feels differently so we are celebrating. There's even a tree, a bushy green giant that should be relaxing in a forest somewhere instead of drying up on the living room tile but it's not like I chopped the thing down myself. It was already sitting in a parking lot beside scores of other sad trees. At that point the best destiny any of them could hope for was to be decorated with glass balls and lights before getting tossed into the woodchipper by New Year's Day.

"Did I show you the ornament my mother gave us?" Susanna asks as she stands in front of the tree with one hand pressed to her back.

I join her, sliding my arms around her waist from behind. There's a faint tap from within her belly when my hand grazes over the surface. The last ultrasound gave no hint whether the occupant is a boy or a girl. The baby faced away with its legs closed. Susanna was disappointed. She really wants to know and she wants to pick a name. I don't have a preference. I just want it to be healthy.

But I really need to stop thinking of the baby as 'it'.

You could have knocked me over with a feather when I looked at the imaging screen and saw the shape of a tiny head and then wiggling arms and legs. I've become a little more comfortable with the idea that I'm going to be a father but it's still a shock to think there's an actual person growing in Susanna's belly. Then I remember that this person is also half mine and I'm dazed all over again.

Susanna points to the tree ornament, a cartoonish ceramic couple dressed for winter with our names written on their snowcaps. The Susanna figure has a big stomach and scrawled upon it are the words 'Baby Malene'.

"When did your mom give you that?"

"She and Keith drove out here this past Saturday while you were gone."

"While you were gone."

I could be misunderstanding the clip in her voice when she says those words. I know she's less than thrilled with my new job but it's not like I can be a work-from-home trucker.

I try to steer away from that subject. "Your mom's real excited, huh?"

"About the baby? She's overjoyed beyond reason." The tension is gone and Susanna relaxes against my chest. "She's very big on looking young so I wasn't sure in the beginning how she would feel about becoming a grandma, but she couldn't be more delighted."

"That's good." I mean it. This kid's not going to have a lot of grandparents to choose from. It's not as if my own mother is going to have a change of heart and start knitting baby hats or something.

I have not talked to her since the wedding and I don't plan to ever talk to her again. I'm not surprised by anything she has to say to me, but I'll be damned if she's going to make Susanna or my kid feel like shit. If Tori has spoken to her again then Tori knows better than to mention it to me.

"Did you feel that?" Susanna squeals and presses my hand to the center of her belly.

"Little one sure knows how to kick." If someone were to take a picture of me now I'd probably look pretty goofy with this huge grin on my face.

She swivels to look at me. "Do you have any new name suggestions?"

I was told to thumb through this huge book of baby names and haven't done it yet. "How about Mike?" It's just the first name that came to mind. "Or Mikayla. That's a girl name, right?"

Susanna raises an eyebrow. The curse of having a smart wife is that she can guess when you fail to do things like study the baby name book. "It is a girl name, yes." Suddenly she winces and makes a face. "I'll be right back."

My panic meter skyrockets. "What's wrong?"

"Nothing. I just need to pee for the twentieth time today."

While she heads for the half bathroom, I take a seat on the couch. I need to displace a couple of fat red and green Christmas pillows in the process. Susanna has framed some of our wedding photos and added them to the wall. She looks breathtaking. I look like a blue-eyed penguin with teeth. I guess Susanna doesn't mind. She married me anyway. I'm still amazed that I'm the one she wants.

Within a minute, Susanna emerges from the bathroom. She's very festive in a red maternity top patterned with silver snowflakes. This is one of those moments when I'm bowled over at the sight of her. Not just because she's beautiful, which she is, but because everything about our lives was transformed overnight and I'm still catching up.

"You feeling okay?" I ask her when she sits beside me.

She tosses her long brown hair over one shoulder. "I feel great for now. That might change in a few weeks when I hit the third trimester. Tori says she needs Jace's help to roll out of bed and her constant heartburn is awful. Did she tell you about her doctor visit yesterday? She's measuring ahead and she's one centimeter dilated. I told her I'm a little jealous that her due date is only ten days away. I feel like I have forever still to go."

That's weird because on my end it seems like Susanna's pregnancy has accelerated at warp speed. Sometimes I expect to turn around and discover that someone is handing me a crying infant.

Then again, I can understand her point of view. She's the one who has to deal with being pregnant, plus she's known about the baby for longer than I have, which is a fact I really try not to mention.

Susanna gestures to the dining room table. Squatting in the center is a bluish green empty vase. "Did you notice the new addition? Tori said Gloria's husband gave it to her for one of their early wedding anniversaries and she always cherished it. Tori insisted that we should have it so Gloria can watch over us."

I remember the vase. It sat on top of the piano where Tori always took music lessons. If I squint at the thing for long enough, I can imagine that Gloria's patient smile will be the next thing I see when I turn my head. Gloria was more of a parent to me than my own parents cared to be. I regret never saying thank you.

Susanna lets out a soft noise of contentment when I start rubbing her shoulders.

"Are we still going out tonight?" I ask her.

She moves closer to get a better massage. "That's the plan. We'll spend Christmas Eve with Tori and Jace at their house and then my mom and Keith are coming over tomorrow. Oh, and Rochelle texted me. She and Carrie are spending Christmas with her family, but she wants to know if we can get together next week to exchange gifts. She offered to drive out here and Tori said she'd host at her house."

This is a bad time to bring up a sore point but I'll need to tell her soon anyway. "I have a cross country job next week."

"What?" She whips her head around. "But you just got back two days ago."

"I'm sorry, baby, but I've got the least amount of seniority so when the boss calls, I need to accept the job."

Her face falls. "Will you be gone for New Year's?"

"I'll do my best to be back by then."

Susanna chews on her lip. "Maybe this job wasn't the best idea."

"It's good money."

"But we're not hurting for money. There's nothing owed on the house and between my inheritance, the proceeds from the sale of my condo and the money you've squirreled away, we're sitting on an impressive nest egg."

"What do you think I should do for work instead?"

"I don't know. Something closer to home would be nice."

She must realize I don't have a ton of career paths. I have no fancy degrees or titles. I'm doing what I can.

"It's not my style to sit around on my ass, Susanna. Don't ask me to."

She sighs. "What if I go into labor while you're on the road?"

"Then I'll turn right around and come back."

"If you remember to check your phone," she mutters.

She has a point. I need to do better when it comes to being available. For so long I was completely alone with no one to answer to and I'm still adjusting.

Susanna rests her head on my shoulder. "Never mind. We'll figure it out. I don't want to argue with you on Christmas Eve."

"I don't want to argue with you ever."

She lifts her head and smiles. "Then kiss me. No arguments."

I can do that. And then once I start I don't want to stop. Her doctor says the pregnancy is very healthy and sex is fine for as long as she's comfortable. She prefers being on top these days. Anytime we're together it always feels crazy good.

My hand goes between her legs and she melts in my arms. The waistband of her stretchy cotton pants is elastic, easy to access. I use my thumb to stroke her gently over her panties. She loves this, getting flushed and breathless in a hurry.

"Let's go upstairs," she suggests, trying to pull my shirt off.

Yesterday she asked if I was bothered by the fact that we stay in her old bedroom instead of moving downstairs to the much larger master suite. When I said I didn't care which bedroom we slept in and that she ought to decide because it's her house, she got upset and said I should care because it's *our* house. To me, this still seems like Coach Toledo's place. But I don't have to let her know I feel that way.

I get my shirt off and toss it over the couch. I stand and extend my hand to help her up. "To the bedroom?"

She eagerly accepts my hand. "To our bedroom."

We're not even at the stairs when I hear my phone go off and I know from the ring tone that it's Jace. Thinking of my sister and the fact that he doesn't usually call in the middle of the afternoon for no reason, I hunt the thing down where I left it on an end table.

"How do you feel about getting a nephew for Christmas?" Jace asks, sounding jumpy enough to blast to the moon.

"*Now?* She's having the baby now?"

"Very soon. We're at the hospital already."

"We're on our way."

He blows out a heavy breath. "Holy shit, Colt. I'm about to be a father."

I grin. "That's one lucky kid. Now go take care of my sister."

Susanna overheard the conversation and is already collecting her purse and my keys. On the way to the hospital, she calls Rochelle and I can hear Carrie squealing with delight as the news is relayed. Susanna pats her own belly and smiles at me. I know she's thinking that in a few months it'll be us in the delivery room. I hope by then I feel more ready than I do right now.

Christmas Eve looks like a popular time to have a baby. There are a bunch of people in the waiting room, pacing around anxiously and awaiting word that a new member of the family has arrived.

Jace looks pretty frantic when he runs in here to tell us that Tori will be able to push soon. There are a couple of gasps from people who recognize him. One old woman is actually brazen enough to approach and ask for an autograph. It's pretty ballsy to ask a man to sign a random piece of paper while his wife is in labor but Jace is too keyed up to object and instead of telling the lady to piss off he scratches out his name on the glossy scrap of a magazine that was shoved in his face. Then he runs back to the delivery room.

Rochelle and Carrie have abandoned their Christmas Eve plans in favor of waiting on the arrival of Mason Zielinski, which is the name Tori and Jace have chosen for their son. Carrie is so excited she can't sit still and entertains the waiting room by performing dances from her recent role as Clara in The Nutcracker. Susanna and Rochelle huddle together and talk about baby things. The staff brings everyone donuts and hot chocolate.

And then, an hour before midnight, the best friend I'll ever have in this life or any other returns and now he cries tears of overwhelming joy.

"He's here," Jace chokes out. "He's perfect."

"And Tori?" Rochelle asks anxiously.

Jace beams. "Also perfect. She's incredible."

As everyone explodes into cheers, I seize my best friend in a crushing hug.

"Congratulations, pal."

He can't talk. He's too emotional. But he nods.

Susanna hugs Jace next. She asks if we will be allowed to see Tori and the baby tonight. Carrie is ready to sprint through the corridors to hunt for her baby nephew whether she's allowed to be there or not. Jace gets permission for all of us to visit once Tori is settled in her hospital room.

It's one thing to hear that I'm now a proud uncle. But I'm caught off guard by the sight of my sister holding her infant son while Jace stands nearby, gazing at his precious little family.

"Colt, we have to tell you something..."

They held hands that day as they sat on Gloria's couch, both of them equally nervous to break the news to me that they had become something much more than friends.

Even after all the years of heartache and separation they still found their way here. I'm so fucking proud of them that I'm going to be the next one to start weeping.

Tori and Jace. They were made for each other.

Susanna hugs my arm and lays her head on my shoulder. Carrie begs to hold baby Mason and is allowed, under the close supervision of Rochelle.

"Oh, I love you so very much," Carrie coos and the baby yawns.

His parents have some additional news to share. Once again, they hold hands and Tori is the one to speak first.

"We have to tell you something. His middle name is Colt."

"Mason Colt Zielinski." Jace looks at me. "After his uncle. My best friend in the world and the best man I know."

I don't even know how to respond.

"Damn, you guys," I mutter and lower my head so that no one can see my chin trembling. "Thanks for that."

I'm the last one to take a turn holding the baby. It's not until Jace places the tiny bundle in my arms that I realize I've never actually held a baby before.

"Your day is coming." Tori smiles as she reaches out to touch Susanna's belly. "I can't wait to see you two as parents."

Susanna takes a deep breath and smiles down at her stomach. "I can't wait either."

My nephew's eyelids flutter. He peers up at me, seems to become unimpressed with what he sees, and opens up his mouth to discharge a high-pitched wail. I have zero clue what I should do to help him. Luckily a nurse pokes her head in. She suggests that Tori should try to breastfeed and reminds us that we can't hang out in here for much longer.

Jace tenderly takes the baby from me and delivers him to his mother. Rochelle and Carrie promise to come by for a longer visit tomorrow. Before leaving, Carrie attacks me with a hug and informs me that I am her favorite big brother.

Tori has decided to take the nurse's suggestion to attempt breast-feeding and I *really* don't want to stick around for that. However, I'm having trouble dragging Susanna away as she stares at my sister with fascination. Finally, she notices that I'm standing outside the door and she joins me in the hallway.

I wave to the Zielinski family. "We'll come by tomorrow. Get some rest."

"Love you both," Tori calls and even though she must be exhausted she's never looked happier.

Jace is so busy studying his wife and son as he perches on the edge of the hospital bed that he doesn't seem to notice our exit.

"That was incredible." Susanna clutches my arm when we reach the parking lot.

"It sure was."

"I'm so happy for them."

"So am I."

When we get to my truck she hooks her arms around my neck. "We'll be back here soon enough," she says with unmistakable excitement. I know she's not talking about the fact that we're returning tomorrow for a visit.

I'd like to be able to say that I'm ready. Ready to be handed another blanketed bundle, this one containing my own child, who I already love without reservation.

"I *will* be ready," I promise my wife, amending the sentiment just slightly.

This is good enough for Susanna and her eyes grow soft. "Merry Christmas, Colt."

"Merry Christmas, baby." I kiss her and open the passenger side of the truck. Then I wait for her to climb in and get her seatbelt on before walking around to the other side.

On the way, I glance up at the sky and the North Star winks at me.

I will be ready.

That has to be true. I'll make it true.

24

SUSANNA

Whenever Colt gets home after zigzagging across the country, he always jumps right in the shower and then collapses into a deep sleep for many hours.

This morning he pulled in just as I was getting into my car to go to work so we only had a minute together. He kissed me first, bent down to kiss my belly, and waved as I drove away to face another rewarding but exhausting day at Arcana High School.

He's just waking up when I arrive home in the late afternoon.

"Hey, beautiful," he yawns as he thuds down the stairs. He's freshly shaved and wearing only an old pair of jeans.

I drop my tote bag on the floor and sink down on the sofa, keen to get off my aching feet. Once my shoes are slipped off, I try to get comfortable but the size of my belly limits my ability to maneuver. Usually, I prefer to relax with my legs tucked under me but that's no longer possible.

"There's most of a pizza in the fridge," I tell him. "Jace dropped it off last night. In fact, he's brought me food three times this week. Did you tell him to do that?"

He flashes a grin. "I might have asked him to look in on you."

"Baby Mason is smiling now."

"I know. Tori sent me a picture. You want a slice?"

"No, not hungry. My stomach's a little off today."

Colt disappears into the kitchen and I hear him rummaging in the fridge. He returns with a cold slice of pizza in one hand and a can of ginger ale in the other. He sits beside me and hands over the can.

"Maybe this will help your stomach," he says, his expression a little anxious.

"Thanks." I smile at him because I love it when he makes thoughtful little gestures like this. I open the can and take a sip.

Colt bites off half his pizza slice, chews, and appraises my stomach.

"I'll be there for your doctor's appointment tomorrow."

"My appointment was yesterday."

"Oh." His brow furrows with distress. "Can't believe I screwed that up. How did it go?"

"Everything is proceeding like clockwork. We're down to the last eight weeks."

He relaxes. "I promise I'll be around for next month's appointment."

"I'm now going every two weeks. Are you going to be in town in two weeks?"

Uncertainty flickers in his eyes. "I'll check the schedule."

I look away because I'm sure my face registers annoyance. "Did you apply for that local job we talked about? The bakery factory that needs delivery drivers?"

"Not exactly a local job. Those routes go all over Texas."

"At least you'd be in the same state," I grumble under my breath.

"What?" he says.

"Nothing."

He's chewing on his pizza again. "How'd you like those pictures I sent you of the Northern Lights?"

"I couldn't see much."

"Yeah, there's really no picture that does the view justice. I pulled over to look at the lights and then lost track of time. They don't call it big sky country for nothing. Never gets old, being out there."

I don't want to hear the longing in his voice when he talks about being out on the road. Colt has never shied away from admitting that he is afflicted with a serious case of wanderlust. It's who he is.

"There's nothing permanent about me, Susanna. I'm not a guy who sticks around."

Maybe I shouldn't have assumed that he would be immediately transformed, that he would become more like me and yearn for a constant home. He's trying. I know he is. But sometimes, like right now, I get the feeling he's eyeing his new circumstances with bewilderment and wondering how in the hell he ended up here on a living room sofa beside his pregnant wife.

These insecure thoughts will lead nowhere good. I force them away.

There are other things we can talk about.

"I was thinking that maybe we should sell the house."

He wipes his mouth with the back of his hand. "You want to leave Arcana?"

"No, I don't want to leave Arcana. I'm just not sure I want to live here in this house."

He shovels the rest of his pizza into his mouth and waits for me to explain.

"I can't get over the fact that this is where my father died. And my family was never happy living here. This is where my parents' marriage fell apart. I don't believe in curses but we're surrounded by bad memories and even though I've tried, I just don't feel all warm and fuzzy about raising our family right here."

He manages to frown while he's chewing.

"You don't agree?" I prompt.

Colt swallows the last of his food. "It doesn't matter to me which house we live in. If you want a different house, then you should have a different house."

He's trying to be honest and yet I bristle. "You have zero input on where we live?"

"Not really. I'm used to moving from one temporary dump to another."

"Well, since we won't be raising our child in a temporary dump it would be nice if you took an interest in our destination."

He scratches his head, sighs and crosses his arms. "To me, selling the house and buying another one seems like a lot of trouble to go to for no good reason but if you want to move somewhere else, I'm on board."

The baby elbows hard just beneath my ribcage and I shift my weight to ease the discomfort. "It's just an idea. Sorry, I'm a little irritable right now."

He uncrosses his arms and touches my knee. "You need me to go get you anything?"

"If you could go to the grocery store later, that would be great."

"Absolutely. Make me a list."

The muscles in my belly tighten for a few painless seconds before gradually easing. "And there's something I need to tell you."

He rubs my leg. "I'm listening."

"I saw your mother the other day."

Colt's eyes flare and he jumps to his feet. "She had the fucking nerve to come here and hassle you?"

"She didn't come to hassle me. She drove here because she wanted to see Mason. She's been trying to get back into Tori's good graces ever since he was born."

"She's *never* been in Tori's good graces," Colt mutters.

"Anyway, she stopped by on Sunday afternoon and brought diapers. She was nervous and apologized profusely for the wedding. She said she wouldn't blame me if I hated her."

Colt hisses and shakes his head. "And you let her in here?"

"How could I refuse? She's your mother."

"She has lost the right to claim that title."

"I understand. But I didn't think it was my place to order her off the property. She asked for your phone number and I wouldn't give her that. She didn't stay for long. She claimed to be disappointed you weren't here."

"She shouldn't be. I would have slammed the door in her face."

"Colt." I struggle off the sofa and heave myself to my feet. "I know you have very good reasons to be angry with your mother. But I've learned something from watching my father die. The past must be reckoned with. Be careful when it comes to shutting a door for good or you might regret it later."

His eyes narrow. "I won't regret it."

"I had some bad moments with my father too. I forgave him."

"It's not the same."

"Of course it's not completely the same. Maybe it would help if you talked more about your childhood."

"No *completely* the same? It's not even the same damn galaxy. You need me to tell you why? Because your father loved you, Susanna! He would have moved heaven and earth for you. That was always clear and that was why I couldn't hate him for treating me like shit because I knew he thought he was protecting you. But my mother? She hates my fucking guts. If you want to know about my childhood so badly I'll tell you. When I was a teenager my mother called me worthless and said I'd either die in a gutter or waste away in prison. When I confronted her with the fact that I'd seen her fucking my best friend's father she told me to my face that keeping me was a bad decision. She said no one would miss me once I was gone and that wasn't something she just tossed out there in a fit of anger. She meant it. When Tori and I were kids, she'd forget to buy us food and spend the child support money on herself. Half the time we wouldn't have had any dinner to eat if it weren't for Gloria. So there, that's what I grew up with and it's nothing like the charmed life you had so don't you fucking stand there and lecture me about *reckoning with the past* or whatever the fuck you want to call it!"

He grabs his keys and storms to the door. I'm expecting him to slam through it and leave but instead he throws his keys down and sighs loudly.

My tears are already rolling down my cheeks. "I didn't know, Colt. I didn't know how bad it was."

He turns, sees that I'm crying, and instantly becomes stricken. "Baby, I'm so sorry." He crosses the room, gathers me in his arms and rocks me gently. "I didn't mean to talk to you like that. Please don't cry. I shouldn't have yelled."

"That's not why I'm crying." I sniffle against his shoulder. "It hurts to hear what was done to you."

"It's fine now," he assures me, kissing the top of my head. "I don't think about all that past bullshit. You shouldn't think about it either."

I'm not sure it's true that he doesn't think about the past. There's no way his painful history didn't affect him or influence who he is now. But I won't push him to talk about it if he doesn't want to.

Colt kisses me and, as always, when Colt kisses me, nothing else matters.

"I missed you," he whispers as passionate urgency takes over. "You're never off my mind, Susanna."

He feels so good and I can't stop touching him. I lead him upstairs to our bed. Lately I've been feeling more and more insecure about my heavily pregnant body, but these doubts disappear when he undresses me, kissing me everywhere. I even believe his heated declaration that I'm beautiful. We make love slowly and with extreme care.

Colt is still tired from his trip and he yawns again. He wants to take a nap before going to the grocery store. I'm tired too, but it's a different kind of tired that has more to do with my body than my mind. Instead of sleeping, I just watch him sleep as twilight sets in. He smiles, still asleep, when I skim my fingers across his muscled shoulder.

Colt knows that I love him.

And I know that he loves me.

We began this journey accidentally and we married with haste. But we love each other wholeheartedly.

Which is why the questions inside my head are unwelcome ones.

Is that enough?

Is love alone enough for two people as unalike as we are?

How I wish there was someone around to assure me that it will always be enough.

25

COLT

It's not the most popular move when I call the corporate office and say that I need to be kept off the schedule until my wife gives birth. Immediately, my direct supervisor calls me back.

"We've all got families," he growls. "The routes don't stop for a baby."

This is one of those times when I seem to be failing everybody, but my wife is sitting ten feet away and I know she's listening.

"I need the time off," I tell the man with finality, confident he won't retaliate. They are desperately short on drivers.

He sighs. "Call when you get it sorted out."

My phone beeps with a warning that the battery is down to one percent but right now I can't remember where I left the charger. I shove the phone into my back pocket.

Susanna folds a pastel baby blanket. "Did you get fired?"

She sounds kind of hopeful.

"No, I didn't get fired but I definitely won't be winning employee of the year." I sound like a crabby dick and she rolls her eyes before reaching for another blanket. She's got a whole tower of them on the coffee table.

"Will you finish putting together the crib?" she asks.

"Of course."

She stops and looks at her baby blanket pile. Then she grimaces and puts a hand to her lower back. Her due date is two weeks from today but her doctor believes the baby might come a little early. She's already begun her maternity leave from the high school because being on her feet all day was becoming too difficult.

So, here we are.

She's off from work and I'm off from work. For now we can look forward to being here alone in this big house, waiting for a baby to show up and trying not to snap at each other.

"Can I get you anything, honey?" I ask her, genuinely anxious to see the way she clutches her back and breathes through the pain.

She gives me a tiny smile. "Let's just get the crib finished before the little one makes his or her debut."

We still don't know if the baby is a girl or a boy. And we don't have a name picked out either way. Weeks ago, she handed me a long list of names that she likes. I said they all sounded just fine. This must have been the wrong answer because she got mad and accused me of being disinterested.

The crib is upstairs in the room that is still in the process of being transformed into a nursery. Apparently, a nursery is supposed to have a theme and Susanna wants the theme to be baby animals. There are baby animals on the wallpaper border I hung last week. There are plushy baby animals hanging out on the wooden shelves I installed. The bedding has been washed and folded, ready to be added to the crib, all of it of course covered with cartoon baby animals.

The pieces of the crib were removed from a giant box the last time I was home but then I got distracted with something else. My tools are still in the room. The closet door is open and neatly stacked inside are the gifts from the fancy baby shower thrown by Susanna's mother. I'm told there was a chocolate fountain. I didn't see it for myself. I was on the road.

The crib is a very easy project, however the quality of the materials isn't great, a surprise because it was a gift from Susanna's mother and I know it wasn't cheap. I'm finished in half an hour and I test out the stability before adding the mattress. I take a step back and try to imagine a baby living in there. I could have designed and built something much better. I should have suggested that, and then found the time to pull it off.

Downstairs, Susanna has finished folding the baby blankets and she's fussing with the straps of a car seat.

"We need to install this in my car," she says. "That will be the only vehicle we can use for the baby because there's no room in your truck."

"I told you I'll trade it in for something with more seating."

"Okay. Do that. That is, if you can figure out how to get around to it."

I know she's tired. I know she's stressed. I really don't want to get irritated.

"I finished the crib."

She puts the car seat down and stands with her hand to her back. "Thank you."

"You don't have to thank me for that. This is my kid too."

Susanna's stomach is so huge that her maternity shirt barely covers it. She runs her hand over the giant bump and smiles. The baby is probably kicking. I want to walk across the room, hold her in my arms, feel the thud of our child moving and share a smile with her. There's no reason to stay where I am, staring in silence and feeling like an outsider.

Susanna looks up and notices that I'm watching her. She wears her glasses all the time now. She says her contacts bother her eyes. Her long brown hair hangs down her back in a loose ponytail. She's still my dream girl. She always will be.

"My mother said she'd come stay after the baby is born," Susanna says.

"Might be nice to have some help."

She nods. "How long will you be sticking around?"

I must have heard her wrong. "What do you mean?"

"How long will you be here before you need to go back out on the road?"

"I didn't give the boss a date. I'm not just going to take off the second you give birth."

"When *will* you take off?"

This conversation is going to a bad place. I should defuse it, but I don't. "It sounds like you think I'll be running away the first chance I get."

"Will you?"

"Damn, Susanna. We're married. We're having a baby together. And I'm right here for fuck's sake. What do you want me to do? Break off my balls so you can carry them around in your purse?"

She reddens. "It doesn't help when you say such things."

"And it doesn't help when you assume the worst of me."

"I don't! Is it so terrible that I want you here, Colt?"

"You're acting like I run out the door whenever I can and don't look back."

She lifts her chin but I can still see it quivering. "I don't want to do this."

"Do what? Fight? Great, let's not fight."

"I don't want us to be this way, slowly picking each other apart until there's nothing good left. My parents were like that. I know you think my childhood was ideal, but growing up with two parents who were always at odds was painful."

"We're not always at odds."

"You're gone half the time. More than half the time. And now that you're here, we act like this."

I swallow hard and ask a question I don't want to ask. "Do you think you made a mistake marrying me?"

She shakes her head quickly. "No!"

"But I'm sure as hell not the kind of man you need."

It's a terrible statement to make and she crumples. "How can you say that?"

The sight of Susanna's tears twists my guts like nothing else. It's always an extra kick in the teeth when I'm the one responsible. Anything else I say right now will just make things worse.

"Going for a drive," I mutter and grab my keys.

She doesn't call out or even make a sound.

I hate myself as I get behind the wheel and drive off. I'll hate myself more if I say something else that I can't take back. It's better if we both cool off a little.

Or maybe it'll be worse.

I don't know.

I don't know anything except I'm somehow destroying the best thing that's ever happened to me.

With a punch to the steering wheel, I aim for the road out of town.

The sky is the color of dirty dishwater. There have been storms on and off over the last couple of days, the remnants of some powerful weather system that has been generating unseasonable results. Looking at the sky, I'm not so sure we've seen the last of the weather but there could be a hurricane on the horizon for all I care.

This is where I used to go all the time as a kid. Sometimes with Tori and Jace. Often with just Jace. Now and then just on my own.

And once, more recently, with Susanna.

There's a rumor that a major developer is keeping an eye on this land. It would be a shame to see this scrubby moonscape disappear under asphalt and concrete.

I leave the truck behind and walk briskly all the way out to the flat boulder. Right now I'm really missing football. Whenever things went to shit I could get some satisfaction out of throwing the perfect spiral pass or knocking down the clumsy opposition. Maybe hitting something hard would kick some sense into my head so that I'd know what to say to my wife.

But there's nobody to throw to or hit out here. I'm just an idiot sitting alone on a rock while twisting my wedding ring around on my finger. I haven't taken it off since Susanna put it there.

"Am I breaking your heart?"

When I asked her that she sat right where I'm sitting now. She was stubborn, refusing to ask me to stay because she thought I wouldn't. Hours earlier, I'd carelessly gotten her pregnant but it would be months before I'd learn this.

If I even think about being condemned to spend my life without her, I'm in danger of being unable to draw another breath.

Somehow we need to make this work, and not just because we are about to become parents.

All the detours in our lives have led us back to each other.

That can't be for nothing.

We belong together, just like Tori and Jace.

Suddenly, I remember that I don't just need to sit here by myself and stare hopelessly at the dirt. I'm fortunate enough to have two of the best allies anyone could ever wish for.

I jump to my feet and jog back to the truck with a fresh sense of determination. Because there's more than one reason why I need to see Tori and Jace right now.

My wife was right about something important. She was right and I was wrong.

Ignoring the past doesn't make it disappear.

And the time is long overdue to reckon the shit out of it.

26

SUSANNA

E ven after he closes the door, I'm sure he won't go far. He'll get to the front yard, or maybe as far as the sidewalk, and turn around, full of apologies and promises that we can figure this out together.

I wait for him to turn around.

Then I hear the engine of his truck fire up and drive rapidly down the street. The sob I've been holding back steals my breath and I cling to the nearest wall.

"He'll be back," I say out loud to the empty living room. "He has to come back."

I'm a slow learner when it comes to some subjects. On the subject of love, all I've ever witnessed should have already taught me that there are no certainties.

"Till next time."

My own memories mock me.

I shouldn't count on next time.

I'm too tired to cry for very long. And pain has a way of distracting from tears. The ache in my lower back is ferocious. I need to lie down in the worst way.

The sofa is not very comfortable. The one bedroom on the first floor is my father's room and I've hardly set foot in there since the day he died. The thought of going in there right now is positively morbid.

Climbing the stairs has never been so hard. I have to pull myself along the railing and coax my leg to rise for each step. By the time I reach the top, I'm winded and my back hurts more than ever.

The first door on the left is the nursery and I slowly waddle over. In addition to putting the crib together, Colt inserted the mattress and covered it with the prewashed bedding. The room is exactly how I envisioned it ought to be and with everything in place I should have no trouble picturing our baby occupying it. Yet I can't picture that at all.

I'm afraid.

I'm afraid things changed too quickly and now we can't catch up.

I'm afraid of the things Colt and I say to each other.

I'm afraid we'll end up like my parents.

And I have the nagging feeling that there is another reason to be afraid, a reason that eludes my understanding but exists nonetheless.

Another spasm in my back steals my concentration and I press my hand to the spot where it hurts the most. In a moment the pain passes and I think about calling the doctor. On the other hand, I've been doing more than I should and I have succeeded in tiring myself out. If I can just sleep for a little while, I'm sure I will feel better. If I'm still feeling pain in a few hours, I'll call the doctor then.

Colt should be home by the time I wake up. At least, I hope so. I'll hold my tongue instead of lashing out over things that can't be fixed overnight. I'll remind him that I love him no matter what. I'll ask him to hold me. He doesn't need to do anything or decide anything today. I can overlook all our petty differences if he'll just hold me.

Sleeping at night has become a rather unpredictable endeavor. I can never seem to get comfortable. I sleep in fits and starts, not accumulating more than four hours a night. Naps have become essential.

I carried my phone up here and now I look at the screen, wallpapered with the same wedding photo that is framed on the wall downstairs. Would Colt turn around and come back right now if I asked him to?

Yes, he would. I know he would. But then what? Would we argue? Or worse, would we glare each other in silence?

My tears have given me a headache and if I don't lie down soon, I'm going to fall over. Abandoning the nursery, I take careful steps over to my bedroom.

This is still the room of a teenage girl. Aside from purchasing a larger bed, I haven't changed the furniture or the décor. For the most part, the room has remained trapped in time. It's certainly not a room you would expect to find a pair of married adults living in. No wonder why Colt doesn't feel at home here. I don't even feel at home here.

The bedsprings creak under my weight. I'm intentionally lying on Colt's pillow and I inhale deeply with my eyes closed, imagining he's right here and holding me close as I listen to the steadfast drumbeat of his heart. The baby stirs within, perhaps rolling over to join me in sleep.

I must be tired indeed. Even through the pain in my lower back and the turmoil in my mind, I can feel myself sinking into the welcome void of sleep.

My dreams, however, are vivid.

I've entered the Arcana High gymnasium where a sea of people awaits. Hundreds of blue and white streamers hang from the ceiling to honor the school colors. Everywhere I look there is blue. I'm covered in it. My dress, the one I hate wearing, is also blue. Music plays and people laugh. Faces turn my way, all of them familiar yet elusive. The one face I hungrily search for is nowhere to be seen, although I know he must be here somewhere. I'm uncomfortable, fretting over the way I look and feeling conspicuously awkward.

The voice I hear next is both sincere and immediately recognizable even though I have not heard it in many years.

"Susanna, you look beautiful, honey."

A petite woman with silver hair coiled atop her head smiles up at me and I don't know her well, but I do know she is always kind. She holds out her small hands and I realize she would like me to do the same. My palms rest atop hers and the gym becomes quiet, which is strange because we are in the middle of the homecoming dance and the noise should be overwhelming. But now there is no dance and no music and no laughter.

There is just her.

She looks over her shoulder and whatever she sees upsets her enormously. I don't get a chance to look for myself because she commands my attention again and her terrified expression terrifies me too. Her wide eyes are blue, the same vibrantly familiar shade of eyes I've stared into many times before.

"Susanna," she says with frightened urgency as she grips my hands in hers, "you and the baby need to wake up now. Wake up now, Susanna!"

A loud crash close to my head jolts me awake. My eyes flip open and the dream is over. The woman is gone but my heart pounds and there's pain, a lot of pain.

I reach for my glasses, slide them up my nose and try to focus on what's happening in the eerie yellowish light that filters through the blinds. A crescendo of agony tears through the center of my body, leaving me without enough air in my lungs to properly scream.

Then I look down and understand.

27

COLT

J ace is standing in the front yard with McClane when I
pull up.

The dog barks joyfully and bounds over to greet me
before I even get the door open. He turns around in circles
and jumps up to press his paws to my chest, tail wagging maniacally. I
scratch him behind the ears and this will have to be enough of a
greeting for now.

Jace stares straight up. "The sky looks weird, don't you think?"

"Yeah, I guess."

He forgets about the sky and looks closely at me instead. "Jesus,
what's wrong?"

I don't even try to keep the despair out of my voice. "I'm fucking
up, Jace. I'm fucking everything up."

My best friend doesn't hesitate to put his arm around my shoulders and steer me into the house. "Come on, buddy."

McClane, who is far more tuned into the moods of people than
most dogs, appears to understand this is not a social call and
becomes properly subdued, following us indoors and choosing to
quietly curl into a ball beneath Tori's piano.

My sister, drawn by my voice, walks in with her baby son in her arms. She's smiling until she gets a look at my face and then she glances at her husband with alarm. He moves to take the baby from her and Tori is now free to run to me with a hug.

"What happened? Is it Susanna?"

She relaxes a little when she hears that Susanna is safe at home. Still, it's not everyday that I show up on her doorstep on the verge of bawling my eyes out. She's anxious as she drags me over to the couch and forces me to take a seat.

"He still needs to burp," she informs Jace as she sits beside me.

Jace shifts his tiny son to his shoulder and lightly pats the little blanket-swaddled back.

Tori looks at me with loving concern and I'm flooded with a thousand childhood recollections of the girl who was always loyal to her little brother no matter how much trouble he caused and whether he appreciated her or not. I might have struck out when it came to drawing the card for parents but having Tori as a sister was my saving grace.

There are some things between me and Susanna that are too private to share. The things I do share right now could not be said to anyone other than Tori and Jace. I'm hanging by a thread and I know it. This is the ultimate crossroad and whatever happens today will determine the course of my life. Along with Susanna's. And that of our child.

"I don't know how to become good enough for her," I admit after a brief explanation of what led me here. "I spent too many years being the center of my own universe."

Tori winces. "Stop it. You're better than you know." She pounds an angry fist into the couch. "Damn them!"

"Who?"

"Our parents. They did this to you. Mom has always been a lost cause but Dad would have listened if I'd confronted him about the way he treated you."

"Tor, I wasn't his son and everyone knew it. That had to be humiliating for him. Every time he looked at me he saw betrayal. Maybe he just did what he could."

"It wasn't enough. And don't even get me started on *her*. I begged her to look for you after you ran away."

"Well, she said no one would miss me if I left."

Tori's chin trembles. "I really missed you, Colt," she says the softest, most heartbroken voice. "I was devastated when you were gone."

"I'm sorry. At the time I really thought you'd be relieved. I wouldn't have blamed you. I wasn't the best brother."

She stubbornly sets her jaw. "But you are to me because you're *my* brother. I felt like I should have understood how miserable you were but I was too wrapped up in my own sorrow after Jace and I broke up." She takes a deep breath and struggles to speak through her sudden tears. "Colt, I had a miscarriage when I was seventeen. It happened the night of the rivalry game between Arcana and Bredon. I didn't even tell Jace until we were reunited after so many years. I was depressed and shattered. I pushed Jace away. I pushed you away. I never talked about it at all. Believe me, I wish I had."

Hearing the whole story of my sister's agony is terrible and I can't find any words right away.

We've all kept secrets.

I've kept a big one from them while allowing it to eat away at my soul.

Perhaps if I'd chosen differently, then I wouldn't have ended up turning my back on the people I loved. Maybe my sister wouldn't have begun a torturous path of suffering her trauma in silence. She might have called me when her boss nearly killed her in San Diego or when she became addicted to painkillers. She could have asked her only brother for help when she found herself with no resources and nowhere to go before making a desperate move to the last refuge she could think of; Gloria's house. That's where she found Jace. That's where their next chapter began. Not just theirs, but mine too.

Jace pulls a chair right next to the couch and sits down with the baby on his shoulder. We all have our own memories of what happened back then, our own personal demons to wrestle with. Now here we are again in our little circle, much changed and inspecting each other with sorrow.

Jace, ever the philosophical writer, once told me that the three of us had been lost without each other in the years we spent apart. We should have found our way back sooner.

Yes, we definitely should have.

But we're here now. That's what counts.

Jace reaches for his wife's hand. He lifts it to his lips and kisses it. She smiles through her tears.

I look to my best friend. "Do you remember the day we met my wife?"

"Sure," he says immediately. "Dave's Tacos."

"Yeah. Dave's Tacos." I take a deep breath. "Less than an hour before that I saw my mother having sex with your father."

His eyes widen with shock. This is not news he was expecting to hear.

Tori gasps. "You *saw* that? How?"

"Remember how I snuck back into the house to steal money from her purse? I heard them in the living room. They were arguing, both of them drunk. She ridiculed him, saying it was a good thing she didn't rely on him for child support since he'd just lost his job again. I heard a crash so I ran in and there they were, fucking like animals on the living room floor."

"Shit." Jace is stunned. "You never said a word."

"I ran outside and puked in the bushes. Then I went to go catch up to you guys down the street. I didn't want to talk about it, didn't even want to think about it and put the pieces together of what it all meant. And I thought I was protecting you both by keeping it to myself."

Tori shuts her eyes and squeezes her husband's hand.

The truth is here.

Someone just needs to say it out loud.

"We're brothers, Jace."

He nods. "Yes."

"You suspected, didn't you?"

"Not until recently. I found some old photographs and learned my folks had been staying with my grandparents while my mother was pregnant. You would have been conceived in that time frame. My father and your mother knew each other in high school. Meanwhile, my parents' marriage was an unhappy one and your mother's husband was away on the other side of the world. I asked my dad directly the last time he was here. He admitted it was a possibility but refused to confirm and said it made no difference at this point anyway."

I remember that visit from Jace's dad. I was staying here in town at the time. I remember Jace looking at me real funny and asking if I ever wanted to know who my father was but I shut down the conversation.

"My mother confirmed it," I tell him. "She confirmed it to me."

"When?" Tori wants to know.

"Long time ago, right before I left home. She said...well, it doesn't matter now what she said. Nothing good."

Tori lowers her head and breathes deeply.

I think that now I too can breathe deeply. Despite my efforts to suffocate the truth about that summer day, it's been a festering infection for a long time.

Baby Mason, perhaps disturbed on some infant level by today's revelations, whines in his sleep. His father soothes him, kisses his cheek, and he calms down.

I chuckle in Jace's direction. "Hey, did your wife ever tell you the story about how I pissed my pants the first day of school?"

He laughs through his nose. "No."

"I promised you I would never tell," Tori reminds me. "I never have."

"Yeah, you found me crying behind the dumpster and swearing that I'd never set foot inside that school again. You hugged me and started pulling me home. You told me everything was going to be okay and because you said it, I believed it. Maybe that's why I'm here now. I need my big sister to tell me everything's going to be okay."

"Colt." Her tears threaten to spill over again but she holds them back and folds me into another soft hug. "We love you. *She* loves you. She loves you so much. You and Susanna belong together."

She's right. Whatever I did before and whatever I thought I wanted or didn't want no longer matters to me. Nothing will ever matter again if I lose Susanna.

That's why I'm quitting that damn job. I never should have taken it in the first place. I'll do something else, anything else. Hell, I'll run around with a push broom and sweep the freaking streets of Arcana if that's what it takes. Susanna and the baby are my home now. I belong with them. I'm ready to beg for another chance and do everything right every day.

"Everything is going to be okay," Tori assures me with unshakable confidence, the same way she did when I was five.

She looks to Jace to reinforce her words but Jace isn't listening. He's left his chair with the baby in his arms and he stands stiffly at the front room window.

Something is wrong.

Tori knows it too.

"What?" she asks.

Her question is answered by the urgent shriek of the storm sirens.

28

SUSANNA

I'm not even confused when I see that I'm soaked and the bed is wet. My water has broken while I slept.

After a moment the powerful contraction eases and I sit up. It's a good thing I glance down at the floor before stepping down. The area beside the bed is littered with sharp shards of turquoise ceramic.

But this really is confusing because I recognize the broken pieces. This was Gloria's vase, the one that is kept downstairs on the dining room table. The sound it made as it fell to the floor was responsible for jolting me awake. I don't remember bringing the vase up here. Colt must have done it and I hadn't noticed.

The digital alarm clock beside the bed is blank and I don't see my phone, although I could have sworn I left it on the nightstand. The lighting in the room is odd, like how I would imagine dusk in an area surrounded by fire. I think the power is out. My uneasiness grows when I hear no sign that Colt has returned.

Carefully climbing off the bed, I wonder how far apart my contractions are. There's no reason to panic. I'll find my phone. I'll call Colt. Labor and delivery for a first baby often takes many hours. There will be plenty of time to get to the hospital.

Once I've avoided stepping on the broken fragments of Gloria's vase, I spend a moment mourning the loss of an heirloom. Gloria received the vase from her husband, the original Jacek Zielinski, in the early years of their marriage. Colt must have relocated it in order to protect it and I can't imagine how it could have been knocked over. There is certainly no wind in here, although it is windy outside. A ferocious gust slams into the house, explaining the power outage.

The wet fabric of my leggings sticks to my skin and I pull a clean pair out of the dresser. I've just finished changing when a fresh contraction begins to build and by the time it peaks I can hardly breathe. I might not have as much time as I thought. Luckily, I've been keeping my neatly packed hospital bag in the trunk of my car, just in case. It's a shock to realize that within hours I will be meeting my child. The thrill of excitement mixes with sharp anxiety.

Colt, our baby is coming. I need you.

I still can't find my phone and I don't understand. I'm sure I brought it in here with me. The only option is to go downstairs. There is still a landline hooked up in my father's old office. I'll be forced to use it if my phone is still missing.

Once my feet are pushed into my shoes, I try to breathe evenly as I walk to the stairs. The railing is clutched for dear life as I gingerly descend one step at a time and hope my next contraction holds out until I'm on flat ground.

I've just made it to the bottom step when the sirens begin screaming. The sound would make anyone's blood run cold. I've only ever heard them in the movies, never in real life, but I know what they are for. A tornado is nearby. The wind accelerates and batters the north side of the house. Another contraction hits and the pain is horrible, so horrible that I vomit all over the floor.

Don't panic.

Reasonable words, but futile. I'm in labor, I'm alone and there's a tornado coming.

Panic is completely justified.

Going outside makes no sense but the world has become rather nonsensical right now. Tornadoes are not common here and it's not the season for them anyway. Yet the sirens insist that one is here and I fling open the front door, perhaps to see for myself.

The air is already thick with dust and debris. Trees bend this way and that, threatening to break in two. Above the wail of the sirens is a roar that could be a jet engine but isn't. It's the merciless scream of nature-born fury.

A window screen hurtles out of nowhere and a sharp edge catches my right temple. By some miracle my glasses aren't knocked off and I press my fingers to the damage. They come away with blood.

But the next contraction is the worst one yet and I can't worry about a scratch on my face. I'm doubled over, sinking down to my knees, depleted by the agony. Returning to the house makes sense but I'm afraid. I don't want to be alone. I gasp for breath and squint at a figure running down the street.

It's Namra's oldest son, Faizal. He must have been out when the sirens began and his mother is a beacon in pink medical scrubs, frantically waving her arms at him in her front yard. I shout my neighbor's name but there is far too much competing noise.

Faizal has nearly reached his yard when he happens to spot me. He points and Namra's head turns. I see her gasp and clap her hand over her mouth in horror at the sight of me bleeding and staggering around outside. Faizal barrels across the street at full speed, undeterred by the monstrous wind. He wears an Arcana High Football jersey and somehow this is a strange comfort. He lifts me up and with a firm, strong arm around my waist begins to halfway carry me. The wind is too loud to bother talking and anyway, there's no time. When his mother catches up, she braces my other side and the two of them rush me across the street to their house.

While Namra opens the door I look over my shoulder. The swirling grey cloud spins at the north end of the street and swallows up a house. It's a monstrous thing to behold and I shut my eyes so I do not have to see it anymore.

"The basement!" Namra shouts when we cross the threshold.

Faizal holds onto me as we descend the narrow staircase and Namra closes the door at the top of the steps. Her other two sons are already down there and they are frightened as it is, but seeing their bleeding neighbor is too much. The youngest boy, Rashid, begins to cry.

"Get her to the sofa," Namra says in the decisive tone of someone accustomed to dealing with emergencies. Her son doesn't question her at all.

"Thank you," I say to the boy who might have just saved not only my life but my baby's life.

Faizal gives me a nervous smile and retreats to the other side of the room to comfort his brothers. Meanwhile, his mother launches into full nurse mode and crouches down to examine the cut on my head.

"Okay, the cut looks superficial, but you'll need stitches."

"I'm in labor."

Her deep brown eyes widen. "How far apart are your contractions?"

"I don't know. I was asleep and there was a crash and I couldn't find my phone and-"

Another contraction hits and I grip the arm of the sofa.

Namra holds my hand. "Breathe, Susanna, breathe."

A deafening series of noises collide overhead, the sound of an innocent neighborhood taking the brunt of the storm's wrath.

"What if the house falls?" Rashid asks.

"It won't," his oldest brother promises, although he flinches when the walls rattle.

"What about Dad?"

"He's all the way in Plainsfield. He's still at work."

Namra wipes the blood from my face with a clean cotton cloth and tries to comfort us all. "I've seen tornadoes before. It'll be over soon."

I don't know how she can be so calm. My terror exists on so many levels I can't unpack it all. Colt said he was taking a drive. He's partial to the wide open spaces outside town. If he was out there when the tornado hit...

"Another contraction?" Namra asks with sympathy when I shudder. She holds my hand.

"The wind is dying down," Faizal announces with a loud sigh of relief. "The sirens have stopped."

His mother listens. "Sounds like it."

There is a narrow rectangular window near the ceiling. Within a minute it goes from being completely dark, to mildly grey, to bleakly sunny. Faizal wants to run upstairs to see if all is clear but his mother begs him to wait just one more moment.

I feel another contraction coming and brace for the peak, doing my best not to scream and scare the boys.

Namra has been keeping track and now she grows worried. "Less than two minutes apart. We need to call an ambulance. Can you still walk?"

I can still walk, just barely. She helps me up the stairs and tells the boys to be careful where they step because there is glass from the broken windows.

There are sirens all around now, not the piercing howl of the storm sirens but the sound of many emergency vehicles blending together as they race to nearby destinations.

Namra sits me down in a comfortable armchair. She shouts at the boys not to go outside. There might be downed power lines. I can hear her calling 911.

Her three sons cluster together and regard me with worried expressions. I try to smile at them but my heart hurts too much. I won't be capable of smiling until I know that Colt is safe. My belly tightens and I whimper my way through another contraction. The pain recedes for the moment but it will be back and it will be worse.

Namra finishes murmuring on the phone. "They will try to get here soon. Just keep breathing, Susanna."

There must be all kinds of terrible reasons why no ambulance is available to come immediately. I don't want to think about those reasons. I shut my eyes and try to breathe like Nama says but I feel a tear roll down my cheek. I need Colt. I need to tell Namra to call him right away.

"SUSANNA!"

My eyes fly open.

The scream comes from outside and it is the most tortured, distressing sound I have ever heard. I'm reminded of the day he showed up at Arcana High and thundered through the halls while shouting my name. That day he was frustrated and confused. Now he's desperate and heartsick.

Labor or not, I'm out of the chair and at the door before anyone else even has time to react. I fling Namra's front door open and I see terrible things but they hardly register because I also see him.

He's on his knees, the picture of grief, in front of the pile of ruin that used to be our house.

"COLT!"

He turns slowly, almost like he's afraid to look in case the sound of my voice isn't real. I want to run to him but I can't because the new wave of pain is unbearable.

Colt is on his feet now and he tears across the street, leaping over debris along the way. He skids to a halt four feet away and stares at me for a second, already crying before he sweeps me into his arms.

"Oh honey, thank god, I thought I lost you." He breaks down completely, sobbing so hard his body shakes.

"Don't leave me." I cry too as I cling to him. "Please don't leave me, Colt."

"Never!" He kisses me fiercely. "I swear I'll never leave you again, Susanna. Never."

Now he holds my face and sees that I've been hurt. I've forgotten about the cut and I tell him it's nothing, nothing at all. I'm on the verge of explaining that there is something much more critical to worry about right now when the next agonizing wave crests.

"The baby is coming," I gasp out.

Colt inhales sharply and picks me up in his arms.

"Bring her inside," Namra orders from the doorway. "I don't think the ambulance will get here in time."

Colt carries me into the house. I am gently laid atop a cushion of blankets in a section of the living room that has been cleared of furniture. Someone helps pull my pants off as my body threatens to split open.

Namra has managed to connect with an obstetrician at the Plainsfield Hospital where she works and he will talk her through the delivery. Namra is an ER nurse but she has been present for births before.

"Do you feel the urge to push yet?" asks the doctor, who has been placed on speaker phone.

"Yes!" I'm gritting my teeth and squeezing Colt's hand. "HOLY SHIT THIS FUCKING HURTS!"

My husband looks around wildly. "What the hell should I do?"

"Sit behind her." Namra examines the progress between my legs. "Hold her, help her bear down."

Colt obeys and I lean back against his strong chest.

"You can do this, baby." He kisses my cheek. "I love you so much."

"Another one's coming," I sob and think longingly of the lovely epidural I was planning to have. I feel like I'm being ripped apart.

"You're crowning," says Namra. "When you feel the next contraction, push hard."

I squeeze Colt's hand with all my might. He should be thanking his lucky stars that I'm not very strong or he'd have a bunch of broken fingers.

Half a dozen excruciating pushes later and I feel an immense moment of pressure, followed by the strangest sense of separation.

And then, seconds later, the robust cry of a new life.

"It's a girl." Namra smiles as she continues to work. "Congratulations."

"A girl," I repeat softly and turn my head to look up at my husband. "Colt, we have a daughter."

He can't say a word. He's been struck speechless by the sight of the tiny creature who is now being placed in my arms.

She had been crying but she stops when she feels me holding her. She opens her eyes. My daughter and I gaze at each other for the very first time.

"She's so beautiful," I breathe and fall in love with the sight of her perfect little face. "Don't you think she's beautiful?"

Colt finds his voice. "Of course she is. Just like her mother."

Namra has already shooed her boys out of the room to give us some privacy. She now gets to her feet and smiles at us before following them.

"Thank you," I mouth silently.

She touches her hand to her heart.

Colt reaches out a gentle hand and our daughter immediately grasps his finger in her miniature palm, almost like she's claiming him.

He bravely tries not to cry as he introduces himself to our daughter. "I'm your daddy," he says.

I touch her cheek and marvel over the satin feel of her skin. "She needs a name."

Colt plants a kiss on my head. "I've always liked the name Emily."

"Emily." I try out the sound.

"We can pick something else," he assures me.

"No, we can't. Emily Malene. That's her name. I love it." I lift my face in search of his kiss. "And I love you."

He kisses me passionately, then tips my chin up. "I meant it."

"What?"

"I'll never leave your side again, Susanna. You and me. We're forever."

"You and me and Emily."

"My family," he whispers and wraps us tenderly in his arms.

That's exactly where we'll stay.

29

COLT

Six people lost their lives in Arcana on the day of the storm.

One of them was Richard Salenger, my former English teacher. He'd come home only minutes earlier and he was inside his house when it collapsed on top of him. If he'd arrived five minutes later, he would likely still be alive.

Susanna wanted to attend the funeral of the man who had been her father's friend before he became her colleague, but she was still exhausted after giving birth only days earlier. I persuaded her to stay home with baby Emily and promised to pay respects on her behalf.

Jace has stepped up to provide financial relief to the victims and he's participating in a fundraiser to help rebuild the parts of town that suffered the most damage. The story of Arcana's deadly tornado would have made national news just because of the catastrophic nature of it but the coverage became far more extensive due to the fact that this is the hometown of former NFL star Jace Zielinski. Add to that the story of his sister-in-law's narrow escape from the storm and emergency birth at a neighbor's house and it's a recipe for massive interest. Susanna has been overwhelmed by all the calls and pleas for interviews, all of which she declined in favor of a simple statement expressing her gratitude to her hometown and especially to the neighbors who saved both her life and the life of our daughter.

Eventually the press will move on to something else but for now there are still news trucks hovering on the downtown strip and reporting from the cemetery ten miles away where some of the storm victims will be buried today.

My mother saw an opportunity to jump right into the middle of things and managed to get her face in front of some cameras. She carried on about how blessed she is and how she can't wait to meet her new granddaughter. I allowed Tori to send her some pictures but that's all she's getting. If Emily really wants to meet her grandmother when she's older then we'll see.

The news even reached Jace's dad where he's been bumming around in a Mexican beach town. Despite the fact that the truth is now out in the open, I'll never be able to think of him as anything other than 'Jace's dad'. He asked Jace to pass his phone number along to me. I said no thanks.

The principal of Arcana High stands beside her college aged son while a sincere eulogy for her husband is delivered by Jace. Jace credits Richard Salenger for faithfully encouraging his students, past and present. He says he is proud to count his former teacher as a friend and he mourns the loss to the Salenger family, to the school and to the community.

Tori and Jace's son begins to fuss while the eulogy is still underway so I ask my sister if she'd like to try giving him to me for a little while. Lo and behold, my little nephew quits crying as soon as he's transferred to my arms. It turns out I'm really good at holding babies. Emily always settles right down when I cradle her against my shoulder. We walk up and down the hall in the middle of the night while Susanna gets some rest.

Richard Salenger's son cries as he listens to Jace say what a good man his father was. I'm sure he was also a good father. His son is clearly heartbroken. He'll be missed everyday by the family he had to leave too soon but from the sound of it, he made the most out of the time he did have.

Tori joins Jace while he speaks quietly to the Salengers. I know he's telling them to let him know if there's anything he can do. Those aren't just words to Jace. He's never insincere.

My sister returns to retrieve little Mason and tells me how people keep bringing her donated items for Susanna and the baby. She asks if she and Jace can bring everything over later today.

"Sure," I tell her, both touched and surprised by all the generosity. When the house was destroyed, all the stuff we had for the baby was destroyed with it. Susanna needed eight stitches to close the cut on her face and she and Emily spent a night at the hospital just to make sure there were no complications. Ever since then we've been making do and staying at Gloria's house. Among the random things that were salvaged from the disaster were our wedding photos and Susanna's cell phone.

The weird thing about the cell phone was Susanna was looking for it right before the storm hit and couldn't find it anywhere. I got sick to my stomach when I heard that she might have remained upstairs a moment too long if not for the fact that she was searching for her phone. Jace was the one who found the thing sitting atop a twisted pile of debris, almost as if someone had deliberately placed it there.

Jace and Tori are puzzled when I say that I want to take a walk in the cemetery. I tell them to go on ahead and leave without me. There are a couple of people I want to visit.

The mourners have drifted away and I keep my eyes trained on Tori, Jace and Mason as they move toward the parking lot. The love I have for those three people is eclipsed only by my fierce love for my wife and daughter.

Once they are out of sight, I do take my walk.

First, I stop by the grave of Eric Malene. I want to tell him that I'm a father myself now and that someday I'll take my daughter camping, like he took me. I'll make sure she knows what country music sounds like and how to navigate by the stars. And wherever he is, I hope he's not worried about Rochelle and Carrie. They are part of our family. Carrie has a dance recital next month and we all plan to show up to let her know how important she is. Lastly, I let my dad know that if he were here, he would be so proud of both of his daughters, Tori and Carrie. And maybe he would have a few reasons to be proud of me too.

My next stop is Drew Toledo's resting place. Someone has left a football and an Arcana High felt pennant for him. He should hear that he's now the grandfather of a beautiful baby girl. I hold up a picture of Emily on my phone, just in case it's possible for him to see it. I promise to be an excellent father and a loving husband. And I'll talk to Emily about her grandfather. She doesn't need to hear about his flaws. She just needs to know that he would have loved her so very much.

Last of all, I go to see Gloria Zielinski. This time the words don't come easy. Jace is sure she knew she was my grandmother but there was little she could do about it when no one would acknowledge the truth. In any case, my childhood was far better than it would have been without her living right next door and looking out for both me and Tori.

I believe she's still looking out for us.

The day after our daughter was born, Susanna asked me when I'd moved the vase that she kept on the dining room table. I told her I hadn't moved it at all. She went pale and told me about her dream. Just before the storm hit, she was dreaming of Gloria and in the dream, Gloria was yelling at her to wake up. The sound of a crash did wake her up. It was the sound of the vase hitting the floor. And then she thought for sure she'd left her cell phone nearby but couldn't find it. That's why she needed to go downstairs. Seconds later she heard the sirens. Susanna concluded it must all be a strange, inexplicable coincidence. Just *one of those things* as people like to say.

I don't think that. Jace doesn't either.

In the end, I just touch the top of Gloria's white marble headstone and say thank you. Next time I visit I'll bring Emily and Susanna. I'll remember to bring flowers too.

As soon as I step away from Gloria, Susanna texts with a photo of our sleeping daughter. She asks if I'm going to be home soon. I smile and text her back right away.

I'm coming home right now.

Because I don't intend to miss a single moment.

30

SUSANNA

Colt gently fastens Emily's diaper onto her wiggling body and snaps up her pink onesie while I watch them from the couch. There's nothing I love to see more than the way his face shines as he smiles down at our little girl.

"Guess who is eight weeks old today?" he croons and he lifts her into the crook of his elbow. "Daddy's little angel, that's who."

He looks up when he hears the snap of my cell phone camera.

"I couldn't resist," I explain and feel my heart skip when I look at the priceless photo captured on my phone. I send it to my mother, who has swiftly become the world's most devoted grandmother as well as Colt's biggest fan. She has even insisted that he needs to start calling her Mom. She responds immediately with a line of hearts.

"You want to feed her before company arrives?" Colt asks.

I'm already unbuttoning my shirt. "That's a good idea."

Emily is wide-eyed and alert when Colt sits down and transfers her to me. She gurgles and smiles and my heart melts into a puddle. She latches onto my right breast and I cup my palm across the back of her little head, feeling the tickle of the light brown hair that has begun to fill in.

Colt sits back and watches us while one hand runs thoughtfully over his jaw. Every day he becomes a little bit more ridiculously handsome. Every day I love him even more.

He quit his trucking job and I'm on maternity leave so we've had a lot of time to spend together as we learn how to adapt to our new little family unit. Right now the plan is for me to remain home through the summer and then I'll return to my teaching job at Arcana High in the fall. Colt balked at the idea of sending Emily to daycare. He'll take care of her while I'm at school and in the meantime he's working on some ideas he can start building on here at home.

"What are you thinking?" he asks me.

"I'm wondering if you're going to keep your latest beard."

He grins. "Do you want me to?"

"You're absurdly sexy either way. But I'm really growing attached to the beard."

His blue eyes glimmer, just for a second. We've been locked in a grueling newborn care routine but at last week's doctor visit I received the green light to resume *all* activities. Colt, forever patient with me, has been waiting for a signal that I'm ready. I know he won't mind at all that my body is still bouncing back after the pregnancy. There's no reason to feel shy in front of my husband.

Emily finishes nursing and when I move her to my shoulder she promptly burps. The doorbell rings. Colt jumps off the couch to answer it.

On the other side of the door are Jace, Tori and Mason Zielinski.

With a charming smile and a shock of black hair, little Mason resembles his father more and more. He laughs in his mother's arms when his Uncle Colt makes a funny face at him and then his chubby arm reaches for his uncle.

McClane has also come over for a visit. After relishing a proper greeting from Colt, he trots over to the sofa with his tail wagging. He behaves exceptionally well when he's near the babies. Tori says the dog now spends most of his time gazing at Mason with adoration and waiting to see what the baby will do next.

"Hello, McClane." I pet him with my free hand and he flattens his ears, sniffing at Emily's pink blanket while his tail continues to thump.

Earlier, Colt prepared a variety of pierogis for everyone. They just need to be reheated. The recipe is Gloria's, and these dumplings were a staple in her kitchen. Early in her marriage she learned how to make them for her husband when he grew nostalgic for his home in Poland.

I'm ready to offer Emily to anyone who wants to hold her. Her loving aunt practically runs across the room to scoop her up with eagerness.

"There's my gorgeous girl." Tori nuzzles her cheek to Emily's and sits down next to me. "How's she been sleeping?"

"Better. Last night she had a six hour stretch and when she woke up a four a.m., her daddy raced to her room."

"We read *The Cat In The Hat* together," Colt adds as Mason laughs at him again. "Then she fell asleep for another hour."

Tori looks over at her brother in a way that I can only describe as pure amazement. I don't blame her. Colt Malene amazes me too.

Jace, always the quiet observer, takes a seat in the chair that was his grandmother's favorite place to relax. He mulls over the sight of his family with a smile while McClane curls up at his feet.

"Do you want to tell them?" Tori asks.

Jace winks at his wife. "You can have the honors."

Tori needs to give Emily back to me so she can rummage through the diaper bag. She extracts a manila folder, which she passes to me.

I look to Colt and he shrugs. Evidently whatever is happening is also a surprise to him. I open the folder and see pages of tightly worded legal documents. I only need to read a few sentences before I understand what these documents represent.

"Wait, you're giving us the house? How?"

I'm aware of the stipulation in Gloria's will that her house was to be left in three equal shares to Jace, Tori and Colt with a clause that prevented a sale to outside parties. She did this in the hopes that the three of them, long estranged, would somehow be reunited.

We've been staying here since Emily was born but our intention was always to buy another house in Arcana. We were just waiting for the insurance money to come through from my dad's house. Anyway, there haven't been many homes for sale locally because of all the storm damage. We have felt very fortunate to have the opportunity to stay here, especially because the house holds so many happy memories for Colt. But we never planned to stay forever because the house wasn't really ours.

Tori can't wait to explain the paperwork. After thorough consideration, Paul Elkins determined that from a legal standpoint there was nothing preventing Tori and Jace from gifting their ownership shares to Colt and, by extension, to me as well.

As Tori talks, I fall in love with the idea of staying here. This is not a large house but it's perfect for us. It's one story and Emily's room isn't far from the master bedroom where Colt and I sleep. The large grassy backyard features a lovely garden and fruit orchard. We're within walking distance to the downtown district and to the high school. Yes, I could happily live here forever.

Still, whether or not to accept a gift of this magnitude from Tori and Jace has to be Colt's call.

He's thinking and he studies me as I hold Emily. He raises an eyebrow and I realize he's asking me how I feel about living here for good. I nod my head once and he smiles.

Tori and Jace have been nervously watching us, trying to gauge our reactions.

"What would Gloria think?" Colt asks Jace.

Jace is ready with an answer. "Gloria would be thrilled. This was already your home. We're just making it official."

"We'll never be able to thank you guys enough."

"You already have," Jace says. "Just by being our family."

Tori considers the matter settled and says that I ought to redecorate and update the house as I see fit. Honestly, I like the vintage style of the place and I can't think of anything I would change. Tori likes that answer. Then she stands up, declares that she's hungry and asks her brother what she has to do to score some pierogis.

He starts walking to the kitchen with Mason still in his arms.

"Follow me. I'll let you help if you promise not to mess up my kitchen."

Tori snorts, rolls her eyes, and trails after her brother.

There are sounds of plates and glasses being removed from cabinets as the two of them bicker in a good natured sibling way. It's not often that Jace and I find ourselves alone together and I feel like I need to say something to him.

"Thank you, Jace. I promise that I will treat your grandmother's house with the care it deserves."

He becomes wistful as he looks around. "Gloria would love that you've made this house your home. This was always a happy place full of love. I enjoyed growing up here. Emily will enjoy growing up here too."

I look at the wall of family photos. In one that has faded with time, Gloria and her husband Jacek stand together in the front yard in a long gone year when they were young. Ever since the storm, I think of her often. When I remember my dream, a cold shiver runs up my spine. As a scientist, I like sensible explanations, however I've never been able to come up with one that would account for what happened that day. I'm left wondering if sometimes the power of love might just be more formidable than anything else.

Yes, I think maybe it is.

Emily, still in my lap, waves her arms and makes a soft cooing noise.

"Would you like to hold your niece?" I ask.

Jace grins, perhaps thinking about the fact that he gets to be Emily's uncle twice over. First, because he's married to Colt's sister. And second, because he's Colt's half brother.

"Yeah, I would love to hold her."

He extends his arms. I hand over my baby girl.

"Someday I'm going to teach you how to play football," he promises Emily. I can definitely see a little bit of Colt in his smile.

There's no formal dining room here so we decide to eat casually in the living room on paper plates. Colt and Jace hold each other's babies the whole time and when I glance at Tori, she's already looking at me. As I gaze at my wonderful family, a dreamlike sense of astonishment sweeps over me and I'm sure that everything I've done all my life was meant to happen in order to lead me right here. I think maybe it's the case for us all.

Little Mason begins to get fussy at sundown so Tori and Jace decide to bring him home. Colt holds Emily in one arm and keeps his other arm around me while we wave goodbye to the Zielinksis.

"Till next time," calls Colt.

His sister blows him a kiss.

After they drive away, we bring Emily to the backyard to watch the rest of the sunlight disappear. As the stars begin to twinkle their way into existence, Colt names them for Emily and I could swear she is listening and learning.

We've figured out that she sleeps better if she receives a bath with lavender baby soap right before bed. We bathe her together, marveling at how pleased she is to splash warm water around in her little pink tub. Shortly after I nurse her once more in a rocking chair built by Colt in the workshop he set up in the garage, she falls asleep. I tuck her into her crib in the room that once belonged to her Uncle Jace, switch on her overhead musical mobile and just stare at her, overwhelmed with indescribable tenderness. Someday she'll hear her parents' story and learn of the tumultuous day of her birth. I wonder what she'll think.

She will always be my little miracle. Mine and Colt's. She is us.

I turn on the baby monitor and leave her door open a crack.

Colt is cleaning up in the kitchen. He doesn't hear when I quietly leave Emily's room and take a few steps down the hall to visit our bedroom. In front of the bathroom vanity mirror I change into a sensual cherry red satin nightgown. My mother went on a shopping spree and gave it to me last week, perhaps understanding that I might be searching for a little help to feel desirable and sexy. Sometimes she understands me better than I understand myself. I shake my hair out of the elastic band that was keeping it tied up and I brush it carefully.

When I sneak into the kitchen in my bare feet, Colt is drying the dishes. He's wearing grey sweatpants and no shirt. He doesn't know I'm there until I plant a kiss on his bare shoulder.

He turns his head, notices the red nightie and gets real interested in a hurry. He drops the dishtowel and puts his hands on my hips.

"Haven't seen this before." His eyes rake me over.

"Do you like it?" As if I need to ask. He's practically drooling.

"You kidding? I need all my self control not to bend you over the counter and fuck the daylights out of you."

I slip my arms up over his shoulders, already feeling giddy with anticipation. "Will you settle for going down the hall to our bedroom and fucking me there?"

He groans and crushes my body to his, showing off the hard evidence of how badly he wants this. I rise up on my toes and deliberately rub against him.

"You have no idea," he growls as he lifts me, wrapping my legs around his waist, "how much I've missed doing nasty things to this body."

I like this game. I nip playfully at his neck. "How much?"

"I have to jerk off three times a day just to tame the beast."

I flick out my tongue to tease his lips. "Show me."

Colt doesn't need any prodding. With my legs firmly around his waist, he charges straight to the bedroom and tosses me down on top of the covers. He drops his pants before I can even sit up on my elbows. I bend my knees open and he curses a hot blue streak when he sees that I've done already done him a favor and left my panties behind.

"Fuck, you're everything, baby." He lowers himself between my legs and flashes a crooked grin. "I'll hold out as long as I can but I'm like a motherfucking damn that's about to break."

"Don't worry." I move my hips. "I'll be ready to come the second I feel you."

His expression becomes serious. "Kiss me."

I pull him down closer and give him my tongue. We make out like a pair of eager teenagers for a minute and Colt pushes my legs farther apart.

I break the kiss and stop him with a hand on his chest. "Wait."

"What's wrong?"

I smile up at him. "Tell me you love me."

"I love you, Susanna." He groans loudly when I reach down to guide him inside and he says it again. "I love you."

"I love you too, Colt Malene."

Though he's ready to explode, he enters me slowly.

The months of deprivation catch up and the orgasm is a freight train. Colt loses control as soon as I'm finished trembling. I watch his face the entire time, until he's so spent and shattered that he drops his head to my breasts and tries to catch his breath.

"I love you," I tell him as I thread my fingers through his sweaty hair. It's true that I just said that to him a moment ago. It's also true that I can never say it too much.

He raises his head. He kisses me softly. "I love you forever."

I tickle his skin. "Promise?"

He knows I'm remembering that night over a year ago when passionate words were exchanged on the side of the road. He grins, then grows completely solemn before acknowledging how far we've come since then.

"Yes, Susanna. I can promise you forever."

EPILOGUE

COLT

3 years later

"**D**addy, they're here!" Emily leaps from her seat beside the front window where she's been keeping watch. She scampers over to the door and begins trying to pry it open.

"Hold on." I hurry over and flip the deadbolt that's too high for her to reach.

Emily jumps up and down while her uncle, her cousin and her favorite dog make their way up the front yard walkway. McClane whines with excitement but he's far too disciplined to barrel ahead at full speed.

"Uncle Colt!" Mason bounces beside his dad. "Emily! Emily, I'm here!""

"Mason!" Emily shrieks and waves wildly.

You might think the kids had been separated for months instead of playing together just yesterday. My eyes meet Jace's and we exchange a grin.

Emily's ponytail has come loose and I reach down to fix it, making one extra loop of the elastic band to ensure it stays in place.

McClane presents himself to be pet and Emily rubs her little hand across the top of his broad head. The dog licks her cheek and she giggles. Mason joins in on the petting of McClane. The dog shuts his eyes, the picture of bliss.

Jace snaps McClane's leash on. "You guys ready to take a walk to the park?"

Emily runs into the house and returns promptly with a stuffed armadillo. "Mr. Bubbles wants to go to the park too."

I try not to wince. "Ah, you know what? Mr. Bubbles looks kind of tired. How about we leave him here to take a nap on the couch?"

Emily stares into the beady plastic eyes of the beloved toy she received for her recent birthday. Her Aunt Carrie gave it to her so it's especially precious. When I asked my daughter why she calls him Mr. Bubbles, she looked at me like I might have a few screws loose and said, "Because that's his name, Daddy." My kid is a freaking riot.

"He can take a nap," Emily agrees and then shoves him into my arms. "Cover him with a blanket."

I do as I'm told and tuck one of Gloria's homemade afghans around the thing's stuffed grey body on the couch. The kids want to hold McClane's leash for the walk to the park and Jace says that's fine as long as they can share. They each agreeably clutch a section of the red leash and start walking.

"Don't get too far ahead," I warn, although there's not a chance they could outrun us.

Jace elbows me. "What do you have against Mr. Bubbles?"

"Mr. Bubbles gets into too much trouble. Last time he went to the park he almost got kidnapped by some other kid and he came home with grass stains all over his backside, which took me an hour of elbow grease to undo."

Jace snorts. "Listen to you."

I'm indignant. "Hey, what kind of dad would I be if I failed to take care of Mr. Bubbles?"

Jace cracks up.

"Did you finish your book yet?" I ask him. He's been working on the third installment in his zombie apocalypse series and I'm not being bias when I say that it's damn good. Even the critics agree.

"I've got one chapter and the epilogue left," he says and sounds quite pleased with himself. I always get the impression he's way more proud of his books than he is of his Super Bowl ring.

I ask him if I can expect to see the first draft soon and he estimates he'll have it done by the time I'm back from my trip.

"That reminds me," he says, "I know you already checked over the RV thoroughly, but I topped off the gas tank for you. I might have also ordered a complete collection of Johnny Cash for you to listen to on the road."

"Thanks, I'll try to sneak that in when I'm not being force fed *The Wheels On The Bus* for the six thousandth time."

He laughs.

"Still okay if we pick the thing up tomorrow?" I ask.

"It'll be ready."

Tomorrow is the last day of school, meaning Susanna's summer break is about to begin. The day after that, we're taking Emily for a two week trip in the luxury RV we are borrowing from Tori and Jace. I can't wait to show my girls the open road. And the Grand Canyon. And Yellowstone. And the clarity of the night sky far away from the city lights. This is our first big family vacation ever and I'm determined to make it unforgettable.

Just ahead, Emily and Mason are having a fine time walking a very well behaved McClane, who seems content to proceed at a very slow pace to match his little buddies. They are the best of friends, more like siblings than cousins, and I hope that will always be the case. Mason is an easygoing, bright little boy who strongly resembles his father in every way. As for my Emily, with her brown hair in a ponytail and a pair of brand new pink-framed glasses on her face, she's a miniature Susanna. But she does have her daddy's blue eyes.

Jace and I keep an eye on our children and when we're about to make a turn that will lead to tiny downtown Arcana, he gets a little misty eyed. "There's nothing I wouldn't do for them," he says like he's echoing my thoughts.

I look at my brother, my best friend. "We've come a long way."

Not just the two of us but all of us. He nods and I know he understands.

Jace takes McClane's leash since we're now coming to an area that's going to be full of people. I offer a hand to each of the kids because we'll be close enough to the street to exercise caution. There is no longer any evidence in sight of the tornado, only a bronze plaque in front of the Arcana Community Center that lists the date and the names of those who perished.

The first place we stop is the office of Paul Elkins. The man's nearly eighty now and shows no sign that he's on the cusp of stepping down from solving the various legal dilemmas that afflict Arcana's citizens. Tori claims his mind is as sharp as someone half his age and she would know since she works right alongside him every day. She has become the leading local real estate agent and though she could easily move to her own office, she prefers to work out of Paul's.

My sister, now six months pregnant with her second son, must have been watching for us. The kids run to her as soon as she steps outside. She crouches down to three-year-old height and asks Mason if he ate his breakfast without a fuss after she left this morning. Next, she tells Emily that she looks fabulous in her new glasses.

Jace holds out his hand to help his wife stand up again and once she's upright he gives her belly a loving pat.

"How are you feeling?" I ask my sister.

"Great. Even though it feels like this one is turning cartwheels in there. What are you guys up to?"

"On our way to the park." I wink and lower my voice to a whisper. "Then maybe some ice cream."

Emily squeals. "Ice cream! I want ice cream!" She bounces up and down.

Mason bounces with her. "I want ice cream too!"

"Now look what you've done," Jace deadpans.

"Don't be such a killjoy," I tell him.

He silently mouths the words, "Up yours, Malene."

"Eat shit, Zielinski," I silently mouth back. Our standard insults going way back for a lot of years.

Tori understands every word and shakes her head. "Behave, both of you."

"I don't know what you mean, Tor. We're just two stay at home dads living our best life."

Jace laughs. Tori tries not to laugh and fails.

"Aunt Tori!" Emily demands my sister's attention. "I'm going on a trip."

"I know and you must be so excited."

Emily nods solemnly. "I heard my daddy say he's taking me to see The Gronkin."

"The Grand Canyon, sweetheart," I correct her.

Thanks to me, the kids insist on visiting the ice cream parlor before going to the park. Emily ask for butter pecan. I hand her a little plastic cup full of butter pecan ice cream and she reminds me that this was her grandfather's favorite flavor.

"You're right," I tell her and we take a seat at one of the outside tables. After four bites, Emily has had enough and asks for permission to give the rest of her ice cream to McClane, who is very grateful.

When we finally reach the park, Emily notices Arcana High in the distance and wants to know if we can go visit her mother.

"Mommy will be home in a few hours," I assure her. "But right now she's busy teaching classes. Why don't you go on the swings with Mason?"

She sticks her lower lip out. "I don't want to go on the swings. I want to play football."

"What do you know?" Jace says as he produces a little foam football from the drawstring knapsack that was slung across his back. "I've got a football right here."

Emily leads her uncle over to the open grass while I push my nephew on the swings.

"Higher, Uncle Colt," he demands.

Jace tosses the football to Emily and cheers wildly when she catches it. She beams and giggles and fires the ball right back at him. He pretends to miss, collapsing in the grass. Both Emily and McClane pounce on him.

"You win," Jace declares when Emily seizes the ball.

"Daddy, I won!" she yells.

"That's my girl!" I yell back.

Jace sits up and we share a smile that's packed with all of our hard won friendship and brotherhood.

Mason still naps in the afternoons and after an hour at the park he's getting tired so we decide to pack it in. Jace carries his sleepy little boy back to Tumbleweed Lane while I help Emily manage McClane. Along the way, Jace mentions that Tori posted a photo of the coffee table I built as a gift for their last anniversary on one of his social media accounts. People went berserk with questions, asking where they could order one. It's definitely an ego boost to hear that my work is being appreciated but I've already got more orders than I can handle. My custom furniture business is a small enterprise and I only work on it during weekends and random times when I'm not busy taking care of Emily. My sister says I could expand with ease and that's good to know but for now I'm not interested. I'm simply happy to have a side venture that brings in extra money while I enjoy my family.

Jace asks what time I want to pick up the RV tomorrow. Most likely in the afternoon. Susanna will have an early day since tomorrow is the last one of the school year.

Unlike Mason, Emily now refuses to take naps. We enjoy a snack of cheese flavored crackers and juice boxes at the kitchen table while she works on drawing a picture of McClane.

"I'm sending it to Nana Kelly." She shakes the paper in my face.

My juice box makes a gurgling sound. "Nana Kelly will love it. We'll stick it in the mail before we leave on our trip."

Soon Emily grows bored with coloring and runs to her room to pluck a book from a shelf that used to hold all of Jace's favorite books.

"I want to read you a story," she declares, giving me one more reason to feel amazed by my own kid. She began insisting on learning how to read right after her third birthday. It's an understatement to say she catches on quick. This is how we figured out we needed to get her eyes checked, when she had trouble seeing the print if it wasn't held right up to her nose. Emily decided she didn't mind wearing glasses once her grandmother produced some old photos of Susanna receiving her first pair of glasses at exactly the same age.

Emily prefers to hold story time in the living room. She makes herself comfortable in my lap and immediately begins reading. She only needs help with a few of the words and she's extremely proud of herself when she reaches the last page.

"Such a smart girl." I hug her. "Just like her mama."

Emily pats my arm. "You're smart too, Daddy."

"You think so?" I have no shame, eagerly trying to extract praise from a three-year-old.

"Yes," she answers without a second of doubt. "You can do anything. You even made a cradle for Mr. Bubbles."

Emily hears the car pull into the driveway before I do. Her face lights up and she runs to the door, waiting with her arms outstretched as the doorknob turns.

"Mommy, I missed you!"

Susanna Malene, love of my life, drops her tote bag and lifts our little girl up. "I missed you too, sweet Emily."

Watching this mother and daughter daily reunion never fails to turn my heart to mush. Emily adores her mother and always gets first dibs while I patiently wait my turn.

When I get it, I take full advantage and pull my wife into my arms. "I also missed you."

Susanna leans into my kiss and we could be getting hot and heavy real quick if not for the fact that Emily dances around at our feet.

"Mommy, did you know that Mason is going to be a big brother?"

Susanna breaks the kiss, but she stares into my eyes while answering our daughter. "Yes, I did know that. Mason will be getting a baby brother."

"Can I have a baby brother too?"

Susanna's mouth twitches. "Maybe someday."

"Sisters are also nice," I add.

"Shh," Susanna warns but Emily is already jumping up and down.

"Oh yes, I want a sister!"

I place my hand deliberately on my wife's stomach and she smiles because we have a secret. We're going to tell Jace and Tori the news tomorrow. Susanna is ten weeks pregnant. We saw the telltale flicker of a tiny heart beating at her ultrasound last Friday.

Emily is going to get her wish, although we won't know for a little while yet whether it will come in the form of a brother or a sister.

I glance at the set of keys hanging on the hook by the front door. From here I can see the small piece of silver that was given to me years ago by the girl who was destined to become my world. Susanna's charm has worked its magic. I'm lucky in all the ways a man can be lucky.

And I'll love every minute and take nothing for granted.

"Can we get pizza for dinner?" Emily has already moved on to another topic and hangs on my arm.

"Sure, if it's all right with your mom."

Susanna pulls a clip out of her hair. "Sounds perfect."

"Daddy." Emily is suddenly dismayed. "I forgot to tell Uncle Jace about the flowers we planted in Grandma Gloria's garden."

"You can tell him next time, Em," I promise my daughter as I lift her up for a hug. "Next time."

DEAR READER:

I'm not sure I've ever been sadder to finish a story and step out of this world.
Susanna and Colt have owned my heart and nothing pleased me more than to give them their happy ending.
Thank you for taking this journey with them.
Love,
Cora

Start from the beginning with Jace and Tori's tumultuous love story in TILL IT HURTS , available now!
"No one would say that our story is pretty.
But we were in love before we hated each other.
And we were friends long before that..."

ALSO BY CORA BRENT:

Made in the USA
Coppell, TX
21 December 2021

69710572R00197